HEART
BREAKER

HEART BREAKER

a novel

JENSEN PARKER

Elite Wrestling Entertainment
Book One

Made for More Publishing, LLC

HEARTBREAKER

Copyright © 2025 by Jensen Parker

All rights reserved.

Cover Design: Jensen Parker

Alpha'd: Ashley Vaccaro, Samantha Ivy, Miriam Al-Qhowdhaib, and Alexandra Cowell

Editing: Sophie B. Murphy, Eloquent Inkblot LLC.

ISBN (e-book) : 979-8-9931781-1-0

ISBN (printed) : 979-8-9931781-0-3

Published by Made for More Publishing, LLC.

https://www.jensenparker.com

For those of us who lost ourselves along the way, it's never too late to start anew.

And B+N,
your strength, determination, and resilience
show in everything you do.
I am beyond grateful for your friendship.

AUTHOR'S NOTE

Heartbreaker is the first book in the Elite Wrestling Entertainment Series.

This book contains scenes with discussions of mature subject matter, including on-page physical violence (scripted and non-scripted), on-page sexual content, drinking, divorce, and explicit language, and is intended for mature audiences.

Should you need it or have an interest in a more detailed description of certain terms than what is provided in the context of the story, I have included a Glossary in the back of the book that you can reference.

"Showstopper" is a short story that leads into the events of *Heartbreaker*. Originally included in the Romantically Yours Con 2025 anthology, you can find it at the back of the book.

— Jensen

Playlist

Bow Down - I Prevail
someday, someone - Kenzie Cait
No One - Aly & AJ
Milestones - Anne Wilson
American Honey - Lady A
Stand - Rascal Flatts & Brandon Lake
We're Not Friends - Ingrind Andress
Feel Invincible - Skillet
Sound of Madness - Shinedown
What's Your Country Song - Thomas Rhett
More Hearts Than Mine - Ingrind Andress
Stuck in Your Head - I Prevail
F**k My Life Up - Clara Park
Better Mistake - Teigen Gayse
Wait For You - Elliot Yamin
Feed the Machine - Nickelback
No Good - Kaleo
What Have I Done - Dermot Kennedy
Lights Down Low (feat. gnash) - Max
Because of You - David J
Outnumbered - Dermot Kennedy
MONSTERS - Shinedown
I Remember - Forest Blakk
How Honest Do You Want Me to Be? - Ingrind Andress
Rock and A Hard Place - Bailey Zimmerman
A Drop in the Ocean - Ron Pope
Before You Leave Me - Alex Warren
Don't Throw it Away - Jonas Brothers
Second Chance - Shinedown
when the party's over - Billie Eilish
Skip This Part - Alexandra Kay
Hear You Me - Jimmy Eat World
I'd Come For You - Nickelback
Grew Apart (feat. Alexandra Kay) - Logan Mize
My Oh My - James Smith
Yard Sale - Alex Warren
The Crow & the Butterfly - Shinedown
Who Am I - Jenna Raine
When You're Gone - Shawn Mendes
Awaken - Breaking Benjamin
What If I Never Get Over You - Lady A
Loved You Better - Jonas Brothers & Dean Lewis
Scars - Miley Cyrus
Stay With Me - You Me At Six
Version of Forever - Matt Hansen
Sorry - Jonas Brothers
Heart By Heart - Joe Jonas
Over and Over - Three Days Grace
When You're Gone - Avril Lavigne
Rome - Dermot Kennedy
It's Not Over - Daughtry
I Dare You - Rascal Flatts & Jonas Brothers
The Last - Alexandra Kay
Love You Anyway - Luke Combs
Ordinary - Alex Warren

Apple Music

Spotify

THE CARD

 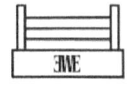

The books in this Series follow characters employed by Elite Wrestling Entertainment, a pro-wrestling company. Below is a list of the wrestlers you'll meet throughout this event, including both their real name and ring name.

John Brooks - *Brooks Taylor*
Savannah Williams - *Savvy Skye*

Current Roster
Brody Wilder - *"The Reaper" Brody Wilder*
Raelynn Carson - *"The Queen of Roses" Rae Rose*
Bennett James - *"The Gladiator" Wolf Bennett*
Harper Valentine - *Harper Valentine*
Austin Murray - *Spencer Austin*
Viviana Murray (formerly Viviana Ridley) – *Viviana Austin, formerly Fortuna*
Cassandra Tate - *Moxie*
Grady Chandler - *"The Lunatic" Grady Chandler*
Miles Drake - *"The Anarchist" Damian Drake*
Colin Montgomery - *Colin Ryker*
Hollis Black - *Nohea Nakoa*
Asher Slade - *Asher Slade*
Callista Kennedy - *"The Diamond" Cali Kennedy*
Nora Hayes - *Calla Lily*
Taylor Kerrigan - *Kerrigan Tate*
Maci Davenport - *Roxanne*
Ava Wilson - *Ava Anderson*

EWE Corporate
Amos Rafferty
Chelsea Rafferty
Theo Rafferty
Xander Collins
Tim Cass
Noah Callahan

Media Team
Jude Paul
Scott Harrington
Joanna Valence

Veterans
Juliet Briggs - *Juliet Briggs*
Ezekiel Slade - *"The Great" Fata*
Sheldon Goodwin - *"The All-American" Sheldon Goodwin*
Clarence Kennedy - *"Top Dollar" Clarence Kennedy*
Holly Kennedy - *Holly Graham*
Juliana Torres - *Luna Haze*

*Welcome to
Elite Wrestling Entertainment...*

PROLOGUE

Savannah

MONDAY, APRIL 8, 2019
ORLANDO, FL

It all started with a bet. A risk. Putting everything on the line with no way of knowing how it will end. Sometimes, the loss is so insignificant, it doesn't matter, but other times it means losing everything...

"*You think you can beat me*?" Austin Murray—better known to the world by his ring name "*The Showstopper*" *Spencer Austin*—scoffs on the monitor in front of me. He shares a look with Viviana, his wife both on and off screen.

The crowd chants a chorus of "Aus-tin," bringing another smirk to the current Elite Wrestling Entertainment Champion's face. The oversized leather belt rests on his left shoulder. The EWE logo sits on the large golden center plate, which is riddled with gemstones to make it shine beneath the bright stadium lights. On either side are two smaller golden plates that contain the initials S.A. in delicate script—a weird choice considering the man who holds the belt, but who am I to judge? He won the title six weeks ago, unseating former champion "*The Reaper*" *Brody Wilder* in a triple-threat match between the two of them and *Brooks Taylor*.

The defeat left *Brooks* itching for revenge...

"*You hear that, Brooks?*" *Spencer* practically spits the name. "*They don't want you. They're tired of you.*"

The monitor switches to show the man he's been heckling for the past five minutes. *Brooks Taylor*, better known to me as John Brooks—but to the world, he's just Brooks. He towers at the top of the steel ramp that leads down through the crowd and straight to the mouth of the ring dressed in jeans and one of his vintage *Brooks Taylor* T-shirts from almost ten years ago. The black material clings to his figure, showing off his strong, athletic build. The wings of an eagle spread across his broad chest, outlining his name. *Built for this* is written in bold, capital letters at the bottom. It's a simple concept for a not-so-simple man...

Brooks looks unamused, glaring down the ramp at the wrestler who has been a thorn in his side for the last three months. While *Brooks Taylor* might not find any of this amusing, I can only assume the person behind the mask of this performance is eating it up. Mischief swims in those dark blue eyes, the same ones that used to stare into my soul and say, "I love you."

A bold-faced lie.

"*And you know, I think it's comical you think you can beat me. You couldn't even beat Vee with a hand tied behind your back!*" That makes me roll my eyes. This whole thing has been embarrassing, even by EWE standards.

When I saw the disastrous match between *Brooks* and *Viviana* two weeks ago, I couldn't believe Noah was okay with it. Noah Callahan is the Chief Content Officer and husband of Elite Wrestling Entertainment darling, Chelsea Rafferty. But it wasn't his idea at all; it was Amos Rafferty's. Amos is the man who started the Elite Entertainment Wrestling empire over thirty years ago, and what Amos wants...Amos gets. Case in point, the storyline between *Brooks Taylor* and the *Austins*. Spencer and Viviana have been married for six months now, and while Noah might have found their on-screen relationship stale by now (his words, not mine), Amos has allowed them to keep going with it.

"*Should we see a clip? I think we should. Roll the clip!*" *Spencer's* demands are met when a recap of their match appears on the screen...

The referee tied Brooks's hand behind his back. Brooks tested the give of the rope before he rolled his neck and shoulders, loosening up. Austin whispered to Viviana from the apron—the outermost part of the ring—and she cracked her knuckles, bouncing on the balls of her feet. The referee motioned to ring the bell, and Austin jumped to the floor. Viviana moved toward her opponent, chopping Brooks across the chest three times, backing him into the corner. She jumped up on the ropes on either side of him, providing some extra leverage as she wailed down on him. Looking out at the crowd, Viviana landed a final blow and jumped down as Brooks slumped farther into the corner.

Jumping down from the ropes, she stalked back into the opposite corner, watching. When he began to stir, she sprang into a somersault that landed a hard kick on his chest. The impact sent him back into the ropes. The force springboarded him back into the ring, straight into her foot.

With her opponent down, Viviana took a moment to celebrate, and it gave him the chance to recoup. She attempted to kick him on his way back up, but he caught her foot and twisted instinctively, about to go for his signature move, the Legacy Lock. She yelped in pain, and Brooks dropped her foot at the sound.

"*Enough, Vee!*" *Brooks yelled.* "*Enough, I'm not going to fight you.*"

"*Finish him," Austin said from under the bottom rope, and the crowd began to chant the same thing. As Brooks tried to talk sense into her, Viviana climbed the top rope and landed another dropkick, this time to his head. Brooks fell to the mat, and in a quick 1...2...3, Viviana was declared the winner.*

The camera pans to *Viviana*, and her growing smirk is met by a loud chorus of "boos." *That's interesting...* This is the first crowd that has mostly been behind *Brooks* since the start of their feud.

"*You didn't even try, Brooks,*" *Spencer* practically whines. "*You could've at least tried to put up a fight, given her something to work with.*"

Brooks stands tall and confident, maintaining that stereotypical *Brooks Taylor* façade—the one I had always admired but hated all the same. I wanted to see him crack sometimes, give in to the feelings he buried deep inside...but that wasn't who the man behind the mask thought *Brooks Taylor* was supposed to be. The character of *Brooks Taylor* was supposed to be a larger-than-life superhero who got back up when he was down and kept going no matter what.

There isn't anyone like John Brooks in this company, no one who can oust him from his place on the throne of EWE... No one is prepared to take his place because no one is willing to do what he does. Not even the man standing in front of him, despite how much Spencer thinks he wants it. He has always believed he's better than Brooks, better than most of the locker room, and has vied for the top spot in the company for as long as I've known him. But, just like everyone else, he's failed to prove himself worthy.

"*Are you serious?*" *Brooks* asks. The sound wraps around me like a blanket in the winter, warming my body to the core. It's the first time I've heard his voice not on a television screen in over two years, and it still has the same effect on me that it did the first time we met.

"You ready?" A voice cuts through the spell I've been under for the last ten minutes. Noah Callahan.

With a small smile, I shake my head. Noah chuckles, giving me a thumbs up, and motions me toward the black curtain separating the gorilla post—the operations center backstage—from the timekeeper position. Once I walk through that curtain, there's no going back…

Taking a deep breath, I grip the black material between my fingers. I have no idea what waits for me on the other side, but more importantly, I have no idea what waits for me when I come back through it.

A deep wave of nausea rolls through my entire being as I step into the waiting area. Feeling a little nauseous—a little nervous—before you walk out is normal, maybe even expected, because once you step out on the other side, all of that gets replaced by pure, unadulterated adrenaline. It's a high unlike anything in the world, and even though I know that, my body hasn't quite caught up to my brain, and I'm almost certain I might throw up. I haven't felt like this since my debut nine years ago. Garbled voices come from the earpiece in the timekeeper's left ear, counting down until it's time to kill the lights.

Brooks's voice is closer when he speaks this time, and it makes the hairs on the back of my neck stand on end. Goosebumps rise across my skin despite the black hoodie I'm wearing—the one I had to wear to maintain anonymity backstage. "*I wasn't going to fight your wife. Are you insane? Vee is good, but I refuse to do that.*" There's a spark in the air following his words. A hum in the crowd as I imagine a smirk lifts the right corner of his mouth.

I strip the hoodie from my shoulders and drop it to the side of the room seconds before the timekeeper gives me a single nod.

Brooks has no idea what's about to happen. None of them do. My return to EWE has been something Noah and I have kept close to the vest for the last two months.

I can imagine the look on his face, wetting his lips with a growing smirk, as *Brooks* says, *"But I know someone who will."* *Showtime.*

PART ONE

1

Savannah

SUNDAY, AUGUST 3, 2008

CRIMSON VALLEY, TX

"For the love of all that is good and holy...stop pushing!" I smack away the dainty but strong hands shoving me through the parking lot of Ash & Thorn—the local dive bar on the outskirts of our college town. Crimson Valley is a small town in central Texas centered around Thornebrooke University, one of the largest and most prestigious universities not just in Texas, but in the South. Thornebrooke excels not only in academics, but also in athletics, having been named in the top five of D1 schools for the last twenty years. I used to cheer for the Thornebrooke Bobcats until I successfully tried out for the darlings of the NFL, the Alexandria Wildcats, two years ago.

"Then move your ass!" Cassandra gives me one final shove, and I jump forward to tug open the heavy wooden door. My best friend doesn't waste a moment, taking hold of the door and pushing me inside, practically stepping on my heels so I have no possible way to escape.

Cassandra and Kingsley showed up at my apartment at seven o'clock on the dot, dressed and ready for a night out, ordering me to get up and get ready. I had only arrived back at my apartment two hours earlier, and I planned to spend the night watching some of my favorite movies with the company of two men named Ben and Jerry, but my best friends had other plans. I turned twenty-one four days ago, and with no cheer practice this weekend, I took advantage of the rare opportunity to go home for more than one night. It's a pleasure I'm not afforded often, being a professional cheerleader *and* college student. And while it was nice to see my family, the real reason I decided to make the two-hour drive was so I wouldn't have to worry about running into my ex-boyfriend on my birthday. Before you start feeling sorry for me, my older brothers made sure I celebrated this milestone properly. Crew and Nash would never allow me to skip out on such a momentous occasion.

"You need to get *him* out of your system," Cassandra said earlier, meaning my ex-boyfriend, as she rummaged through my closet. She pulled out a pleather mini skirt and a black mesh long-sleeve shirt. That was an immediate no. After thirty minutes of going back and forth on different outfits, we compromised on dark denim jeans and a black crop top, with a black blazer and heels. The right amount of sexy, but kept things modest, and if anything happened to be shared, I wouldn't get in trouble with the Wildcats. I had an image to uphold, and I wasn't looking to find myself on the other side of Coach's desk because Cassandra wanted me to "let loose."

"You're so lame." Cassandra sighs when I order a beer, earning an eye roll from me and Kingsley. At least I know she has my back. Kingsley is also a Wildcat and knows that even when we're not in uniform, we're expected to maintain a certain appearance—something our friend doesn't always understand.

And with only five days before the start of preseason, I'm not trying to have any marks on my record. Besides, I already had my good time with my brothers, in a safe space where I wouldn't have to worry about the possibility of doing anything stupid that the team might find out about. Being a cheerleader for a professional football team is fun, and it's been my dream for as long as I can remember, but it comes with a lot more rules than I expected.

"How was home?" Kingsley asks when we finally settle into a table. Her ruby-painted lips pucker before she pulls away from the rim of her martini glass. She glances back at the bartender. "Damn, they're pouring heavy tonight."

"And that's why I got a beer," I say, looking pointedly at Cassandra. "We have practice tomorrow, and I'd rather not feel like shit when they decide to kick our asses."

"I don't know how you guys do it. I would've quit after the first year," Cassandra says.

"You would've quit after the first day." Kingsley laughs, attempting to take another sip of her drink.

"Oh, give me some credit! I would've at least made it to the second day." Sure, if that's what she needs to tell herself. We've been friends since eighth grade, when Cassandra's family moved to my hometown of Celestia, Texas, from San Diego, and if there's one thing to know about my best friend, it's that she doesn't do sports. Doesn't watch them and certainly doesn't participate. Despite her hatred of physical activities, she has always been supportive of my dream to be a professional cheerleader, never missing a single one of my competitions. And while she hasn't quite figured out what to do with her life, I'm here to support every one of her failed endeavors.

The rest of the night goes by without mishap, and it does exactly what they had been hoping for: it takes my mind off Conner. It's not like I don't know the breakup was my fault, but that doesn't make it hurt any less. The writing was on the wall almost from the mark of our first anniversary; the relationship wasn't going anywhere. We barely saw each other due to the difference in our work schedules, and barely spoke because of them, too. The occasional text here or there, the quick phone calls in between appointments…it wasn't enough. If I'm going to *feel* single, I might as well *be* single.

Conner didn't put up much of a fight when I suggested taking a break, and I think that's what hurt the most. His reaction is what brought about this depressive mood I've been in since he and I made the time to sit down two weeks ago. There was no pushback. He simply agreed that ending things was for the best and walked out of my apartment without a second glance.

Kingsley finishes her third martini, and I can see the glaze coat her big, blue eyes before she leans across the table and begs Cassandra to go outside for a smoke. Kingsley knows better, but she's a big girl, and I'm not here to babysit. Cassandra downs the final sip of her second martini before they rise to go outside, and she gives me a confused glance when I stand alongside them. I've never joined them for a smoke, not since my first and last cigarette at a house party our freshman year of high school. But her confusion dissipates when we part halfway to the door, and I turn left to the bar. Waiting for the bartender—who seems to have gotten slower as the night goes on—I notice someone else walks up to the bar, but he doesn't seem to care about ordering a drink. His focus is on me, constantly shifting his weight, fidgeting against the bar, and looking my way every few seconds.

Stop flirting with those girls and get my fucking beer. I catch sight of the bartender at the other end, chatting it up with two girls in matching skin-tight dresses. If they lean over another half inch, their boobs are going to fall out of the top. Not that he, or half the population in here, would care.

"Your friends call it a night?" the presence beside me asks. Looks like he finally worked up the nerve to speak.

"Nope," I say, popping the last syllable, holding my glare on the bartender. "They'll be right back."

"That's too bad. I've been waiting for them to leave so I could work up the courage to come talk to you."

Against my better judgment, I glance at him. He looks familiar, but not in a truly memorable way, like maybe I've passed him on the street or seen him in a class before. He has round features that remind me of the young boys who walk onto a college campus before they lose their cherub cheeks and the real world starts to hit them.

"I'm Jordan." He extends his slim hand and smiles. "I've seen you around campus. You're...Samantha, right?"

"Yes, Samantha." I shake his hand briefly. *Good, he doesn't know my name.*

His shyness, bit of avoidance, and trouble with names, paired with the round eyeglasses, remind me of the man I'm supposed to be forgetting about. My ex-boyfriend wears the same glasses because he thinks they make him look smarter, wiser. That feeling was exaggerated every time I did or said something he deemed annoying, or "not smart." He'd pull the wire rims from his nose, wipe the lenses with the gray cleansing cloth kept in his pocket or desk drawer, and replace them with a slight huff before promptly telling me how and why I was wrong.

Finally. I sigh when the bartender returns, sliding my beer across the counter and turning on his heel in one swift motion. I swipe it before Jordan can. A glance around the room shows no sign of Cassandra or Kingsley. I'm going to kill them if I get sucked into a full-blown conversation with this guy because of a fucking cigarette.

"You wanna grab a seat? We can get to—"

"Sorry I took so long." A warm voice comes from behind me, matching the weight that appears at my lower back. A hand comes around my left side, resting on the bar with a beer in hand. While I should recoil from the new intruder, I decide to lean into his warmth, and relief washes over me when I see Jordan's eyes widen behind his glasses. "You okay? This guy bothering you?"

"I—I didn't...I didn't know. I just saw—"

"No, he's fine," I say, not bothering to hide my smirk, and lean further into mystery man's chest. His hand glides from my back to my hip, giving it a gentle squeeze.

"I had no idea. I'm sorry, I—" Jordan stammers, stepping back a few paces before he turns and runs through the crowd back to whatever corner he crawled out of.

Even after Jordan has disappeared, the newcomer doesn't release his hold on my side. Normally, I'm not into the whole male show of dominance thing, but there's something about this man that brings me a sense of safety and security. Despite the intense draw I feel toward him, I know I should end this before my friends come back, but the least I can do is offer to buy him a drink.

Turning in his arms, I'm ready to thank him for saving me from the torturous conversation and having to break Jordan's heart on my own, but the words get caught in my throat. Eyes the color of the cerulean sea stare ahead, locked on something, or someone, before they blink down at me. They have to be the prettiest color I've ever seen. This man is not from around here, and while he looks familiar—more familiar than Jordan—I can't remember where we could have met. I'm about eighty (maybe seventy-five) percent sure I've seen him before, though. He's handsome and towers over me, having to be at least six feet with broad shoulders and thick arms hugged by a dark gray Henley shirt. Light brown hair that is the perfect length to run my hand through, but not too long. His hand still lingers on my waist, and his thumb lazily moves against the exposed skin above my waistband. The touch ignites a spark inside me. "T-thanks...for saving me. Bad time for my friends to go have a smoke break, huh?"

His eyes narrow slightly before a soft chuckle rises in his throat. He looks ahead one final time before he smiles back at me. "I don't know. You seem like the type of girl who can handle her own if needed."

"Then what are you doing here?"

"Oh, you *looked* miserable, and I *was* miserable listening to my friends bitch about work...So, I decided, why not make us both less miserable? Besides, that poor bastard clearly wasn't getting the message."

You think?

"You're not from around here, are you?" I ask.

A toothy grin spreads across his face. "How can you tell?"

"You don't exactly look like a college student, but you also don't give Alexandria vibes. So, I know you're not from here."

He shakes his head. "No, I'm here for work."

"So, is this your shtick?" I ask. My hand comes to rest over his arm, still on the bar. "Go to a local bar wherever you're in town for work, find the most miserable-looking girl, and say, 'Her! She's the one.'"

"Actually, you'd be the first. I don't usually pick up women in bars."

That seems hard to believe. This man is the definition of tall, dark, and handsome, and he doesn't pick women up in bars? Every eye in here has turned his way at least twice since we started talking—men and women alike.

"Yet, here you are, doing just that."

"Is that what I'm doing?" he asks with a smirk that stirs the butterflies in my stomach. However, it must be a different breed of butterfly because their presence doesn't make me nervous. He doesn't make me nervous. He makes me feel... safe. Comfortable. Sexy. Confident. So many words run through my mind, each one true.

"You tell me." I haven't felt this bold when talking to a guy in years. What is happening? "I'm Savvy," I say, extending my hand in the small space between us.

"John." He takes my hand and presses it to the back of his lips before his eyes glance over my left shoulder. "Your friends are back."

When I do the same, I see Cassandra lead Kingsley through the door, her eyes frantically sweeping across the room until finally landing on me. Us. Her eyes widen, and her mouth drops. She forces Kingsley to look in my direction before I shoot them a wink, turning back to John. "So it would seem."

John glances over his shoulder where his own friends are too busy heckling the guy sitting at the far end of the table to notice he's gone—well, except for one of them. The stone face of the man at this end of the table unmistakably stares straight at us, watching with a level of uncertainty. He's darker than John, but I can't tell whether the deep gold color of his skin is natural or a spray tan. The bronzed tone almost looks too perfect to be natural. Grey eyes flicker from John to me, and the chill that accompanies it reminds me of Cathy, the assistant coach of the Wildcats. Cold, calculating, overly observant.

"Don't mind him." John chuckles, turning away from his friend. "He's just mad because I left him to deal with those fools."

I play with the opening of his Henley before my hand trails up around his neck, and his hands find my waist again. I'd be lying if I said there isn't a spark of something new when he pulls me flush against him.

He leans down to my right ear and whispers, "You want to get out of here?"

I'm not sure Cassandra meant this when she said I needed to get Conner out of my system, but who am I to deny myself a night of pleasure with a guy as good-looking as this one?

"Lead the way," I say.

John slaps a hundred-dollar bill on the bar and places my untouched beer on top of it. He takes my hand to lead me past the table my friends have been watching from and out the door.

He's staying at the Crimson Valley Resort? What in the hell does this guy do? "The Resort," as locals like to call it, is one of the most luxurious places within at least a hundred miles, sitting equidistant between the Valley and Alexandria. This is for people who can afford multiple hundred dollars a night, or people who want to pretend they can. The Resort is where you'd find someone like me working behind the front desk to make a little extra money. It isn't The Plaza in New York, but it seems close.

I'm surprised by how easily the conversation with John has flowed since we left the bar. We've managed to discuss our likes and dislikes, the number of siblings we have, why I was at Ash & Thorn in the first place, and whether we like pineapple on pizza—the only correct answer here is yes, no matter what he says—but the one thing we've seemed to avoid mentioning is work. Not that I minded. It's nice, considering the next four months my life will revolve around school and the 'Cats.

"Your job puts you up in the Resort? Are you the CEO?" I ask when John offers his hand to help me step out of the SUV. His only response is a laugh, and I can't hold back my own smile. "Is this one of those if you tell me you'd have to kill me things?"

"Sure." He laughs again. "Let's go with that." John thanks the valet, handing him the keys and a twenty, and rests his hand on my lower back to guide me through the revolving door.

I cannot believe I'm doing this right now. I've never done something like this. What in the hell am I doing? This isn't me...Then again, wasn't that the point? To do something out of the norm and forget about the shitstorm I've created?

John leads me through the expansive lobby to the left back corner labeled "South Tower," and before he can hit the elevator call button, the doors slide open. A man not much shorter than John stands on the other side, wearing a suit and tie. Interesting choice of apparel for...I glance at my watch and realize it's almost midnight. Where in hell is he going at midnight dressed like that? I probably wouldn't have thought anything of it, nor paid him any attention, except for the look in his eye and the nod he gives the man beside me, like they know each other.

"Brooks," the man says. Brooks? I thought his name was John? You know what...None of my business.

"Theo." That's all the exchange consists of before the man named Theo steps off the elevator, and John pulls me inside, letting the doors close.

"Friend of yours?" I ask.

"Yes and no," John answers with a shrug. "Think more of a close acquaintance on the corporate side of things." The answer only serves to bring more questions to mind, but I tell myself they don't matter because after tonight, I'm never going to see this man—or Theo—again.

John stands on the opposite side of the elevator, hands gripping the handrail behind him, his eyes cast on the floor. I can practically see the swirling thought cloud hovering above his head. There's a war inside him, and I can't help but wonder if he's having second thoughts...or maybe I'm just projecting my own insecurities, my own worries, onto him.

One final ding signals our arrival on the twentieth floor.

His gaze trails from the floor up the length of my body. Warmth radiates from his darkened stare, and any sense of hesitation I'd been feeling moments ago dissipates. Without warning, John steps forward, claiming my mouth with his own. The railing digs into my back, the metal cool against my burning skin as my jacket bunches. The kiss is all-consuming. I feel him everywhere, despite one hand being firmly planted on my waist and the other on the wall behind me. It's not enough, I need more. I need him, all of him.

John groans when I pull his bottom lip between my teeth, eyes on fire when they meet mine, as his hand slams against the door when it begins to close. His other hand moves from my waist, threading his fingers through mine to drag me down the hallway. I can barely keep up with his long strides before coming to an abrupt stop in front of his room. He waves the keycard over the little black rectangular box fixed on the door, but a red light blinks alongside a derogatory beep.

With an amused huff, I fall back against the wall, watching him continue to wave the card. Each attempt is met with a red light. He curses under his breath, and I reach for the card. My hand envelops his much larger one, slowly guiding it over the lock. letting it rest there instead of waving it frantically like he'd been doing, and a second later, it blinks green, followed by the sound of the lock opening.

John opens the door, but doesn't walk in. He pulls me into another kiss on this side of the threshold. It's softer, sweeter, and more inviting. It draws on something buried so deep, I've never felt something like it before. It's warm and bright, intimate and familiar, and I never want it to end. I can't hide the soft pout when he puts a small space between us. His lips have a slight red tint to them from my lipstick. *God, please tell me it's not smudged across my face*, I beg quietly, using my thumb and index finger to wipe the edge of my lips. They come back clean, and I offer a silent word of thanks, meeting his stare again. "Are you sure about this, Savvy? I don't—We don't have—"

"John." The sound of his name brings a halt to his rambling. "Stop talking."

Blue eyes darken again before he does just that. He captures my lips in a kiss that silences any second thoughts either of us might have as we step over the threshold. Warm hands slide down my back and palm my ass, and a soft squeal escapes me when he lifts my feet off the ground. Shrugging out of my jacket, I let it fall in a heap on the floor before I reach for the hem of my shirt and tug, pulling it over my head. His eyes drop from mine to my newly exposed skin, drinking in every inch. His throat bobs as he swallows before lifting his gaze back to mine.

"You are beautiful, Sav."

The way he says it...I know he means it and not just because he's trying to seduce me. The soft look in his eyes tells me he genuinely thinks so. If we're supposed to walk away after tonight, he's going to have to stop saying and doing things like this. What would someone say who was trying to keep it...casual?

"You have too many clothes on."

Good. Well done, Savannah. That wasn't a dead giveaway to your anxiety at all.

John breathes out a soft chuckle, and his brow raises knowingly before my back hits the mattress. His hand reaches behind to the nape of his neck and pulls the fabric over his head in one swift motion. *Holy shit.* My eyes travel the planes of his bare chest, and I'm almost certain I've never seen anything more magnificent. How is this man real? I reach my hand out to touch him, tracing the dusted freckles on his shoulders and the single tattoo on his right side—a cross made up of three thick railroad spikes. It's the kind of tattoo that you know bears a heavy weight and meaning behind it, a story that feels too intimate to ask about for a one-time thing.

I feel like I should be nervous right now, half naked in front of this beautiful man (if that's even the right way to describe him), but the way he's looking at me makes me feel like I'm the only woman on the planet. And for now, that's more than enough—it's more than I ever felt with Conner, and certainly more than my other ex, Jaxon. The warm skin contracts beneath my fingertips, a sharp inhale as my hands travel farther down his stomach, and the ache between my legs grows.

He takes my hand in his when I reach the waistband of his jeans, bringing each one of my fingertips to his lips, maintaining eye contact the whole time. A tingle radiates from each finger down my arm, and my body begins to vibrate with anticipation. John leans down to press a hard kiss on my lips before his mouth trails down my jaw. His tongue caresses the skin, dipping into the joint of my collarbone.

"John," I gasp when he softly nibbles the skin, setting my nerves on fire. The flames spread with every kiss, bite, and lick, moving down my chest until he reaches the valley between my breasts. John brings my nipple to his mouth, capturing it through the fabric of my bra, and my spine arches, pushing further into the feeling of him. His hand cups my left breast, kneading the flesh through the black lace, before he tugs down the fabric and takes the hardened peak into his mouth. His tongue swirls around it, sucking greedily.

With a simple flick of his fingers, the button of my jeans comes undone, and I don't know whether to be impressed or intimidated. It shouldn't have been that easy, right?

He peels the denim from my thighs, shoving it down my legs until I'm left in only my underwear. A soft curse under his breath. His eyes shine with hunger when he looks up at me. "You're fucking soaked, baby," he rasps, one of his hands coming to graze my core, a thin layer of wet fabric the only thing between his fingers and me.

"Tease." A breathy chuckle turns into a moan as two of his fingers push the fabric aside, slipping between my folds.

"What was that?" He licks his lips, gaze lingering on my body.

"You're a fucking tease," I say, and he slides another finger inside me. The pad of his thumb finds my clit, circling the swollen bud, and heat pools in my belly, a coil already begging to be released. I feel so full with just his fingers, but something tells me nothing will compare to having his cock inside me.

John brings his lips to my exposed nipple again, sucking the peak into his mouth. The mixture of teeth and tongue alongside the steady rhythm of his fingers sends me soaring, and I can feel my arousal coat the insides of my thighs. I audibly gasp when he bites down on my nipple, and the sensation pushes me closer to the edge of my orgasm. I've never been one to associate pain and pleasure—or maybe it's because I've never considered it before—but the next time he bites down on the already sensitive bud, my back arches and I cry out from release.

A hum of satisfaction fills the air, and I open my eyes to find him sitting back on his haunches, sucking on his fingers. The sight alone is almost enough to make me come again. Why is that so fucking hot? John's eyes roll back in pleasure before he opens them to meet my gaze, and anticipation prickles beneath my skin. "You taste even better than I thought."

My teeth rake over my bottom lip, and I sit up on my elbows. John leans down to kiss me, brushing the hair off my face. His tongue sweeps across my lips, and I open to him— tongues tangled together in a desperate and eager embrace.

He parts from me too soon, stepping off the bed to undo the buttons of his jeans. Even from here, I can tell his body is...firm. Masculine. Like he's dedicated hours at the gym and only ever eaten the right foods, curating a body he can be proud of. Oh no, I hope he's not one of those crazy juice heads…

No, stop, Savannah. You're never going to see him again. So, what if he is? That's not your concern.

As he shoves denim, along with his underwear, down his legs, I can't take my eyes off the sharp pair of lines that lead from his hips down to his now fully exposed groin. His cock is huge, maybe the biggest I've ever seen. Long and impossibly thick—how in the hell is that going to fit inside me?

There's no time to ponder it, because when I draw my gaze back up to his, the look in his eyes makes my heart beat rapidly inside my chest. A hurricane of hunger…desire… want…need swirls in his cerulean eyes. I meet him at the edge of the bed, reaching to unclasp my bra and rid myself of my underwear. John cups my face in his hands, bringing his lips to mine in a soft, gentle kiss. I sigh against his mouth, and he guides me back onto the bed. A newfound sense of urgency flares between us.

"Shit, just look at you." John sighs, staring down at my figure, and my breath hitches when the head of his cock brushes against my center. My eyes snap shut when he rubs against my clit. "So wet, so needy. Just for me. Look at me, Sweetheart."

I meet his gaze, and he leans forward to capture my lips as he pushes inside me. I moan against his mouth, adjusting to the sudden fullness of him. He rocks forward, and I realize he's not even fully inside yet. Holy shit, there's no way he'll fit.

"You can take it, Sav," he says with such certainty that it quells some of my nerves. "It'll fit, I promise."

I nod fervently, still not sure if I believe it.

"Relax, baby. I got you," he whispers, and rocks his hips, sliding in further inch by inch until he's fully seated inside me. There's a moment of stillness when he lets me adjust before he begins to move again. He pulls out almost completely and pushes back in, filling me to the hilt at a delectably slow pace. Soft moans of his own fill the space between us, and it's the sweetest sound I've heard. Rough hands grip the flesh of my thigh, hitching it higher on his side, and he begins to roll his hips a little faster. "Fuck," he hisses, looking down where our bodies are connected as one. He watches as he slams in and out of me, slick arousal coating his cock every time. "You're so fucking wet, so warm...You feel so good, baby."

My head falls back against the mattress, eyes shut, listening to the chorus of sounds that fill the room—sounds of wet skin mixed with soft moans of pleasure—as pure ecstasy fills my veins. The unrestrained sounds that fall from his lips—sounds that he's making *for* me, *because* of me—only beg the coil deep in my core to tighten further.

"You take me so fucking good, Sav. Like you were made for me." The words pull a whimper from me. Neither of my exes was ever very vocal in the bedroom, and truth be told, neither was I, but this open dialogue, hearing these words of praise...I never realized it's something I'd been missing in these intimate moments before. His forehead falls against mine, but his fingers still dig into the skin of my thigh with bruising force.

My nails rake down his forearms and his back, digging into the flesh. I grasp for anything I can hold on to as he rolls into me. His lips find the small space between my neck and collarbone again, and my fingers trail down between us, circling my swollen clit. His name comes out of me in a strangled cry as the waves of ecstasy crest and my body seizes beneath him in what might be the most powerful orgasm I've ever experienced.

"Don't you dare stop," he whispers in my ear when I try to release the swollen bundle of nerves. "Keep going."

Whimpering, I force my hand back between us, continuing to move my fingers in slow circles around my clit as I ride out the waves of my orgasm. With only a few pumps, John groans as he comes, and I can feel the warmth of his cum inside me. The sensation is almost too intense, but he holds me in place so I can't writhe away from him as he finishes, continuing to fuck me through his orgasm. We had been so caught up in the moment, I hadn't even thought to ask him if he had a condom, and right now I can't bring myself to care...

His lips find mine in a sweet kiss. I relish in the soft tickle of his breath as he takes his time, exploring my mouth, our tongues moving in a languid dance. No pressure, no rush, just enjoying being tangled in each other. Gently, he pulls out of me, dropping onto his back and pulling me into his side. Eyes closed, he takes three slow, deep breaths, letting his chest rise and fall with each one. His fingers trace along the center of my back, sending a shiver down my spine.

My thumb skates across his jaw and his lips before a smile lifts the corner of his mouth. There's still a slight red tint to them from my lipstick. When I look up, I meet his soft gaze, and he smiles. "What do you think? Is this my color?"

"Oh, definitely." I laugh, mirroring the soft rumble in his chest beneath me.

This was supposed to be a one-time thing, yet it feels the opposite. Every passing moment I'm in his arms, it feels like it's only just the beginning of something bigger.

2

Savannah

THURSDAY, NOVEMBER 27, 2008

CRIMSON VALLEY, TX

One of the hardest things about being a professional cheerleader is the schedule. Sure, I had done what I set my sights on from the first time I picked up a pair of pom-poms. I made it to the top, becoming a cheerleader for one of the most well-known, most sought-after squads in the league, but the more time that passes, I find myself longing for something...more. Something different. Cheerleading isn't the only thing I've been questioning in the last few months. I've contemplated picking a new major and a new fallback career—sports medicine was never what I wanted to do, anyway, even if it made sense. When the time comes to retire from performing, I wanted the option to stay involved in the cheer world, but now, I don't think that's what I want to do anymore. Or maybe I'm just a little more over it than normal because today is Thanksgiving, and where am I? Not at home.

The Wildcats are scheduled to play Knoxville in a home game, which means cheerleader attendance is *mandatory*.

No exceptions.

Cassandra is home for Thanksgiving, and Kingsley is

spending time with her family, who made the trip from Oklahoma because she couldn't. With two hours before I have to leave for the stadium, I have plenty of time on my hands, and I should probably go for a run, but lying in bed and watching one of those classic black and white movies with Audrey Hepburn sounds better. It's a holiday, after all. I deserve this.

I've lost count of how many times I've seen most of these classics. Growing up, my mother watched them all the time. Her father was from Chile and spoke virtually no English when he moved to the States as a twenty-something with a dream and three months' worth of rent. He fell in love with a young college student who lived in the same co-op building, and they married a year later. She helped him learn English by showing him movies, and they continued watching them well after he learned the language. Their shared love for those movies was passed down to my mother, who shared them with us. Movies like *Roman Holiday* bring a sense of comfort when I need it most, like when I'm away from home on the holidays.

Gregory Peck's character smiles on screen, taunting the young Princess Ann for her new haircut. I mouth the words of her response with her: "What would they say if they knew I spent the night in your room?" The words strike a chord in me, bringing the image of a man I've been trying to forget to the forefront of my mind. It's been at least three months, almost four, since we parted ways outside of The Resort, and I still think about that night and the next morning more than I'd care to admit...

Waking up in a strong embrace was a good indication that the night before was far from a dream, as if the three times we'd found ourselves tangled in the sheets weren't reality enough. I buried myself further into the plush mattress and his side, unable to force myself out of bed. His embrace tightened before his fingers traced up and down my side. Neither of us said anything, lying in the stillness for a few more minutes before we'd have to get up and face reality.

It was the opposite of everything I'd ever been told about a one-night stand, at least from the perspective of Cassandra and my brothers. I had every intention of leaving that night. Calling a cab and going home after we were done, because sleeping over was a big no-no in this situation, right? Except I couldn't bring myself to leave, couldn't force myself out the door, and he didn't seem to mind. That night was the first and only time I've done something like that...but I'd be happy to take that sentiment back if it came to getting lost in the sheets with John again. My pulse quickens just thinking about that morning...

"Mornin', Sweetheart," John had mumbled against my hair. Normally, I'd cringe at the use of that particular pet name—it had always seemed superficial, lazy even—but when he said it, a warmth spread through me. It moved down my spine and spread like a wildfire across the network of nerves beneath my skin. "What time is it?"

Pushing up from his chest, I glanced at the clock. "Seven."

"Fuck." He groaned, scrubbing a hand down his face. "I'm sorry to say this, but I have to go," John said before he sat up and pulled my mouth to his for a series of quick kisses. The last one lingered, warm and soft as he plied my mouth open. His tongue danced against mine, stroking it in an eager embrace. I couldn't contain the soft whimper when he parted from me, earning a soft chuckle in reply. "Trust me, I'd much rather stay here and find all the ways to make you squirm."

The words made my cheeks warm, and I was certain he could see the blush growing on my skin by the way he smirked. But he wasn't wrong...I needed to leave, too.

"Technically, so do I. Duty calls at the coffee shop before rehearsal."

Probably shouldn't have said that. The man obviously had an important job—a career—one where they put him in nice hotels and he's friendly with the suits. He doesn't want to know that the girl he brought home is the same one who will probably be serving him coffee later on.

You're not just *a barista*, I thought. *Being a professional cheerleader is a career, too.*

"Rehearsal?" John asked, pulling on a pair of gym shorts.

"I thought we weren't discussing our private lives." Even though we'd done just that on the drive back from the bar.

"You started it, Sweetheart." He winked, disappearing into the bathroom.

"Cheerleader," I answered, lifting my arms into the sky and leaning from side to side in a much-needed stretch.

He poked his head back into the bedroom, about to put his toothbrush in his mouth. "You're a cheerleader?"

"Wildcat."

He stared at me a moment longer, lifting his brows in surprise, before he stuck the toothbrush in his mouth. I climbed out of bed to get dressed, and looking down at the clothes I had readily available, it dawned on me that I'd be late for my shift at the café. I couldn't wear a crop top, and I certainly couldn't wear high heels.

"You don't remind me of any cheerleader I've ever met," John said a minute later, putting his toothbrush into his bag. He pulled out two white shirts, extending the second one to me.

Wait, was he giving me one of his shirts?

"You meet a lot of them?" I asked, fingering the fabric, but I didn't take it immediately, unsure of the protocol in that situation. I was never supposed to see him again. I couldn't take his shirt...could I? I looked up to meet his gaze again. "Cheerleaders, I mean."

"No." The answer came quickly and made me smile. He

pushed the shirt toward me again. "Here, take this, you'll be more comfortable." John's attention returned to the bag after he pulled his own shirt over his head, methodically packing things into the suitcase that had barely been unpacked to begin with. He was leaving already? That was a quick trip...

"You're never getting this back, by the way," I said, tying the back of the vastly oversized shirt into a small knot and tucking it inside the back.

"It's yours now." John laughed. "I'm sorry I have to run, but...I can drop you off at home first." His face when he looked at the clock said otherwise, though.

"You don't have to. I can manage to get a cab."

He smiled weakly—grateful almost—which told me he didn't have the time to drop me off, but the offer was sweet. "I really should go."

"It's okay, go."

He stooped down to capture my lips in a deep kiss, snaking his arm around my waist to pull me further against him. That was not how one-night stands end, but you want to know something? I wasn't complaining. Not when it felt so right being in his arms. The way he made me feel...it was like walking on air while being tethered to the Earth at the same time. Standing there, his lips pressed firmly against mine, it started to hit me that I'd never see him again...

"C'mon," John said. "Least I can do is get you a cab." I didn't argue, following him out of the room, his fingers interlaced with mine as the door closed behind us.

And when I walked into Adler Training Center that afternoon to begin what I liked to call hell week—the week leading into preseason—it was the furthest place from where I wanted to be...How was I supposed to worry about following routines and working on tightening up our weak spots when my head was in the fucking clouds all day? It was fair to say I'd been on autopilot most of the day, going through the motions at the café and barely able to comprehend the words I put on the page for the paper due for my single class of the summer semester. Despite my attempts to put it on the back burner, I hadn't been able to get him out of my head.

A loud bang echoed from the other side of the locker room door of the training center, and I stopped short right before it burst open. One of the only blonde girls on the squad stormed out, and another followed two steps behind. I rolled my eyes as they passed by. I should've known it was them. They were always fighting over something—usually over a guy. The same guy. A similar situation happened two months prior, and I just hoped it didn't take the coaches to separate them.

The rest of the squad seemed to be in good spirits when I finally walked into the locker room, despite what awaited us on that field. Wide grins split their faces as they filled each other in on the latest drama and gossip. I waved at them when they called my name before I dropped my bag on the floor, sinking into the chair in front of the mirror near my locker.

"So, how was last night?" Kingsley appeared out of nowhere, leaning back against the lockers. I glanced her way but rolled my eyes. "Oh, c'mon, Sav! You go home with one of the hottest guys to find his way into the Valley in like...*ever*, and you give me the silent treatment?" Her freshly manicured hands fell to her hips. "Cass and I tried to text you, but...Oh my gosh. Wait, was it bad? Tell me it wasn't bad. Oh, sweetie! I'm so sorry. Your first one-night stand, and it sucked."

"Kins, breathe!" I laughed, pulling my hair into a ponytail. "It wasn't bad. I just...I don't have anything to say."

"That's all I get?" Kingsley's blue eyes narrowed, and she groaned dramatically when I shrugged. "What am I going to do with you, Savannah Williams?"

"You wouldn't have me any other way," I said, swapping out my long sleeve for a tank top. "Look okay?"

"Yeah, just don't let Cathy see that thing on your chest."

What is she talking about?

The smirk that spread across my friend's lips made me paranoid. Turning back to the mirror, my eyes were immediately drawn to the dark discoloration of skin on my shoulder. If either coach saw it, I'd never hear the end of how having a hickey in such a prominent place was not ladylike and not appropriate Wildcat behavior. The idea to curse John came to mind, but as soon as I thought about his mouth on my skin, it killed the impulse entirely.

"I'll take that as evidence you had a *great* time last night," Kingsley said, trying to hide her smirk.

I glared at her, replacing the tank top with my long-sleeve practice top. "Shut up."

"Hey, mission accomplished, right?" She looped her arm through mine after I double-checked my appearance in the mirror to make sure no more surprises were waiting for me. "We went out to take your mind off Conner, and it seems like we succeeded. So, mission accomplished!"

Holy shit, she's right, I thought as we walked out to the field. I hadn't thought about Conner once since John had come to my aid. I had been too busy thinking about the one man I knew I couldn't have.

Kingsley and Cassandra finally stopped asking questions about that night about a month ago. They'd randomly bring it up, trying to pry any information from me they could, especially when I'd turn down anyone who came up to me when we'd go out. But the truth was, I don't want to start hooking up with other guys—John or no John. That wasn't me.

My phone vibrates from somewhere on the bed, ripping me from the memories, and before I can find it, there are five more dings. That can only mean one thing: the Williams sibling group chat. Years ago, my youngest brother, Bodhi, had properly named it The Inner Circle.

The first message is from my second-oldest brother, Nash. It comes with a link to an application for tryouts at Elite Wrestling Entertainment set to take place next month. He cannot be serious. Nash is a lot of things, but a professional wrestler is not one of them. When we were little, Nash and Crew were obsessed with wrestling; without fail, they would watch EWE every Monday night and Saturday morning. Somehow, I always found myself caught in the middle of their matches, until Crew grew out of it by the time he turned fifteen and got a girlfriend. Nash, though, never did. He still watches every week, but he has finally come to accept that it's not real...I think.

Nash Williams
You see this?

Elite Wrestling Entertainment Tryouts
ewe.com

Bodhi Williams
No, but I'd pay good money to see you step foot in the ring with those guys.

Blake Williams
He wouldn't last five minutes.

Bodhi Williams
That's generous.

Crew Williams
Come on. Be nice.

Nash Williams
Thank you, Crew.

Crew Williams

We all know he wouldn't even make it up the steps.

A wave of laughing faces floods the chat after that.

He'd make it up the steps, but he'd probably trip and fall climbing through the ropes. He'd make it really easy for his opponent.

Nash Williams

Dickheads.

Love you

Nash Williams

Fuck you

You guys talk a big game for people who wouldn't even consider it.

Blake Williams

I am quite literally the least athletic person in our family. WHY would I put myself in that position?

I'm a professional cheerleader. What more do you want from me?

Bodhi Williams

Get punched in the face < Go to college.

Crew Williams

I get enough excitement around the ranch. I don't need to go prance around in tights in front of millions to get my kicks.

Nash Williams

Exactly, SJ. You're already a professional athlete, so why don't you try out?

Oh, come on, Crew, I'm sure Amara would find it sexy.

Ummmmm...because I'm not into that shit? You weirdos are the ones who like it, not me.

Bodhi Williams

Imagine SJ as a wrestler. 😬

What is that supposed to mean? I could be a wrestler if I *wanted* to be. Between my background in cheerleading, volleyball, and dance, I could hold my own in the ring.

Blake Williams

At least she has her brains to fall back on.

That one stings a little, but I know the twins don't mean it the way I'm taking it. Blake and Bodhi are the youngest Williams siblings. They came as a surprise, born five years after my parents decided they were done having kids. They're good boys, but too smart for their own good, and sometimes think they're better...no, smarter than their older siblings. Mamá and Papá would never admit it—refuse to, actually— but they spoil the twins, and in my humble opinion (not that it matters), I think it's setting them up to be crushed by the real world sooner rather than later. Sometimes, I worry for them when they go off to college in two years.

I try to think of a response, but the only one that comes to mind shocks me. Their remarks ignite a desire within me to not only prove the twins wrong, but all four of my brothers.

And proving them wrong would mean…trying out for EWE. What am I saying? That's crazy. I'm not going to try out for EWE.

Nash Williams

I dare you to do it.

Crew Williams

What are you talking about?

Nash Williams

I DARE our sister to try out for EWE.

Crew Williams

You've got to be kidding.

Get your ass back to work, Nash. Stop fucking around.

Mom wants us home in time for dinner.

Nash Williams

She won't do it.

See?

She hasn't even responded

Crew Williams

Because you're being a jackass. She's probably getting ready for the game.

Leave her alone.

Nash Williams

Nah, she's scared.

Blake Williams

Bodhi Williams

I know they've been going back and forth for a few minutes now, but my brain hasn't moved on from Nash's text *daring* me to try out. The longer I stare at it, the more I think I'm starting to consider it...No, what am I saying?

"Fuck it," I say, opening the link Nash sent earlier. What's the harm in trying? "Not like I'll make it anyway." My fingers tremble slightly the whole time I fill out the required information. One of the questions stops me: *How many years have you been wrestling?*

Is that a requirement? Surely not. It can't be *that* hard. Whatever moves they throw at me, I can figure it out. And if all else fails, I'd follow what everyone else is doing.

Taking a deep breath, I enter a zero in the space before coming to the end. The bright red "Submit" button stares back at me, but my thumb only hovers over it. Am I really going to do this? This isn't me. This isn't even close to what I want to do with my life, but maybe that's the point. I've been trying to figure out what I want to do after college, but I can't find the answer. I've been thinking about stepping down from the Wildcats after this season. This will be my third season with the team, and I'm not sure I have another one left in me. I'm supposed to graduate in May, which leaves me only six more months to find something else to do if I decide not to stick with the team, and I've procrastinated lining up a job after graduation.

Maybe this is the change I've been looking for.

My thumb presses down, and in less than a second, the confirmation page appears. *Thank you for submitting your application to Elite Wrestling Entertainment. We will be in touch with your next steps!*

Holy shit, I did it.

The conversation between my brothers has finally died down, but something tells me it's about to start up again. Fortunately, I have to get ready to leave for the stadium, which means I won't have time to answer the slew of texts about to hit my phone. A smile tugs at my lips as I type the words and hit send, followed by a picture of the confirmation page, before tossing my phone in my purse.

Wanna bet?

3

Savannah

SATURDAY, DECEMBER 20, 2008

CELESTIA, TX

Christmas at Willow Pond Farm is anything but a silent night, especially with four boys running amok. By some miracle, Coach made the last-minute decision to change practice from the normal evening start time to first thing this morning. Even though the squad was tired after the Los Angeles game last night, not a single one of us complained. How could we? Practice would be over by noon, and we'd have the next three days off. By early afternoon, I was in the car, driving two-and-a-half hours straight to my family's ranch just outside of Celestia.

When I arrived at my family's ranch two hours ago, Mamá was prepping dinner, and I've been wrist-deep in a variety of dishes since I walked in the door. Green bean casserole, homemade mashed potatoes, stuffing, mac'n'cheese, salad, and Easter bread are just a few of the staples we prepared.

My sixteen-year-old twin brothers finally dragged themselves out of bed about an hour ago, and when I glanced at my mother with a cocked brow, she wiped her hands on her blue-striped apron and started loading food into the oven, pretending not to notice. I didn't have to say it for her to know what I was thinking. She'd heard it more than enough times, but it never ceased to amaze me the difference in how the twins get away with things my older brothers and I could never.

Speaking of my older brothers...they *still* haven't shown up. Mamá said they were out in the field moving the cattle, which meant they could be home in an hour or maybe three, depending on how much they fucked around. Without Papá joining them, Crew and Nash are more likely to mess around while they work. Not that I blame them, it keeps the day from dragging. My brothers chose to work on the ranch after high school, while I decided to pursue college and cheerleading. However, Nash recently accepted a job as one of Celestia High School's football and lacrosse coaches, which gives him some purpose outside of the ranch, and I think it's been good for him. I always knew he'd get bored with the farm life, unlike Crew. Our oldest brother enjoys his simple life; it was obvious when we were kids that he'd take over one day. He enjoyed being on the ranch, liked working with the animals, with his hands, and with Papá. Sometimes I wonder if he ever thinks about life outside Celestia—of all the things he could be doing—but when I asked him about it a few years ago, Crew said the ranch was his home and working here gave him a purpose.

Speak of the devils.

There's a loud commotion outside the back door before Crew shoves Nash inside and smacks him on the back of the head. *Typical. Wonder what he did this time.*

Nash rubs his head, glaring at our brother, before he notices me. His grimace lifts into a smile before he shares a knowing glance with Crew. With a nod, they split the difference, coming around either side of the kitchen island. *Shit*, I know what's coming.

"Well, well, well, look who finally decided to show up," Nash says, knowing that I have nowhere to run. I try to use my mother as a blockade to get away, but he grabs hold of my waist, hoisting me onto his shoulder. He spins in a circle at least five times before I lose count.

When I beg for help, Crew's only response is a hearty laugh. He pulls one of the chilled water bottles from the fridge that Mamá keeps ready and waiting for them. "Better learn how to get out of it if you're going to be a wrestler, Sav," Crew says.

Nash comes to a complete stop, but my head doesn't. The world continues to spin long after he sets me back on my feet. Even with my eyes closed, I can see the way his eyes bug out of his head, looking between me and Crew. I hear Mamá chuckle to herself from somewhere behind us. "What did you just say?" Nash asks. "Did you just say...Savannah! You're going to be a...Holy shit! You mean you actually did it?"

I glare at Crew. "Thanks, I was saving that for later."

"Sue me," he says with a shrug. Mamá swats at his hand when he swipes a green bean from the platter beside her and says a few scolding words in Spanish. He laughs, popping the vegetable in his mouth before he walks back outside, probably to join Papá at the grill.

"Are you punking me?" Nash asks.

"Nope," I say, and straighten out my shirt after his assault. "I got the call on Thursday."

Exactly one week after tryouts, I got a call from Xander Collins, head of Talent Relations at Elite Wrestling Entertainment. While I thought the tryout went okay, I decided to be realistic about my chances of getting a callback. I wasn't as qualified as some of the others who were there, but I wasn't the worst by any means. From the second I stepped into the ring, I was surprised by how much I enjoyed it. Standing in the squared circle—a term I learned through my quick internet search of basic wrestling moves—was like a shot of pure adrenaline to my nervous system. A rush like I'd never experienced, and the longer I was there, the more I wanted to stay. Getting the phone call from Xander made missing practice—and the scolding from Coach the next day—worth it. One practice in three years wasn't the end of the world, but you'd think I'd committed a felony. Their response was the final nail in the coffin for the relationship between me and the Wildcats. No matter the outcome with EWE, I wasn't returning to the team after this season.

"You're going to do it, right?"

"I was thinking about it," I say with a shrug.

"You have to!"

I laugh. "I said, I'm thinking about it."

"Nash," Mamá cuts him off before he can pester me further. "Leave your sister alone. Go outside and see if your father is almost done with the *asado*. The three of you need to wash up before dinner."

"But, Mamá—"

"Now," she says. "Go." Mamá shoos him outside despite his pleas to stay. I'm sure he has a million questions. Like, did I meet any famous wrestlers? Was it hard? Was it fake, or did the punches hurt?

"You still owe me $100," I yell before the door closes on his backside.

Mamá mutters to herself, wiping her hands on her apron, and when she looks at me, her shoulders rise and fall with a heavy sigh. This is how it always is around here. The boys give my parents a run for their money, not to say I haven't a time or two, but they wouldn't have it any other way. She motions to the dishes covered in foil that sit on the counter. "Help me move this food over to the table. Not long before the rest will be done."

We move them over in silence, but I know her own

questions are bubbling beneath the surface. Questions I know she has wanted to ask since I told her about the call two days ago, but she waited until we could be face-to-face. Truthfully, I'm surprised she lasted this long. My mother is nothing if not persistent, and when she wants something, she has no issue making that fact well known.

"Do you want this, Sav?" she asks, dropping the final baking dish on the table. "You know that your father and I support you in whatever you decide to do, but...I just— We want to make sure this is what *you* want. Just because you made it doesn't mean you have to go. You still have the Wildcats and your degree and—"

"I know, Mamá." I toy with the fabric of the red tablecloth draped over the long table my father built years ago. He built most of the furniture that fills these rooms, some with our help, and others as experiments.

"When do you have to make a decision?"

"Monday." I wrap my arms around my torso. "I'd start in their developmental program at the end of February...It's in Florida."

"Florida?" My mother's outburst makes me flinch. She flies into a rage of Spanglish as she paces between the dining room and the kitchen. I knew this was coming the moment Xander told me I'd have to move to Tampa, where their training facility is located. She finally pauses at the island, her hands wringing the fabric of her apron. "There is no way, Savannah! You won't graduate. You can't just—You can't move across the country! All of...All of your hard work gone to waste. You won't—"

"I know, Mamá. I know!" Taking a deep breath, I rub my eyes and meet her intense stare from across the kitchen. "I know, okay? But this is...I don't know. It's hard to explain. When I was in that ring, it felt...good. Right. Like I'm supposed to be there."

"*Ay*, Savannah." She shakes her head, eyes drawn to the ceiling.

"I see you broke the news to your brother," Papá's voice booms when he walks inside not two seconds later. He's a bigger man, the kind of man you'd expect to see on a ranch, with a rugged face and graying beard. His skin is permanently tanned from years of work in the sun. He towers over my mother by at least six inches, and he passed that gene onto my brothers, while I land somewhere in the middle.

Mamá points at me. "Wesley, please talk some sense into your daughter. She's talking about leaving school to go do this silly wrestling thing."

"I can always transfer. I don't have to drop out," I say.

"Now hold on a second, let's back up," Papá says, stepping between us. "What's all this about?"

I look over my shoulder, but my mother only glares at me. Her arms cross over her chest with a raised brow, waiting to hear not only my explanation, but my father's response. It takes everything in me not to roll my eyes. "Mamá is upset because *if* I decide to join EWE, I have to move...to Florida... in February."

"February?" His dark brows arch toward his graying hairline. "That means you'd have to leave Thornebrooke."

"Or transfer," I say, quickly. "I can finish my last semester in Tampa after I get settled. I'll have to take the next semester off, but I can apply to some schools there...I can still graduate. It's no different from what I'm doing now!"

Papá's features soften. He places a hand on my mother's shoulder, giving it a gentle squeeze, and she covers it with her own. The look on her face tells me that Mamá thinks she has won this argument, but his eyes tell a different story. "Will you get paid while you're training with EWE?"

"More than I make with the Wildcats."

"Well, it would seem you've already thought it all through."

"Wesley!" Mamá shouts. There's a fire in her eyes that tells me she is ready to stand her ground on this, but my father lifts his hands, quieting whatever protests she had in mind.

"So, what's the problem, Savannah?"

The problem is that I can't seem to find a problem. The longer I search for a reason not to do this, not to join EWE, the more I find reasons to say yes. The only thing left to do is pull the trigger.

"Is this what you want to do?" Papá asks.

Mamá refuses to meet my stare when I look between them. She's hurt, and I think it has more to do with the fact that starting this new career means moving across the country and less to do with the college thing. If I do this, I'll be the first person in our family to "officially" leave the nest. I won't be a quick two-hour drive anymore; it will be more like twenty. All four of my brothers still live at home. Crew and Nash occupy the guest house within walking distance of our childhood home, and the twins have two more years before they go to college. The thought of being so far away from them scares me, but not enough to say no.

My index finger scratches along the surface of the island, eyes glued to the Corian countertop. This wasn't supposed to happen. I wasn't supposed to want this. It was only supposed to prove my brothers wrong. I sigh. "It was supposed to be a joke."

"That's not what I asked."

"Yes. This is what I want to do," I say, finally lifting my gaze.

The guest house is the opposite of what you'd expect from

two bachelors, especially when those two bachelors are my older brothers. It's clean, tidy, and the air carries a warm, woody scent with a hint of floral. However, the furniture is exactly what you'd expect. "'Cats seem to be doing okay this year," Crew says, handing me a beer before he plops down into the dark chocolate leather recliner beside the matching couch.

Papá built the guest house a long time ago for when the rest of the family came to visit. It eventually became our hangout spot until I begged my parents to let me move my room out here during my sophomore year of high school. Crew moved in not long after I went to Thornebrooke, and Nash joined him when his apartment lease ended last year. Yesterday, though, I overheard Papá talking with Mamá about giving my oldest brother some land to build on. If that happens, they'd be one step closer to officially becoming empty nesters. I'm not sure my mother is quite ready for that, though.

"Might even make it to the Super Bowl."

Oh, goody.

Don't get me wrong, it would be amazing to be part of a championship team, but that means I'll have to stick around for two more months after the regular season, and I was looking forward to having some time off before heading to Tampa. He's not wrong, though. The Wildcats have had an incredible season, and with only two games left in the regular season, it's become glaringly obvious that we are headed for the playoffs.

"You don't look too happy about that, SJ," Nash says over his shoulder, using the nickname reserved only for my brothers, and occasionally Mamá. A combination of my first and middle names: Savannah Josefine. He's been flipping through television stations to find something to watch for the last twenty minutes, and if he doesn't find something in the next five, I'm turning it off.

"I'm not *not* happy about it."

"But?" Crew pushes, sipping his beer.

"I'm just ready for a change."

"Well, you're about to get the change of a lifetime."

"Hey, look!" Nash finally stops on a channel, and my annoyance only grows. He's picked *Monday Night Rage*—Elite Wrestling Entertainment's weekly Monday night spectacle. Before I can protest, he says, "You should probably start watching these, y'know? Get used to it because this is about to become your life."

"What she needs to watch is the old stuff, back when *Juliet* and *Holly* were still around," Crew says, igniting the conversation further. They start naming off a slew of different characters. Some sound familiar, and others I've never heard of in my life. The more they talk, the more I realize Nash isn't wrong...I should be watching. It's no different than a football player watching tapes to see how they can improve or study their opponent. I haven't watched EWE in years, at least a decade, which means it might be a good idea to start.

A woman appears on the screen carrying an oversized white belt with an intricate design made from gold, jewels, and pink accents, with the EWE logo front and center. She must be the champion. Beneath her image, the name *Moxie* appears on the screen. Her clothes are a mixture of black and neon colors with a leather jacket over her shoulders; the whole ensemble has a preppy-punk vibe. She's talking to the backstage interviewer about her upcoming match against someone named *Luna Haze*—that name sounds familiar, unlike *Moxie*. I think this is what they call a "promo," something meant to help build the tension and momentum leading up to the big match.

Moxie laughs when the interviewer asks if she's worried. She oozes confidence, leaning into the other woman, and I half expect the interviewer, whose name I didn't catch, to take a step back, but she holds her ground, poised and graceful. She barely even flinches when the wrestler gets in her face. *"What is there to be worried about? Luna Haze is a washed-up has-been trying to stay relevant when she needs to go back to the old folks' home before she gets herself hurt."* The champion scoffs, walking away from the interview without another word. The camera pans to follow her strut down the hallway before fading to the show's commentators sitting at a ringside desk.

"She's hot," Nash says, and I realize my brothers have halted their conversation. "You think you can introduce me to her when you get there?"

"First off, she probably has a boyfriend," I say, twisting the top off my beer. "Secondly, he's probably a wrestler who could most definitely beat your ass."

"Hey! I could take one of them."

"Now that's something I'd pay to see," Crew says, and I can't help but laugh when Nash throws the remote at his head. The remote flies over the back of the chair when Crew ducks just in time, and while he could easily respond with an old-fashioned raise of his middle finger, my oldest brother decides that's not enough. Just like when we were kids, they lock up in the middle of the floor, and Crew overpowers Nash within seconds. He puts Nash into a submission hold that, from my spot on the couch, looks extremely uncomfortable. Their legs are a tangled mess, with Nash on his stomach as Crew squats down to practically sit on Nash's back. "Ask him, ref!"

"Oh, for crying out loud." With an exasperated sigh, I slink down to the floor to act as referee. As much as I want to hate being pulled into their antics, I can't. This kind of thing excited me when I was little. I loved being included in anything my older brothers did. But as the years passed, I found myself more interested in things like cheerleading, going to the mall, dance, and just being a teenage girl, and the idea of professional wrestling seemed…juvenile. I don't know if that's the right word, but it's the first that always came to mind. Now look at me, eating my words because in less than three months, I will be walking into my first day of training as a professional wrestler. "What do you say, Nash?"

"No!" He shakes his head furiously despite the clear pain written across his face.

Crew adjusts the grip on our brother's legs, keeping them locked together, and sits back further. He glances over his shoulder to taunt Nash. "Come on, man. Don't try to be the hero."

This is how it's always been. Nash rarely gets the upper hand or wins, but he always puts up a good fight. And per usual, he refuses to tap until he just can't take it anymore, or until Mamá comes in and tells them to knock it off before they break something—themselves or one of her decorations. Despite how rough they can get with each other, there's only been one trip to the hospital that I can recall. I'll spare you the details, but let's just say there was a roof and a table involved.

I start to ask Nash whether he concedes, but he beats me to it, slapping the palm of his hand on the floor numerous times. "That's it, he taps! Break the hold."

Crew untangles their legs, stepping out of the hold like it was nothing. He takes a long drink of his beer before he glances over at me. "Well, if nothing else, you'll make a good referee."

4

Savannah

WEDNESDAY, FEBRUARY 25, 2009

TAMPA, FL

I'm here...I made it. I left central Texas, left the Wildcats, left the only life I've ever known, and in just a few minutes, I'm going to walk through those doors and officially become an Elite Wrestling Entertainment wrestler. If you want to be technical about it, yes, I became a wrestler the day I signed the contract, but this—standing here in front of the NextGen training center—makes it feel *real*. If only sixteen-year-old Savannah could see me now, she might have a heart attack.

The Williams family goodbye was harder than expected, but I'm not sure who it was harder on: me or them. I know (and I think they do, too) it's for the best. The entire drive from Celestia to Tampa, I was excited and nervous, maybe even a little nauseous, but as we got closer to my new home, the nerves turned into something else...something more raw. Something I can only remember experiencing one other time, in the moments leading up to my very first cheerleading competition.

The Wildcats went on to the Super Bowl, where they lost to New England by a single point. It was a disappointing blow, but at least I can say I cheered on a championship-level team. Whether or not they won doesn't matter to me; the experience alone was worth the two extra months. After the loss, I spent a few days at home before my parents helped me drive across the country and move into my new apartment.

I don't know what I expected the training facility to look like, but I know it wasn't this. The building looks more like a warehouse with solid, white-washed walls and only a few windows in what I think is the lobby area. For an organization that prides itself on being extravagant and over the top, this is extremely underwhelming. Compared to their headquarters in Houston, where they held tryouts, this is the off-brand, prototype version. No, it might be worse than that.

Headquarters was housed in a beautiful building with walls made of glass and a wrestling belt the size of the state of Tennessee sitting on the front lawn. The inside was just as awe-inspiring, with glass walls and stark white floors that shone in the sunlight streaming in from the skylight above. Auditions were held in the basement, where they had a permanent ring set up. It seemed odd at first to house a wrestling ring in the basement of a corporate office, but then again...this is a wrestling empire. Why wouldn't they have one?

"Fucking hell," comes from across the parking lot, followed by the slam of a car door. The same voice mutters loudly before I see a woman with long black hair digging through the trunk of a beat-up Volkswagen. She groans, cursing under her breath, and slams the trunk probably harder than necessary. She huffs, crossing her arms, and glares at the car, as if it will magically give her what she wants if she waits long enough.

"You okay?"

"Fine," she says, finally peeling her stare from the trunk to look at me. "I forgot my damn knee pads, and my hairband just broke, and I can't wear a damn clip in the ring." She groans, combing her fingers through her hair. "I don't feel like dealing with all of this in the ring today."

"Knee pads?" Was that a requirement? Because if so, I never got the memo.

"Yes! I forgot them...somewhere." She twists her hair into a quick knot before letting it fall down her back again. "I'm always losing those things. I should buy stock in them at this point because I swear I buy a new set every damn week. I'd lose my head if it wasn't attached." Lucky for her, I may not have knee pads, but I do have a spare hairband. Pulling it off my wrist, I offer it to her, and she looks like she could cry when she realizes what it is. "You are my new best friend." She pulls long, black locks into her hands, threading them through the band in three quick strides, and tightens them into a messy bun on top of her head. She exhales a long, steady breath before extending her hand to me. "I'm Raelynn."

"Savannah."

"You're the cheerleader, right?"

"I'm scared to say yes."

Raelynn laughs. "I started last week with a few of the others. They told us you'd finally be here today."

Great, now I'm going to be playing a game of catch-up. I'm already going to be behind, considering I haven't been doing this for the last ten years. From what I read online, most people who come into this have been wrestling for many years prior. It consumes their life from a young age. Sure, there are a few here and there who have a background in something else—a few models, a few soccer players, a few cheerleaders—but most everyone comes from the "indies." That's what they call the independent circuit, or the smaller, more regionalized companies not associated with the bigger ones like EWE. And wouldn't you know, there are hundreds of them all across the world.

"Don't worry, I'm sure you'll be fine." Raelynn waves her hand in dismissal, with a quiet pfft. "Cheerleading and wrestling are basically the same thing."

That's a lie; cheerleading and wrestling are completely different things, but I appreciate the sentiment. I've been concerned that my lack of wrestling background and surplus of cheer experience will make it hard for my future colleagues to take me seriously, but Raelynn doesn't seem to mind at all.

Glancing back at the center, I can't help but feel like I'm about to walk into a detention center instead of a professional wrestling gym. I ask, "Why does it feel like if I walk in there, I might not walk out?"

"Depending on who's running the show, you might not." Raelynn laughs. "It's better on the inside, I promise. Not as sketchy. Okay, maybe a little sketchy, but it gets the job done."

"Well, whoever it is, they can't be any worse than my last assistant coach. I think she was a warden in a previous life."

"Then you'll feel right at home with Fata," Raelynn says, snaking her pale arm around my shoulders. Fata. Why does that name sound so familiar? I consider asking her, but decide not to let my ignorance show within my first five minutes.

"Great, can't wait," I say with a tight smile.

"Come on, we'd better get inside. He hates when people are late."

"Late?" I check my watch. "It's not even 7:30."

"First rule: Always be here and in the ring at least fifteen minutes early. That applies to any of the trainers, but especially on the days when Fata is here."

Did she just say Fata?

Before she guides me inside, Raelynn does one final sweep of the parking lot and sighs. "And let's hope Bennett shows up on time, or you're going to get one hell of a welcome gift."

A memory that has been buried deep bubbles to the surface when I step inside the training center and come face-to-face with someone who used to fill the screen of our CRT television on Saturday mornings. Juliet Briggs—one of the biggest names in the history of women's wrestling. Moments pass before my brain finally catches up to the reality I'm currently living, and I take the hand she extends. That's the other thing my quick internet search told me. Shake hands with everyone—it's a sign of respect, and the most important unwritten rule of the sport. Her handshake is soft, yet firm all the same. Juliet is smaller than I thought she'd be, standing about my height, with shoulder-length chestnut hair and warm brown eyes that remind me of my grandmother, but she doesn't look a day over thirty. I know she has to be in her late thirties, though. It's been at least thirteen years since the last time I saw her on EWE.

I follow two steps behind the veteran through steel double doors into what I imagine is every wrestler's dream. It reminds me of the Alder, but instead of a football field, there are three rings placed in a clover pattern. Multiples of every exercise machine you can think of line the far right and bend round the corner, where human-shaped punching bags stand in a line. Black curtains conceal a doorway in the opposite corner, leading deeper into the building, and two steel doors beside it lead into what I imagine are the locker rooms.

After giving me a quick tour, Juliet pokes her head through the curtains. Satisfied, she pulls them to the side and ushers me through. On the other side is a fourth ring, but this one looks cleaner, less exhausted than its counterparts. A black skirt hides the belly of the ring, with the EWE and NextGen logos displayed on alternating sides.

"This is where they hold shows for the kids in developmental," Juliet says. We walk down the small ramp into the perimeter squared off by metal barricades and surrounded by stadium seating, with only five or six rows of chairs on the floor. "It's a great way to test your character... See what works with a live crowd, what doesn't."

"They're televised?" I ask, noticing the camera a few rows up.

"Once a month, they put it out there, but it's mostly for you guys to watch back."

Raelynn's description of the place is pretty spot on... Sketchy, but not too sketchy, and gets the job done. The Wildcats had the best of the best of everything, but if I had learned anything in my time with the 'Cats, it was that determination and spirit make a person the best, not the things they have.

"You were a cheerleader for...Alexandria, right?" Juliet asks, but I know from my conversation with Raelynn outside that she knows the answer. Everyone does, but I'm not here to make waves, at least not yet, so I'll play along.

"Born and raised a Wildcat," I say.

"My parents are in San Antonio, but they're diehard Wildcat fans." Her eyes roll into the back of her head, and I can imagine that comes from the mere mental image of game days with her parents. Wildcat fans can be...intense. "Pop couldn't believe they went all the way this year. Normally, they choke in the final rush to the finish line."

"Well, they kind of did," I say, laughing. Sure, the 'Cats had made it to the big game, but they hadn't been able to pull it out in the end. "I think the only reason we got there was the new offensive line coach. He wasn't messing around, came in and brought new life to the team." Not to mention, he wasn't too bad to look at from the sidelines either. Just because we couldn't touch, didn't mean we couldn't look, and he'd caught Kingsley and me looking on more than one occasion.

"Well, looks like Barbie finally decided to grace us with her presence!" A loud voice booms from behind us, where a hulk of a man walks down the ramp.

You've got to be kidding. Did he call me *Barbie*?

The smirk hasn't left his lips since he walked through the curtain. He gives me a quick once-over, and I wonder if he thinks it will intimidate me, but I've been under the scrutinous eye of professional cheerleading coaches, and there's nothing harsher than that. "I've heard all about you, Pom-Poms."

Great, another nickname.

"I wish I could say the same," I say, and his face falls.

Juliet stifles a laugh behind her hand, clearing her throat. "I think you might have met your match, Fata."

Fata?

Holy shit, it is Fata. I barely recognized him without the hair and in costume. I should've known by his size alone. Ezekiel Slade, better known to the world and me as *"The Great" Fata*. Mental note: he prefers to be called Fata. Underneath his black sweatsuit, I know there's warm, brown skin covered in black ink—the tribal markings of his heritage. The Slade family has been part of the wrestling industry for decades, spanning back further than the founding of EWE. Fata used to sport a head full of curly black hair that reached the middle of his back and a face full of scruff, both gone in favor of a clean-shaven face and head.

"Be nice, Fata," Juliet continues. "Don't run her off before she ever gets in the ring."

Fata laughs before he winds an arm around her petite frame, practically swallowing her whole in his embrace. "If she wanted to run, she would've done it the moment she took a look at the outside of this shit hole."

Juliet rolls her eyes and slaps him on the chest.

Extending his hand to me, Fata says, "It's nice to meet you, Savannah. I've heard good things."

I'm sure his words are meant to be comforting, but they do the exact opposite, melting my insides into a puddle beneath our combined hands. What does that mean? And why has my presence been such a big topic of conversation?

Following him and Juliet back through the curtain, Fata continues, "I look forward to seeing if the guys at corporate were right. From what I hear, it was between you and Caitlin Dubois."

"Yeah, and it should've been Caitlin." A female voice scoffs, drawing my attention to the middle ring where two women hang over the ropes. It's almost impossible not to guess who said it. Her almond-shaped eyes glare down at me while her counterpart looks down at her feet. "Just because you decided to hang up your pom-poms for wrestling boots doesn't mean you deserve to take the place of someone who *knows* what they're doing. Cheerleaders don't belong here. It's people like you who give real wrestlers a bad name."

"Oh, give it a rest, Harp," Raelynn says, coming to stand beside me. Looks like she found her kneepads, after all. The black squares now cover her knees beneath her capri-length leggings.

"You know it's true!"

A small crowd has formed now, and I only recognize one person from tryouts last December—Colin, I think? I'd never forget him or the electric blue color of his eyes that pierced straight through to your soul. They're the opposite color of a different set of blue eyes I think about more than I'd like to admit. Colin catches my stare over the crowd before he offers me a single nod. I return the gesture before Fata finally decides to break up the argument. "Harper, you seem extra peppy today. Why don't you take the lead on laps?"

I can see the complaint building in her face, but she bites it back, swallowing whatever she was about to say. Her full lips pull into a thin line, and she releases a hard exhale before stepping through the middle ropes and jumping down from the outside edge of the ring—I believe we're supposed to call it the apron? Harper's counterpart, whose name I still haven't caught, follows suit, and they walk with their heads held high toward the open garage doors that lead out to the parking lot.

"Go on, Pom-Poms," Fata says, urging me to join the single-file line that now follows Harper. "Oh, and Savannah, don't come in last."

A heavy dullness weighs down my feet with every step into my apartment. My body feels stiff yet alive at the same time, with a pulsing ache deep within every fiber of my being. I heave my duffle bag onto the kitchen island before I fall face-first against the cool countertop, relishing in the moment of silence and stillness. Turning my head to the other side, I spot bright green numbers that tell me it's just past six o'clock. Just enough time to shower, stretch, eat, and sleep before I have to get up and do it all over again tomorrow.

I knew this was going to be hard—physically, maybe a little mentally—but I didn't expect it to be just as emotionally draining. When I pulled into the parking spot reserved for my apartment, I hadn't expected the wave of emotion that overpowered me. It started with a prick in the corners of my eyes and only continued to build from there until I was sobbing in the front seat of my car. The emotional toll that today had taken on me was something I wasn't prepared for, and as I sat there, I couldn't help but wonder if I could actually do this.

My phone rings inside my bag, and I search blindly until I find it. I answer without looking because I have two guesses: Mamá or Nash. My father would wait until I called him, and Crew would wait until at least Saturday.

"How was it?" My second-oldest brother's voice rings out over the speaker. "Was it amazing? Was it terrible? Was it—"

"Nash, breathe," I say, finally pushing up from the counter and taking a deep breath myself. Guiding my arms over my head, I swear I can feel the rush of tingling lactic acid through my muscles, leaving a simmering fire in its wake.

"Okay, but how was it?" Nash pushes. "Did you meet anyone? What did you do? Do you like it?"

I laugh, opening the fridge to take inventory of its contents before pulling out only a water bottle. I'll figure out food after I take a much-needed shower—hell, maybe even a hot bath.

"It was great. I worked with Fata and Juliet. We just started with basic bumps, easy takedowns, running the ropes…stuff like that," I say. It's not the answer he's looking for, but I don't have the energy to detail my entire day for him.

I now knew this was something you had to experience to understand. I knew it would be a different kind of physicality, but I thought all of my experience in cheer would lend some favor…

I was wrong.

Twenty laps around the building—including the entirety of the exterior, back inside around the "ring room" (as I had so eloquently named it), and up and down the various steps of the television room—had been a cakewalk compared to the rest. I lost count of the number of squats somewhere around two hundred and fifty.

Two more trainers joined somewhere between laps ten and eleven: "The All American" Sheldon Goodwin, another EWE veteran I recognized almost instantly, and Jack Cameron, head trainer at the facility. They were working with the more experienced wrestlers—the ones who would be moving up to the main roster soon.

Once we finally got into the ring to start on the basics—like bumps, takedowns, roll-throughs, and rope running—

Juliet observed from the outside, while Fata joined us inside, offering more hands-on guidance.

Nash all but screams into the phone. "You trained with *Fata*?"

"Here we go." I chuckle, shaking my head. I plant my hands on the island and take two steps to stretch out my back. I knew this would happen as soon as I told him.

"I can't believe you met *Fata*, like the *Fata*! What was he like? Is he as big as he looks? Is he nice?"

"Bigger," I say, followed by a beat of silence. I consider telling him that I need to go so I can get ready for round two tomorrow, but he beats me to it.

"You didn't answer my question."

"Which one?" I ask, standing up straight.

"Do you like it?"

Do I like it? I sit back against the edge of the counter and take a long sip of water. It's different than what I imagined it would be, but with every challenge they threw at me today, I felt the desire to not only face it but to overcome it tenfold. To prove to them—and the more experienced trainees—that just because I had "traded in my pom-poms for wrestling boots" didn't mean I couldn't hold my own.

Do I like it? Despite feeling completely and utterly drained, I've never felt more alive. The moment I stepped foot in that ring today, the same rush I felt during tryouts filled my veins, and I knew that no matter what happened, this was where I was meant to be.

Do I like it? A smile creeps its way into the corners of my lips, and I nod.

"Yeah...Yeah, I like it."

"I'm proud of you, SJ." The words wrap around me with a tight squeeze in the way I imagine my brother's arms would if he were standing next to me. Warmth coats my eyes, and I clear my throat, trying to keep the fresh round of tears at bay.

"You're going to be the best fucking wrestler to ever step foot in that ring."

A tearful laugh crawls out of my throat. "I don't know about that."

"I do. We all do. You are the kind of person who has to be the best at whatever you do; I mean, look at your track record. You were the youngest person to join the Wildcats. You earned a scholarship to Thornebrooke for cheerleading—that's unheard of! You—"

"Yes, Nash, okay. I get the point."

"Besides, you're training with Fata and Juliet, two of the greats. If anyone can turn you into a professional wrestler, it's them."

The fluorescent lights flicker to life as Raelynn, Bennett, and I walk into the training center on this beautiful Friday the thirteenth. The weather is perfect, and I only wish we weren't working today so we could go to the beach before the city is overrun by spring breakers next week. Today marks two and a half weeks since I first walked through these doors, and I've continued to fall in love with this sport every day since. Rae and I were surprised when Bennett pulled into the parking lot seconds after we did. He's usually racing through the door seconds before we're supposed to be here. Even Juliet asked him if he was feeling okay when we met her at the door. He rolled his eyes, not answering, and held the door for the three of us to walk inside. Raelynn had introduced me to Bennett on my second day, and maybe it was because he reminded me so much of my brothers—specifically Nash—but we had an instant connection. The three of us have been almost inseparable since. We hang out together on our off days, work out together, and help each other practice.

Bennett James, nicknamed Wolf from his high school football days, has been part of NextGen for almost two years, and from the reaction he got two weeks ago during the live show, I think it's safe to say he's a crowd favorite. NextGen hosts live shows every other week, giving fans the chance to see some of the new talent. Curious to see some of my more experienced colleagues, I snuck in to watch, and I was pleasantly surprised by the number of fans who showed up. The place was packed. Not an empty seat in the house. It was electric inside that room. I've never experienced anything like it before, and it only made me want to know how it felt to be on the other side even more. After what I saw that night, I don't think it will be much longer before Bennett gets called up to the main roster, despite his hesitations.

My only grievance with him is his taste in women. He's infatuated with Harper Valentine, the one person I cannot stand here. Raelynn and I have a theory that it's because she reminds him of his ex-girlfriend, but Bennett vehemently denies it. We brought it up once, the same night we saw the picture of his high school sweetheart, who dumped him when he dropped out of college to pursue his true passion—wrestling. They had been together for five years, and she dropped him like a hot cake, too quick for someone who had been talking about rings and houses two months before.

Even though Harper knows about his crush, she doesn't give him the time of day, which is probably for the best. And that's the one nice thing I have to say about her.

"You want to tell me why you're here so early, Wolf?" Raelynn asks for the second time this morning, walking out of the locker room. As if on cue, one of the steel double doors swings open and Fata walks in, followed by a man in a deep maroon-colored suit. Xander Collins, Head of Talent

Relations. The same man who called to offer me a job at Elite Wrestling Entertainment last year.

"Wolf," Fata yells our way. "Office. Now." Raelynn and I look at Bennett, but he ignores our wide-eyed stares and nods at the legend. "Mornin', ladies," Fata adds before he disappears back out the door with Xander and Bennett on his heels.

"What the fuck is going on?" Raelynn asks.

"Do you think..." I trail off. There are only two reasons I can think of why Fata *and* Talent Relations would want to talk to Bennett together. One, he's in trouble, which I don't think is the case; or two, he's being moved up.

"Okay, ladies," Juliet calls out, returning to the ring room. "Let's do some warm-ups. Start with some rope running, bumps, and then ten up-and-overs."

"You're out for blood early today, Juliet," Rae calls over her shoulder, rolling into one of the rings. I chuckle, sliding beneath the bottom rope of a nearby one. On mornings like this, when we have the whole place to ourselves, we like to split up. With a special show tonight—appropriately named Hell Night in honor of it taking place on Friday the 13th—most of our comrades won't be training today because they'll be preparing for their matches. Bennett is supposed to be taking on Asher Slade for the NextGen title, which he was supposed to win, but now I'm wondering if that's still going to happen.

On the outside, rope running looks easy. That's what I thought, anyway, until I did it. Do you know what makes up the ropes of the squared circle? Steel cables encased in a rubber hose and sealed with colored electrical tape. On one hand, it doesn't sound so bad until you hit them the wrong way and those ropes bite back. The bruises I had after tryouts were enough to make me respect anyone who steps foot in a ring, regardless of whether I made it or not.

"Five laps, ladies. And I want clean footwork, got it?"

The last part is meant more for Raelynn, but I appreciate the reminder. "And don't bounce off them like a damn trampoline. Respect the ring and it will respect you."

From the center of the canvas, I take a few running steps forward and reach out with my right arm to grab the top rope and pivot, leaning into the ropes. There isn't much give before they snap back, launching me forward into a rebound. Three large steps, and I reach for the top rope on the other side, pivot, and lean in. *One.* I count the beats between rebounds, now a fluid motion that makes me feel like I'm walking on air. Normally, we'd be doing this with two people, running in opposite directions, and if you're not paying attention or fall behind, you're likely to collide with your ring partner.

"Start over, Rae!" I overhear Juliet yell. "You've been doing this long enough. You should know your footwork better than Savannah."

Rae has been a wrestler for almost five years, joining one of the indie promotions at eighteen. Despite all of the miles she's put on the canvas over the years, you can always count on Raelynn Carson to mess up her footwork at least once a day. Being a wrestler was always her dream, despite the one her parents had for her. They wanted her to be a doctor or a lawyer or a CEO...anything other than a wrestler. She says they came around to the idea a year or so after they watched her first match, but I'm not sure I believe her—she didn't sound that convincing.

Finishing lap five, I come to a stop in the center of the ring, chest heaving, arms burning. My system is already buzzing with adrenaline.

"Hit the mat, Williams. You're not done yet."

On command, I fall back onto the mat. Arms out, chin tucked, spine flat. Bumps are one of the first things you learn how to do when you walk through these doors, because taking a fall properly minimizes the risk of serious injury. If you hit a hard landing wrong, it can change your entire life in the blink of an eye.

"Again," Juliet calls out to me before she tells Rae to hit the mat. "Already winded, Carson?"

I scramble to my feet and do it again. Up. Down. Up. Down. Seventeen more times to make twenty total. By the time I'm done, my legs tremble, aching from the impact of each hit, but I force myself up anyway. Wrestling is a business built on pain. There is no escaping it. You learn to live with it, but practice to avoid and minimize serious injury. Practice is protection. The hesitation that comes along with trying something new is merely a mental hurdle, one that I can't let stop me, because that's the difference between protecting myself and the other person in the ring. *Get out of your head or get out of my ring*, as Fata says.

Without looking my way, Juliet says, "Hit the ropes again, Savannah. Then, when you're done, get over here with Rae and do the up-and-overs together."

One—two—three strides, reach for the rope, and pivot. It's clean, shoulder turned, with my right elbow over the top rope. The rebound hits harder this time, sending me forward. I let its momentum fuel my pace. Sweat soaks through my shirt as I cross the ring again. Tight. Controlled. Crisp. Moves that prove I belong here just as much as anyone else, and just because I didn't spend the last five years on the indie circuit, I can still be as good as them. On the days when I wake up sore and tired, I remind myself that I have to work harder than the others. People looked at me like I was someone who would fade to black when I took my first bump. Well, joke's on them. While I don't know how to do everything or understand everything on the first try, I do whatever it takes to prove I belong here and get stronger in the ring. Besides, who cares what the others think, as long as the trainers and the company see improvement?

"That's how you run." Juliet claps. "Beautiful, Sav. Keep it up and you'll be able to outrun the rest of the roster."

Hitting the ropes one last time, I land in the center of the ring and suck in a large breath. When I look over at the ring Raelynn occupies, she's starting her second round of ropes, and I hope she doesn't fuck it up this time. Then again, maybe I do—Juliet *might* let me breathe for a second.

It's a smooth transition sliding beneath my ropes and straight under the ones of the ring next to mine. I prop myself up in the corner and watch her feet, counting the beats of her steps as the ropes slingshot her forward.

"Nicely done that time, Rae," Juliet says. "Alright, get into the up-and-overs."

I roll my shoulders and crack my neck before Rae and I lock up. Our fingers latch around the backs of our necks and elbows in a collar-and-elbow lock-up. I backpedal into the corner before she breaks the hold, grasping my arm to prepare for a whip. She tries to launch me forward, but I plant my feet, turn my hips, and reverse the momentum to send her flying toward the opposite corner—Irish Whip. She runs straight into the corner, gripping the rope on either side of the top turnbuckle, and jumps. Her legs come up to her chest before she kicks back, and I run beneath her legs into the turnbuckle.

"Lock it up," Juliet yells, and we do, starting the sequence over again. This time, Raelynn reverses my hold and slingshots me across the ring. "Closer grip, Savannah." My hands automatically adjust, moving in tighter to the top turnbuckle before I jump, lifting my knees to my chest and then kicking out as Rae moves under me. We do that ten more times each before Juliet calls it.

By the time we're finished, Bennett walks back through the double doors, and when his gaze lifts from the floor to meet ours, a shit-eating grin splits his face.

5

Savannah

TUESDAY, APRIL 7, 2009
TAMPA, FL

Raelynn grips the backs of my thighs, lifting my feet off the mat in a double-leg takedown. Not wasting time, she forces me to roll onto my stomach. Dropping my legs, she sits on my back and wraps my arms around her thighs. She laces her hands together beneath my chin and pulls back—the pressure extending my neck and torso. Raelynn's choice of landing spot, while not perfect, is still optimum for the chance to grab the bottom rope and force her to break the submission hold. Hands outstretched, I grasp the air, narrowly missing the bottom rope. Realizing her error, Raelynn releases her grip, and I barely catch myself before I face-plant into the canvas. She kicks my side twice and drags me to the center of the ring before reapplying the hold, showing little mercy in her movements.

"What do you say, Sav?" Juliet questions from underneath the bottom rope. My only answer is a furious headshake.

"C'mon, Sav. Tap!" Rae's voice echoes, pulling back further. I attempt to lift my left leg, trying to stand, but fail. "Tap!"

"Gotta do something, Sav," Juliet says.

There's a commotion from the other side of the room, near the lobby doors. It drowns out the sounds of Bennett and Austin Murray, better known as *"The Showstopper" Spencer Austin*—a main roster wrestler who occasionally joins us when he's home from the road—grappling in the center ring. Bennett has been traveling with him recently, ever since he found out that he'd be making his official main roster debut at the end of this month.

Whatever is going on distracts Rae, and she loosens her grip just enough to allow me to bring my left knee forward, followed by my right. Gripping Rae's calves, I force myself to stand and run backward, slamming her back into the turnbuckle.

"Good, Sav!" Juliet yells over the continued noise.

I do my best to ignore the commotion; whatever it is will have to wait because I need to finish this match first. Raelynn rubs her lower back as she uses the ropes to pull herself up. At the same time, I climb to the top rope of the opposite turnbuckle.

"Finish it!" An unfamiliar voice rings through the air. Baritone and heavy, but smooth like a good whiskey. Was he the cause of all the racket moments ago?

Focus, Sav. Finish the match, then you can figure out what's going on.

Jumping from the top rope, I extend my legs and kick Raelynn as she begins to cross the ring—dropkick. It drops us both to the mat, and I land on top of my left arm. Ignoring the twinge in my elbow from the landing, I crawl on top of Rae, and Juliet slams her hand down on the apron for the three count.

"Nice job, ladies!" Juliet claps her hands together as I roll to my opponent's side, both of us trying to catch our breath.

"Fuck, Sav," Raelynn groans, sitting up.

"Same to you," I say, rubbing my lower back, sore from

her submission hold. It's definitely going to be sore tomorrow from the way she overextended during that last hold. Raelynn offers me her hand, and I take it, hoisting myself up to my feet. When we glance outside of the ring, piercing eyes stare back at me. The man beside Juliet looks oddly familiar, but I don't know where we would have met. His intense gaze mirrors the sharpness of his features—strong jawline, broad shoulders, and muscular arms covered in black ink are crossed over a wide chest—with a face made of stone. When he narrows his gaze, the realization hits me.

This is the same man from the bar when...*Holy shit. There's no fucking way. But if he's here...then that means—*

"Raelynn, Savannah, I'd like to introduce you to Brody Wilder," Juliet says, interrupting my thoughts. His gaze narrows even further. "He's one of our legacies here at EWE and is currently on the main roster."

"I know who you are. I fucking love you," Raelynn says without warning, and her hands quickly cover her mouth. The outburst seems to break whatever spell Brody and I are under, drawing our attention to her. "I cannot believe I just said that. I am so—Oh my gosh, I'm so embarrassed."

Brody chuckles—a deep, gravelly sound—and I swear it sends a shiver down Rae's spine. He rubs at his chin and bites down on his bottom lip, looking Raelynn up and down. "I'm guessing you're Raelynn?" My friend nods, cheeks now a cherry tomato-red color. I can practically hear her heart explode when he smiles at her, but the small gesture falls when his gaze returns to me. "And that makes you...Savannah."

A chill runs down my spine when his eyes narrow, the same way they did that night in the bar, and his head tilts to the left ever so slightly. What is going on? Why is he here? And if he's here, does that mean John is here? He said they worked together, didn't he? Is Brody going to say something, right here and now? In front of the entire NextGen locker room? I hope not. I don't need these people thinking I got my foot in the door because I know either one of them.

After what feels like the longest moment of my life, the corner of Brody's lip quirks up and his tongue pokes out to wet his lips. Taking a breath, he shakes his head before looking back to his number one fan. "It's nice to meet you both. I'll be seeing you around. Jules, I'll see you at Fest?"

"You know I won't miss a chance to see you get your ass kicked."

Brody rolls his eyes. "Ha. Ha."

"Brody!"

My heart stops. No. This cannot be happening.

"What the hell are you doing over there?"

"Should've known he'd be here, too." Raelynn scoffs, not sounding impressed in the slightest.

My gaze falls from my friend to Brody, who, despite his friend's calls from the other side of the room, stares straight at me. The small smirk in the corner of his mouth never falls before he glances at the hand that just landed on his shoulder.

"I know you're desperate after Alex, but I didn't think I'd find you over here flirting with the rookies, Brods." John laughs, slapping his friend on the back before his gaze travels up to finally meet mine. What was surely meant to be a quick glance turns into a long, hard stare. His face falls, and his blue eyes narrow, homing in on me. I can see the questions rising to the surface—the same ones running rampant in my own mind.

"Brooks, this is Raelynn and Savannah, two of Juliet's best and brightest," Brody says, and without looking, I can picture the look on his face clear as day. The smirk overtakes his features, mischief twinkling in his gray eyes. He is living for this right now.

Brooks. That's what the man we saw in the elevator called him. Wait...what was his name?

Theo.

You've got to be kidding me. How could I be so stupid? How could I not put two-and-two together? While I've never met or seen the son of the man who started this organization, I've heard all about Theo Rafferty. The playboy heir to the company who doesn't mind getting his hands a little dirty when it comes to the female talent. His father has come to his rescue on more than one occasion over the years, according to the rumors. They say Theo is good at his job and never goes after anyone who didn't initiate first...at least that's the official story.

Brooks...Is that what I should call him? But that's not what I know him as.

John...Brooks...whoever he is, I watch his throat bob with a hard swallow, more questions than ever swimming in the cerulean sea of his eyes.

Juliet's best and brightest.

While I would normally be ecstatic to receive such a compliment from someone like Brody—someone on the main roster, and not to mention a legacy in the industry—right now, I can barely digest the words.

"Nice to meet you, Brooks," Raelynn says, still a hint of annoyance in her voice.

"Um, yeah," he says, tearing his gaze away from me. "You too, Raelynn." Turning back to me, his voice seems to falter, and his hesitation catches the attention of everyone around us. "S—Savannah," he finally sputters out.

"Brooks." The name feels foreign on my tongue, and I instantly hate it. That's not who he is...not to me.

I catch a quick glimpse of the look Juliet and Brody share, the knowing one that tells me we have been anything but subtle. She chuckles, shaking her head before she shoos both men away. "Alright, boys, enough distracting my girls. Go on, get."

"Yes, ma'am," Brody says, offering her a mock salute. "We'll see you in a few weeks!" He grips John's shoulder and turns him away from the ring, away from me, and away from the impending storm I feel brewing.

And when they're finally out of earshot, Raelynn turns on her heel toward me with a suspicious glance. "Okay, what was *that*?"

"What?" I ask.

"Oh, I don't know, maybe the way you and *Brooks Taylor* were just eye-fucking each other in front of everyone."

I roll my eyes. "No, we weren't."

"Uh, yeah! You were."

I ignore her continued pestering to climb out of the ring. I have to get out of here. Right now. I don't want to have this conversation, but I especially don't want to have it here. Not with Rae. She isn't exactly subtle. The last thing I need is someone like Harper overhearing. When my feet hit the ground, Raelynn is already there, blocking my escape.

"Juliet, back me up here," Raelynn pleads. "Were they not just eye-fucking each other?"

Juliet chuckles, crossing her arms. "You know, I'm not usually one to stir that pot, but you'd have to be blind to miss *that*. And even then, I think a blind man could see it."

"You guys are being ridiculous." I scoff. "Are we done?"

The smirk that lights up Juliet's face only serves to make the knot in my stomach grow ten times bigger. I am so screwed. Goodbye, EWE, it was nice knowing you. "Yeah, you guys are done. Make sure you stretch and ice that back, Savannah."

I wave her off, picking up my pace. The whole way to the locker room, Raelynn tries to pry the answers out of me, almost like she *knows*, but she wants me to admit it. I glare at her, ready to tell her to shut up, but my attention is drawn to Brooks, standing near the lobby doors. His attention wanders from his conversation with Fata to me. I command my feet to move, to walk into the locker room, but they don't listen. At the same time, Raelynn turns to see what has captured my attention, and Fata does the same. His stark white smile slowly creeps onto his face. After a moment, he chuckles, slapping a hand on John's back, and guides him through the double doors.

"You still want to tell me nothing is going on?" Raelynn asks, and this time, when I meet her stare, I don't deny it.

A sense of overwhelming dread washes over me when I park in front of the whitewashed metal walls. I've never felt like this, not even on my second day when I thought I was going to die as I dragged myself out of bed. No, not even the aching pain deep in my muscles could deter me from getting out of the car, but this...this could. How did this happen? How did I not know? How did I not figure it out before now?

I hate to admit it, but after practice last night, I went home and looked him up on the internet. Is that creepy? Probably. But I had to know what I was dealing with. What I found only stressed me out more. Somehow, I missed the part where the man I'd been thinking about for the last eight months is one of the top wrestlers at my new job...No, not just one of them. He's *the* top wrestler.

John joined the main roster of EWE four years ago, and once he gained his footing, he took the wrestling world by storm. However, he's been out for an injury for the last six months after tearing his Achilles when an aerial landing went awry. That's why I haven't seen his face on any programming, but now that I know...I see him everywhere.

In the midst of it all, I called my best friends back home

because I needed someone to talk me off the ledge, and I sure as hell wasn't going to tell any of my brothers what was going on.

"He's going to think I'm a fucking stalker, for fuck's sake." I sighed, pacing the length of my living room. A split screen showed Cassandra on one side of my laptop, and on the other, I could hear Kingsley rummaging around her bedroom in the background. "What are the chances that when I change careers, it would be *his* career, too?"

"You know, I think you should take this as a sign," Cassandra said, and Kingsley's voice sounded from the background in agreement.

"A sign?" I scoffed. "A sign of what?"

"That you guys were supposed to meet." Cassandra's eyes glittered on the screen. Her jaw hit the floor as I detailed the events from yesterday, from my initial interaction with Brody to seeing John, to what Raelynn and Bennett had said outside before I drove away. "It's just like you said. What are the chances? You have a one-night fling, never expecting to see him again, and then he walks into your new job! Sounds like destiny."

Ever the optimist.

I dropped my face into my hands with a soft groan. "And he's one of their biggest fucking stars."

"A bonus!"

"He's going to think I knew who he was. That I'm a fucking psycho."

"Don't you think you're overreacting just a little bit?" Kingsley asked, returning to the screen.

"No," I snapped.

"It's been…What? A year?"

"Eight months."

"If you were a stalker, you would've been there long before now," Cassandra said to further prove her point. "Sav, you *didn't* know who he was. It's not like you're some groupie who has been following these guys around. I guarantee the thought never even crossed his mind."

But a terrible thought entered mine. Could this ruin my career before it even begins?

Juliet was right, you'd have to be blind not to notice something was going on, and that was only confirmed by Bennett when Raelynn and I walked outside. Bennett stood in the space between my car and Raelynn's, waiting to throw his own two cents in on the matter. And amid his flurry of questions, I realized that if *he* noticed, that meant it was likely that everyone else did, too. Despite their constant badgering, I maintained my innocence.

"What if they kick me out?" Eyes locked on the ceiling, my thoughts began to spiral, thinking of all the ways this could ruin me.

"They're not going to—"

"If he sees me as some wacko and wants me gone, I think they'd make that happen."

"I think you're overthinking this whole thing," Cassandra said. "Did he seem weirded out when he saw you?"

"I don't know. Maybe." I sighed, trying to remember how he reacted. A thousand-watt smile that slowly fell into a thin line, matching the look in his eyes. He studied me with a narrowed gaze, trying to piece together what was going on. It wasn't exactly the welcome I had anticipated if I ever saw him again, but I can't say I blame him. This wasn't exactly how I expected a reunion to occur. "He didn't really...say anything. Not that I wanted him to, because the last thing I need is someone thinking I'm fucking my way up."

"So, you're not going to fuck him again?" Kingsley asked.

"Kins!" Cassandra and I shouted at the same time.

"Don't *Kins* me. I'm just asking what we're all thinking, and in my humble opinion, I agree it seems like the universe is offering you a chance to get another taste of it."

Cassandra sighed, rubbing the space between her eyes. "Fuck him, don't fuck him, whatever. But I think you should at least *talk* to him."

"I'm overreacting," I finally said. I wasn't sure who I was trying to convince more—me or them? "It's not even a big deal. I probably won't even see him again."

Kingsley laughed. "Until you get called up."

"And then you'll be working with him four or five days a week," her counterpart added.

"Seems very unlikely that he'd be working with a rookie like me. I think it's better if I keep my distance—"

"I think that's a bad idea," Cassandra said, drawing out the last syllable.

"I concur. Avoiding it is a bad idea, Sav. You need to face it," Kingsley said. "Talk to him."

I rolled my eyes, mouse icon hovering over the big red button that would end the call. I needed some time to think about this on my own. Time to figure out what I was or wasn't going to do. "I'm not going looking for this man. That *would* be stalkerish."

"Okay, then the next time you see him, commit right now that you'll talk to him. You'll make sure he knows you're not some groupie stalker chick." Cassandra sat with her arms crossed, brow raised. I knew she wasn't going to let this go until I did. I groaned, rolling my eyes again, and begrudgingly said okay before I ended the call.

Now, staring at the training center from behind my steering wheel, I don't feel any more confident than I did yesterday. With one final breath, I open my car door and get out. Baby steps—each one will get me inside eventually. It doesn't help that today we are combining all classes of trainees to work on promos, and I am not looking forward to it. If there is one thing I don't think I anticipated about this new career, it's the amount of acting that I have to do. Wrestling is storytelling, and wrestlers tell a story in and out of the ring. Delivering promos is just one of the ways to do that, and you have to make them believable and interesting, keeping the audience engaged the whole time. Promos are one of the areas of this circus where I have yet to feel confident and comfortable.

Tugging my bag across the center console, I throw it over my shoulder and close the door. I turn and walk straight into the chest of none other than the one man I'd been hoping to avoid. *John Brooks.* John? Brooks? Brooks Taylor? What in the hell am I supposed to call him?

So much for keeping a distance.

His brow quirks as he stares down at me, followed by his mouth. A mouth I'd come to know all too well during our night together, and I'd be lying if I said I didn't think of how good that mouth made me feel. I avert my gaze down to the ground, and it occurs to me that he isn't wearing a boot or any kind of protection on his foot. Does that mean he's healed? You mean to tell me all of this is happening because he came here to—

"Mornin', Sweetheart." His voice draws my eyes forward, and his use of that name chips away at the mental barrier I put in place.

"John." His name is barely a whisper. "I—I swear I had no idea. I didn't...I didn't know you worked here."

He laughs. "I know."

"I'm not a stalker."

"Well, that is something a stalker might say." The words draw a glare from me. "I'm kidding, Sav. I believe you. I had a feeling that night when you didn't flinch seeing me or any of the guys in the bar. You only confirmed my suspicion when you saw Theo and couldn't give two shits."

"If I had known—"

"If you had known—what? You wouldn't have joined the

company? Savannah, I'd never ask that of you. I am curious, though. What happened to cheerleading?" John tucks his hands into his pockets. "I thought you were with the Wildcats."

"I was," I say a little too quickly. "But the longer I was in it, the more I wanted out. I'd been wanting out, I just didn't know what I wanted to do instead."

"So, you picked *wrestling*?"

My shoulders lift gently, hands tightening a little around the strap of my bag. "Not exactly. My brothers made a bet that I wouldn't try out when one of them saw the posting." I laugh, realizing how stupid the whole thing sounded. "It wasn't supposed to mean anything. This wasn't supposed to happen, but the second I stepped in that ring...I don't know, it just felt right." The words draw a genuine smile to his face, and I notice he takes a step closer, hands still restrained inside his pockets. "But these damn promos are killing me."

"I've heard."

"What do you mean, 'you've heard?'"

"We all talk." John shrugs, finally peeling his hands from his sides, folding his arms over his chest. "I was asking how the new people were looking, and Fata mentioned that you needed some help."

"I think we all do, that's why we're here today."

"Funny, so am I."

The moment John and I walk into the training center together, I can see Raelynn and Bennett immediately enter a frenzy from their place on the apron on the other side of the room. Eyes bug out of their sockets before they start giggling like schoolgirls.

"Brooks!" Fata's voice booms, and he slaps a hand on his back. "Glad you could make it. Am I interrupting something?" The legend looks between us, and I realize we're standing closer than two people who aren't supposed to know each other should be.

John clears his throat, but doesn't move away. "No, I just happened to run into Savannah in the parking lot."

Fata's brow cocks, along with his mouth. He nods slowly before his tongue pokes out to wet his lips. "Well, I hate to interrupt, but I'd like to discuss the game plan for today. Do you mind if I steal him, Barbie?"

I force my mouth into a smile and shake my head. John offers me a small smile and a subtle wink before he follows the legend back into the lobby. When they're gone, I finally let out the breath I've been holding before heading for the locker room with Raelynn hot on my heels.

"Did you guys...you know?" Her brows wiggle when we get inside.

"No, Rae. We did not '*you know*.'" I roll my eyes, tossing my duffel into the locker. Barely six inches sit between us when I turn around. "Ever heard of personal space?" I sigh when she doesn't budge. "Nothing is going on. We just happened to walk in at the same time. It's not that deep. Now come on," I say, urging her back a few steps. Her eyes narrow, as if she can tell a truth from a lie just by looking at me. "C'mon, before we're late. I don't feel like going first."

When Juliet initially told me the trainers were planning a full day of promo work, she said they were bringing in Luna Haze to help Sheldon coach us, but Fata had other plans. The moment he saw John yesterday, he invited him to help the rookies with their delivery, and all the trainers agreed that if he was going to interrupt practice, they should put him to work. In all my research last night, it became obvious that *Brooks Taylor* had a knack for solid promos and eleven-out-of-ten character development. While he may not be the best wrestler on the roster, there's a reason he's at the top, and he can hold his own in the ring even with the best technical boys out there.

And that's how we end up here.

The rookies surround the ring, watching and waiting for their turn to climb in and deliver a thirty-second promo in front of everyone. John and Sheldon work with each person, taking time to go through where they went wrong and what they did well, sometimes making them start over until the veterans are satisfied.

When my name is called, I dig my nails into the palms of my hands and remind myself it's only thirty seconds. I can do this.

And those thirty seconds feel like thirty hours, much longer than any other time I've delivered a practice promo. My words are awkward and stilted, and the whole thing reeks of nerves. I can only think of one reason why, and it's sitting in the corner. In the end, it wasn't terrible, but it wasn't great. At least Sheldon didn't tell me to start from the top halfway through.

"That was better, Savannah! Much better. I can tell you've been working on it," Sheldon says, his hands coming together in loud claps. His words of praise make a small swell of pride rise in me because he's been working with me the most on promos. "But—"

"Do you want to know what your problem is?" John asks from the corner of the ring. Elbows resting on the top of the ropes, he's made himself comfortable, leaning back into the turnbuckles. His hand scratches the small amount of stubble on his jaw as he stares straight at me. He pushes off the ropes, taking one slow step at a time like a predator stalking its prey until he stands in front of me. "You don't believe it. You don't believe what you're saying. You don't believe in yourself."

"I believe in myself." I cross my arms, but I know he doesn't believe me any more than I believe myself.

"Maybe in a physical aspect, but not like this."

"Because she thinks she's better than all of us," Harper says under her breath, and her eyes roll so hard they almost end up on the floor.

"Shut up, Harper!" Raelynn hisses across the ring.

"Tell me I'm wrong, Rae." Harper doesn't wait for a response, her glare turning back on me. "Am I wrong, Savannah? You think you're better than the rest of us because of where you come from. But the reality is you got *handed* this opportunity because you have big tits and a nice ass, while the rest of us had to work twice as hard to get here."

"Okay, that's enough," Sheldon says before I can respond. "Go on, Sav. You're done for the day." He shoos me out of the ring, but not before I catch John's eye and his small headshake, retreating to his corner. Climbing out of the ring, I take my place between Rae and Bennett as Colin Montgomery is called in for his turn.

John's presence has made everyone act... differently today. Okay, I take it back. His presence has only made the other girls act differently today. Every time I catch one of them gawking at him, drool pooling in the corner of their mouth, I remind myself no one can know how it affects me. It wouldn't take a genius to see the look in their eyes and know exactly what they're thinking. Instead, I dig my nails into my palms and force my attention on Colin, who delivers a heel turn promo in the center of the ring.

I hate that it makes me jealous. Who am I to be jealous, anyway? What he and I shared was a one-time thing. It wasn't supposed to leave the walls of The Resort. Besides, let's be real, he has probably slept with plenty of other women since then.

The mere thought of him in bed with another woman

makes my skin crawl and sends a shudder down my spine.

A movement from the corner draws my attention away from the ring, and I find myself lost in a sea of blue. John smiles when I meet his gaze, and I only briefly return it before his attention turns back to the task at hand.

Fucked. I'm so fucked. How am I supposed to concentrate and work if he looks at me like that?

"Don't look now, but someone is staring *again*," Raelynn whispers, and the words earn a snicker from the man standing on my other side. Her hand reaches behind my back to slap Bennett on the arm, glaring at him for possibly drawing attention our way.

"You two seem to be having a good time over there."

Shit. I roll my eyes, ready to take two steps away from them, because I am not about to get roped into this. I already endured my thirty seconds of hell; I'm not looking to go through it again.

Lifting my gaze from the mat, I expect to find Sheldon's heated gaze on the three of us, but instead, he's staring down at Harper and her crony, Ava, on the other side of the ring.

"Since you're feeling chatty today, Miss Valentine, why don't you get in here and show us how it's done?" Sheldon's suggestion makes Rae snicker. The way she always does when Harper gets called out. It happens more often than not because she can never seem to keep her mouth shut, especially when it comes to me. She hates me, and she's never had an issue letting everyone know it.

Harper mumbles to herself the whole way up the stairs, stepping through the ropes Sheldon holds open for her.

"Okay, Harper. Let's pretend it's the *Monday Night Rage* right after Wrestlefest. You just won the championship the night before from our current champ, *Ivy Jade.* Now you have to go out in front of a pissed off crowd because their golden girl lost the title to you."

"You could have at least given me something hard," Harper says.

Sheldon takes a deep breath and shares a tight smile with John over his shoulder. John rolls his eyes, settling back a little further into his corner, waiting for the show to begin.

Harper takes a breath before she breathes out a soft chuckle. "I feel like I've said it so many times, but I'm going to say it *again*. I was right." She smirks. "I was right, and you were wrong! I said I was going to walk out of Wrestlefest with this title, and I did." Sheldon and John offer soft boos, playing the part of the audience. Bennett, Raelynn, and a few of the others join them. "You people are what's wrong with this company! No, I take that back. You don't know any better. You go along with whatever this company shoves down your throat. Whatever they tell you to like because as long as she has boobs and an ass, you don't care!"

Another chorus of boos.

"This company needs a reality check. This title means everything to me, and those Barbie dolls pretending to be wrestlers don't deserve it. They haven't done what I've done. They haven't fought the battles I did to get here! All this company wants is a pretty face to stand there and do what she's told. Newsflash, this isn't the '50s, and we're not here to be your playthings anymore. If this company really cared about women's wrestling, they'd stop hiring models and *cheerleaders*."

Harper stares directly at me when she says it, and while she means to try to intimidate me, it does the opposite. She only manages to piss me off. She has done nothing but harass and tear me down from the second I walked in the door, and why? Because her bestie Caitlin couldn't cut it. And instead of facing the fact that her best friend wasn't up to EWE standards, she uses my background as her excuse to tear me down. Raelynn came from the indie circuit, too, but she's never held my years as a cheerleader against me. Neither has Bennett, or any of the trainers. Sure, they might call me Barbie or Pom-Poms, but they've never purposefully made me feel out of place.

"I didn't win this title because I'm pretty." She bats her eyelashes. "Or because I'm a legacy." Her venomous stare is now on Callista, the daughter of two EWE legends, who stands on the other side of the ring. "Or because I fucked the right people. I earned this title. I worked my ass off for this, unlike the rest of those bobbleheads backstage. Unlike your precious *Ivy Jade.*" Harper smirks, glancing around the room at every single face, including John, who she winks at. He only chuckles in return, shaking his head. "But no more! I am here to save the women's division, and I am going to rebuild it brick by brick." Her gaze finds me again. "Just try and stop me."

I do my best not to react, but my jaw clenches and my tongue presses against the roof of my mouth. Taking a deep breath, I rip my gaze from hers, only to land on John, who I know has been watching me the whole time. His brow quirks, but I look away, rolling my lips between my teeth, and keep my mouth shut. It's not my place to say something. This isn't a real storyline. It's just practice—even if Harper can't separate the two.

"Savannah," Sheldon says, and I meet his wide grin. "You're up. You are now the other half of this brewing feud. Your character is the antithesis of Harper. Go."

Bennett doesn't waste time, lifting me onto the apron as if I'm as light as a feather.

Why couldn't he pick Rae? An inward groan resonates through me as I wipe my shoes on the apron and climb into the ring. *Just let it flow, Sav. Make it believable.*

Without thinking, I begin, "You're here to 'save' the women's division?" I scoff. "That's funny considering how you barely show up for work."

A low snicker sounds around the ring, but I'm locked in on Harper. If she wants to play games, fine. I'll play. While she might have come from the indie circuit, she is far from the best of anyone standing here. How she manages to keep her job is beyond me because there have been too many times she hasn't shown up or shows up halfway through the day. And that's not how this is supposed to work.

From day one, it was made clear that you show up, you put in the work, and you try your hardest. You respect the ring, respect your peers, and respect the sport. You may fail, but you get back up and keep going. That's how you get to the main roster one day. That's how you make a name for yourself. And those who didn't want to put in the work? Those who didn't want to show up? Those who didn't want to show respect? They were supposed to be out. So why hadn't she been tossed out yet?

Rae has her theories—so do I—but Bennett doesn't say much. It's one of those situations where you keep your head down and mind your own business unless you want to put yourself on the chopping block.

"You know something, Harper? You're right. This company does need a reality check, and so do you. You think I'm not worthy to be here just because I was a cheerleader, but—"

"Pretty much."

"You wouldn't last a damn minute on that field. And let's face the facts, Harp. The only reason you're mad is because you've had to work for years before this company ever considered you. Not to mention two failed auditions before that. But all it took was one look at me, and they knew they wanted me."

I force my gaze to remain on Harper, but I want to look over my shoulder and see the look on John's face when I hear him laugh. He tries to cover it with a cough, but it's obvious.

"These people don't care about boobs and ass—"

"Yes, we do!" Colin calls out, earning a few laughs from those around the ring.

"Okay, maybe some of them do, but are you sure you're not just bitter because the Good Lord didn't bless you? Doctor Nassif did." I smirk when her face falls, eyes wide in horror. A chorus of "holy shit" rings out around us.

"You bitch!" Harper cries.

"No, Harper. I'm just honest. The majority of these people couldn't care less as long as we put on a good show. And if we look pretty doing it, that's just a bonus. The sob story is old. Pretending like the rest of us can't do this because we didn't spend years in the circuit doesn't make you better than us. It just makes you pathetic." My feet move on command, circling her, the same way John circled me earlier. I guess some good did come out of his presence after all. "You feel threatened by us because we see behind the mask. And no matter how hard you try...you'll never be anything more than a sniveling, pathetic excuse for a woman from Ohio." Her face set in stone, eyes blazing with fury. "So, no. You're not here to *save* the division. And if you think I'm going to let you stand there and disrespect the hard work every one of these women has put into it, you're sadly mistaken. You want to see what a real woman looks like? I'll show you. And I'll start by taking that title."

"You'll never get your hands on—"

"Just try and stop me," I say, stepping into her. My heart beats so hard in my chest, I'm sure it's going to jump out any moment. Finally, I take a step back and take a deep breath. I don't want to let the others see how I feel, like I'm either going to pass out, throw up, or both from the sheer amount of adrenaline pumping through my veins.

It's quiet for what feels like hours before a slow clap resonates from the corner. *John.* All eyes are on him as he stands from his makeshift seat and walks closer, a shit-eating grin on his lips. "Where have you been hiding that? Because that...that's what I want to see."

6

SUNDAY, JANUARY, 10, 2010
ATLANTA, GA

"You know," Brody draws out. "Call me crazy, but you could always *talk* to her. Have you considered that?"

I roll my eyes as we walk through backstage toward the media room. Tonight is Battle of Champions, the first of two premiere events this month. This show sets the stage for Wrestlefest every year, and at least two storylines will officially be booked to come to a head on the grandest stage in all of EWE in three months.

This is the same conversation I have with my best friend every time he finds out a certain NextGen rookie will be backstage. I don't know how he knows she's here; neither Raelynn nor Wolf mentioned anything when I ran into them earlier. Usually, when she's around, the three of them are attached at the hip.

"God, the universe, Cupid, whatever you want to call it, has given you a chance to get to know this girl. Weren't you the one who said you wanted to try and figure out who she was? I don't understand why you haven't taken advantage of it."

He's right, I *did* want to find her. I know it's crazy to say that I felt a connection with her, this girl I'd never met before, who I had a one-night stand with, but it's true. She had a softness in her eyes, and from the very first time I looked into them, I felt an intense connection to her. I'd never felt something so intimate before, and I was certain she felt it, too.

Or maybe I haven't pursued her because of my past. I'll never deny that I was—for better or worse—a bit of a... fuckboy? Playboy? Whatever word you want to use, I was one when I first joined EWE. Can you blame me? I had been a small-town, Midwestern boy surrounded by the same girls since kindergarten. When I joined this company, I was introduced to a new league of women, and I'm not talking about just my female counterparts. Did that make it right? No, but that's not who I am anymore—not for a long time. No matter what some of the rumors might say. I had my fun, but who didn't in their twenties?

"You're friends with one of her best friends, why wouldn't you—"

"Oh, hello, boys!" A shrill voice interrupts us before Harper Valentine jumps down from one of the black production crates, abruptly ending her own conversation with Ava Anderson—the crony who only gets screen time when doing Harper's bidding. "Where are you headed?"

"Media," Brody says. "We're already late, so if you'll—"

"Oh, what a coincidence, so am I." She bats her lashes, shifting her stare between us. "What are the chances?"

"Apparently, pretty good," I say under my breath, earning an elbow to the side from my best friend.

Harper is a decent wrestler, not the best by any means, but her confidence makes up for what she lacks in the ring. I don't know a lot about her resume, except for the little bit that Wolf has told us as we've gotten to know him. I have a bad habit of tuning him out when he talks about their "relationship."

I like to think of it more as a situationship, because I can't think of a better word to describe them. They are all of the things you want—good morning texts, safe sex, and a reliable dinner date—without the label. Except he wants more, while Harper...Harper wants her cake and to eat it, too.

"So, if you'll excuse us. We really have to be going, because—"

A fit of laughter echoes down the hallway before three people appear in the doorway where Brody and I were supposed to be two minutes ago. Not just any three people: Raelynn, Wolf, and Savannah.

"See, I told you." Brody chuckles, staring straight at me. I pay him no mind, too focused on the woman walking down the hallway. But she's too preoccupied with whatever story Wolf is telling, hands waving wildly in front of him, to notice me.

"Oh, you've got to be kidding. Who let her in?" Harper scoffs, and my gaze falls to the dirty blonde blocking our path. She looks over her shoulder at her crony—and sometimes friend, depending on the day, maybe even the hour—Ava. "Is she debuting tonight?"

Ava shrugs in reply and rolls her eyes when Harper turns away, but when Ava meets my gaze, her eyes widen, realizing she's been caught. I always had a feeling that she hated Harper, but her loyalty keeps her face on television, and around here, screentime is the most important thing you can have.

"I wish Wolf would stop hanging out with those two. It makes him look bad," Harper says.

"Worried he might find someone else, Harp?" Spencer fills the gap between me and Brody. He lifts onto the balls of his feet to drape his arms around our shoulders, but still stands at least four inches shorter. "I've always thought he had a thing for Savvy."

My hands flex at my sides, but I force them to uncurl. I

know that's not true. I know that Wolf has only ever had his eye on one person, and it's not Savannah.

"Well, I heard she doesn't want to date wrestlers," Harper says.

"Say that again?" Spencer laughs.

"You heard me. Wanna-Be Wrestler Barbie thinks she's too good for the likes of a wrestler boyfriend. She seems like the stockbroker type. I mean, she came from Alexandria, or something, didn't she? Everyone down there is rich and snobby."

I share a glance with Brody, who shrugs.

"Everyone knows it's almost impossible to date someone outside of the business," Harper continues. "Oh well, guess she'll just have to learn the hard way."

"Whoa! It's a party over here," Wolf says, breaking away from Raelynn and Savannah, who finish their own conversation at a safe distance. He wraps an arm around Harper's waist, going in for a kiss, and she returns it. That's strange. Normally, when he tries to show her affection in front of other people, she pushes him away. "Hey, they're waiting for you guys in there."

"Yeah, we were just on our way, but got interrupted," Brody says.

"Hey, Wolf, you'd probably know...Is it true that Savannah doesn't want to date wrestlers?" Spencer asks without pause.

"Dude." Brody sighs, pinching the bridge of his nose.

"What? I'm just curious. Don't stand there and act like you don't want to know. It seems a bit extreme, if you ask me."

"Where did you hear that?" Wolf chuckles, looking around the group with slight hesitation, but when he lands on the woman beside him, his eyes narrow slightly.

So, it is true, and not just some random piece of gossip Harper scrounged up. Savannah doesn't want to date a wrestler, and I'm...a wrestler. While I respect the idea, it's not easy being with someone outside of the industry…They don't (can't) understand it. I've seen too many people try and fail to make it work because this life isn't meant for everyone.

"Whether Savannah wants to explore her options backstage or not is her business," Wolf says. "However, I will say this, if you're looking to make your move, I think you're the last person she'd consider, Spencer." A brief smile tugs on his mouth, and his gaze falls to the ground before he blinks and meets my own.

"Well, Brooks and I better get goin," Brody says, stepping out of Austin's grip. "We're already late, and you know Martin hates to be kept waiting."

Martin is one of the content photographers for EWE, and has one of the biggest crushes on Brody I've ever seen. He's harmless, and it's nothing more than a schoolyard crush, but that doesn't stop the others from using it to make the fearsome *"Reaper" Brody Wilder* blush.

"He's got the baby oil ready for you, Brods." Wolf chuckles, and his words do the trick, cutting through the tension that has crept its way into the conversation. Even Harper laughs, and not one of her ear-piercing cackles to remind you she's still there if you haven't paid enough attention to her. This was a real one.

"Fuck off, Wolf." Brody lifts his right hand over his shoulder, middle finger raised high. "Afternoon, ladies," he says, walking past Raelynn and Savannah.

Raelynn rolls her eyes before turning to me, a few steps behind. "Brooks, make sure you keep an eye on him. Martin is feeling extra spicy today."

"Yes, ma'am," I say, and lift my left hand to my forehead in a salute. When I drop my hand, I catch Savannah's gaze. The lift in the corner of her mouth is so slight, you'd miss it if you weren't standing right next to her.

"You remember my friend, Savannah, right?"

With a soft hum, I touch my finger to my chin, pretending to think. It's been months since I've seen her, and you'll have to forgive me for taking advantage of this rare opportunity to let my eyes roam freely. The pink bandage dress she chose for tonight hugs her body in all the right places, and I want nothing more than to caress the defined curve of her waist. She's bulked up since the last time I saw her, and the little bit of extra mass looks good on her. Toned muscles exude nothing but power beneath her warm, tanned skin. Trailing my gaze back up the length of her body, I meet her stare, and it takes everything in me not to toss her over my shoulder and carry her back to my bus for the rest of the evening. Fuck the show.

A slow smirk tugs on my lips. "You were...Pom-Poms, right?"

Savannah rolls her eyes, this time not even trying to hide a smile. "One of the many nicknames I have earned from Fata, yes."

I extend my hand, and she looks between it and my face before returning the gesture. My palm swallows hers whole, and my pointer finger extends, grazing the skin of her wrist. Her breath audibly catches, but she holds my stare. "It's good to see you again, Sweetheart. I hope to see more of you around here soon."

7

Savannah

THURSDAY, APRIL 22, 2010

NASHVILLE, TN

Tonight is the annual special edition of *Thursday Night Commotion* before Wrestlefest, the biggest event of the year. I liken Wrestlefest to the Super Bowl of the wrestling world. All of Elite Wrestling Entertainment, along with hundreds of thousands of fans, descends upon a major city for a week-long celebration, ending with the big show where anything can, and does, happen. I had the pleasure of experiencing my first Wrestlefest last year from one of the corners backstage with the rest of the NextGen trainees, but this year...I have a front row seat to the action.

This year, I'm making my debut on the main roster during Wrestlefest week, and it's happening tonight. *Thursday Night Commotion* is EWE's weekly Thursday night event. The show is televised bi-weekly, but every other week it's simply a live event without the extra glitz and glam, giving the talent more opportunity to try out new things in front of live crowds; except for the weeks of Wrestlefest and Beachbash, when it's televised regardless.

Current women's champion *Moxie* issued an open title

challenge at the beginning of the month, welcoming any woman in *all* of EWE (NextGen included) to step in the ring and give it their best shot. Defeat her and you could be walking into Wrestlefest as champion to face *Fortuna*, also known as Viviana Ridley.

My system has been on edge since Talent Relations and Creative pulled me into a meeting last month and disclosed the plan. I told myself not to get too excited because things change all the time around here. They could decide to postpone my debut at the very last minute and throw someone else out there to fight *Moxie*. I've seen matches change or get cut moments before they were supposed to take place on more than one occasion. The uncertainty of it all will keep you on your toes. But it's still hard not to be excited, and a little nervous.

The only thing that has helped keep my nerves (somewhat) at bay is knowing Moxie would be by my side. She has become someone I look up to in the company, and besides Rae, who was called up two months ago, she's the only other woman I've gotten close to backstage. Like so many of those in EWE, Moxie—known to the government as Cassandra Tate—has allowed her stage name to become her go-to identifier and thank the Lord for it. Can you imagine having to remember two different names for the number of people who work for this company?

Despite being backstage a handful of times at some of the bigger shows—like Wreck the Halls, Mayhem, Fall Brawl, and Beachbash—I haven't seen John since he helped us work on promos. And why would I? From the moment *Brooks Taylor* made his grand return post-injury last year at the *Monday Night Rage* after Wrestlefest, he's been thrown to the wolves.

No, I take that back. I ran into him once.

It was Beachbash last year, the mini version of Wrestlefest held at the end of the summer every year. I was mid-conversation with Moxie and Jo Valence—one of the backstage interviewers—when I saw John and Brody approach from the corner of my eye. His eyes brightened when I met his gaze down the hall, and his hand swallowed mine, not letting go immediately like he had with my counterparts. A brief, fleeting moment, but it was enough to make the two women question how I knew *the* Brooks Taylor.

"We met at the training center," I said, a simple shrug paired with a nonchalant smile. I wanted to get off the topic as quickly as possible.

Raelynn is the only person I finally opened up to about John, not even Bennett knows, and she agrees it's best to keep it quiet. Some people here, as nice as they seem, are plenty ready to stab you in the back if it means taking your place or gaining favor with the suits. They could take something as innocent as an accidental meeting in a bar and twist it into something much worse.

"You ready?" Juliet asks, leading me through the maze backstage. Over the past year, she has imparted a lot of knowledge about EWE and wrestling. She used to let me stay as late as I wanted, or come in early, and was always there to help guide me or answer questions. I don't know how I would've made it without her.

Juliet's arm comes to rest around my shoulders, giving me a comforting squeeze, but it does nothing to calm my nerves. Nausea builds in my throat, and my stomach has been in ever-growing knots from the moment I opened my eyes this morning, but I do my best to push it all down. I remind myself of the words I spoke to my reflection this morning: *It's no different than working a show at NextGen.*

Except it is.

This is way different.

This is it. The main roster, and somehow, I was chosen to make my debut against the women's fucking champion.

I don't say any of that, simply mustering up the best smile I can, and nod at the woman who has become my mentor. "Sure, if you consider 'being ready' feeling like I can't breathe and want to throw up all at the same time."

"Sweetie, if that's all, then you're doing great." Juliet laughs and guides me through the black drapes that lead into gorilla. This is where you'll find the producers and writers during the show, alongside Amos Rafferty, the man behind the whole operation, and typically his children, who work in the company, Chelsea and Theo. Gorilla is the in-between of backstage and the talent entrance to the arena.

The lights are dimmed, but the room is lit up by the multitude of monitors that showcase different angles of the ring and arena. And in the corner: none other than Amos. A pair of black-rimmed glasses sits on the edge of his nose, a headset rests over his ears, and his intense stare is on the monitor in front of him. Chelsea, beside him, pushes long red hair off her shoulder and leans forward to whisper in her brother's ear. They laugh to themselves before the Darling of Wrestling sits back in her chair with a satisfied smirk. Before I can look away, their father glances my way and offers a thumbs-up. The gesture only makes the nausea creep further up my throat.

"*So, who is it going to be tonight?*" *Moxie* asks, her voice echoing over the speakers on the other side of the wall. The screen hung in the corner shows her in the center of the ring, focused on the ramp. "*Who thinks they can come out here and take this title from me?*" She lifts the title high above her head.

Juliet takes hold of my wrist, dragging me further through the camp toward another set of drapes, leading to the timekeeper's area. "Hoodie," she says, motioning for me to hand over my jacket.

Unzipping the black jacket, I stare down at my ring gear made specifically for tonight. It's a nicer version of what

I've been wearing at NextGen, but still, it reminds me of a sexy cheerleader outfit, albeit less trashy than one you'd find at a Halloween store. Honestly, I could get behind the top. It reminds me of one of my old cheer uniforms, sporting a keyhole cut in the center of a warm pink-and-white checkered pattern with solid baby pink on the sides. However, it's the rhinestones scattered throughout the pink sections and the shorter-than-short, hot-pink pleated mini skirt that drives me crazy. I get it, they want us to look sexy, but do I have to be one step away from fulfilling some weird fetish?

Despite my hard work to get away from the nicknames I was given on the first day I walked in—Barbie and Pom-Poms ring a bell?—I haven't been able to shake them. The brilliant idea Creative had when the discussion of my advance began was to continue the cheerleader gimmick. *Very original*, but as a rookie, I don't have much room for argument. I'm just happy they think I'm ready. They could've told me I'd be dressing up like a clown, and I would've asked, *Rainbow hair or burnt orange*?

At least I have a lot of experience with the type of character they want me to play: the bubbly airhead with lots of energy and pep in her step. And just like Crew said when I told him about it, if I do what they want for now, I can show them why it needs to change.

Juliet offers me one final smile before she disappears back through the curtains. The production aide hands me a microphone, and I swallow down the bile coating the back of my throat. My stomach twists even tighter when the older man gives me a subtle nod.

"*I guess nobody thinks they can beat—*" Moxie's words are cut short by a catchy, upbeat, pulsing opening to a pop song. Again, not my first choice, but it matches the character.

Air rushes through my lungs, filling every nook and cranny it can find as my chest expands, until I release it and take my first step over the threshold. I swear I feel the physical transformation from Savannah Williams to *"The Hellcat" Savvy Skye* occur. It's a strange sensation, almost like walking through a thin veil between backstage and the crowd-filled arena where we are meant to be these larger-than-life characters.

The roar of the crowd is louder than anything I've ever experienced at NextGen. Our showroom holds two hundred people max, and this is at least one hundred times that. It takes my breath away and allows the nerves to dig through my mental block, but I shut them out. The response surprises me. I expected a quiet welcome; instead, the fans dance and sing along to my music, and most of those sitting along the ramp barricade reach out toward me. It's a surreal feeling, one that will be embedded in my brain for the rest of my life. It's a high that I never want to come down from.

Moxie stands in the center of the ring with a cocked brow, the EWE Women's title slung over her shoulder now. She watches every step I take down the ramp, looking me up and down when I finally step through the ropes.

"This is the best they could do?" she asks and circles me. When she stops, her face contorts in a dubious frown. She looks back at Jude Paul and Scott Harrington, the show's commentators. *"Really, Theo? This is the best you can do?"* She asks, looking past me up the ramp. Her words were meant for Theo, who plays the "General Manager" of both *Monday Night Rage* and *Thursday Night Commotion*. *"Wannabe-Barbie? Come on, man. You gotta do better than this!"*

Moxie glances back at me with a sweet smile. She wraps a delicate, yet firm arm around my shoulders and guides me back to the ropes, a small nudge in the direction she wants me to go.

"Listen, Spirit Squad, I wouldn't want you to break a nail or bruise your fresh blowout. So, why don't you go back to

where you came from and send someone out here who knows what they're doing?"

I take hold of the top rope to steady myself when she shoves me forward, and for a brief moment, my character considers it. But only for a split second before I turn back around to face her again.

"Y'know something, Mox?" I chuckle. *"I appreciate your concern, but you can keep it. You see, while the rest of the women around here seem to bow down and take your shit, I'm not going to do that. I'm the one who's going to take that title off your shoulder and walk not only in, but out, of Wrestlefest as the women's champion."*

"You're gonna..." Moxie scoffs. *"You? Miss Yay-Rah Pep Squad, you think you're going to beat me? Don't make me laugh. Ha. Ha. You need to stay in your lane, sweetheart. Go back to the sidelines and leave this to the professionals. You're trying to shine under the wrong stadium lights—your glitter won't get you far out here."* The champ shakes her head, glancing at the crowd. *"Now, get out."* Her face only twists further in irritation when I refuse to budge. *"C'mon Pep Squad, time to go."*

"I'm not going anywhere. You issued the—"

Her hand collides with my cheek, sending me stumbling back a few paces. *"Get out of my ring!"*

Clutching my cheek, I glance at *Moxie* over my shoulder.

"This is my ring, Skye!" she yells, lifting the belt into the air. *"You don't belong here, and you never will. Go back to the sidelines!"*

Without warning, I run straight ahead, spearing her in the midsection. The impact sends us flying across the ring, and my opponent folds in half. The crowd erupts. Sitting up on my knees, I push the hair from my face and run my tongue over my teeth, glancing around the crowd. The microphone in the corner catches my attention, and I reach for it, staring down at the champion. *"Sidelines, huh?"* I chuckle. *"Welcome to the main event, bitch."*

I throw the microphone out of the ring as she stirs beneath me, and finally, the referee joins us. He swipes the title from *Moxie*'s side and hands it to the ringside aide before signaling to ring the bell and officially start the match.

Moxie uses the ropes to pull herself up, glaring at me the whole way to her feet. She shrugs the black leather jacket off her shoulders, tossing it outside the ring.

We circle each other, and she tries to hide the smirk tugging up the corner of her plum-colored lips. She's impressed with my show. A brief nod and we surge forward, colliding in a collar-and-elbow-tie-up. We both fight for dominance, but I win. Ducking under her arm, I pivot out of her hold and yank her into a side headlock, coming down to one knee. She hisses in frustration, jerking against me, but I cinch my grip.

Moxie swings her right leg, attempting to kick out my left knee, but misses. She does it again, and this time I feel the air rush past my leg, narrowly missing. The champion tries to push me off, but I sink my weight further into the ground, resisting.

The air escapes my lungs when she lands a right hook into my ribs. She does it again, and this time I don't have a choice but to let go. Shooting me into the ropes, *Moxie* prepares for a standing dropkick, but I shoulder tackle her on my return and lay her out flat on the mat. I run the ropes, looking for extra momentum in my counterattack, but she pops up to hit a hard clothesline on my rebound. My back slams into the mat, knocking the wind out of me, but I roll through, coming back to my feet, and I meet her wide stare.

"Seriously?" *Moxie* snaps.

She dives forward, grabbing both my legs for a double-leg takedown, and goes for a quick roll-up. She tugs on the waistband of my skirt, trying to force my shoulders to stay down for the count. The referee drops to the mat, but only gets to the one count before I kick out, shoving *Moxie* off. She rolls through, but when she tries to stand, my boot collides with her jaw in a hard superkick. Her body crumbles beneath her, and the crowd gasps. Standing over her, I place my boot on her throat and grip the top rope, using it as leverage.

Moxie claws at my ankle as I twist my ankle to make it look like I'm grinding into her windpipe, and the referee counts off. I have five seconds to let go before he'll disqualify me. He makes it four when I finally break free, arms flying into the air to show I give up, only to do it again when he steps away.

"*Come on, Skye! Get off the rope*," he yells, and I glare at him, this time only stepping off once he gets to five.

Hauling the champion by her hair to her feet, I attempt to whip her toward the ropes, but she plants her feet and sends me flying forward instead. *Moxie* ducks low to miss my clothesline upon rebound, and on my second return, she leapfrogs over my head. When I turn on my heel for another attempt, she catches my arm and drags me over her side to land back-first on the mat.

She scrambles to her feet and climbs to the top turnbuckle, waiting until I'm back on my feet, and soars through the air for a crossbody. I sidestep, and she crashes face-first into the mat. Hooking her leg, I press down on her chest to keep her shoulders on the mat for the pin.

The referee slams his hand down on the mat. There's no movement beneath me until after the second one, when *Moxie* shifts her weight and lifts her left foot onto the bottom rope. One foot on the rope, even if you're pinned with your shoulders down, means the referee should stop counting. The problem is the referee doesn't *see* it, even though he should, and he's about to hit the damn three count.

"*Ref, the rope!*" I hear *Jude Paul*'s voice ring out from the commentary table. I begin to lift off my opponent, and *Moxie* lifts her shoulders off the mat, but it's too late…His hand has already slapped the mat for the third time, ending the match.

Holy. Shit.

That wasn't supposed to happen.

Chaos is the only way to describe the sound that erupts throughout the arena. People cheering. People yelling. Some people don't say anything at all. The commentators go back and forth, trying to make sense of what to do next. Because this wasn't in the script.

I sit back on my heels and meet the distressed gaze of Scott Harrington, unlike the calm demeanor of Jude Paul, the more senior announcer. Jude's hands chop through the air matter-of-factly, speaking to his counterpart. He's most likely saying the referee should've seen *Moxie*'s foot, and he's right. The referee *should* have seen it because her foot on the rope was a planned spot. So, what in the hell happened?

Moxie looks pissed, following the referee around the ring. She repeats the same sentiment to him over and over: "*My foot was on the rope!*" But he doesn't seem to care. He all but ignores her, reaching out for the belt from one of the ringside aides.

Holy shit, I just unseated the champ three nights before Wrestlefest.

Holy shit, I just unseated the champ three nights before Wrestlefest. I'm going to be in so much trouble. I've fucked up my career before I even started.

"*My foot was on the rope, Jimmy!*" *Moxie* yells again, still following the referee as he walks the title over to me. She blocks him, inhibiting every path he tries to take.

"*I didn't see it.*"

"*Play it back, right now! My foot was on the rope.*" The former champ whips her head around to me, a pleading look in her eye, and mouths, *What the fuck?*

What does she want me to do? I lift my hands in the air.

Maybe it's not the best response, or the proper one, but it's the only one I have. I lean back against the ropes, letting Moxie vent her frustrations from a safe distance. She continues to bombard the referee with insults and never lets him get anywhere near me.

"*Whoa!*" A voice rings out—Theo. "*Hey! Hey, Mox, chill out. Moxie!*"

To the crowd, Theo is here to save the day for one of us. He's the one making all the decisions, because out here there's no Creative. Out here, this is all *real*. He stands at the top of the ramp wearing his signature suit and tie—today's color palette is navy blue and gold.

"*Chill out?*" She practically chokes on the words. "*Theo, my title was just stolen! My foot was on the rope.*"

He takes a few more cautious steps forward, but keeps a safe distance from the middle of the ramp. *Theo* glances my way before turning back to the distressed champion...sorry, distressed *former* champion. "*I think we all need to take a deep breath.*"

The referee tries once more to hand me the title, but *Moxie* rips it from his hands. "*This is my title. My foot—*"

"*I heard you,*" *Theo* says. "*We all heard you. Your foot was on the rope. The problem is...*" He sighs, pinching the bridge of his nose. "*There's no footage of your foot being on the rope.*"

The crowd boos in response. How could there not be footage of her foot on the rope? How many fucking cameras are there around here? Did they magically forget how this match was supposed to end?

"*You're fucking kidding me, Theo!*" *Moxie*'s shoulders slump, and even from here, I see the tears well in her eyes. I feel bad. She's supposed to be walking into Wrestlefest on Sunday as the champion, not *Savvy Skye*. The now former champ clings to the belt, holding it so tight there are sure to be indentations from her nails on the leather strap.

"*The only option is for you to enact your rematch clause, right here, right now.*"

Another fucking match? You've got to be kidding me.

"*My rematch?*" Moxie scoffs. "*Theo, I didn't lose.*"

He shrugs. "*Take it or leave it, Mox. But it's not really up to you, it's up to the champ to accept it or not.*" All eyes turn to me. "*What do you say, Savvy? You open to a rematch?*"

A glance around the outside of the ring proves that just about everyone here is interested in the idea. I know that I should say yes, it's the right thing to do…right? Or I could just as easily say no and force *Moxie* to accept this fate.

Something tells me if I do that, I'll walk out of here tonight with more enemies than colleagues, and I don't want to start issues this early. I don't want to give Harper more ammunition to cause issues backstage for me. Pushing off the ropes, I glare straight at *Moxie* and say, "*Let the crowd decide.*"

"*Let the crowd decide?*" *Theo* asks, almost in disbelief, and I nod. He scratches at the scruff on his chin with a slight chuckle. "*Alright then. What do you say, Nashville? Should we have a rematch, right here, right now?*"

An overwhelming, thunderous sound erupts. It reverberates in my chest and the soles of my feet, shaking the ring beneath us.

"*It looks like you get your wish, Mox,*" Theo says. His eyes linger on me for a moment too long before he chuckles, turning back up the ramp.

When he disappears, I smile at *Moxie* with a simple shrug. "*Looks like we're doing this.*"

Moxie glares, shoving the belt back into the referee's hands. Her words have an extra bite to them when she says, "*Don't fuck it up this time.*"

The mental wall between *Savvy Skye* and Savannah Williams comes crashing down two steps before I reach the mouth of the backstage. My stomach is in knots at the thought of what I could face on the other side of that curtain. I'm probably going to get my ass chewed, maybe even fired, for screwing up the match. Did I screw it up, though? It wasn't my fault the referee didn't do his job; he forgot the spot that should've kept the match going. Something tells me that doesn't matter. A fuck up is a fuck up, and I just fucked up my debut.

Gorilla is silent when I walk through the curtain, and the first person I see is Fata, his left leg crossed over his knee, sitting in one of the chairs that line the left-hand side of the room. He shakes his head with a low chuckle, turning his attention back to the television in the far corner of the room. Theo does the same when I meet his stare over his monitor, in his normal spot, two seats down from Amos. His sister, Chelsea, sitting beside her father, never looks my way. Amos's gaze hasn't left me since the moment I walked in; his eyes narrow, darkened by the shadows that dance across his features from the screen in front of him. Amos looks pissed, but he hasn't beckoned me to his corner yet, so I guess that means he's not too pissed. I've heard stories about people who get called over for a quick chat after their match, where either a verbal lashing or quiet words of praise await them. Since it doesn't look like I'm in line for either, I take the opportunity to get the hell out of dodge before the man who signs my checks changes his mind.

"Holy shit!" Raelynn's voice rings out when I step into the hallway. Her arms and legs wind around me in an embrace, practically knocking me back through the gorilla curtain. "You just won and lost your first title at the same time...and on your debut! You looked like a total badass."

"I botched a few times, not to mention I almost cost

Moxie her title."

Bennett—or *Wolf*, if you ask anyone else around here—approaches from my right with a slow clap. I roll my eyes as he drapes his arm over my shoulders, and we begin a light stroll down the hallway. "You didn't do shit. That was on Mox. She's gotten lazy. You did her a favor."

Bennett shrugs when Raelynn shoots him a glare. I'm happy to be back with the two of them again; it was getting boring around NextGen without them. Bennett has been on the main roster for almost a year now, and he hasn't had any issues fitting right in. I think it helps that he formed a bond with John and Brody after they met last spring—and yes, he continues to ask me what's going on between me and John. I wonder if he does the same to John.

"Savvy!" a voice rings out from behind us. Moxie runs down the hallway, the title clutched tightly in her hands.

"Remember what I said," Bennett whispers, and I elbow him.

"Good match," Moxie says.

"You sure about that?" I ask, feeling a little hesitant considering how things just went down in the ring. Not to mention her comment before we restarted the match: *Don't fuck it up this time*. "You seemed pretty upset."

Moxie chuckles. "All part of the act, Sav."

"But you almost lost the title."

"Well, technically, I did," Moxie says. Her words make my heart stop. I didn't even realize until now...I was *technically* the EWE Women's Champion for the five to seven minutes we spent trying to figure out what happened next. "Good practice for Sunday, I suppose."

"You're dropping?" Bennett asks, seeming a little more shocked than I expected, considering his words minutes ago.

"Yeah, I've decided to go on a small hiatus."

"You didn't re-sign." His voice dips low—sad—almost,

and it brings an equally sad smile to her lips. "Mox, why—"

"I've been doing this for seven years, Wolf. I want a family, I want kids. And this life...It isn't very conducive to that. Besides, I'm leaving you in very capable hands." She smiles at me and Raelynn. "These two are about to take EWE by storm."

"Come out with us to celebrate," Raelynn says, reaching her hand out to the champion.

"As fun as that sounds, my bed is calling my name. I have a long day ahead of me tomorrow." Moxie pulls us into a quick hug and leaves before Raelynn can convince her otherwise.

"You're coming, right, Wolfie?" Rae asks.

"I'd love to crash, but I'm supposed to meet Harper." Bennett rolls his eyes when he sees the same *ick* face Rae and I share. He's been dating Harper (if you can even call it that) for the last three months, and if you think it improved the relationship between her and me, you'd be wrong. We're... cordial when we have to be, but we do our best to ignore each other most of the time. "You guys promised you would be nice."

"And what about her?" I ask.

"She's not that bad. You'd know that if you just gave her a chance."

"She's only nice to you because you can give her something we can't."

"And what's that?"

"A dick to suck and fuck."

"Savannah!" Bennett gasps in horror as Raelynn high-fives me in a fit of giggles. His phone illuminates in his hand, catching his attention, and he rolls his eyes. "That was rude, and normally I'd have more to say, but I really have to go."

"Yeah, wouldn't want to keep your booty call waiting," Raelynn says, and I bite down on my bottom lip to stifle another laugh.

Bennett looks between us and breathes out a sharp exhale,

lips drawn into a thin line. He's tried to build the bridge between the three of us, but no one is looking to go over it anytime soon. Eyes closed, he shakes his head, and when he reopens them, there's a newfound sincerity there. "Sav, I really am proud of you. You did great tonight." He kisses the top of my head, glancing at Rae with an eye roll, before he jogs down the hallway.

Raelynn and I agree to meet in twenty minutes, because I'm in desperate need of a shower before I go anywhere, even if it's just the hotel bar. Different people littered throughout the hallway congratulate me, applauding my performance and offering words of praise. I try not to sound rude when my only response is a quick *thank you*, but I need to get to the locker room before I'm the one making Raelynn wait. If that happens, I'll never hear the end of it.

I grasp the handle, ready to sprint inside, when a slow clap bounces off the walls. I glance over my shoulder, my breath catching. What is he doing here?

"Quite the debut you had out there."

Try as I might, I can't hide my smirk as I step back from the door. "Watching me, Brooks?"

"Brooks, huh?" He chuckles with a soft shake of his head before his face turns serious. "But in all seriousness, you looked good, Sav." I think about making a witty comeback, but something tells me now isn't the time. That isn't what he came here to say, not really.

"Thank you, John," I say, and the corner of his mouth lifts again.

"Can I make one suggestion, though?" There it is. "Make sure you're protecting your neck. That bump from the top rope during the second match looked pretty brutal. Too many of those and you'll find yourself benched before you even get started."

"So, you *were* watching me," I say, but I know he's right. I felt it as soon as I landed. However, there wasn't much I could do; it was the way she threw me off the top rope.

"Savannah, I'm—"

"I know." A small smile of my own. "I appreciate you looking out for me."

"Savannah, come on!" Raelynn yells. She stands at the far end of the hall, looking extremely annoyed. "Normally, I'm all for you two making googly eyes at each other, but for once, can you not? I'm starving!"

The flames rise in my cheeks immediately, and I cover my burning face. Why did she say that?

"Sounds like you have a hot date. I wouldn't want to keep her waiting," John says, and I peek through my fingers to see the smile on his lips. He chuckles, taking a small step to close the space between us, and kisses my forehead. "I'll see you around...*Skye*."

8

TUESDAY, DECEMBER 28, 2010

CELESTIA, TX

My stomach tangles in knots when Wolf flicks the lever and the left turn signal ticks on the dashboard. He lifts his hand in a quick wave to a pickup truck that passes by before turning into the driveway of a gated property. There's nothing on either side for miles, but that doesn't seem to bother him. He appears perfectly at ease driving down the desolate Texas highway. He didn't even use the GPS, relying solely on his memory to find his way, much to the dismay of our comrades in the backseat.

Willow Pond Farm hangs above the open gates in bold, ornate letters made of wrought iron. Cream-colored pillars blend seamlessly with shorter stone walls to frame the sides of the iron gate. Flag poles stand at attention on either side— one with the American flag, and the other bearing the Texas state flag. Beautifully curated garden beds flank the sides of a gravel driveway, framed by a thick tree line with lush green canopies winding deeper into the property. The display oozes Texas grandeur and pride; it reminds me of the homes I used to look at and dream of when I was a kid.

My family of four lived in a modest two-story home in Indiana. It had enough room for my sister and me to have our own rooms, and our parents to have separate rooms after they finally grew tired of each other when I was around fourteen. We lived on what you might call the wrong side of the tracks in our small town. Dad was too much of a cheapskate to move us to the better part of town, even after he made his fortune. And when he left Mom after my sister turned eighteen, he took it all with him and moved into one of the wealthiest neighborhoods in the state on the northern side of Indianapolis. That was four years ago, and I haven't talked to him since. Truth be told, I stopped speaking to him before that, after he…Well, it doesn't matter. The past is the past. No sense in rehashing it when we're supposed to be enjoying our week off. Not just that, there are plenty of other things I'd rather be thinking about, like the woman who awaits us at the end of this gravel road.

Wolf maneuvers the oversized SUV down the winding drive until the trees open and the house comes into view—a picturesque farmhouse with a wraparound porch, surrounded by acres of untouched land. It's the kind of house you'd expect to find on a ranch—white siding, black shutters, chimneys made of stone, a black front door, and rocking chairs line the front porch. Maybe fifty yards from the house, there's one barn, and I can see another peeking around the corner. There's even a pond in the distance with what I can only assume are willow trees planted at one end. This is where Savannah grew up? I would've never guessed. She said she grew up on a farm, but I thought she meant a small plot of land on the city outskirts where they had horses, maybe chickens, but not an actual farm.

Raelynn is the first to jump out of the back seat before Wolf can put the car in park, running to greet two boys— twins from the looks of it—who run out of the open garage doors.

"Thing One and Thing Two!" Raelynn squeals, embracing them.

"Blake, the queen is here!" the taller of the two says.

"All hail the queen," the one I assume is Blake says, and they both hinge their hips in a bow. Raelynn rolls her eyes when they refer to her gimmick name, *The Queen of Roses*, and shoves them playfully.

As the rest of us filter out of the car, I meet the stare of the other twin and watch his eyes turn into wide saucers. He smacks his brother, interrupting the now-quiet conversation they're having with Rae, but Blake ignores him. His twin pinches his chin and forces him to look my way.

"Holy shit, you're Brooks Taylor," Blake says.

"And Brody Wilder!" his brother adds. And before I know it, they're talking in sync. "What are *you* doing here?"

Brody laughs, clamping a hand down on my shoulder. "We're friends of your sister."

"*You* are friends with *our* sister?" Blake asks.

"Seems unlikely." Twin Number Two says. I really wish they would tell us his name. I guess I could just call them *Thing One* and *Thing Two* like Raelynn, but I'd rather know their names. "She's not exactly *Juliet* or *Holly Graham*, or even *Moxie*. If you know what I mean." The last sentence is said together once again: "She's good, but she could use some help."

Wolf scoffs. "They didn't act like this when they first saw me."

"That's because you were a nobody the first time they saw you," Raelynn says, with a pitying smile. "Okay, Things, where's your sister? I told her we were on our way."

"Back forty." The answer comes out simultaneously, and I wonder if this is something that's going to happen often.

"She and Crew went out to see what kind of damage

happened during the storm last night," Blake adds.

"Blake, Bodhi!" a feminine voice yells out with a slight accent. All heads turn toward the house where an older woman with long dark hair pulled into a braid over her shoulder stands on the porch. She wipes her hands on her jeans, muttering to herself in what sounds like Spanish, and tromps across the yard. "Boys, where are your manners? Don't just leave our guests out here. Bring them inside! *Apúrate.*" She gestures in a "hurry up" motion before pointing to the open trunk, long forgotten amid our conversation. The twins groan, but do as told before the woman turns to greet us.

I notice she has similar features to Savannah—the dark hair, the shape and color of her eyes, the high cheekbones, the warm color of her skin, and the strong jawline. It makes me wonder if Savannah got anything from her father. "Come on inside. Savannah and Crew should be back any minute, but you guys can take a load off and—"

Gravel crunches behind us when a large pickup truck pulls up the drive. It swings to the left and parks in front of the detached garage near another barn I hadn't noticed earlier. How many buildings does this place have? The driver cuts the engine and practically trips over his own feet getting out.

"Shit!" The word echoes across the yard, and I hear Savannah's mother mumble under her breath.

Raelynn takes off toward him and jumps into his awaiting arms. He spins her wide before he sets her back on her feet, laughing the whole time. They share a quiet conversation only for them to hear, and I notice the tension building in Brody's frame. If his jaw clenches any tighter, he might chip a tooth.

"Fix your face," I whisper, and he glares at me. I've had a feeling that he's had a thing for Raelynn since we met her at NextGen last year. It's cute, but he denies it anytime I bring it up, which lately has been more often than not. Her constant presence since moving up to the main roster has only made his crush more obvious.

Even from here, I see the man's eyes widen beneath the brim of a baseball cap as he scans over our group. He stops short on Brody, and then on me. He whispers to Raelynn before she slaps him on the arm, starting a flurry of giggles, and she pushes him toward us.

"All be damned, SJ said she was bringing home some friends, but I just thought she meant Rae and Wolf...not the whole damn roster," he says.

"For those who don't know, this is Nash, Savannah's older brother," their mother says. "*Mijo*, please help your brothers with the bags, huh? We need to get them inside so our guests can settle into their rooms."

"Sure, Ma," Nash says, unwinding his arm from Raelynn's shoulders. He joins the twins, who have been going back and forth near the trunk about whether they could carry everything in one trip. Trust me, it's not possible. Why these girls need so many bags for only a few days is beyond me. They do just fine with a single suitcase being on the road every other day of the year. Why couldn't they do that now? "These all yours, Rae?"

"About eighty percent of them," Wolf says.

"Shut up, traitor." Rae pushes him. "You're supposed to be on my side."

Savannah's mother sighs, shaking her head with a slight smile. I get the distinct feeling this is her normal, but she loves every second of it. When Nash and the twins leave, promising to return for the rest of the bags shortly, she turns back to us and says, "I'm sorry about them. They're still getting used to the whole...their sister works on television thing." She does another once-over of the group before she extends her hand toward Harper. "I don't think we've had the pleasure of meeting before. I'm Laine, Savannah's mother."

"Harper." She introduces herself. "It's nice to meet you,

Mrs. Williams."

"Harper?" Laine glances at Wolf. "*The* Harper? I've heard all about you."

Harper's brow reaches the sky, and Wolf turns a bright shade of red. She's heard all about her? How many times has Wolf been here? I knew he and Savannah were close, but I guess I didn't realize how close.

"I'm Brody Wilder, ma'am," Brody says when Laine turns her attention to him.

"Laine, please." The older woman smiles up at him, and I suddenly realize how far we tower over her. She can't be any taller than five-foot exactly, and when she looks up at me, a different smile spreads across her lips—a knowing smile. One that says she knows exactly who I am without any introduction. "That must make you..."

"John Brooks." I extend my hand.

"Brooks." She chews on the word for a moment. "Why does that name sound familiar?" The small smirk in the corner of her lips tells me that she knows, but she doesn't want to out her daughter in front of everyone.

"Brooks Taylor," Brody says, oblivious to what is going on.

"Oh! Yes, my boys love you." Laine covers our still-joined hands and laughs. "You'll have to forgive me, I don't know much about all of this. It was never my thing...My husband, however, he's the one who got the kids into it."

"Savvy, too?" Harper asks.

"Oh no, Savannah was never that much into it. She'd watch occasionally when she was younger, but lost interest." That must be why she didn't recognize any of us at the bar a few years ago. "She was much more involved in cheerleading. From the moment she picked up her first set of pom-poms, she knew she wanted to be a professional cheerleader." A nostalgic smile graces her lips before she wraps her arms around her torso against the cool December breeze. "Anyways, she and

Crew should be back soon. It's a bit chilly today. Come inside and get warm." She holds her arm out to Raelynn, who steps into the embrace, and they walk toward the house.

Brody and I hang back to sort the rest of the bags. "Rae seems pretty close with them," he says, picking through the bags, but never settling on one.

"You mean she and *Nash* seem close," I say, and laugh when he glares again. "Why don't you just say something to her?"

"Why don't you?"

Touché.

He picks up his half of the remaining bags, and I close the back of the SUV when the roar of music tears through the tranquil air.

A Jeep barrels out of the tree line at the far end of the property, and even from this distance, I know who's sitting in the front seat. Her hair whips around from the wind and speed, only settling on her shoulder when the Wrangler comes to a stop beside Nash's pickup. She climbs out, and all I can do is stare. The dark denim jeans show off her delicious curves, even beneath the oversized plaid jacket. I fold my hands into my arms, trying not to think about how it feels to run them down her sides, remembering the sounds she made as I traced the planes of her body.

She plucks a hat from the back seat and sets it on her head before the man beside her hits the brim, knocking it off. Savannah swats at him, picking it up and laughing at something he says. Crew, I assume. She shoves his shoulder, trying to stifle her laughter when her gaze finally lands on us.

This is the first time in months that I've seen her, and I'd be a liar if I said I haven't been thinking about her. I've watched her matches—every one that I could—and occasionally I send her a quick text with feedback when I feel like she needs it, but we haven't *seen* each other. EWE is like that, though.

You could go a long time without ever seeing someone in the same building, if you really wanted to.

Her lips fall into a soft smile, and she embraces Brody first. It's quick and friendly, and I wonder if she meant to do the same thing to me because ours isn't anything like that. From the second I pull her into my arms, inhaling the heavenly scent of *her*—a musky yet floral and citrusy scent that's fresh, warm, and captivating—I know I'm in for a long weekend. Arms tighten around my neck, her face buried there, and she releases a contented sigh, like she needed this just as much as I did. Only the clearing of her brother's throat breaks us apart, and even then, her fingers remain wrapped around my wrist. We haven't been this close since the first night we spent together, and now that I've gotten a small taste to remind myself what it's like...I don't know how I'm supposed to keep my distance from her. I know I should, but I don't know if I can.

"Brody, Brooks, this is my oldest brother, Crew," Savannah says, introducing us, and I hate the choice of name she used for me. Her hesitation before she says it tells me that she isn't sure how to introduce me. We never talked about it.

"Nice to meet you," Crew says, much calmer than his younger brothers. He extends his hand, and Savannah drops her hold on me so I can return the gesture. The oldest Williams sibling keeps an observant eye on his sister, while watching every move I make, almost like he's analyzing even the breaths I take.

"Did my other brothers see you already?" Savannah asks.

Brody laughs. "Yes, it was...interesting."

"Damn," Crew groans. "I wish I could've seen the look on their faces. We tried to get back before you guys got in, but got sidetracked."

Savannah rolls her eyes. "What Crew means to say is *he* was too busy yapping, and we lost track of time."

"That's funny coming from you."

She sticks her tongue out at him, repeating the words in a mocking tone. Crew only laughs, adjusting the backwards cap on his head. He and Nash look the same, except for Crew's much larger body mass. Their complexion is lighter than Savannah's and their mother's, similar to the twins. I assume that comes from their father. Their rugged features are a stark contrast to the feminine ones of their sister. But the one thing they all share for certain is the dark brown color of their eyes.

"Everyone else inside?" Savannah asks.

"Mamá is probably making them empanadas."

"Then what are we still doing out here?" Brody looks around like we're crazy, and he's not wrong. A home-cooked meal sounds amazing after a long day of traveling.

Crew pats Brody on the back, taking one of the bags from him and guiding him toward the house, but not before he gives his sister a subtle glance.

Savannah rocks back on her heels, folding her arms over her chest, and waits until they're far enough away. "I hope they weren't too obnoxious. I didn't tell them you were coming because...Well, because I didn't know you were coming."

"Wolf said it was okay." In fact, he all but begged me to come, promising that it had been okayed with the woman standing before me. He said he didn't want to spend the weekend as the only man in the house, failing to mention that all four of the Williams boys would also be here.

"No, yeah. It's fine. I told him he could invite whoever he wanted. He just failed to tell me who that was."

"So, you didn't invite us?"

"I didn't *not* invite you." She smiles. "Truthfully, I didn't think you'd want to come. Why would you want to hang around a bunch of newbies?"

"Why wouldn't I want to hang out with you?" The question draws her eyes back up from the gravel beneath our feet, and I feel a tug of an invisible string between us. It draws me closer, just like it did the first night we met. The feeling is strange, hard to explain, but every time I look in her eyes, there's a deep sense of familiarity and comfort. I can't remember a time when I've felt so connected to someone, let alone someone I've technically only met a handful of times.

A blush creeps into her cheeks, or maybe it's just from being in the chilly December air for too long, but I'm almost certain they weren't that red before. "We, uh...we better get inside before Mamá sends a search party."

I motion for her to lead the way, restraining my hand from reaching for her lower back when she walks ahead of me. Something tells me this weekend is going to be more than either one of us bargained for.

"I swear she'd lose her damn head if it weren't attached," Brody says beside me in the back seat. Savannah slouches in the driver's seat, picking at her nails, but she glances back with a small snicker. Raelynn disappeared through the automatic double doors of the drugstore about three minutes ago because she had forgotten to pack something. Actually, she forgot a lot of somethings. Thirty minutes ago, she walked into the living room, rattling off the list—toothpaste, hairbrush, contact solution, and a razor—and Savannah said she could help with the toothpaste, but would need to go into town for the rest. Brody jumped at the opportunity to tag along, offering my presence as well, but Wolf and Harper declined. They feigned exhaustion, too tired from travel, but I think we all know what that really means.

"I'm surprised she made it to the airport on time," Savannah says, and I share a pointed look with my best friend. "She said she was on time!"

"If you call running down the hallway yelling to hold the door 'on time,' sure."

Almost ten minutes later, Raelynn jumps into the passenger seat with three bags full of stuff, clearly not just the things she had forgotten. Savannah eyes the bags, asking, "Did you buy the whole damn store?"

"You know we're not going home before Monday, right?" I add.

"I'm sure she has enough room in the three bags she packed," Brody says, and the three of us break out into a fit of laughter, but Raelynn doesn't find us comical.

Savannah shakes her head, pulling out of the parking lot and driving the opposite way we came. "You guys mind if I run by the coffee shop?"

Raelynn points at the clock on the dashboard. "Savannah, it's like seven o'clock. You'll never go to sleep."

"Says the girl who downs three energy drinks a day."

"Three?!" I can't stop my outburst. How is she downing three energy drinks *a day* and hasn't keeled over yet?

"Not every day!" she defends. "Just some days."

"That's terrible, Rae," Brody says, igniting a conversation between them about making good choices. The whole thing reminds me of a worried boyfriend and a nonchalant girlfriend. I catch Savannah's eyes in the rearview mirror, and she rolls her eyes playfully.

Savannah drives in silence through the small town of Celestia, Texas, a charming farm town with a population of 5,001, according to the sign I saw on the drive in. Driving down Main Street reminds me of Mayberry—the idyllic small town. Everything is clean and tidy, the landscape is perfectly manicured, the storefronts are stocked full, and everyone waves hello as they pass by. I get the sense that life moves at a different pace here, and the people like it that way.

At the end of Main Street, Savannah pulls into the parking lot of a small white house. There's a pep in her step when she jumps out of the front seat, bounding up the unvarnished wood steps and straight through the front door. A bell jingles above her head, signaling our arrival at *Celestia Coffee*.

Brody and Raelynn place their order before they walk arm-in-arm down to the end of the counter. It's too late for me to want caffeine, but I step forward when Savannah beckons me to place my order. Instead, I hand over a one-hundred-dollar bill to the cashier, and his eyes light up even more than they did when he recognized Brody. Savannah's heated stare warms my cheeks, but I ignore her, telling him to keep the change.

"You didn't have to do that," she says when I drape my arm around her shoulders, pulling her away. "I'm the one that's supposed to be picking up the tab and showing you around town, not the other way around."

I chuckle. "Can't a guy do something nice?"

"When a guy is 'nice,' it usually comes with some kind of expectation." Her tone isn't snarky, but it's got a small bite nonetheless.

My steps falter, and I pull away to look her straight in the eye. I don't know what kind of guys she's been around in her past, but that's not me. It's never been me. "I have no expectations of you, Sweetheart. I did that because I wanted to, not because I want something in return."

Savannah gnaws on her bottom lip, tucking a piece of hair behind her ear, and I think she's going to say something further, but her attention gets pulled to the back corner. Raelynn's laughter echoes in the mostly empty café, I'm sure in response to whatever face Brody just made after trying the drink he ordered on a dare from her. From the sound of it, when he was reading it off the chalkboard menu, it wasn't something I'd ever expect him to order, but he wasn't someone to turn down a challenge.

I watch Savannah as she watches them, taking measure of everything about her: the tension in her back, the clench of her jaw, the tight smile on her lips when Raelynn looks our way, and the way her shoulders rise and fall with a heavy sigh before she turns back to me.

"Brooks, I, uh..." *Brooks*? I thought we were past the Brooks thing. "Look, I don't want things to be weird." They're already weird; she just called me Brooks. "And you have to admit—"

"Why would they be weird?" I ask, and she gives me a knowing look. "Sweetheart, it doesn't have to be weird. And if I've come across that way to you, I'm sorry. Yes, we slept together, but that was before all of...this. Even if it wasn't, that doesn't mean we have to make it weird. There's no reason we can't be friends."

Savannah wets her lips, taking a breath. "Does anyone know?"

"Brody."

"What about the others that were there?" She chews on her thumbnail. The lights above us turn her eyes a lighter shade of brown as she stares up at me from underneath long lashes.

I don't mean to, but I feel my gaze narrow. *What about the others*? That hurts a little. Or maybe this is what they would call a bruised ego. Let's be real, everyone (or at least everyone thinks everyone) sleeps together. That's the nature of backstage...I think this might be the first time someone didn't want to yell from the rooftops that they had been with me.

Shaking my head, both in disbelief and answer to her question, I ask, "Raelynn?" She hesitates, but shakes her head. That's a lie.

My gaze narrows, and I notice a slight blush in her cheeks—she's been caught. I don't understand why she would lie; she's allowed to confide in her friend.

I clear my throat, folding my arms over my chest. "Well, my lips are sealed. You don't have to worry about me outing your secret."

"I didn't...Brooks, it's not like that." Savannah stumbles over her words, reaching out for my hand without hesitation. "I just...I don't know. Maybe we should keep our distance. I don't want people to think I got this job because of you. Or that I did this for you. Harper is already suspicious. I'm sure you being here has only made her more so."

I'm sure Wolf has his own suspicions, and I highly doubt he's kept those thoughts to himself. Or maybe they are only rooted in whatever Harper has said to him, because he's never outright asked me. He and Savannah are close, though. It surprises me that she would tell Raelynn, but not him.

"You know as well as I do that if people find out the truth, it's the first thing they'll say."

"And?" I laugh. "Let them, Savannah. Fuck them and their opinion. As long as you know it's not true, why does it matter what they think?"

"It's do—" Her rebuttal is cut short when another patron taps her on the shoulder. We both look over her shoulder to meet the gaze of another man, whose smile only widens when he realizes it *is* her.

"Holy shit, it is you! I thought it was, but—"

"Jaxon?"

Jaxon? So, she knows him.

The intruder looks down at her, his arms open at his sides like he's waiting for an embrace. One that doesn't come. Savannah remains in place, arms folded over her chest, and it might just be my imagination, but I swear she takes a step back toward me.

"It's good to see you! How long are you in town for?" he asks, letting his arms fall.

"Only a few more days," Savannah says.

The young kid behind the counter sets her coffee and an iced water on the counter. She thanks him, and he reminds her to come back before she leaves town, to which she enthusiastically agrees. He gives me a small smile before glaring at Jaxon, and I chuckle when he turns on his heel to get back to work. Glad to know I'm not the only one who gets a bad vibe from this guy.

"I think this is for you." She hands me the water, and the action draws the eyes of our guest to me. This is the first time he's acknowledged my presence since he interrupted us. His narrowed gaze moves over me, but locks onto the space where our hands meet on the plastic cup. Dropping her hand, Savannah takes another subtle step closer to me, her side now leaning into my own, but surprisingly, she doesn't pull away when my hand lands on her waist. The whole thing reminds me of that night at the bar in Crimson Valley, and I give her waist a gentle squeeze. "I have some friends visiting before we head to Philadelphia on Monday."

"Oh, right, you're doing that wrestling thing. I heard you were dabbling in that."

Dabbling? Is he serious?

"Well, if you find yourself with some free time in the next few days, we should hang out."

Savannah's hand comes to cover mine when my grip tightens, her fingers delicately weaving between my own. This is the complete opposite of what we are supposed to be doing. Not even two minutes ago, she said we should keep our distance, and now...Her fingers grasp mine when I try to remove my hand from hers, her grip almost as tight as the smile she offers the man before us. "Jax, I'm not going to have a lot of time."

The barista sets another coffee down without a second glance, not even a curt nod to his customer. Jax takes a sip of the coffee, his mouth turning up in disgust. He glares over his shoulder at the young kid, but surprisingly, doesn't say anything. Clearing his throat, he musters up his best smile. "Oh, c'mon. For old times' sake."

I don't have to look to know Savannah wants to say no, but for some reason, she accepts his invitation. Why doesn't she just say no? From the moment he walked up, it was obvious he made her uncomfortable. Why not tell him to get lost? I've never seen her like this before, so...compliant.

Jaxon promises to call her before glancing my way one final time. He pushes by me to leave out the side door. Savannah stands there a moment longer, lost in thought. Before I can ask her what that was all about, Raelynn and Brody make a joyous return with bright smiles on their faces and laughter in their words. Rae asks if we're ready to go. Without answering, Savannah untangles herself from me and walks out the front door. Head on a swivel, Raelynn looks between her retreating figure and me before she runs after her friend.

"You might want to fix your face," Brody says with the hint of a smirk. I let out a sigh, rubbing the space between my brows. "Something happen?"

"No."

"I believe that like I believe Noah isn't fucking Chelsea."

He means Noah Callahan, one of the producers for EWE, who people widely speculate has been sleeping with Chelsea Rafferty under her father's nose. Is it true? I can't say for certain, but that doesn't stop the rumor mill from churning out gossip. Either way, I will say I've caught them on more than one occasion talking in a flirtatious manner or sharing a longing glance.

"Who was that guy?"

"Not sure, but he's pushy," I say.

Brody chuckles. "Was he pushy, or are you just jealous?"

Am I jealous? No...I'm not jealous. I'm simply looking out for my friend who seemed uncomfortable in the presence of that douchebag. I glare at my best friend and roll my eyes. "Shut up."

9

Savannah

TUESDAY, DECEMBER 28, 2010
CELESTIA, TX

Somewhere in the back of my mind, I considered the thought that maybe, just maybe, Bennett would invite John to the ranch. But then I reminded myself that while he and John were friends, that didn't mean the biggest name in EWE wanted to spend a week with the new kids on the block. That's why I didn't invite him or Brody in the first place. This wasn't supposed to be a big deal, just a few friends hanging out and ringing in the new year together before we had to return to our hectic life on the road. Originally, it was only supposed to be Raelynn, Bennett, Jo, and maybe Jo's boyfriend—who ended up bailing at the last minute, just like I knew he would, which meant Jo bailed, too.

"I'm the lone wolf, once again," Bennett said two weeks ago when he asked me who would be joining us in Celestia for New Year's.

"Is there someone else I should've invited?"

"Well, no, but another guy in the mix every once in a while would be nice."

"Jo's boyfriend will be there," I said, and he deadpanned.

My brothers would be around, too. Granted, Crew and Nash would probably be working most of the time, and the twins usually kept themselves busy, especially now that they're seniors in high school. Okay, so maybe I saw his point. "So, who would you suggest?"

"I don't know...Brody?"

My brow raised. "Did you just say Brody?"

"I thought you liked him."

"I do, but I doubt he wants to spend the holiday with a bunch of newbies."

Bennett shrugged, pursing his lips. "We're not *that* new. Besides, I don't know if you've noticed, but he doesn't seem to mind finding us in a crowded room over practically everyone else in the company." That was true and had happened on more than one occasion. The real problem I faced with inviting Brody was having to invite John, too.

We still hadn't addressed the elephant in the room; in fact, I hadn't seen much of John since my debut. Not that I was surprised. Whether or not it was intentional, I knew he was busy, constantly on the go, always being pulled in a million different directions, finishing one thing just to be whisked away to handle another. I guess that's part of being the face of the company. But I had been just as busy trying to keep my head above water and stay relevant enough with the people in charge to keep my face on television. I didn't want to make my debut only to be pushed to the back of the line again.

"Look, B." I sighed. "I don't care who you invite. Just know that if they cause problems, *you* get to deal with it." The statement rang true for anyone he invited, but mostly Harper, whom he'd practically gotten on his knees and begged to be allowed to come. That was before he started in on the "lone wolf" nonsense.

Now he's far from a "lone wolf," but has been too far up Harper's ass to enjoy it. Which means Rae and I have to deal with it...Not that I mind, but it's the principle.

I should be in bed, getting some sleep so I can play the proper hostess tomorrow. Not only that, but I should be in bed catching up on the sleep I haven't been getting while on the road. Everyone else turned in about an hour ago, but I've been sitting on the porch taking some space to think. Think about my conversation with John—I mean Brooks—earlier. I've decided I should probably call him Brooks—everyone else does. Calling him John would indicate a deeper, more personal relationship, but we're just co-workers, maybe friends. And he isn't the only thing on my mind...The unanswered text message on my phone reminds me of the plans I agreed to earlier.

I can't believe I said I'd consider hanging out with my ex-boyfriend. I should've just said no, but Jaxon is nothing if not persistent, and charming, though his usual charm was slipping today. His smile faltered when he saw the way Brooks pulled me close, a presence between me and Jaxon, keeping him at bay. Still, I knew the only way to get him to leave was to agree to whatever he wanted. Was it fucked up? Yes, but the last thing I wanted was for him to say something that might cause John—*Brooks, I mean Brooks, damn it*—to show him what "dabbling" in wrestling really looked like. *Insert eye roll here.* Jaxon's condescending outlook on my newfound career doesn't shock me, but he could have at least tried to hide it.

A slight prickle raises the hairs on the back of my neck when I hear the soft rustle of grass in the distance. At this time of night, I can think of a few things that might be lurking around, but it's hard to make out anything in the surrounding fields when the moon hides behind a blanket of clouds. Squinting, I can make out a black silhouette against the inky field, and even shrouded in darkness, I'd know that stance anywhere. The same man who has held permanent residence in my mind since we met walks toward me, almost like I'd plucked him straight from my thoughts by thinking his name too many times. Let's hope Jaxon isn't next.

"Thought you might want one of these," Brooks says when he finally reaches the wooden stairs, a blanket in his arms. I can't fight my smile. His next steps are cautious as he ascends the porch. "I don't mean to intrude, but I was coming out for some air and saw you sitting here."

Mamá insisted that he and Brody needed something more comfortable to sleep on than an air mattress and a couch, so she coaxed Crew and Nash out of the guest house for a few nights. I wouldn't say my brothers were happy about it—any of them really—because it meant close quarters in the twins' bedrooms, but they complied with her request anyway.

"Thanks," I say, and take the soft material from his hands. I recognize it as the Wildcats blankets I gave Crew a few years ago, identical to the one I have tucked away in my blanket basket in Tampa. I drape the soft material over my legs, which were in fact freezing. Why I didn't bring one out with me in the first place is a great question, but I thought I would be okay in my sweats.

"You okay?" Brooks asks.

"Yeah." I push a hand through my hair before lifting my arms skyward into a much-needed stretch. "Just thinking."

Brooks shifts his weight, shoving his hands into the crooks of his elbows against the warmth of his crewneck sweater. His gaze travels back toward the guest house, and I can see the wheels turning, wondering if he should stay or go.

"Do you want to join me?" I ask.

"Is that a good idea?"

Probably not, but he's already here. I shift to make room for him on the couch, lifting the blanket to offer him the space beside me. "We're just two people thinking, right?"

Brooks hesitates for a moment longer before he gives in, falling into the spot on my left. As I cover his legs with the

147

blanket, the warmth of his body calls to my bare feet, and I bury them beneath his leg.

"Holy shit!" His body jolts against the newfound coolness, absorbing his body heat. "Your feet are like blocks of ice."

I cover my mouth, trying to contain my laughter, and hope that no one inside heard. Papá is a light sleeper, and he won't be happy if he gets woken up, especially considering the time. He'll be up in a few hours to start work, and he treasures every moment of sleep he gets.

"And you're like an oven," I say.

Brooks chuckles and covers my ankles with his hands, instantly warming the skin.

"Fuck," the word comes out somewhere between a hum and a moan. "That feels good."

His grip tightens around my joint, and even in the shadows, I see the flash of something familiar cross his features. Brooks rolls his lips between his teeth, looking away from me as his hold loosens. He moves his arm to rest along the back of the couch, keeping a space between his fingertips and my shoulder, but I feel him there regardless. A current fills the space between us, trying to draw us closer.

Silence envelops us for a few heartbeats, and despite his distance, I settle further into the newfound warmth. And this time, when I take a deep breath, my eyes flutter closed. I could fall asleep right here.

"What's got you up this late?" Brooks asks, waking me from the small trance.

"I could ask you the same thing," I say, eyes still closed. He doesn't answer, and it tells me that I already know the answer, or maybe I don't. Maybe the thoughts consuming him aren't the same as mine. Maybe he has other shit going on, and I'm just being self-centered, thinking it has to do with me. "I just have some stuff on my mind...and Jaxon texted me."

Why did I just tell him that? Brooks doesn't care that my

ex-boyfriend texted me.

"Coffee shop guy?"

Or maybe he does.

"He wants to have coffee," I say, picking a loose string on the blanket.

"So, a date."

"Not a date," I say a little too quickly. "It's not. We're just two high school acquaintances catching up."

Brooks hums in response, a slight scoff.

"What?"

"That guy isn't looking to just 'catch up' with you, Sweetheart." He's not wrong, but the way he says it—like I don't know what Jaxon really wants—pisses me off.

"Is that a bad thing?" I challenge, and Brooks meets my stare for the first time since that familiar look crossed his eyes. This time, though, his gaze narrows and his jaw clenches for a completely different reason. Is he jealous? "What's it to you, *Brooks*?"

I swear there's a small flinch when I say his name before he takes a deep breath and says, "I'm just looking out for a friend."

"Is that what we are—*friends*?"

"We can be whatever you want us to be, Savannah." There's weight to his words, implying so much between the lines. I feel a heaviness settle in my throat, blocking whatever response I had ready to shoot back. That is not what I expected him to say. "Look, you said earlier you think we should keep our distance, and if that's really what you want, I can go right now. But..." He seems to grasp for the words, trying to find the right way to say what's on his mind.

But what? I know what I want, but I know I can't have it. Not right now. Not yet.

"But I don't want that, Savannah. I want to be...friends."

Friends. He wants to be just friends. Of course, he does.

What else would he want to be? Why did I think he was going to say something else?

"And as your friend, I want you to be careful. You want to go on a date with this guy? Fine. But don't pretend like you don't know what he wants. He made that obvious by the way he couldn't stop eye-fucking you earlier."

I won't deny I felt a little uncomfortable under Jaxon's intense stare, but I know him. I've known him since we were kids. Jaxon is a shameless flirt, and he has no problem making it well known when he wants someone. He's a sweet talker, and he has a way of getting you to do what he wants, even if you don't want to. A way of convincing you it's what you wanted all along. But he's harmless.

We dated in high school because that was what cheerleaders and football players were supposed to do. The squad pressured me to say yes when he asked me on a date the second week of school, and that ignited a terrible cycle of ups and downs until senior year, when I decided I didn't want to do it anymore. Will Jax try to convince me we should give it another go? I don't know, maybe. He tried it once before, when I came home from Thornebrooke my sophomore year, but Crew put a stop to it before he could get the words out. And this time, I know better. I've broken the cycle twice before, and I have no intentions of going backwards. This is exactly what I said: two acquaintances catching up over a cup of coffee.

"It's just coffee, Brooks."

"Don't call me that."

A soft laugh. "Don't call you by your name?"

"I am not *Brooks* to you." His face pulls into a tight line. "Not you." Those words tell me everything I need to know—confirm what I already know. He wasn't going to say *friends* earlier, but he did because that's what I need right now. I reach out to smooth the lines of his cheeks with a small smile and nod.

"It's just coffee, John."

"Yeah, better be careful. You might hurt yourself lifting those hay bales," Crew says, mocking Papá's warning from moments ago. "Make sure you lift with your knees."

"Shut up, Crew. At least I know how to use my knees." A deep sense of dread fills me the moment I say it, and a grin spreads across my brother's cheeks. Shit.

"And what *have* you been using your knees for, SJ?"

Papá rolls his eyes and keeps walking when I jump on Crew's back, snaking my right arm around my brother's neck. I clasp onto my other bicep to put him in a classic sleeper. Crew reaches out for help, his breath coming out in desperate gasps, even though I put no real pressure against the column of his throat.

"Tap!" I demand, but he shakes his head, calling out to our father instead.

"If I was you, I'd do as she says," Papá says without looking. He continues further down the main hall of the barn toward the stalls he and Crew are supposed to be cleaning. We're behind on chores this morning, mostly because Crew and I have spent a good majority of the time putzing around and picking on each other. I'm surprised Papá hasn't told us to knock it off, but I think he's missed it too much to care. He raises his hand, waving down at the end of the barn. "Oh, Brooks! Good morning."

At the name, my grip loosens, and Crew takes my temporary moment of distraction to break the hold. He grasps my left ankle, undoing the knot I tied with my feet on his abdomen, before reaching around to my sides to tickle me. A squeal bursts from me at the sensation, and I immediately drop my hold, jumping away from him. My brother laughs as I stumble upon landing, crashing into a nearby large wooden storage crate.

The sudden commotion catches the attention of both our father and John, who stand at the far end of the barn. Papá rolls his eyes, saying something under his breath before his voice carries down the hall, "Crew, you guys get out to the coop yet?"

"Sorry, Pa, what?" Crew asks, still chuckling to himself.

"You get out to the coop?"

"Haven't done it yet. *Someone* has been distracting me all morning."

I raise a contemptuous brow at my brother. "I have not! I've been helping."

"Sure, if you call getting in the way help. You ran off to Hollywood and forgot how to do chores."

Before I can respond, our father breaks us apart. "Savannah, you and Brooks go get some eggs for your Ma, huh?"

"But, Pa, I'm going to—"

"You were going to get those eggs."

I blow out the rest of my argument with a huff, earning a chuckle from my brother. I shoot a glare over my shoulder before doing as I'm told, walking between my dad and John, who gives me an apologetic glance and follows me outside.

The chicken coop isn't far from the barn, but right now it feels like one hundred yards. The only sound is the crunch of our steps against the crisp morning grass that has yet to be thawed by the sun. After a moment, John says, "You were up early."

"So were you." I open the coop and reach in to grab the wire basket hanging on the wall, handing it to him. "I saw you go out for a run this morning."

He shrugs. "Figured the fresh air might do me good."

"Something else on your mind?" I ask, and glance over my shoulder when he doesn't answer. The muscles in his throat contract, swallowing down whatever he might have thought to say, and he shakes his head. "Well, you'd better get some rest while you're here. Mamá will never let me hear the end of it."

"I'll do my best."

I shoo away a few of the chickens and reach down into the first box to pull out two eggs, gently placing them in the basket. When I glance back at him to ask how he slept (once we finally turned in for the night), his gaze is locked on the wall, his mind somewhere else.

"John?" A second later, the realization churns in his eyes before he meets my stare. "Is everything okay? You seem distracted."

"Oh, yeah. Everything is...Everything's fine."

"Well, as your *friend*, I'm here if you want to talk," I say, reaching into another box. So far, we've collected six eggs, but I'm not going to make him stand here and wait for me to clear out this whole coop. Shooing another chicken out of the way, I feel it as soon as I step down—the odd angle my foot lands in—and when I try to avoid stepping on the animal, I stumble over my own feet.

A strong arm wraps around my waist, catching me before I can eat dirt—or in this case...well, I don't really want to think about it. John's hand holds tight to my side as he steadies himself. Wide, inky blue eyes meet mine before flickering to my lips briefly, his tongue poking out to wet his lips.

Wait, is he...Is he leaning in? Or is it me? If it's me, he hasn't pulled away. Should I pull away? Shit, if we get any closer, we're going to—

"What the hell?" His body jolts as if struck by lightning.

It doesn't take long to figure out the culprit behind the intrusion...At our feet, Buddy the Chicken squawks loudly. He stares intently at John's denim-clad leg, and without warning, he leans in and pecks it.

John jumps out of the coop, and I double over in laughter. A big, bulky guy, over six feet tall, running out of the chicken coop because of a teeny, tiny chicken. That might be the funniest thing I've ever seen.

"Looks like Buddy wanted to say hi," I say, covering my mouth to try and hide the laughter still on my lips. Still chuckling, I reach into a few more boxes, collecting eight more eggs before I leave the coop and drop them into the basket John still holds. "C'mon, that should be enough for now. I'll get the rest later."

10

Savannah

FRIDAY, DECEMBER 31, 2010

CELESTIA, TX

"You cannot be serious," Cassandra says, pushing through the crowd to catch up to me and Kingsley. My best friends drove from Alexandria to join us for the New Year's celebration. After all, Kingsley could hardly pass up an opportunity to witness the Taco Drop again.

What's the Taco Drop? It's our little town of Celestia's version of the Ball Drop to ring in the final moments of the year. A giant taco, decorated by the high school senior class, descends a 120-foot pole placed in the middle of town square. This year, the seniors chose Candyland as the theme, and they went all out. The seven-foot-wide LED taco is slathered in a rainbow of candies, and I've heard more than once how it looks good enough to eat.

The twins ran off the moment we arrived to find their friends and fellow seniors; they wanted to watch their handiwork and bring in the new year together. My older brothers have helped me keep my friends entertained, including Nash, who can't stop flirting with Rae. Every time they seem to get lost in each other, I notice that Wolf and

John glance at Brody, who ignores them. Mamá and Papá are in charge of one of the stalls, selling Mamá's homemade empanadas and a flurry of other homemade snacks—they're always a hit at these events.

"Savannah, please tell me you're joking about meeting your ex-boyfriend tomorrow," Cassandra pleads, and I roll my eyes. They had sequestered me from the rest of the group under the guise of finding some spiced wine, but I knew it was really to corner me about Jaxon. I made the mistake of telling them about running into him, and that he invited me to coffee, and that I said yes.

"What is the point of going?" Kingsley asks.

"That's what I'd like to know. What reason could you possibly have for meeting up with Jaxon Gallagher?"

"He's not that bad, Cass," I say, pushing through the crowd when I see one of the spiced wine stalls up ahead. Cassandra, unlike Kingsley, knows him, because we went to high school together. She moved to Celestia the summer before sophomore year, and we've been friends ever since. We were roommates the first year at Thornebrooke, and when I joined the Wildcats, Kingsley turned our duo into a trio.

"He's a dickwad, and he treated you like shit in school."

Was Jaxon kind of a jerk sometimes? Yes. Was he a cocky, teenage football star who thought he was better than everyone? Also, yes, but he wasn't *that* bad. He never cheated on me. Never called me names. Jaxon was just a self-absorbed kid who wanted a trophy wife, not a partner, and as time went on, that became abundantly clear. Unfortunately for him, that wasn't me. Unfortunately for me, he had a way with words, and that's how he always managed to pull me back in...until I ended things once and for all after a big fight at the state championship game our senior year. I said some not-so-nice things to him right before he went on the field, but hey, we still won. Still, he offered to give me a ride home from a party that night, and we had the same conversation, minus the yelling. We agreed ending things was for the best, and then he started dating Olivia Jakes two weeks later.

"Seriously, Sav. You have a beautiful man right in front of you, and you're going to chase some old high school fling—"

"What are you talking about, Cass?" They both give me a knowing look. "Who, Brooks? You guys, we are not—"

Kingsley dismisses me. "First, let's not pretend like you call him *Brooks*. You are the only person I have ever heard call him John. Second, why not?"

"Because we're just friends. And—"

"Who slept together."

"And I don't want to date someone I work with. That could really complicate things."

"Sounds like an excuse to me," Cassandra says, stepping up to the counter of the small hut selling wine. "Hi, Mrs. Daniels!"

"Evenin', girls. Savannah, glad to see you could get some time off," says Celestia's resident town gossip, Mrs. Joyce Daniels. A Cheshire smile extends past her eyes that twinkle beneath the multicolored lights of her bungalow.

"It's been good to be home," I say, offering a tight smile of my own.

"Rumor has it you brought some of your more famous friends with you, including two very strapping young men. One of them yours?"

Cassandra looks right at me, and I roll my eyes. "No, ma'am. We're just friends."

"Too bad. That one is a tree I'd like to climb." Mrs. Daniels turns to the steaming pots of spiced wine along the back wall, and I try to ignore the snickering on either side of me. I cannot believe she just said that. Actually, I can. While Joyce Daniels has been happily married to the same man for the last thirty years, that's never stopped her from looking. "Just three wines, then?"

"Yes, ma'am."

She waves me off when I reach into my pocket. "On the house, sweetie. Just promise you'll lock that one down before someone else does."

"Just out of curiosity," Cassandra says, taking her wine. "Can I ask which one you mean?"

Oh, for the love of God.

The older woman's eyes light up again. She cranes her neck to look over the crowd, and I know she's found what she's looking for when the smile creeps back onto her lips. Mrs. Daniels turns to me. "He's quite tall—well, they both are, but he's not as tan as his friend. No tattoos like the other one, either. I want to say I've heard his name is B-Brian? No, that's not right."

Cassandra's smirk only grows. "Brooks?"

"Yes, that's it! Brooks." Mrs. Daniels raises her brow, pointing a single blood-red nail my way. "Honey, I saw the way he was looking at you earlier. We all have. And I'm serious, you better lock that down."

"If she doesn't jump on that man, I'm going to," Cassandra adds, and I shoot her a glare.

Kingsley shakes her head, rubbing the space between her brows. "Stop talking, Cass."

"I'm just saying. He's too fine not to."

I grumble in response, taking my wine, and use the growing density of the crowd to escape. The crowd has started to fill the square in preparation for the countdown set to begin in one minute, according to the clock tower of City Hall. Swimming through the crowd with a mixture of "excuse me" and "pardon me," I try to get back to where we left my coworkers and two oldest brothers.

There's a tug on my hand just steps before I reach the edge of the crowd, and it pulls me back a step, holding steady when

I try to rip from its grasp. I twist, ready to disarm whoever is on the other side, but my defenses fall immediately. Blue eyes sparkle beneath the light of that damn LED taco. Faintly, I can hear the countdown begin, starting at fifteen. He pushes a lock of hair behind my ear, and my eyes flutter closed when his fingers trace the curve of my jaw, leaving a trail of fire in their wake. "John, what are you—"

"Savannah." He dips down, his lips barely brushing mine. I can smell the faint mixture of mint and cider on his breath.

The countdown grows louder now as they reach the count of ten.

"What if they see?" I breathe out. There's no guarantee that Cassandra and Kingsley aren't looking for me in the crowd after I left them with Mrs. Daniels, or Raelynn, who might be wondering what's taking so long.

A soft chuckle rumbles in his throat, and when I open my eyes, I'm greeted by his bright smile. "Let them."

Our lips meet as the crowd yells out "Happy New Year!" I'm not sure who leans in first, but what I do know is this feels right. The kiss is soft and warm, igniting the sensors in my brain and filling me to the brim with warm dopamine. This is exactly what we're not supposed to be doing, but I don't care. The feeling of him against me is too good, too right, to let it go. We part too soon, and a soft whimper escapes me. Gazing up at him, I have so many questions—*What in the hell was that?*—but I don't have a chance to get them out before he kisses me on the forehead and disappears into the crowd, leaving me standing there confused and conflicted.

11

SATURDAY, JANUARY 1, 2011

CELESTIA, TX

"Speaking of pathetic," Nash says before taking a quick swig from the bottle in his hands. He points a finger at his older brother and swallows down what has to be warm beer for how long he's been nursing that thing. "Did *you* see the way Jaxon was eyeing our sister yesterday?"

Glad to know I wasn't the only one who noticed.

"I couldn't be bothered to notice," Crew says with a dramatic roll of his eyes.

If the height of the moon is any indication of the time, it has to be close to midnight. Brody and I decided to stay outside with the older Williams brothers a little longer after everyone else called it a night around ten. Normally, if I had the chance to catch a few extra hours of sleep at night, I'd do the same, but getting to know Crew and Nash has been one of my highlights of this trip. Growing up with my little sister as my only companion at home made me long for the connection that comes with having a brother, someone who understands the trials and tribulations of navigating the teenage boy world. And let's be honest, Ari probably felt the same way.

I had friends in school, but I never felt that connection with anyone until I met Brody in developmental at EWE. We didn't have NextGen back then. It was just a handful of guys in a dingy gym with a single ring and two trainers. A lot has changed over the years, and the introduction of NextGen was the love child of Noah Callahan and Theo Rafferty. They were tired of new guys coming in and falling flat because they didn't have anyone teaching them the ropes—literally. Noah and Theo wanted to give new kids a place to go where they could learn what it meant to be an EWE wrestler—indie or not. They could work not only on their wrestling skills, but also on promos and character development.

Brody and I became best friends almost instantly and have been inseparable ever since. Always looking out for each other, always there for each other, always cheering one another on in our careers. There has never been any jealousy or ill feelings when someone seemed to get ahead.

That's how it feels to watch the Williamses, and they made us feel like part of the family from the second we set foot on the property. But the thing I liked most about the family is the way each of the brothers looks out for their sister. God save anyone who tries to mess with her.

I guess I forgot people like this exist, because I haven't met many in the last six years. Backstage is a competitive place. People are constantly vying for a morsel of acknowledgement or TV time, and it's always been that way. If you're not willing to step on a few throats, you won't make it in the business. You can't worry about the chances someone else isn't willing to take.

Nash swallows another sip of warm beer and shrugs. "All I'm saying is Jaxon always finds a way to weasel his way back into Sav's life."

Brody and I share a look, knowing that he's already tried to do just that.

"That was in high school, Nash. Besides, Savannah isn't dumb enough to fall for his shit again."

I try to hide a chuckle behind my beer, but it's not subtle enough, earning a glance from Crew, but before he can ask, Nash spills the beans on her morning activities earlier today. "She went on a date with him this morning!"

Crew's head whips back to his brother. "What are you talking about?"

"I heard Mamá telling Pa about it," Nash says, lifting his hands in a shrug. "Something about SJ was gone and back by the time everyone got up, told Mamá she went to breakfast with Jaxon."

The oldest Williams scrubs a hand down his face. "You've got to be kidding me."

I think back to this morning, when I walked into the kitchen after a run to find Laine gathering ingredients to prepare another large breakfast, with coffee already brewing. The sight made my heart ache as it had for the past three mornings. The Williams family was what I had hoped my family could be, but my parents were the epitome of people who stayed together for the kids. They finally divorced when my sister Ari turned eighteen, and they didn't see each other again until she graduated from college. And try as she might, my mother is the opposite of Laine Williams in every sense of the word.

"Good morning, Brooks!" Laine beamed over her shoulder from her place at the stove. "Saw you out there runnin'. I figured you'd still be in bed after last night."

Last night was the New Year's Eve festival in town, and the exact reason I needed that run. I had to work through the events of the night—more specifically, the event that transpired moments before the clock struck midnight. Savannah and I were supposed to be friends...Hell, maybe even acquaintances, and people who were acquaintances did *not* kiss.

As the clock counted down, I couldn't get the idea of kissing her out of my head, and with only two minutes left until midnight, my feet moved on their own through the crowd to find her.

"What if they see?" she asked with only seconds remaining, but the question didn't faze me. I didn't care if anyone saw us. I didn't care if someone took a photo and posted it on the internet or sold it to a gossip magazine. Let them. None of it mattered, because in that moment, I only cared about the woman in my arms.

The kiss ignited a spark in my brain, and it screamed at me to hold on to her and never let go. My run only jumbled my thoughts more. Every scenario I came up with ended with telling Savannah I don't want to be just friends...I want her. We only spent one night together, one fleeting moment, but I still thought about it often. Still thought about the girl from Crimson Valley with the bright eyes and beautiful smile. There was something behind that smile calling out to me, and it made me want to know her. It felt like the universe was giving me the chance to do just that, except there was the issue of her rule: No dating wrestlers. Then there was the issue of her date with Jaxon this morning—okay, so maybe that wasn't the word she used, but let's call it what it is—and instead of doing what a good *friend* would do, I had gone and blurred the lines...again.

Why was this happening? I'd never experienced anything like this before, never felt this...I couldn't get her out of my fucking head. It was driving me insane.

"You see Savannah out there?" Laine asked, handing me a cup of coffee. "She wasn't in bed, and she wasn't in the barn with Crew and Wes, either."

"No, ma'am. Can't say I did."

Her mother hummed in response, tapping the rim of her

coffee mug. With a small shake of her head, she cleared her throat. "Well, I have to go round up some more eggs. Breakfast will be done shortly."

Not a second later, the door swung open to reveal Savannah dressed in blue jeans and a basic white T-shirt hidden underneath a black jacket. Her eyes met mine almost instantly before her mother bombarded her. "*Buenos días,* Mamá."

"Where were you this early?" Laine drew out the question.

"Oh, I…I met a friend in town," Savannah said, pouring a cup of coffee.

"*¿Un amigo?*" Laine asked and glanced at me briefly. "*¿Quién?*"

"Jax." The name came out barely audible over the rim of Savannah's mug, but it sent her mother into a tizzy. Her eyes looked as if they were about to pop out of their sockets.

"Savannah Josefine! How could you—"

"Mamá, please."

Laine dropped her voice into a harsh whisper. "You have guests here, and you went out with *Jaxon*?" Savannah stood with her back to me, but I could see the tension mounting in her shoulders as her mother continued to chastise her. While they were both preoccupied, I made a break for the door. "Why would you want to see that boy, huh? He's nothing but a troublemaker, and you know it."

"I ran into him in town the other day, and he invited me to catch up. That's it."

"Ay, Savannah!" From the door, I saw Laine throw her hands up in the air before she walked away. She shoved her arms into her jacket sleeves, muttering to herself in Spanish the whole way out the door.

Brody's voice brings me back to the fire pit with the brothers. "What's the deal with this kid? Jaxon, is it?" Brody asks, and I glare at him. "What? You act like you don't want to know."

"It's none of our business," I hiss.

Crew scoffs and glances my way. "Oh, please, Brooks. You're dying to know. Don't think I haven't seen the way *you* look at our sister."

Brody tries to cover his laugh with a cough.

"I could tell from the second you saw each other the other day."

"I don't know what you're talking about. Nothing is going on." The words flow off my tongue with a small bite to them. Maybe it's because of that small bit of jealousy I feel knowing she went on a date with her ex-boyfriend while we're here... while I'm here. Or maybe it's because the words are the truth. Nothing is going on. We're not dating. We're barely even friends. However, I'm not sure it's the right time to tell them I *have* seen the most intimate parts of their sister...

"It's not like it's not reciprocal," Nash says.

"Your sister doesn't date wrestlers," Brody answers before I can.

They share a laugh over the fire, but the joke seems lost on me and Brody. "Jaxon was a football player *and* a wrestler in high school," Nash says, still laughing to himself. "He was—"

"Jaxon Gallagher was a cocky son of a bitch who thought he was God's gift to mankind," Crew interrupts.

"That doesn't mean he wasn't good," Nash argues. "He got a full ride to UT."

"Yeah, and as soon as he got up there with the big boys, what happened?" Crew asks, but Nash only clears his throat in response. "Exactly."

"What happened?" Brody asks for both of us.

"Jax thought he was going to get up to college and still be running things the way he did in high school, but he learned real quick that's not how it works outside of our small town. The very first time he got put on the field, he was knocked on his ass by A&M and ended up breaking his leg. He's never been back on the field since."

"Scored the touchdown, though," Nash adds, earning an eye roll from his brother.

"His dreams went out the window, and he became an accountant instead." Crew takes a sip of his beer, shaking his head. "The kid was an asshole to Savannah, but for some reason, he's always been able to talk his way back into her heart. When you're in high school, you think that's the only thing that matters…you don't realize there's a whole world out there just waiting for you to discover it. She was a cheerleader, so Savannah thought dating a football player was the thing to do, and from what Jaxon told her, he'd always had a crush on her but was too afraid to say anything."

Brody laughs. "That should've been her first red flag."

"You would think, but our sister likes to see the good in people."

"There's nothing wrong with that," Nash defends.

"There is when it comes to someone like Jaxon Gallagher," Crew says. "That kid broke her heart on more than one occasion. She would never admit it, but seeing him go after Olivia Jakes two weeks after they broke up for good crushed her."

Damn, what an asshole.

I'm starting to understand why they are so against her hanging out with him. He sounds like nothing more than a washed-up football player trying to relive the glory days, ex-girlfriend included.

"Alright, that's enough talk about Jaxon," Nash says. "I knew I shouldn't have said anything."

"Well, if she's gonna start dating the fucker again—"

"I didn't say that!"

"You just said she went on a date with him this morning."

"But I didn't say they're *dating*."

Crew stares hard at his little brother, and then looks at me and Brody. "Is it even realistic to try and date someone outside of the industry? I mean, you guys are gone over half the year. That can't be good for a relationship."

"It does happen. Some people are better at making it work than others," Brody says. "But it's hard. People who aren't in this...they don't get it."

"They can't," I add, seeing Crew's eyes flicker to this brother again. "Unless you're part of this...you can't understand."

"Most times, people end up breaking up, but like I said, some make it work."

The brothers nod in unison. I notice Crew's thumbnail picks at the label on his bottle, and he chews on the inside of his bottom lip. He takes a deep breath, and when he blinks, his eyes look up from the flame straight into mine. Eyes slightly narrowed, he continues to stare at me without saying a word, but he doesn't have to...He's trying to piece together whatever he thinks is going on between me and Savannah. *Don't think I haven't seen the way you look at our sister.* Was it really that obvious?

"Is she doing okay?" Nash asks, and I rip my gaze from the oldest Williams. "Sav, I mean. I'd like to think she'd tell us,"— he looks to Crew for confirmation—"but I don't know. This is a first...SJ is the first one of us to move farther than two hours away. Hell, even the twins are just going to UT in the fall."

"And you think she'd tell us?" Brody chuckles. "You're better off asking Rae or Wolf."

"I think she's doing okay, all things considered," I say, and all heads whip in my direction. "Getting accustomed to the life, being on the road all the time...It's hard on anyone, like we said earlier, but she's kicking ass. If she keeps it up, I think she'll be one of the top women in the division within the next year."

It's quiet for a moment, and I look from the dwindling fire

to the barn in the distance, where a light still shines through the window of the upper floor. Savannah left not long after the others. I assumed she was going to bed, but instead, she took a water bottle from the cooler next to her brother and walked straight to the barn. That's partially what started the whole conversation about Jaxon—her brothers going through a list of things that could have bothered her enough to make her want to go up in the barn and hit the old punching bag.

"You guys will keep an eye on her, right?" Nash asks. "Since we can't be there."

Brody laughs. "Your sister can take care of herself."

"Oh, we have no doubt," Crew says. "But if she needs something, we're not just down the road anymore. I can't be there in a quick drive if something happens."

"I have no doubt you would be if she called," I say, turning back to the three of them, and it makes him laugh. He nods, unable to deny it, but no one continues the conversation further.

After a moment, Crew slaps his hands on his knees and stands from the lawn chair, stretching his limbs, and we all follow suit.

"Goodnight, gentlemen. We'll see you in the morning for breakfast before you leave," Nash says, picking up the cooler and dumping the melted ice water onto the remaining flame. A quiet sizzle follows before he offers a final nod and leaves.

"Brooks, you mind if I get a word?" Crew asks before I can do the same. Brody chuckles, shaking his head without so much as a supportive glance, and walks toward the guest house. "Look, I didn't mean to call you out...about Savannah."

"No harm done," I say, except for the fact that apparently I'm not as good about hiding how I feel about her as I thought.

"I'm just a little concerned."

Concerned?

"You understand where I'm coming from, right?"

"I don't think I do."

"Well, you know, you're known for being a bit of a...How do I say this? Manwhore."

"You mean I used to be known as that, but you can't believe everything you hear."

"So, you weren't sleeping with Chelsea Rafferty to get in good with her father?" Crew's brow raises, arms crossing over his chest.

I don't even try to hide my scoff. Is that supposed to be a joke? "Y'know, I've heard a lot of rumors about myself, but this is the first time I've heard that one. No, I have never—and would never—sleep with Chelsea Rafferty. But I especially wouldn't sleep with Chelsea to get in good with Amos. I don't know what you think you know, Crew, but I've worked my ass off to get where I am." I shake my head, glancing toward the barn where the window still shines like a beacon in the night. "When it comes to Savannah, I've kept my distance from her because that's what she wants—"

"You seem pretty attached for someone who just met her a few months ago." His dark brow cocks a little further.

Remember when I said I liked the Williams brothers? I might have to take it back. Don't get me wrong, I get it. If it were my little sister, I'd be doing the same thing, but I'm not the one they need to worry about.

"I care about your sister more than I've cared about someone in a long time. It's hard to explain, and I don't totally understand it myself, but I'm not here to cause problems, Crew. I would never push her to do something she's uncomfortable with. I respect her, and I respect her decision not to date a coworker. Honestly, it's probably the smartest thing she could do, knowing some of the guys we work with. But that doesn't mean I can't be her friend."

Even in the shadows, I can see the small smile tug on Crew's face. Digging his hands into his pockets, he takes a deep breath and nods.

"You're a good guy, Brooks," he says, and it feels like there is more he wants to say, but for whatever reason, he doesn't. After a second, he chuckles. "But if you break my sister's heart, I'll kill you."

12

Savannah

Right hook, left hook, kick. Right hook, left hook, kick. I repeat the motions over and over, waiting to feel some relief, but none comes. I've been wound tighter than one of the rattlesnakes in the field since this morning. Every time I start to unwind, I'm reminded of my conversation with Jaxon this morning.

I could feel John's observant gaze on me all night, and not just his. Rae had clocked my discomfort from across the breakfast table. She cornered me as we strolled through the flea market outside of town earlier, but I brushed off her concern. I didn't feel like rehashing my morning activities, especially not in a place where the town gossips had ears everywhere. Mrs. Daniels couldn't wait to get the next juicy piece to talk about with her friends over tea, and if one of her lackeys heard I was out with Jaxon this morning, they'd run straight to her.

My time with Jaxon had been fine...at first. We met at Celestia Eatery, a small diner in town, and went through the normal topics: work, health, life updates, and family. But as soon as there was a lull in the conversation, he took the opportunity to ask the question he'd really wanted to ask when he saw me at the coffee shop days before. "So." He cleared his throat, wiping his mouth. "What's the deal with that guy?"

"What guy?" I asked, even though I knew exactly who he meant.

"Big bulky dude...He was with you the other day. That your boyfriend or something?"

"Why?" It came out snappier than I meant.

Jaxon shrugged, using his straw to stir what was left of the iced coffee in his glass. "I'm just curious. Way he acted, seemed like more than just a friend."

I scoffed. "Jax, that's—"

"So, you're not dating him?"

"That's none of your business, Jaxon."

"A guy can't be curious?"

No.

"Look, I'm just checking on a friend."

Checking on a friend, my ass. I rolled my eyes.

"He one of those wrestlers or something?"

"Yes." I sighed. "He's a *friend* from work."

"Just a friend?" A sly smirk crossed Jaxon's features as he placed the straw on his tongue.

As much as I'd like to say otherwise, I can't. That's exactly what Brooks said the other night. He wants to be friends... *just* friends. But the way he kissed me last night at the Taco Drop was the opposite of how you treat someone who's just a friend. He and Brody were gone by the time I found the others. Raelynn told me they left before midnight to go back home, but I knew that was only partially true.

"Not that it matters, but yes, he's just a friend."

For now. No, for good. I can't risk screwing things up at EWE, and getting involved with another wrestler seems like a fast track to derailing my career before it ever truly gets started, especially if that wrestler is John "Brooks Taylor" Brooks.

Jaxon's following huff ground away at my nerves. I knew what he was doing. He was trying to see just how far he could push before I exploded.

I sighed. "I'm going to regret this, but what?"

"He just seemed really into you, is all. For just a friend," Jaxon said. "You fucking him?"

I practically spat the drink of hot coffee I'd taken. "What is wrong with you?"

He laughed. "That's not a no."

I stared at him for a brief moment before I shook my head, running my finger over the rim of my coffee mug. "Why did you really want to meet up, Jax?"

"Catch up." He shrugged.

"That's all?" I asked, shocked by the lack of typical Jaxon charm and decorum I'd become so accustomed to over the years.

"And maybe to get under his skin a little." Jaxon's lips pulled into the devilish smirk I had come to know all too well over the years, and it made me sick to my stomach. "You should've seen the way he looked when I suggested you and I hang out. You'd have thought I'd stolen his favorite toy."

Unbelievable. Why had I agreed to this? Oh, right, because I was trying to prove a point to myself and John. Instead, I was only reminded why I had ended things with Jaxon for good in the first place.

"You haven't changed one bit," I said with a soft laugh.

"Never said I did, Sweetheart." Jaxon shrugged and popped a bite of egg into his mouth.

The pet name sounded bitter when he said it and made my skin crawl. It was completely different from the way it rolled silky smooth off John's tongue, gently caressing my skin as it wrapped around me.

With one final roundhouse kick to the heavy bag, I plant both feet on the ground and slump forward against it.

Taking a deep breath, I push away from the bag, ready to start another set of reps, but I'm interrupted by a soft chuckle. "Remind me never to get on your bad side."

My head whips toward the loft door, where the same man who has consumed my thoughts stands with an amused smirk. *You've got to be kidding me.*

"From the beating that thing just took, I'd say your date didn't go well," John says and steps a few feet inside. He folds his arms over his chest, glancing around at the converted gym. It's nothing fancy, just a small part of the hay loft Papá had walled off and added a window air conditioner to give us kids somewhere to weight train or work out when the weather was shit. He even installed a mirror with a ballet bar on one of the walls so I could work on my form for cheerleading and dance.

"It wasn't a date." I take a sip of water and tighten my ponytail before craning my neck side-to-side, earning a crack of relief on both sides.

"No?"

I check the tape on my wrists even though I know it's still in place. "No," I say, planting my feet and raising my hands, geared for another round.

"Wanna talk about it?" His words cement my feet to the ground.

"Do I want to talk about it?" I ask, and find him a few steps closer now. "With you?"

"We're friends, right?" John shrugs. "Friends tell each other about their 'not dates.'" His use of air quotes around the words makes me roll my eyes.

Maybe so, but not us. We're not those friends. Imagine telling him the real reason Jax had invited me to coffee...The thought of having to admit he was right and that it had been a setup is humiliating. Jaxon only invited me to get underneath John's skin, and *that* got under mine.

I swipe my tongue over my teeth and turn back to the bag. "It was just coffee."

"You seem pretty tense for just coffee." He's closer now. I can feel the weight of his presence at my back. The tug of that invisible string begs me to turn around. The same pull I've felt every time I'm around him, the same one I felt that first night at Ash & Thorn, the same one the other night on the porch, the same one I felt last night before he kissed me...But instead of giving in, I let the annoyance win over.

"Why are you here, *Brooks*?"

"I already told you—"

"Bullshit. Why are you here? At my parents' ranch. In this gym. Right *here*." I step toward him, less than a foot apart now. A wave of heat washes over me, but it's not the same one that normally accompanies his presence. "We've barely spoken the last eight months, and now you show up here, on my vacation with my friends, like we're old friends that are just catching up. But we're not, John. So, why are you here?"

John doesn't answer. I don't even think he blinks, just stares at me, gnawing on the corner of his mouth. And without warning, he takes the final step, closing the space between us, and captures my lips. It feels like our first kiss all over again. There is no hesitation, no holding back as he explores my mouth. His tongue caresses mine with the same authority and dominance I remember from our first night together. This is not like the kiss we shared last night; it's not soft or slow. It's hard and passionate, possessive almost, pulling my desire for him to the forefront of my mind. He bends his knees slightly, slides his hands under my ass, and lifts my feet off the ground, wrapping my legs around his waist. My back hits the mirrored wall, and I gasp at the cold glass in contrast to my burning skin.

"Savannah," he breathes out. His forehead falls against mine, and when his eyes open, I get lost in his endless sea. There are so many words behind those eyes, but he settles for: "You have too many clothes on."

"Do something about it, then."

His eyes darken at the challenge, but he doesn't lean in like I expect him to. The muscles of his throat contract, and he searches my face. What he's looking for, I'm not sure, but if it's any signs of uncertainty, he won't find any.

My right hand clenches the fabric of his sweater as my left slides up his chest, gliding around the side of his neck, and I pull his mouth to mine. The soft moan that escapes him sends a shock through my system, straight to my core.

He lifts my shirt over my head before attaching his lips to my shoulder. My head falls back against the glass, and a moan fills the air when he undoes the front clasp of my sports bra. His hand kneads the flesh of my right breast before he bends down to capture my nipple with his mouth. His tongue swirls around the bud, sucking greedily, every so often letting his teeth graze the skin.

John drops my legs, letting my feet fall to the floor, and brings his mouth back to mine for a quick kiss. "Take these off," he demands, fingers toying with the waistband of my sweats. He does the same, reaching behind to pull his sweater off in one motion, and the sound of his belt buckle hitting the floor builds the anticipation inside me further. Without missing a beat, his hands find me again, one dipping between my legs, and his fingers push between my folds. I gasp at the sudden fullness, and he smirks, kissing my chin. His thumb circles my clit once. "That's the face I like to see," he says, and just as fast, he pulls his fingers from me, sticking them in his mouth with a moan of satisfaction. "I've missed the taste of you. And as much as I want you to ride my mouth, that's going to have to wait."

He cradles my face and kisses me, his tongue sweeping over mine in a soft, possessive embrace. A moan rumbles in his chest when I wrap my hand around his cock, stroking the velvety skin. We kiss for what feels like hours, mouths molded together in a mixture of slow, languid strokes, soft nips, and exploration, until he guides me down to the ground.

I brace my palms against his chest when his hands dig into the flesh of my hip, pulling me to straddle him. The head of his cock rubs against me, and the anticipation is fucking brutal. The realization of just how long it's been since I've had this man creeps in with every passing moment. He must be thinking the same thing because he doesn't waste another moment, pushing into me with a shared gasp.

"Fuck," I breathe out, lowering down inch by inch until he's fully seated inside me. His hands caress my sides, reaching down to squeeze my hips, my ass. The movement begs me to move, and I do. I slowly roll my hips against his, and with the first stroke, John's head falls back against the cushioned floor beneath us.

"Just like that, Sav." A soft moan in his exhale. "That's it, baby. Ride me." The words spur me on, making me feel sexy...beautiful...confident. My hand traces up my stomach, cupping my breast as I rise and fall, over and over again. My other hand reaches behind to grasp his thigh, and a small tingle forms along my arm where my ponytail swishes over the skin, the sensation heightened by the euphoric state we're in. I trail my fingers down my stomach until they find the space where our bodies meet, circling my clit. I feel my walls clench his dick. His head lolls, eyes rolling into the back of his head.

After a moment, John winds his arms around my back and sits up. I wrap my arms around his neck when he captures my lips in a bruising kiss. One hand on my lower back, he forces my hips to move in a fluid motion.

Heat fills my cheeks and pools in my core when I look down to see where our bodies connect, watching as his dick moves in and out of me with each roll of my hips. The sheen of sweat makes our bodies slick against each other.

John lifts my chin to meet his gaze, and he smiles before kissing me again. His hands fall back to support our weight as I ride him—a slow, steady pace that fills my veins with adrenaline and ecstasy, bringing me higher with each stroke. My hands explore his arms, his chest, and his neck. Anywhere I can reach.

Without warning, he leans forward again, wrapping his arms around my midsection to pull me flush against his chest. John rocks his hips and mine in tandem. It's sloppy and uncoordinated, without much room to move, but this new position applies delicious pressure against my clit.

"John," I gasp, clutching his shoulders, and my nails dig into the flesh.

"Eyes on me, Savannah." His large hand cradles the side of my face, and when I open my eyes, his eyes stare straight into mine. "You trust me?" John asks, the corner of his lips quirked. "I want you to lean back," he says when I nod. He pulls my mouth back to his for a quick kiss before I do as I'm told, allowing him to guide me exactly where he wants me. This new angle is deeper, opening me further to him, as he lifts his hips, thrusting into me.

"Yes, John. Don't stop," I cry out, and my nails dig into the cushioning under my fingertips. I can feel it, my orgasm reaching its peak, and I reach down to rub at the swollen bud between my legs. His name is a soft whimper on my lips when I feel the wave crest. "I'm close."

"Give it to me, Sweetheart." His hand reaches out, wrapping around my throat, and applies a light pressure on the sides. "I want to feel you come all over my dick."

John's words are the final push over the edge—my back

arches, body convulsing, as I clench around him and ride the waves of my orgasm.

Somewhere in the back of my mind, I swear I hear the creak of the barn door downstairs, but there's no way. Everyone is in bed by now. It's just my imagination—the fear of being caught in such a...compromising position.

"C'mere." His voice is pleading as he pulls me back into his lap, back to the moment. With his hand still on my throat, John brings my mouth to his. My nails rake down his forearms, his shoulders, his back, scraping over the flesh. I grasp for anything I can hold on to as his hands dig into my hips, moving me exactly how he needs to find his own release. His lips find my neck, sucking on the skin before soothing it with his tongue.

"Savannah?" A voice calls out from downstairs. *Motherfucker*. You've got to be kidding me. What the fuck is my brother doing here? "You still up there? It's getting pretty late. Are you—"

"W-what do you want, Crew?"

If he comes up here, I am so fucked.

"I just wanted to check on you because you seemed—"

"Fine!" I slam my hand down on John's shoulder and suppress a moan as he rolls his hips up into mine. "I'm fine. I'll...I'll be inside shortly." John grips my throat and forces my stare to his darkened blue eyes, his other hand forcing my hips to continue moving. "You are not helping," I hiss at him.

"Who said I wanted to help?" He smirks.

There's another creak on the staircase before Crew says, "Are you—"

"Yes!" I glare at John when the word comes out louder than it should, and he pecks my lips. "I'm fine, Crew. Just go. I-I'll be done in a few m-minutes."

"Don't count on it," John whispers in my ear, and it tightens the coil in my abdomen again.

It's quiet for a moment before I finally hear Crew's mumbled rebuttal and the shuffle of his feet at the bottom of the stairs, followed by the squeak of the barn door closing again.

"You fucker." I slap my hand onto John's bare chest, but he catches it with his own, bringing my palm to his lips. The sensation sends tingles down my spine.

"This is everything I need, Savannah," he says, and my heart aches. That's all I want, too, but we can't...I can't. "You are everything I need."

"John," I whisper, pressing my forehead against his as the fire grows between us. He reaches down to apply soft pressure to my clit.

"Fuck." He breathes out, his forehead dropping to my shoulder, and I run my fingers through his short hair. "Sav," John whimpers.

I'm mere seconds from coasting the waves of ecstasy again, but this time I want to do it together.

"Wait for me," I beg.

"No," he says. "No, I want to come inside you, and then I want you to climb up and ride my face."

His words wind the fucking coil even tighter. Is he serious? "John, I haven't even showered."

"I want to taste you." He kisses me and forces his hips up from the mat in a hard thrust that makes my head spin. His hands grip my back. With one final thrust, I can feel the twitch of his dick as he comes, and his moans resonate straight to my core. "Now," he orders and lifts me with ease, leaving me feeling empty, but not for long. As he slides his back to the ground, John pulls me up to his face. "Grip the barre."

I do, and at the same time, he wraps his hands around my thighs and pulls me down to his mouth. "Holy fuck," I cry out, my fingers white against the grain of the wood. I immediately catch sight of my reflection. Normally, it would make me blush and look away, but for some reason, I can't. His tongue moves against me, and slowly, I find my rhythm against him. "John." His name comes out in a whimper, and I swear I feel him smile. "I'm going to come." His only response is a moan, and the vibration sends me over the edge. His hold on my thighs tightens when I try to move away, his mouth continuing its relentless assault until another wave of pleasure rolls through my body.

With hard breaths, I still grip the barre, trying to come down from my high. I didn't think it was possible to feel this spent, but I'd do it all again in a heartbeat. John carefully lifts me from my position and cradles me into his arms, wiping his mouth before he kisses me, and I can taste the mixture of us on his tongue.

"I swear I didn't plan that," he whispers with a soft chuckle, planting a kiss on my forehead.

"I wouldn't have cared if you did," I say with a lazy smile.

As we get dressed, the weight of what we've done hits me, and what bothers me most is the fact that I don't care as much as I should. I should be upset. I should be mad because I have made it clear (to myself and everyone) that I am not dating a wrestler. I promised myself I wouldn't get involved at work...

But when it comes to John, it's so fucking hard to walk away. I've heard time and time again that *it's easier to date someone in the business* and that *someone on the outside can never understand this life*. While all of that might be true, I'm not there to find love...not right now.

When I pull my shirt over my head, I notice him staring.

"You okay?" John asks.

"Fine."

He sighs and crosses the room to me. "Don't do that."

I scoff. "What are you talking about?"

"Don't lock yourself away in your head. Don't shut me out. Talk to me, Sweetheart. What's going on?" John reaches for me, trying to caress my face, but I push him away.

"John, I—I can't—"

"I want this, Savannah." His words stop me. "I want you. I want us." He sighs, skating a hand over his head. "Fuck, I know it doesn't make sense, but you can't deny there is something here...Every time we try to stay away from each other, something pulls us back in. Pulls me back in."

"I don't even know you. Not really. I—"

"Tell me you don't feel something." His burning stare bores into me, and he takes my face in his hands. "Tell me that, and I will walk out that door. We'll never have to discuss it again."

"You know I can't do that." As much as I'd like to deny it, I can't. My shoulders fall, and despite my answer, I take a small step back. "But that doesn't mean anything, John. That doesn't...That doesn't mean we can be together. I can't do this. I made a promise to myself and—"

"Yeah, I've heard about your *rule*."

"If there is one person I would break that rule for...it's you. But I—I can't. I have to make a name for myself in this industry. In EWE. Without you. I have to prove myself, and I don't want it to be because of you. I want to do it on my own. I have to."

"I know." John sighs, scrubbing a hand down his face before he leans in to kiss my forehead. "I know, and when you're ready to break that rule..."

I can only smile at him.

He squeezes my hand before he drops it, turning to leave. Everything in me screams not to let him go, not to let him walk away. I shove the voice aside, putting a wall up between us.

Just before he steps outside, I say, "Don't wait for me, Brooks Taylor."

John looks over his shoulder, and a smile spreads across

his full lips. "Don't tempt me, Skye."

13

SUNDAY, JANUARY 8, 2012
ALEXANDRIA, TX

It's not unusual to hear my name tossed around backstage, but it is when someone calls me by my first name. No one in EWE calls me *John*, except one person, and even though this voice sounds similar to hers, it's not the same. Which means it can only be...

"John!" Laine Williams calls again, and I glance over my shoulder to see the entire Williams family huddled together. All heads turn my way before the twins begin waving wildly. They still look like the high school seniors I met last year, except this time it's a little easier to tell them apart because Blake has longer curls that frame his face. I excuse myself from a conversation with Tim Cass, head of Creative, and greet each member of the family with a handshake, except Laine. She refuses, pulling me in for a hug.

This is the first time I've seen the Williams family since I left their ranch last January. I received an invitation to the New Year's gathering this year from not only Wolf but Brody and Nash, too, but I politely declined. Savannah and I have kept our distance since that night in the barn (a night I've thought

184

about on more than one occasion), and I know myself well enough to know that if I had gone, I wouldn't be able to keep my hands to myself. Crew had eyed me suspiciously when I'd walked into breakfast that next morning, and it was only after I'd seen the dark bruise peeking out from underneath Savannah's sweater's collar, lightly coated with makeup, that I realized he had probably put two and two together. But if he knew (or thought he knew), he never said anything. Not even tonight when I ran into the whole family backstage following Savannah's loss to Raelynn.

Savvy Skye has been the women's champion for the last four months, following her win at Last Stand, the premiere live event in September. Throughout her title run, she has defended her title at least once a week, something I haven't seen a champion do in a long time, maybe ever—and it was something *she* wanted to do. Not a story that Amos or Tim Cass threw together, not one match per month at a premiere event. Every week, she defended her title against one of the other women, including Raelynn's character, *Rae Rose*, who became her biggest opponent. The whole thing was Savannah's idea, from what I heard, and the fans ate it up, firmly cementing her as one of the top women's wrestlers in the company.

The feud between Savvy Skye, "*Queen of the Ring*," and *Rae Rose*, "*Queen of Roses*," began two months ago and is my favorite of her title reign. There is something special about working with your best friend in the ring that allows you to put on some of your best matches. And tonight, the outcome had been kept secret. I'm not sure if the girls even knew who was going to walk out as champion because the winner slot had been left blank on the call sheet, but in the end, *Rae* successfully pinned *Savvy*, earning *Rae* her second women's title.

"Some match you had out there," Savannah's father, Wes,

says.

That's one way to put it. I'm not particularly happy with the storyline I've been involved in the last two months, but I remind myself that sometimes we all get handed the short end of the stick, even me. I was thrown in the middle of a storyline between Chelsea and Theo Rafferty. Chelsea recruited me to be her lackey, for lack of a better term, when she "realized" her brother was planning to "undermine her" and "take over" her position in the company, just below their father. It was a classic case of sibling rivalry gone too far, and tonight I was pitted against "*The Lunatic*" *Grady Chandler*, the wrestler Theo had chosen to stand in for him. The timing of tonight's match seemed rather fitting, considering tonight is Battle of Champions, the first of two premiere events this month.

Whichever wrestler won allowed their sponsoring Rafferty to keep their position, and the loser was banned from the company. It was stupid, but the crowd had been eating it up for weeks. And tonight, it all came to a head when I made *Grady* tap out. Both Rafferty children were ringside for the match, and upon my win, Chelsea jumped into the ring to raise my hand and kiss my cheek, leaving a large red imprint of her lips on my skin. Walking backstage, I could already see the wheels turning behind Amos's eyes, and I knew I wasn't going to like where this was headed...

"You and Chelsea close, or is all that for show?" Wes asks. I notice the way Crew's stare narrows slightly at the mention of her name.

"No, sir," I say, glancing briefly at the oldest Williams sibling. "Just part of the story." Crew bites down on the corner of his lip and shakes his head, looking down the hallway. "Y'all waiting on Savannah?"

"Yes, she had to go to the trainer," Laine says. "Her shoulder was bothering her."

"I was wondering about that."

Savannah took a hard hit during her match, going headfirst into the ring post, and the landing didn't look right. She came out of the corner, favoring her shoulder, but let Raelynn continue to work it anyway and finished the match. Pain etched her features as soon as the bell rang, and she clutched her arm as she rolled out of the ring. I watched on the monitor as she pushed medical staff away, but it was written across her face—something wasn't right.

"You saw the match?"

Before I can answer, Savannah's voice echoes from down the hallway. "Mamá, what are you guys doing? I told you to— Oh." She stops mid-step, meeting my stare. "Brooks, hi."

I sigh at the name choice.

"We were just catching up since you didn't invite him back to the ranch this year," Laine says.

Savannah rolls her eyes and offers me a brief, sympathetic look. "I'm sorry if they've been bothering you. I told them to stay out of the way, but—"

"They're fine," I say. "It's good to see everyone."

"Yes, it was good to see you since you couldn't join us for the holiday this year." Laine turns her stare from me to her daughter, but she ignores her mother.

"I'm sorry I couldn't make it. I was spending it with my sister and her boyfriend."

When Ari heard I didn't have plans to ring in the new year, she insisted I join her and Samuel in our hometown of Ravenswood, Indiana. We compromised—they'd come down to my house in Florida, and could invite some friends to tag along. Their guests included Samuel's sister and brother-in-law, and one of his sister's girl friends, and let's say the third wheels did not hit it off the way the other two couples had hoped.

"Well, I expect to see you there next year. Bring your sister along, we have plenty of room," Laine says.

"Mamá, you can't just order him to show up," Savannah says, looking between us in disbelief. "What if he—"

"I'd love to," I interrupt. Her brown eyes meet mine for the first time all night, and I smile. "If that's okay with you, Sav."

After a moment, Savannah nods.

"How's that shoulder, SJ?" Wes asks.

"Doc wants me to get evaluated further. He thinks I might have dislocated it," she says.

"I wouldn't be surprised," I say. "Looked like it hurt."

Her gaze returns to me with a look of surprise. "You saw?"

"Wouldn't miss it." That makes her smile, and I do the same in return. "Well, I'm sorry to cut this short, but I have to get going. I want to get to Houston before it gets too late."

"You stay in touch, you hear?" Laine pulls me into a tight hug before Wes extends his hand. Each of the siblings pulls me into a quick embrace, too, except Crew, who only offers a nod.

"I'll see you around," I whisper to Savannah, doing my best to ignore that familiar pull between us, and I have a feeling she's doing the same by the way her arms cross over her chest. A twinge of pain crosses her face before she catches herself and offers a tight smile. "Please get that looked at."

Savannah rolls her eyes. "I'll live."

"Sweetheart, please. The sooner you do, the sooner you come back." The nickname rolls off my tongue with such ease, and it catches more than her attention. I notice the look shared between her parents and excuse myself before I can say something else I shouldn't.

Halfway down the hall, I can hear her mother say something in Spanish that I can't understand, but Savannah's response tells me everything I needed to know.

"*Ay*, Mamá." She sighs. "Would you just drop it already?"

Brody and I finally arrived at our hotel in Houston twenty minutes ago and agreed to one drink before we go to bed. We don't typically indulge the night before a show anymore, but my best friend was feeling spontaneous tonight, and I decided to go along for the ride.

The moment we walk into the bar, I immediately regret that decision.

We're beckoned to the table in the corner where Miles Drake, better known as *Damian "The Anarchist" Drake*, Grady, Spencer, and one of the show's announcers, Scott Harrington, sit. And from the looks of it, they're in the middle of welcoming the new kid, Colin Montgomery, or *Colin Ryker*, by making him pay for whatever tab they've racked up. Stupid hazing ritual. I thought we left that shit in 2010.

"Well, well, well," Drake says when we reach the table. "Look who finally decided to be one of the guys for a change." Miles Drake is known for being the backstage asshole, always inserting his two cents where it doesn't belong. Most of the time, he takes the title of "Anarchist" a little too literally, blurring the lines of reality and fiction. He and I have never gotten along; I can't remember a single time we have. Keeping our distance backstage is our version of being civil.

I roll my eyes. I stopped going out with the guys after shows when it became boring; I was tired of the same old thing. Not to mention getting drunk the night before a match wasn't very conducive to getting up at five in the morning and going to the gym before having to get in the ring in front of thousands of people.

"To what do we owe the pleasure?" Drake asks.

"We felt like having a drink," Brody answers. "Figured we'd join you boys since you're here." And because if we ignored them, it would have caused an even bigger scene than the one they've probably already caused.

"Pull up a chair, boys!" Grady yells, half drunk, moving

his chair over to make room between him and Austin. Brody pulls two chairs from a nearby table and ignores my glare.

"Alright," Drake says once everyone is finally settled. "We have something else we need to discuss." He pauses when the waitress appears with a fresh round of drinks and two beers for me and Brody, smacking her on the ass when she walks by him. She winks at him, and the whole display makes me roll my eyes. Something tells me that if he were some normal guy, she'd have him thrown out for the action, but because he's a "celebrity," she feeds into it. Once she's gone, Drake turns back to the table with a serious expression. "*Savvy Skye.*"

My stomach drops. What the fuck is he talking about? When I meet his stare, a devilish grin spreads across his face.

"Our dear *Savvy Skye* has just suffered her first big title loss."

Grady pouts. "Poor thing."

Oh, you've got to be fucking kidding me.

Drake continues, "Which means she's going to be sad and looking for a shoulder to cry on."

He cannot be serious.

"Get to the point, Drake," Austin says, rolling his eyes.

"Isn't it obvious? One of *us* can be that shoulder."

I scoff. As if Savannah would go for any of them.

"Something you want to say, Brooks?" Drake raises a brow in my direction.

Brody does the same from behind his beer and waits to see how I'm going to get myself out of the hole I've just dug. I shake my head, looking away from them. I should keep my mouth shut.

"Didn't think so." Drake chuckles. "Now, as I was saying—"

"I can't do this," I say, and that Cheshire grin returns. "You cannot be fucking serious, Drake? As if Savannah would let any one of you within five feet of her. She has made it abundantly clear that she has no intention of dating anyone on the roster or within this company. And—"

"Who said anything about dating?" Scott asks, his tongue poking out to wet his lips, and that earns a high five from Miles.

I roll my eyes, and glancing over, I notice the waitress hand Colin the checkbook. I snatch it from his hands. "I cannot believe you guys are still doing this bullshit. This kid is barely making enough to pay the bills, and you want him to pick up your tab?"

"We all did it!" Grady argues.

"And?" Just because it's been something we used to do doesn't mean we need to continue the tradition. Some things are better left in the past...

Stuffing my card into the checkbook, I hand it back to the waitress without looking at the total because that would only piss me off further. I don't care what it costs; the relieved look on Colin's face tells me all I need to know.

"Why are you here?" Drake hisses after a minute. "You come in here, acting all high and mighty, like you're better than us...Why even show up?"

"You're the one proponing high school bullshit, Drake. Grow up," I say, signing the returned bill.

"So, you wouldn't take the chance to bend Savannah over the side of the ring and have your way with her if she'd let you?"

"That is enough." I slam the pen down on the table.

Drake laughs, seemingly unfazed. "That's what I thought."

"Brooks, don't," Brody warns under his breath. "Don't feed into it."

My fingers scratch at my denim-clad thighs, picking at the fabric as I do my best to ignore the anger building in my chest.

"You know something, Brooks? You've always been Mr. Get-the-Girl. Why don't *you* take a stab at it? Surely, you of all people can persuade her to change her mind."

"Because I'm not doing something I know she doesn't want."

"She doesn't *know* what she wants," Drake says. "I mean, how could she? She's never given it a shot. Someone just needs to show her what she's missing. You're friendly enough with her, so why not you?"

"Because I'm—"

"Scared she'll say no?" Scott asks, and I glare at him.

"Oh, come on, Brooks. Give it a go," Drake says. My glare returns to him. "How about this...you do the horizontal tango with Ms. Skye by the night of Wrestlefest and you'll earn yourself six hundred apiece."

Oh, you've got to be kidding...Is he making this a fucking wager?

"Take me out of this," Brody says, leaning back in his chair.

"You don't even have to date her, just show the girl a good time. Warm her up for the rest of us," Drake continues.

My fists tighten, nails digging into the meat of my palms, but before I can tell Miles he can take his stupid bet and shove it up his ass, Grady says, "Unless you'd rather it be one of us, of course."

Brody sighs beside me, already knowing what I'm about to do, and it only makes the pit in my stomach deepen. Makes the nausea push further up my throat, and I swallow hard to keep it contained.

"What do you say?" Drake pushes.

"She isn't some trophy, Drake," I say between clenched teeth. "She isn't—"

"It's you or me, Brooks. I'm being nice and letting you decide, but you better pick quick, or it's gonna be me."

I glance at Brody one more time, and he shakes his head. This is a bad idea. I know it, he knows it...but I cannot let one of these fuckers go after Savannah.

"Fine." I sigh, scrubbing a hand down my face. "Deal."

"Fuck." My best friend pinches the bridge of his nose.

An even wider grin splits apart Drake's face, and it makes my skin crawl. I feel like I just made a deal with the devil. "Well, boys, looks like Brooksy here is just like the rest of us, after all. He just needed a little reminder."

Without another word, I push away from the table, and I hear Brody say something to the others before he follows. We walk through the lobby in silence, and it's not until we get into the elevator that he finally says, "This is a bad idea, Brooks." I don't reply. "If Savannah finds out—"

"She won't," I snap, glaring at him, but I can only hold on to that anger for a second. I sigh. "She doesn't need to know because nothing is going to happen."

"What are you talking about? You just—"

"I'm not letting any of those fuckers near her, Brody. I will tell them nothing happened. I can't...I couldn't sit there and let them talk about her like that."

"So you jumped in? Decided to throw your name in the ring? You didn't have to do this, Brooks. You could've kept your mouth shut and just told her."

"It wouldn't have stopped them from messing with her," I say, and my best friend sighs. He stares at me from across the elevator, eyes narrowed into thin slits. He folds his arms over his chest, and the black ink runs together. "The only way to protect her was to insert myself in their path."

Brody scoffs, shaking his head. "I don't like this, man."

"Neither do I."

14

SUNDAY, JANUARY 29, 2012

CHICAGO, IL

My stomach has been in knots since I got the text from Xander Collins, the Head of Talent Relations, earlier. He requested that I meet him and Tim Cass, the head writer for all EWE content, when I arrived at the arena. Today is my first day back after being cleared to return to action since injuring my shoulder at Battle of Champions. I didn't even know it was possible to sprain your shoulder, but it happens more often than you'd think. Aiming for a spear to her midsection, I slid through the middle and top ropes when Rae stepped out of the way. My shoulder slammed into the thick metal ring post, and from the moment of impact, I knew something was wrong. I continued to let Rae work the same shoulder, which only made things worse. By the end of the match, I knew I was in trouble, but I hoped it wasn't as bad as it felt. The doctors told me I was lucky it had only been a small sprain, but it was a sprain nonetheless and would take me off TV for at least three weeks.

And in this business, that can be a death sentence.

So, I can guess what the suits want to talk about—a new

storyline. Or maybe they want to continue the feud between me and Rae (far less likely). Or maybe they're going to keep me off TV for a while (less likely, but still possible). I've been in the title picture since last September after I unseated *Harper Valentine* as the most boring champion we'd seen in a while—don't let Bennett hear me say that, or he'll have my head. He and Harper have been going steady since he invited her to the ranch last New Year's, and God forbid anyone have any criticism about her (constructive or otherwise).

I can't wait for the day their relationship ends.

Before I can knock on the door to the makeshift "corporate" office, it swings open to reveal Xander Collins dressed in his maroon colored suit, per usual. How many of those does he have?

Similar to the first time I saw him at auditions, Xander reminds me a lot of my mother's father, with dark, curly hair and a mustache to match. Bushy eyebrows over warm, brown eyes with small crinkles in the corners when he smiles, just like Abuelo. And I always notice the small quirk of his mouth whenever he catches me speaking Spanish. Even though I know he understands me, he always replies in English. One day I'll get him to respond in Spanish, though.

"Oh, good!" Xander smiles and ushers me inside. "You're both here, we can get started."

Did he say *both*? Who else is here? He must mean Raelynn, which means they are keeping... *What the hell*?

"Savannah!" Amos shouts my name from behind the desk.

Amos Rafferty is the man behind the Elite Wrestling Entertainment empire. He started the company in 1981, taking over a failing wrestling promotion based in Houston, Texas, at the ripe age of twenty-seven. With a lot of hard work (and some occasional backstabbing with a smidge of less-than-ethical practices, but hey, that's business), he turned it into the company we all know and love today. Everything about Amos is loud, from his voice to his mannerisms to his strut; his presence is one you cannot miss when he walks into a room. He's ruggedly handsome with hazel-green eyes that pierce straight through the lenses of his black-rimmed glasses and into your soul. Despite his rough exterior, Amos is one of my favorite people in the whole company.

Xander gives me a gentle push forward when he walks behind me to join Tim in the chairs on the side of the room.

"Glad you could make it." Amos stands and outstretches his hand. As if I had a choice, but his excitement when he sees me never fails to fill me with a small amount of pride. "Sit, we have a proposition for you," he says, motioning to the chair next to none other than *Brooks Taylor*. Amos adjusts his black suit jacket before he sits down and folds his hands neatly on the desk. His use of the word *proposition* is just a nice way of saying they have a new script to follow. But it's the presence of the man next to me that confuses me. Are they putting us in a story together?

"You know about this?" I whisper to John when Amos briefly turns to Xander and Tim. He shakes his head, finally peeling his eyes from his lap. A soft smile melts some of my nerves, and I return the gesture.

"Okay, guys," Tim says. "Let's get down to business. We want to put you in a story together. Savannah will return tonight to reignite and finish the feud with *Rae Rose*. You'll have your rematch at Capitol Punishment next month, but you'll also start joining Brooks out at ringside and—"

"So, I lose my title and I turn into a valet?" I scoff, and a slight knock against the side of my foot tells me to knock it off, but I choose to ignore his warning.

"You're not a valet, Sav," Xander argues. "We want to keep you on television, keep you in the eye of the audience. You're going to help feed into an upcoming feud between *Brooks* and *Ryker*."

"So, a love triangle?" John asks.

"Essentially," Tim says.

You've got to be kidding me. I went from the top woman in the whole division to a fucking valet overnight. *How typical.* The worst part is, as much as I want to fight, to push back...I know that I can't. That's not how this works. There are too many risks involved in that. If I say no, they could just as easily take me off television and put me on the bench until they deem me ready to return. I've seen it happen too many times over the last few years.

However, even though I can't fight back...John can.

"Don't you think that's a little overplayed?" He asks, and his eyes flicker my way. I offer him a soft smile before he returns to the men in charge of our fate.

"You have something else in mind?" Tim asks.

Yes, literally anything else.

I watch John's mouth open and close three times, grasping at straws, before he resigns with a heavy sigh. He glances at me with a sorrowful smile, shaking his head. John knows suggesting anything else could potentially mean pulling me from TV, and he doesn't want to risk it.

"Great!" The writer claps his hands together and looks at me. "Then starting today, you'll be spending a lot of time together."

John stares at each of them for the appropriate amount of time, giving each man his attention, and listens as Tim goes over in more detail how things will play out. I haven't heard a damn word he's said, focused on my nails, and I wish I had gone with a darker color than maroon. When John stands from his seat, I scramble to do the same.

"You put them up to this, didn't you?" I ask once they've dismissed us and the door closes on our backs. I know how dumb it sounds, but part of me believes it might be true. We haven't spoken much in the last year. He kept his word, keeping his distance while I did the same and continued to work my ass off and prove myself in this company. It hasn't been easy, and there has been a lot of pushback, but the moment Amos and Chelsea told me they wanted to give me a title run made it all worth it.

I can't deny that I've craved more than a smile in the hallway or a quick conversation in passing, but I suppose I haven't welcomed more either. Every time we've seen each other, I've kept the interaction brief and moved on. If you ask Rae, *everyone* can see there is something there, but she and Bennett are the only people who have said so. Maybe it's because she's always thought so from the first time she saw me and John together back at NextGen (she's never let that go), or maybe it has to do with the countless times she's caught me watching his matches and promos.

"You caught me, Skye." John laughs, and it melts away a large chunk of the annoyance that's been running through my veins.

"I told you not to wait for me, Brooks Taylor." The words bring a toothy grin to his face.

"How's your shoulder?" His eyes drop from my face to my left shoulder.

"It's okay." I shrug my shoulders a few times without any pain and laugh when his brow raises. "I'm fine, John. They wouldn't let me back if I wasn't clear." We might wrestle while hurt sometimes, but the EWE trainers and doctors won't let us if they *know*.

His steps pause when we reach the end of the hallway, and I can hear the buzz of backstage on the other side of the wall. John turns to face me, and he starts to say something, but stops. Two more times he does that, and I know that I should leave to find Raelynn—we need to put together a plan for tonight—but I'm too curious what's got him so tongue-tied. He takes a deep breath and finally says, "Let's go to lunch."

Well, I wasn't expecting that.

"Are you asking me on a date?"

"You don't date wrestlers, remember?" A smirk. "Not a date, just business. We can talk more about this." He motions between the two of us, and my brow quirks. "Not *this* this. This, as in you and me, our characters...You know what I mean."

I do, but seeing him so flustered is too funny to interrupt.

"Fine." I point my finger at him and say, "But it's not a date."

"It's not a date."

MONDAY NIGHT RAGE

Live Broadcast

JANUARY 30, 2012

LOUISVILLE, KY

"Good evening, everyone, and welcome back to Monday Night Rage! I'm Jude Paul, joined here by my commentator partner, Scott Harrington, and by none other than the former women's champion, Savvy Skye," veteran announcer Jude Paul says, adjusting his headpiece. "You know, I haven't had a chance to ask yet, Savvy. How is your shoulder?"

"Well, if last night is any indication, I think it's doing just fine," Scott says with a hearty laugh.

Last night was the Chi-Town Clash, a special premiere event in Chicago, Illinois. During the women's tag-team match featuring the new EWE Women's Champion Rae Rose and Ivy Jade versus Harper Valentine and Viviana Ridley, Savvy Skye made her return to action. She jumped the barricade and pulled Rae Rose out of the ring before the champ could pin Valentine. Rose landed face-first on the ground before Skye threw her into the barricade. Once the champ managed to pull herself to her feet, Skye hit her with a hard clothesline, sending her over the barricade onto the cement floor. Plucking the title from the production aide's hands, Savvy climbed to stand on top of the same barricade, holding the title high above her head, and the whole time, the crowd cheered.

"I was just reminding Rae who the real queen is," Savvy says, offering her counterparts a sweet smirk. "She might be the Queen of Roses, Jude, but I'm the Queen of the Ring."

A rock ballad sounds through the arena, sending fans to their feet, as Spencer Austin steps out. Harper Valentine clings to his side as they walk down the ramp with wide grins, feeding into the chorus of boos that follow their path.

"Here comes Spencer Austin, still riding the high from his win over 'The Gladiator' Wolf Bennett in their street fight last night at Chi-Town Clash," Jude says.

Savvy rolls her eyes, sitting back in her chair. "Oh, goody. We're blessed with the presence of Spencer Austin. Alert the press."

"Someone's not impressed."

"What is there to be impressed with? When Spencer does something besides the two moves he does every damn night, maybe then I'll have something to be impressed with."

Scott's laugh is drowned out by the guitar riffs of Brooks Taylor's entrance music. Brooks steps out onto the stage, receiving a mixed reaction from the crowd, but the cheers slowly begin to overpower the boos.

"Speaking of impressive," Jude says. "Here comes Brooks Taylor. He and Spencer battle tonight to see who will face current EWE Champion, "The Lunatic" Grady Chandler, at Capitol Punishment at the end of next month."

Brooks steps inside the ring, runs the ropes, and rips his shirt over his head, tossing it haphazardly into the crowd. He glances over his shoulder at Spencer, who has propped himself up on the top rope in one of the corners, arms resting on the tops of his thighs, looking unamused by the display from his opponent. Brooks looks around his opponent to the announcer's table, straight at Savvy Skye. Just for a moment, *but long enough to make it feel intentional.*

Her brow arches, and she smirks before their eye contact is broken when Harper reaches over the table to mess with Savvy's headset.

"Aw, poor wittle Savvy Skye. They finally realized you can't wrestle, so they moved you to commentary. Funny how that works. You started on the sidelines and tried to hang with the big girls, but now you're back where you belong."

"Are you really criticizing me when you're a glorified escort?"

Harper's mouth drops and reaches across the table, but Jude interferes, casting his arm between the two women. "You're a bitch!"

"I'm sensing some animosity," Scott says.

Savvy blows a kiss as Harper stalks away. "Oh no, we're best friends, couldn't you tell?"

"And here we go!" Jude says. The bell rings to signal the start of the match. "Brooks Taylor looks absolutely locked in tonight."

"You know who you're talking about, right?" Savvy raises a brow at Jude. "I think people underestimate the time Brooks Taylor puts into dissecting every opponent he faces. He knows every move they're going to make before they make it."

"This is my time, Brooks!" Spencer yells inside the ring as the men circle each other, sizing each other up. "Mine!"

Brooks only chuckles before they lunge forward, locking up—one palm on the back of each opponent's neck, the other cradling their elbow. Pivoting his hips, Brooks breaks the hold and slides his arm around Spencer's neck, forcing him into a headlock. Brooks tightens the grip on his wrist, reinforcing the hold when Spencer tries to break free.

Spencer struggles against Taylor's side. He slowly frees himself and shoves his opponent forward into the ropes. His back hits the mat when Brooks rebounds with a shoulder tackle.

"Brooks Taylor is setting the pace for this match early. Keeping Spencer right where he wants him," Jude says.

There's a wild look in Spencer's eyes when he jumps to his feet. He launches himself, swinging a clothesline, but Brooks Taylor ducks, stepping behind and wrapping his arm back around Spencer's neck, putting him into a front facelock. Brooks rolls through, dragging Spencer onto his back. He goes for the pin, but Spencer kicks out at the one count.

"There's that technical side of Brooks Taylor that I love to see."

"For all the grief he gets, Brooks Taylor has become one of the better wrestlers over the years," Savvy Skye adds. "He just likes to put on a show most of the time. Entertain the crowd. Give him the opportunity, and he'll get down and dirty. There's a reason he's earned his place at the top of this company. Look, here's the thing about Brooks...He doesn't want to just win—he wants you to know that he knows how to beat you."

"Sounds like you're a fan," Scott says, looking her way.

She shrugs. "He's efficient. Focused. Doesn't flinch under pressure. I like that."

"Spencer is going to break the hold, and he goes for the running knee!" Jude says as the wrestler lifts his knee and makes contact with Taylor's chin. The force sends Brooks back into the corner.

"Looks like the tables are turning in Spencer's favor now," Scott adds, but he retracts the statement when Brooks sidesteps a spear, sending Spencer shoulder-first into the post.

"That shoulder's gonna be a problem now," Savvy says. "I'd know."

Brooks drags his opponent out of the corner by his left arm, the same one that just collided with the metal pole. He glances over at Savvy, a smirk tugging on his lips, before he stomps down on the joint.

"Don't look now, but I think you have an admirer," Scott chuckles.

"Shut up, Scott."

Brooks continues to work the shoulder joint of his opponent. He drops to the mat, wrapping his legs around Spencer's arm, bridging upwards and over-extending the arm in a cross armbreaker. Spencer yells out in pain but refuses to tap.

"Brooks continues to isolate the shoulder with a cross armbreaker, here," Jude comments. *"Spencer is trying to reach the ropes and break the hold, but he's barely out of reach."*

"If he finally breaks the hold, it might give him the break he needs to gain some momentum in this match," Scott says. *"Brooks Taylor has been dominating the entire thing."*

From the side of the ring, Harper yells at Spencer, pleading with him to reach the ropes. When the referee turns his back, she pushes the bottom rope inward, giving Spencer the opportunity he needs.

"Harper Valentine helping Spencer here, but the ref didn't see it," Jude explains.

"Stay out of it, Harper!" Savvy yells, earning a glare from the other woman.

"Break the hold, Taylor!" the referee yells, but Brooks maintains the hold for two more seconds, just before it becomes illegal.

Once free, Spencer rolls under the ropes and out of the ring, where Harper checks on him.

"Get back in the ring, Austin," the referee scolds as Brooks stares down at him. *"Let's go!"*

Tired of waiting, Brooks uses the ropes to propel himself and dive outside the ring.

"Taylor just went headfirst into the barricade! He went for the suicide dive, but he didn't anticipate Spencer moving out of the way," Jude yells as Savvy stands from her chair. *"Spencer not wasting time, throwing Brooks into the steel steps. He's*

trying to wear down his opponent, but he needs to get him back in the ring before the ten count."

"I don't think he cares, Jude," Scott says.

Spencer forces the other man up to his feet and forces him into a standing headlock. He glances over at the woman sitting behind the announcer's desk before he falls backward, driving Brooks face-first into the floor.

"You're just going to stand there?" Savvy yells at the referee, who watches idly from the ropes. "Do your job, ref!"

Spencer chuckles from his seated position, glancing over his shoulder at the lifeless body of Brooks Taylor. Using the barricade, he pushes up from the floor and rolls beneath the bottom rope back into the ring.

"Spencer Austin has certainly turned this match around," Scott says. "There for a minute, I thought this was going to be a shutout, but he has reminded everyone that he's not to be counted out early."

"Get up, Brooks," Savvy whispers.

"You want to say that a little louder for the people in the back?" Scott teases her.

"If the ref would do his job, we wouldn't be in this situation."

"And Brooks Taylor is back on his feet as the referee gets to the eight count. He needs to get back in the ring before ten," Jude says. "And he makes it just in time!"

Brooks rolls under the bottom rope and barely makes it to his feet before Spencer launches from the top rope. He narrowly misses the missile dropkick, moving out of the way just in time, and it gives him the advantage he needs. Grabbing Spencer by the wrist, yanking him to his feet, Brooks whips him into the ropes. On the rebound, Brooks performs a spinebuster, lifting the other man off his feet and slamming his back onto the mat in a hard impact that shakes the ring.

Brooks turns to the crowd, soaking in their reaction, before he glances at Savvy one more time and winks. From the sidelines, Harper slams her hand down on the apron, trying to help Spencer garner any energy he has left to finish the match.

"Spencer still looks a little lost," Scott says when the wrestler begins to stir, crawling on all fours toward the ropes. "I think that last spinebuster is going to give Brooks the opening he needs to finish this match."

Brooks reaches down to force his opponent to his feet, but Spencer counters, sweeping his feet out from under him. Harper throws her hands up in victory and claps as Spencer uses the ropes to stand. He watches Brooks do the same, but on the outside of the ropes, where he now stands on the apron.

"That's not good," Savvy says, already seeing what Spencer is planning.

Spencer drop-kicks Brooks in the back, sending him flying from the edge of the ring onto the ground. He takes a lap, soaking in the mixed reactions from the crowd before the referee berates him, telling Spencer to keep it in the ring.

"Brooks Taylor is still out cold on the floor, and it looks like Harper is looking to give her boyfriend some more advantage," Jude says, watching her creep around the corner of the ring.

"Savvy, where are you going?" Scott calls out when Savvy rips the headset off her ears.

"Wait a second! Our guest commentator, Savvy Skye, is getting involved now," Jude yells. His excitement matches that of the crowd as the former champion rushes to intercept Harper. She stands at the other end of the ring, begging Harper to take another step towards the man who has finally begun to stir.

"I don't think Harper anticipated this," Scott adds. "Jude, I think we might be witnessing the beginnings of a new rivalry."

Spencer slides under the bottom rope, ready to force Brooks back into the ring and finish the match. Savvy stands nearby but doesn't interfere when he grabs his opponent by the back of the neck. Brooks digs in his heels, resisting, and throws a sharp elbow into Spencer's ribs. In a quick flash, Brooks takes hold of Spencer's jaw and drops to the floor in a seated position, forcing his shoulder into his opponent's jaw.

Scott cringes. "That's gonna hurt!"

"Jawbreaker on the floor. That's unforgiving," Jude adds.

"There's no give whatsoever on that concrete."

Brooks shoves Spencer back under the ropes as the referee gets to seven, climbing in behind him. He waits patiently for his opponent to stand on his feet, and the moment Spencer is up, he kicks him in the gut. Hooking Spencer's bad arm, Brooks lifts him onto his shoulders and drives him shoulder-first into the mat.

"Brooks goes for the cover!" Jude yells as the wrestler drops back to the mat, hooks a leg, and pins his opponent. The crowd counts along with each slap of the referee's hand on the mat: One. Two. Three!

"And that's it! Impressive win for Brooks Taylor tonight on Monday Night Rage," Jude says.

The smirk in Scott's voice is evident when he adds, "Very impressive, but I think there's something else on his mind besides that win, Jude."

Savvy Skye steps through the ropes, glancing over at Harper, who coaxes Spencer out of the ring, before she meets the victor's gaze..Brooks stands tall, chest rising and falling with steady breaths, and watches her slowly walk toward him. All eyes on them, waiting to see what happens next. Never breaking eye contact, she slowly slips her hand in his, threading their fingers together before she lifts their joint hands high in the air.

MONDAY NIGHT RAGE

Live Broadcast

FEBRUARY 13, 2012

TAMPA, FL

Spencer Austin shoots Brooks Taylor into the corner of the ring, not only knocking the referee out, but also sending him straight into Savvy Skye, who stands on the apron. Brooks calls out for Skye as she crumples helplessly, both she and the referee knocked out, before he narrowly avoids Spencer's running boot.

"What the hell is she doing?" Jude Paul asks as Harper Valentine lifts the curtain and begins to dig around underneath the ring. Finally, she pulls out a steel chair.

"Well, Jude, that would be a chair," Scott Harrington says.

"The official is still knocked out! He has no idea what's going on. This could be bad news for Taylor."

Harper sets the chair on the apron and steps away, peeking around the corner to ensure the referee didn't see anything. She runs to the other side of the ring and climbs up the apron, right where Brooks Taylor pulls himself up in the corner. Her face is mere inches from his when he looks up, and before he knows it, Harper reaches over the ropes and pulls his face to hers. The crowd gasps, but Brooks shoves her away. Too preoccupied with feigning hurt from his rejection, Harper doesn't notice the movement beneath her.

Savvy Skye swipes her feet out from under her, sending Harper face-first into the apron and then the floor.

"Oh, that's gotta hurt," Scott says.

"Chair!" Savvy yells up at Brooks.

Brooks steps out of the way, missing a strike to the head. He turns on his heel and kicks Spencer in the jaw.

Satisfied, Savvy turns back to Harper, who pulls herself up with aid from the barricade, earning a few taunts from fans sitting ringside. Not waiting, Savvy digs her fingers into the dirty blonde strands of Harper's hair and throws her straight into the side of the announcer's table.

"Savvy, what are you doing?" Jude yells, but she ignores him.

She kicks Harper once, knocking her back down, then again just for good measure. She pulls a chair of her own from under the ring.

"You want to play with chairs?" Skye slams the weapon into Harper's back, sending her crashing back to the floor. She does it three more times before tossing it aside and running to aid the official. Skye pushes him into the ring just in time for the three-count.

"Brooks Taylor picks up the win!" Scott shouts as the referee motions to ring the bell.

"This win re-cements his number one contender spot for the EWE World Championship," Jude explains. "Spencer challenged this after losing to Brooks two weeks ago, and our interim General Manager, Chelsea Rafferty, had no choice but to give him a rematch."

"He wouldn't let her alone," Scott says, with a soft chuckle. "She had no choice."

Savvy climbs into the ring and jumps into Brooks's waiting arms. His hands plant firmly on her hips, and her fingers tangle into his short hair, tugging gently at his nape before she leans in close. She can practically taste the icy mint on his breath, but before their lips touch, a siren blares through the arena. They both share one final glance before she sighs, and her legs slowly untangle from his waist to slink down until her feet are planted firmly on the mat.

"The Lunatic" Grady Chandler stands at the top of the ramp with the EWE Championship belt hanging loosely around his waist. The logo is surrounded by gemstones and gold, making it glitter and shine beneath the bright lights. "Oh, don't stop on my account. I, like everyone else here, want to know where this is going..."

Brooks narrows his eyes and takes a small step in front of Skye, placing a protective arm in front to usher her further behind him.

Grady chuckles, rubbing at the scruff on his chin. "I'm sorry to ruin your moment, but I just wanted to come out and say thank you. You both saved me from having to deal with a real wrestler on Sunday. You've just made my job a whole lot easier."

Savvy scoffs, stepping out from behind Brooks. "Why don't you come down here and say that inside this ring?"

"Oh!" Grady's face lights up in surprise. "You let her speak for you now, Brooks?"

Brooks rolls his eyes, taking the microphone from the ring announcer.

"A man worthy of carrying this title would never let his side piece have a say in his business affairs." Grady scoffs. "How pathetic."

"Keep running your mouth, Grady, but at the end of the day, I'm not the one you should be worried about." Brooks smirks and casually leans over the top of the rope. He glances briefly over his shoulder at Savvy Skye, who glares up the ramp at her partner's future opponent. "When I win at Capitol Punishment next Sunday, when I'm holding that belt high over *my head...you're going to see what a real champion looks like. I'll have the title and the girl, and you...you'll just be a footnote in our story."*

15

Savannah

TUESDAY, FEBRUARY 14, 2012
TAMPA, FL

I've never been one to break the rules, but I guess after tonight, I can no longer say that. I spent most of the day trying to talk myself out of this, while pretending like nothing was wrong every time my best friend asked. Raelynn and I were together for the better part of the morning—first for breakfast, then getting our nails done, before rounding it off with a run down the canal and lunch at my condo—and the last thing I needed was the added pressure from her to make tonight go well. I lied when she asked what I was doing tonight, because if she knew the truth, she would have lost her mind and never would've left my place until she was satisfied with my appearance. I'd already felt a weight on my shoulders since I'd agreed to it, and I didn't need her (or anyone) making it worse. I knew better than to say yes to him, but I couldn't stop it. Like the filter between my brain and my mouth was missing.

Valentine's Day was meant for staying home, ordering pizza, and spending it with two men named Ben and Jerry. But this year I'll be spending it with one man named John Brooks.

Last night, John stopped me after his match, pulling me between some of the larger black production boxes to shield us from any lurking eyes backstage. "Do you want to grab dinner tomorrow?"

"You do know what tomorrow is, don't you?" I asked, but he didn't answer. Whether that was from a lack of knowing or just not wanting to admit it, I couldn't be sure. "Valentine's Day, John. Tomorrow is Valentine's Day."

"Okay." The answer was so simple, so matter-of-fact, I wasn't sure how to feel. Did he forget that we weren't actually dating? It was only a storyline, and you don't go out to dinner with people you aren't *dating* on Valentine's Day. Everyone knows that.

"And you want to go to dinner?"

"Yes."

"Is this you asking me on a real date?"

His tongue poked out to wet his lips before he rolled them between his teeth. "What if it is?"

"John—"

"It doesn't have to be, Sav," he says, shrugging. "It can just be dinner between friends, coworkers, storyline partners... whatever you want."

Whatever I want. What I wanted was the man standing in front of me...who just so happened to be asking me on a date on the annual day of love. I should take it as a sign, right? That's what Cass and Kingsley—*and* Raelynn—would say.

"Don't you dare ask me to be your girlfriend on Valentine's Day, John Brooks. That's corny," I said, pointing my finger at him, and when I laughed, a genuine smile formed on his lips.

Dating a wrestler—a coworker—was never part of my plan. I didn't want to complicate things. I didn't want to make a mess I couldn't escape, but the time John and I have spent together lately has only confirmed what I already knew: he's the one. The one man on the roster I would break my rule for.

And the harder I search for a reason to cancel tonight, the more obvious that truth becomes.

I did what I set out to do. I made a name for myself in the industry and with the fans, firmly cemented myself as a top female wrestler, and had what is already being called one of the top ten matches of the year—the championship match between me and Rae last month. The problem is that the higher I've climbed the proverbial mountain of success, the more I realize there will always be something else, some new challenge to overcome. So, why should I continue to deny myself? Why shouldn't I get the only other thing I've truly wanted the last few years?

John said he would pick me up at five, but my building phone rings at 4:54 p.m., and my doorman tells me I have a gentleman guest who wants to be let upstairs. When I open my door, my breath catches in my throat at the sight of him. Both of us seem equally nervous, and that makes me feel a little less so.

"You look…" His gaze lifts to meet mine, and he bites down on his lip. "Beautiful." It's so simple, but the compliment warms my being. John outstretches his hand. "Shall we?"

A large hand envelops my waist when he meets me on the bow of the sailboat. He pulls me into his side and kisses the top of my head. "Warm enough?" John asks with a slight chuckle in his tone.

When we pulled up to the marina earlier, I glowered at him from the passenger seat. He forgot to mention I'd need a wetsuit for this date. John laughed softly to himself, noticing my glare, and gave my leg a gentle squeeze through the fabric of my white-knit midi skirt. "Relax, we're not going swimming"—he shot me a toothy grin—"unless you want to." His thumb dipped beneath the small slit to caress my thigh, and his touch set fire to my skin.

"I'm fine," I say, settling a little further into his embrace.

"How am I doing on the cliché meter?"

"On a scale of one to ten, this is definitely an eight. But I've never been on a sailboat, let alone a sailboat during sunset, so I'll bring it down to a six."

John smiles. "I half expected you to say eleven."

"You're a cliché, John Brooks, but you haven't officially asked me to be your girlfriend on this commercialized day of love. Unless you do that, you'll remain in the safe zone."

"And what if I did?" He turns me in his arms to stare straight into my eyes, his face serious. "Ask you to be my girlfriend."

The final moments of daylight cast a warm glow on his face, and a hint of green surrounds his pupils, spilling into the blue depths. For a moment, the only sounds are the waves beneath our feet, lapping at the side of the boat, and the captain somewhere below deck whistling a happy tune to himself.

"Is this you asking?"

"No," he says, and another smile spreads across his lips. "Not yet."

"Not yet?"

"Not yet," John confirms. "We do have something else to discuss. Tonight is all about risks."

That's an interesting way to say it.

"So, in that spirit, I'd like to play a game."

"A game?"

"A game. There are three different levels, each one has two options, and the choice you make will determine what we do tonight. So, are you willing to play a game of risk with me?"

I look around at the scene before us. We're on a sailboat in the middle of Tampa Bay watching the sunset with champagne, and you mean to tell me this isn't our date? I meet his awaiting gaze, and ask, "You mean *this* isn't our date?"

John laughs, cradling the side of my neck to pull me in and kiss my forehead. "Sweetheart, this is only the appetizer." The look in his eyes matches the fire that ignites in my core. "Are you ready?"

No.

"Yes," I say, holding his stare.

"Level one: A or B," he says, and my mind goes blank. *Shit.* What am I supposed to say? I thought he'd give me actual options, not pawns to choose from. "Don't think about it, Savannah. Just choose."

"I-I don't—"

"Choose."

"A."

"Okay," John says with a toothy grin. "Level two: square or circle."

"Circle."

"And finally, level three: red or white."

"Red."

John's pace slows when we approach an exit from the Riverwalk, not far from my condo building. He uses our conjoined hands to stop my movements, pulling me into him. His right hand cradles my left against his chest, and his left arm slips around my waist. He moves us in a small sway beneath the city lights, leaning in close until our noses touch.

When he spins me out and back in, it brings us even

closer, and my breath catches as his lips brush over mine for the first time all night. He doesn't close the gap; he kisses the tip of my nose instead.

"Do you want to play one more level?" John asks.

My brow cocks. Another level? It has to be close to midnight. What else could he possibly have planned?

So far, my choices have led to: "A," mini golf; "circle," a visit to John's favorite ice cream shop right outside of Tampa, because apparently he is a dessert before dinner kind of guy; and "red," a private cooking class where we made caprese salad, fresh mushroom ravioli, and a side of broccoli rabe. When John parked outside my building after dinner, he practically jumped out of the driver's seat to open my door before I could. I assumed the date was over, but he offered a stroll down the Riverwalk instead, and that's how we ended up here...

Apparently, still in the middle of our game risk, but so far, the rewards have paid off.

"What are my choices?" I ask.

"Level four: Hearts or Spades?"

"Spades."

The answer comes out so fast it surprises me, and a boyish smirk crosses his lips. John pulls me back into his side, pressing his lips to my temple in a long kiss. We walk through the waterfront park, up the sidewalk toward the street that will lead back to my building.

"So, do I get to know what the alternative date plans were?"

"And why would I do that?" He asks, pausing outside the lobby door. "I don't want to spoil any element of surprise I may have for the future."

The future. As in, this wasn't just a one-time thing. As in, he wants to do this again...with me.

"C'mon, let's get you inside." John's hand falls to my lower back, guiding me through the lobby door. This walk reminds me of the first night we met, when we got to The Resort before spending the rest of the night getting to know each other. But this time, when we step into the elevator, he doesn't stand on the other side of the car. He remains at my side, and his left hand grips my waist, keeping me close, before sliding back to my lower back when the elevator doors open on the thirteenth floor.

"Thanks for tonight," I say, unlocking my apartment, but I don't open the door. "It's been fun."

He's farther away than I remember him being when I turn around, now standing on the opposite side of the hallway. His hands are shoved deep into the pockets of his dress pants. The sleeves of his white button-up have been rolled just above his elbows, and the top three buttons are undone. The muscles beneath the fabric pull it taut against his body, and I've caught myself staring more than once tonight. So has he.

"You have the time?" he asks, staring me straight in the eye.

Why is he asking me what time it is? That's a strange question...Regardless, I pull my phone from my clutch and watch the time flicker to 12:01 a.m. on February 15th. "It's 12—"

Before I can finish, John kisses me.

He pushes me against the door of my condo, and I moan softly against his lips. This is what I've wanted, what I've waited for all night. He maintained a respectable distance throughout our date, and it left me wanting more. I'll admit, I was a little afraid he would walk me to my door and leave without even kissing me. Looks like I just needed to be patient.

Patience is a virtue, Mamá would say, and it's one I'm not good at practicing.

"Isn't it time we break that rule, Sweetheart?" The nickname sends a chill down my spine, or maybe it's the way he whispers it against my ear before kissing the skin where my neck and jaw meet.

"John—"

He pulls back to look at me. "Savannah, I respect the hell out of you, and I will do whatever you want, but fuck...I just want to call you *mine*."

The confession chips away at the last remaining resolve I have left, and I laugh. "Did you really wait until after midnight to ask me to be your girlfriend?"

"You told me it would be corny to ask you on Valentine's Day."

I didn't think he'd taken me seriously, but the fact that he did is cute. "It is corny. You're corny." I laugh, and he nuzzles his face into my neck, inhaling deeply before I feel a soft kiss against my collarbone. "Okay," I whisper, and he returns his gaze to mine. "I always said you were the one man I'd break that rule for...and I meant it, John."

"Wait, let's do this properly," he says, taking a step back. Before I know it, he's down on one knee.

"John Brooks, what in the hell are you doing?" I urge him to stand up. "I swear if you ask—"

"Savannah Josefine Williams,"—*Oh, fuck, I'm not ready for this*—"will you do me the honor of breaking your *one* rule and becoming my girlfriend?"

An involuntary breath of relief escapes my mouth when he says *girlfriend*. "Yes," I say, and laugh, tugging gently on his arm. "Now get up before someone sees you."

The first thought that comes to mind: *Holy shit, I just said yes to John Brooks*. The same man who captured my heart inside a college bar, but I never thought I'd see him again. If only I'd known what the universe had in store for me on that fateful night. Holy shit, I just said *yes* to John Brooks.

I smack his chest playfully as he stands. "Don't do that!"

"What?" His cocked brow matches the smirk on his lips.

"Did you think I was going to ask you something else?"

"No," I lie, and it makes him laugh.

"Sweetheart, one day I am going to ask you to marry me, but it won't be standing outside the door of your condo." He sounds so certain, I have no choice but to believe him. But how can he possibly know that? He only asked me to be his girlfriend sixty seconds ago. John pulls me to him in a hard kiss, claiming my mouth. We tumble inside when I reach behind, twisting the doorknob, but he pulls away briefly. He stares down at me, tucking a strand of hair behind my ear, and sighs. "I want you so fucking bad, Savannah..."

"There's a *but* in there...I can tell."

"But...I don't want to rush things. Not this time."

"I think it's a little late for that," I say, laughing, but he doesn't return it. He's serious?

"I want to do this right, Sweetheart. You mean more to me than just sex or jumping into bed because it's been over a year since I've felt you wrapped around my cock..." The words draw my brows higher and higher. I don't know who he's trying to convince more—me or him. Clearing his throat, he says, "I don't want to screw this up."

A smile pulls on my lips, and I kiss him gently. "I guess you should be going then."

John smirks and swipes his tongue over his teeth, dipping down to whisper in my ear. "Just because I want to take things slow doesn't mean I can't play with you at all." His eyes are darker than the depths of the ocean when I pull away to look up at him, and that simple look lights my skin on fire.

16

Savannah

WEDNESDAY, MARCH 28, 2012

CRYSTAL BAY, FL

"Sav?" His voice carries through the house. The large, opulent place he calls home is tucked away in the back of a gated community in one of the notoriously wealthy areas in central Florida: Crystal Bay. To live here, you'd have to spend no less than $1.3 million. (Yes, I looked it up. Is that weird?)

The Mediterranean-inspired exterior of John's home was not what I had been expecting. I suppose I expected some bachelor pad condo outfitted with an over-the-top sound system, remote-controlled lights and blinds, minimal food, top-shelf alcohol, and an oversized television perfect for watching sports. Instead, what I found was a house full of sophistication and classic charm. A grand entry behind a wrought iron gate and a wall of stucco, with a private courtyard filled with lush greenery, a bench, and a small fountain. Inside, white walls, vaulted ceilings, wrought iron fixtures, dark wood floors, an open layout with arched doorways, a stone statement wall, and a lofted upstairs that overlooked the living space. The house was bright and airy, filled with an abundance of natural light from the rear wall of windows overlooking the backyard and in-ground pool. There were two garages: one three-car that housed his SUV and Porsche, and a single-car that had been converted into a home gym. When he showed me around, the one thing I noticed that was missing was a personal touch—no photos, no quirky momentos, no candles, no plants, no keepsakes of any kind. Everything was a neutral color. If I didn't know better, I would've thought it was a furnished rental.

"What do you need all of this space for when you spend over half the year on the road?" I asked from across the marble kitchen island the first night I spent here. I thought it was a reasonable question. We spend over two hundred days a year on the road with EWE. How did it make sense to have something so...grand, if he couldn't be here to enjoy it? Not to mention it was just him in a six-bedroom, more than five-thousand-square-foot house.

John handed me a glass of wine, checking the time left on the timer for the dinner he'd made. "I wanted something for me, I guess. Somewhere...safe."

"Safe?"

He sighed, folding his hands as he leaned over the island. "It's a long story, and I want to share it with you. I will, but not...not tonight."

"Maybe when I'm older?" I joked. When he saw the smile in the corner of my lips, he couldn't fight his own with a playful eye roll. Our age difference has never been a concern of mine, but it has been his. He's thirty-one, and I'm twenty-four. Seven years isn't a big gap, so I've never seen the issue.

"You can talk to me," I said, placing my hands over his.

"I know, and I will. Just not tonight. I want to enjoy turning this house into a home with you." John came around the island and pulled me into his arms. He kissed me in the middle of the kitchen, only to be interrupted by the timer sounding the alarm. The emotional weight from seconds before dissipated when he pulled away to check on the chicken, but I haven't forgotten the look in his eyes when he said. *Somewhere safe.* What did that mean?

Walking through the foyer into the living room, I find him standing at the top of the stairs just outside his office. He's dressed in his gym clothes, but he doesn't look like he's even broken a sweat. I offered for him to join me at the NextGen center, but he said he needed to get some work done before he could hit the weights, including a podcast interview.

"Sorry, I'm late. I had to run by the condo. Grab some stuff for the road next week," I say, lifting the bag of extra clothes and a change of ring gear options I had picked up at my condo.

"How was the gym?"

"Rae came by. We got some ring time in. I got to work on that new submission move." I drop my bag onto the window bench of the master bedroom, returning to find him now at the bottom of the stairs. He pulls me into a hard kiss, and my suspicions are confirmed when I inhale the fresh scent of his skin. Pulling away, I pinch the fabric of his shirt. "I thought you were going to work out?"

"I was about to, but Ari called." I don't know much about his sister, or the rest of his family, for that matter. They don't talk much—not on the phone anyway. He and Ari text a few times a week, catching each other up on necessary information, but never anything long and drawn out. I've wondered if that's how they are in person, too. If that's how the whole family is. John is cautious when it comes to things concerning the rest of the Brookses, and the one time I asked Brody, he said it wasn't his place to tell.

"How is she?"

"Fine, fine. She was inviting me to the joint birthday party for my mom and grandmother," John says, sinking onto the brown leather L-shaped couch. She invited *him*, not us.

"Mom is turning sixty, and our grandmother will be eighty-five. Everyone is going to be there, apparently, which doesn't happen often, but I suppose the matriarch turning eighty-five is good enough reason."

"I suppose it is," I say, sitting at the far end of the L's stem.

"They're planning it for Friday and Saturday before Wrestlefest week."

"That will be a great way for you to decompress."

His eyes narrow, and he chuckles, pushing up from his spot on the couch to sit beside me. "I think we're having two different conversations here, Sweetheart. I want you there with me. Of course, if you think it will be too much, seeing as the next week is going to be extremely busy, I understand. You're welcome to come back and stay here, get some rest, and I'll meet you in Phoenix."

"You want me to go?" I ask. He wants me to meet his family? And not just his immediate family, he wants me to meet the whole family? This seems out of the blue, considering he's hardly told me anything about these people.

"You don't have to if—"

"It's not that I don't *want* to go, John. I—I do. My concern is that I don't know anything about them. We've known each other for a long time, but I know nothing about these people. I don't even know their names, except for Ari." I run a hand over my hair, twisting the end of my ponytail before letting it fall over my shoulder again. "John, you know my family. You've met them, talked to them…but you've kept everything about your family a secret. The only thing I know for sure is you have a sister, and you would move Heaven and Earth to protect her. You told me that much the night we met."

His gaze remains glued to the blue-gray rug beneath the circular glass coffee table. John rubs the back of his neck before his hand comes down to interlace his fingers together. They hang between his knees, and with a heavy sigh, he finally looks up at me. "Sweetheart, I'm sorry. I never meant to make you feel like I was trying to keep things from you. I just… When it comes to my family, I don't—"

"We all have issues, John."

"Not the Williamses."

"Trust me, stick around long enough and you'll see that's not true. Everyone has something."

I could laugh just thinking about some of the antics that used to get my older brothers in trouble. Our parents still don't know about the time I had to pick Crew up from the middle of nowhere because he and some friends almost got arrested a few towns over for a bar fight, and the kid who caused it left the rest of them to walk home. Or the time Papá kicked Nash out because they found weed in his room while he was still in high school. Or the times I heard my parents whispering in the middle of the night in the early stages of the ranch when they were close to going under water. Sure, it may seem like we're perfect, but life comes for everyone at some point in time. I guess we do a better job at hiding it.

"I won't ever push you to tell me, but when you're ready to open up about it, preferably before I meet them…I'm here." I pat his thigh and press a gentle kiss to his lips. "I'm going to take a shower and change. Then we can grab dinner because I'm starving."

John disappears up the stairs and into his office without a word, the moment we walk through the door after dinner. I stand at the bottom of the stairs, debating whether I should follow, get the conversation over with—or wait.

Waiting sounds like a better idea.

Dinner was quiet, unusually so, but I'm not sure whether it's because of John or me. We both seemed to be locked in our own minds, waging different wars on the same topic since the conversation this afternoon. Sitting across from him, twirling angel hair pasta onto my fork, I decided I shouldn't join him for the birthday celebration in a few weeks.

I didn't know what I'd be walking into, and I didn't want him to feel uncomfortable when he already doesn't see his family often. He should be free to be whoever he needs to be and enjoy his time, without worrying about me or what I might think. Sitting there, I made up my mind to tell him as soon as we got back to his house.

Opening the bottle of wine from last night, I take a sip... and hear the sound of his steps coming down the staircase. Less than a minute later, he joins me in the kitchen with a shoebox tucked under his arm. He slides it onto the counter before he removes the glass from my hand and pulls me into a crushing hug.

With eyes closed, his forehead against mine, he says, "I'm sorry, Savannah. I—I don't want to keep things from you. I don't mean to, but this has always been a...I guess it's more of a sore spot than I realized. But I'm ready to talk about it, I'm ready to—"

"John, you don't—"

"I want to, Sav. You have shown me all of you, and it's time I do the same." He kisses me gently before guiding me to the box on the counter. His fingers touch the lid before he gently lifts it. Inside are countless memorabilia: photos, ticket stubs, a trophy, ribbons, a broken action figure, a smashed snow globe, an old watch, letters, and drawings. Too many things to count, but I can tell each one holds significance to the man beside me, each one with a story to explain who he is. "I haven't opened this in years," John says, more to himself than me.

"How about we start at the beginning?" I say, handing him a glass of wine, before taking a sip of my own.

John pulls out an old photograph—a Polaroid—and his thumb traces over the smiling faces. A young boy with a toothy grin holds a trophy high above his head, *Bobcats* across his chest in white embroidered letters. His father, I assume, stands behind him, hand on the boy's shoulder, with an equally bright smile, wearing a hoodie with the same team's name on it. Both wear their hats backwards. John sets it down and pulls out another photo, this time of the same boy with his parents. Then another and another. Each one depicts different moments in time captured on film to be remembered—for better or worse, it would seem. Finally, he comes across a photo that stops him, and I notice his touch tighten ever so slightly. Rolling his lips between his teeth, he sets it down on the counter so I can see it, too.

"That's my father," he says, pointing to the same man I had seen in the earlier photos. This time, however, there is something different in the way his father smiles. His smile no longer reaches his eyes, no longer portrays the same love and light it did in the earlier moments. "This was taken at my sister's second birthday party, the same day Mom found out about his first affair."

His *first* affair?

"They spent the entire morning in a screaming match right up until the first person showed up for Ari's party." John shakes his head, staring down at the man in the photo, but I can't take my eyes off the one next to me. "Ari was clueless. They told us to go outside and play, but I heard them. I—I heard everything. Obviously, I didn't understand it all. I was only ten, but I knew something bad had happened and I was scared shitless of what it meant."

John puts the photo down, lifting out a thin, square children's book. "They tried to hide the fighting, but they weren't very good at it. Even Ari started to notice after a while. When it would get really bad, she'd sneak into my room, and I'd read her books or tell her stories to try and take her mind off it. Eventually, they moved into separate rooms, and then after a while, they just stopped talking altogether. That was the best thing they ever did because he refused to get a divorce."

What the hell?

Next, John withdraws the base of what, I think, is supposed to be a snow globe. In what should be the inside of the globe, a black bear stands on a mountaintop in front of a serene mountainous background outfitted with a log cabin, pine trees, and a sign that reads *Great Smoky Mountains*. There are dried sparkles cemented to different parts of the base, obviously from when the glass was broken.

"Then, one day, out of the blue...about six years after that first big fight, we came home from school, and they told us to pack a bag. We were going on a family road trip." John runs his thumb over the bear's head. "I could see right through him—them—but Ari...she thought it meant things were going back to normal. They were trying to act like things were normal, like they were happy, until Ari answered his phone and there was another woman on the other end of the line."

The tears that brim in his eyes threaten to shatter my heart. Seeing the hurt—the heartbreak—pouring out of him is more than I ever imagined. This is not what I expected.

"Mom walked in, and Ari told her what happened...I watched that entire weekend implode in less than five minutes. He had just bought this for my sister maybe two hours before that, and amid his tirade, he picked it up and threw it across the room."

"Did he hit you?" I can't stop myself from asking, even though the thought of it makes me sick.

John shakes his head. "No, he never raised a hand to us.

Sometimes, I used to wish he would have. I think that almost would've been better than some of the shit he used to say."

I reach out to cradle his cheek, and he smiles, covering my hand with his. "Why do you keep all of this?"

John shrugs, picking up the watch. He runs his thumb over the face before he drops it back in its hiding place. "Everything in here is a reminder of the happy times, but also the not-so-great times. At some point, I stopped being able to differentiate, but it reminds me of where I came from and who I don't want to be." He finally looks up. "I don't want to be like him, Savannah."

"You're not him, John."

"My mother would've said the same when he told her that he didn't want to be like his father."

I stand on my tiptoes to get as close to eye level as I can with him. "You are not your father, John Brooks. You are your own person. You have your own victories and you make your own mistakes, but despite those mistakes, it doesn't make you more like him. It just makes you...you."

John smiles softly, kissing me. "Thank you, Sav."

"Why doesn't your mom leave him?" I ask, not expecting the soft chuckle in response. John takes one of my hands in his, threading our fingers together and bringing the back of my hand to his lips.

"My parents are divorced. Now." John rolls his eyes. "My father left the day my sister turned eighteen. Took everything with him and moved into one of the wealthiest neighborhoods on the north side of the state. That was...Shit, that was almost five years ago."

"He left on your sister's birthday?"

"Waited until Mom couldn't ask for child support anymore."

"What a dick."

"Ari and I are close, and my mom and I have been working

on our relationship. I'll never understand why she stayed, and for a while, I resented her for it. We didn't need him. I would've done whatever it took to help her make ends meet." John fiddles with the ring on my right-hand ring finger—a gold band with a bead-shaped blue topaz stone secured by four prongs, gifted to me by my parents when I graduated high school. When his eyes find mine again, they're softer. "I begged her to leave him, offered to help with the bills, with whatever she needed. She always told me no. I just wanted her to get Ari out of that situation. When I was gone, I thought it would give her the push she needed to leave...They were living separate lives, but she stayed anyway."

"Until he left her."

"She and Ari came back from lunch to find his shit gone and divorce papers on the counter."

"You're joking."

"I wish I were. And I was in Europe with EWE. I'll never forget that phone call." John bites down on his bottom lip, squeezing his eyes shut and shaking his head as if to rid himself of the memory. "Savannah, I don't talk about this because I still haven't dealt with it all. My dad kicked me out at seventeen because I wasn't going to college. He said he wasn't going to have a son who paraded around in tights for a living and kicked me out two weeks before graduation. I still feel guilty for leaving my sister behind in that mess. And the shit with my dad, I've never gotten closure. We don't talk. We haven't talked in years."

This is a lot of information to process, but it explains so much. John Brooks is a quiet man. He's loud and boisterous when he wants or needs to be, but over the last month, I've come to see him in a different light. I've seen a side of him most people don't. His home, quiet and neutral and serene, reflects the things he's been craving for so long. He has no keepsakes because there are none to have. No photos because they all remind him of the man who abandoned him. He keeps his family hidden the way he was taught to do, because I imagine his father wasn't someone who wanted the whole town to know the truth, but also because he wants to do everything he can to protect his sister. The longing I've seen in his eyes when he looks at my family, wishing for the same. It all makes sense...

"Do you want to talk to him?" I ask, unsure whether it's the right thing to say.

John rubs a hand through his hair, chewing on the corner of his lip. "I don't think there's anything left to say to Leeland Cabot."

Cabot? I thought his last name was Brooks.

"Brooks was my middle name," John says, as if he can read my mind. "I dropped Cabot when I turned eighteen because I didn't want to be associated with him."

"And what about your mom. How is your relationship with her now?"

"We're still mending fences. I helped her buy a house a few years ago. Helped Ari pay for college, get a car, all of the things our dad should've helped with. I don't—I don't say all of this to make you feel any certain way, Savannah. I want you to understand why I am the way I am, sometimes. I've had to step up and make sure my family is taken care of. And I don't—"

"You don't have to handle this alone, John. I'm here, and I'm not going anywhere."

"I know that. I've known that, but it's not always easy to talk about."

"Well, whenever you want to—whenever you're ready to—tell me more, I'll be right here."

"How did I get so lucky to find you?" John asks, tugging me into his arms and kissing my forehead.

17

FRIDAY, APRIL 13, 2012

RAVENSWOOD, IN

We barely make it out of the car before my sister comes barreling out of Mom's house. She sweeps Savannah into a tight embrace and says, "John hasn't shut up about you from the moment he met you."

"Oh, really?" My girlfriend's brow raises in question, glancing my way.

"Well, a month or so later, I guess. You know he used to be a bit of—"

"Okay, that's enough gossip," I say, breaking them up and giving Ari a warning glare. But she doesn't care. She threads their arms together and sticks her tongue out at me over her shoulder, guiding Savannah toward the house. I shouldn't be surprised—I'm not, in fact—I had just hoped I'd have some more time to prepare myself before Ari outed me.

Sometimes I wish I could go back to the man I was on the second day of 2011 and tell him all the things he had to look forward to just by waiting a little bit longer for the woman Ari just dragged inside. I wouldn't want to ruin it for him, though, because nothing could accurately relay the way I've felt the last two months. We've kept the truth about us quiet for no other reason than to enjoy the beginnings of our relationship without being under a microscope. The only people who know the truth are Amos and Xander, because we thought it was only right to inform them, and Brody and Raelynn. No one else has batted an eye at us spending almost every day together, thanks to the storyline. It's made it easy to ignore the scrutinizing eye of Drake. Little does he know, his bet only hurried along the inevitable, and I don't plan on ruining this good thing to keep a couple of hundred dollars in my bank account. He could offer me triple, and I still wouldn't risk this. And after this weekend, there's nothing that could ever make me want to walk away from this woman.

"You don't need to book a hotel room so you can sleep in the same bed as your girlfriend. You're adults, Brooks," my mother says the moment I walk through the front door.

Well, hello to you, too.

Her words are sharp, matching the color of her steely blue eyes. The comforting presence that once emanated from her was lost a long time ago, replaced by the shell of the person she once was. I used to long for that woman, to hear her laugh and sing the way she once did, to feel her warm embrace comfort me in the hard times. However, I was forced to watch her disappear before my eyes, and I'm not sure I'll ever have the pleasure of knowing her again.

Her words halt the conversation between Ari and Savannah, who stand just inside the foyer. My girlfriend looks between us, waiting to see what will happen next. I warned her about this. Warned her that Mom would either have some snarky comments the moment we arrived or ignore us altogether. I could never be sure which version I would get.

"Now go get your bags and cancel that hotel room. You might own this house, but I'm still your mother."

And she never lets me forget it.

Do I own the house we currently stand in? Yes. Do I hold that fact over my mother's head? No. I bought the house after Dad left because I wanted to know that while I was on the road over three hundred days a year, she and my sister had somewhere safe and secure to live. After Ari moved out two years ago, we begged Mom to move my grandmother into the house with her, to make it easier on both of them, but she refused. "Your grandmother likes her independence," she said. While that might be true, Grandma Aggie wasn't getting any younger, and letting her live alone on the farm was less than ideal.

"That's nice of you to offer, Mom, but I think we'll be more comfortable in town," I say.

"You are the most gorgeous creature I've ever seen," my cousin Tommy says. Savannah stifles a laugh behind her hand, staring down at my youngest cousin as he lifts her other hand to his lips. She somehow maintains the elegant smile I've seen her give many people in her tenure with EWE—mostly fans who got a little too close for comfort. Seeing that discomfort roll off her now, I excuse myself from my conversation with a few other cousins.

"Tommy, give it a rest, would you?" my sister says, pushing him away before I can make it there. "Besides, she's taken."

"Taken?" Tommy scoffs. "Well, I sure don't see a ring on her hand." I roll my eyes, coming up behind my girlfriend. Tommy's pupils dilate further than they already are from his extracurriculars, which made him late today in the first place. "Oh shit, John-boy! I didn't know you were coming this weekend."

"Tommy, good to see you're still you," I say, and Savannah leans back even further into my embrace. I hear Ari chuckle at my side, hands on her hips. "I see you've met Savannah."

"Savan—Your girlfriend? This is your girlfriend?"

"I told you to leave her alone," Ari says, rolling her eyes.

"Holy shit, cous." Tommy chuckles, looking Savannah up and down once more. His tongue pokes out the corner of his mouth, wetting his dry lips, before he swipes his thumb over the cracked skin. I give Savannah's hip a gentle squeeze when he meets my narrowed gaze. "I had no idea you were able to pull such a hottie."

"Leave that poor girl alone, Thomas!" Grandma Aggie shouts across the yard when she walks out the back door, followed by my mother. "Don't run her off before we even get the chance to know her. Lord knows, two seconds talkin' to you and John'll never be able to convince her to come back."

My cousin scoffs, ignoring our grandmother. "Listen, Sweetheart, when you're ready to have a good time, give me a holler." With a final glance my way, Tommy stalks off to bother someone else, and probably ask them for money.

"I thought you said he wasn't coming, Ariana," I say when he's gone, and this time she rolls her eyes at me.

"Don't you *Ariana* me, *John*." Ari points her finger at me.

No one in my family calls me John except my grandmother—and Tommy when he's trying to get under my skin. Everyone has always called me by my middle name: Brooks.

"Keep in mind, I have a million stories about you just waiting to be shared." That earns a laugh from Savannah. "I can almost guarantee you haven't told her about that time you set yourself on fire in chem lab and they had to—"

"Okay, time to go." I wrap my arm around Savannah's shoulders, trying to guide her away, but she slips out of my grasp.

"Actually, I'd love to hear more about this," she says, looping her arm with Ari, and without a second glance, they walk away in a chorus of giggles.

"I like her," a voice dripping with honey comments before a thin hand wraps around my arm and squeezes. Grandma Aggie. "She handles this family well. Better than your last girlfriend."

"The last time I brought a girl to one of these was in high school."

"And she hated every second of it," Grandma Aggie says, looking up at me. "She was ready to leave the second you pulled up the drive. And when she realized we'd be eating outside, she 'bout had a coronary. But this one, she didn't even bat an eye."

"Savannah was raised on a farm."

"So I heard." She smiles. "Your sister hasn't stopped talking about it since you told her you finally asked her out. Savannah said her family owns a big ol' piece of property down in Texas. We were trading stories of life on the farm earlier. Your mother seems fond of her, too."

"I wouldn't know. She's barely said anything to me unless it was giving me shit for booking a hotel or reminding me that *my* name is on the house."

"Oh, John. You have to ignore her," she says, waving her hand through the air. "She'll always have something to say about that because of how things went with your father. It just is what it is."

"That was six years ago."

"And for many years before that. She put up with a lot from that man, including holding that house and the food on the table over her head."

"I would never do that," I say.

Grandma Aggie pats my hand. "I know, Sweets, but unfortunately, I think it's going to take a lot more than a few simple words to undo the years of conditioning she endured under your father."

Savannah's laughter draws our attention her way. She's doubled over as Ari continues to tell her whatever outrageous story she's pulled from the depths of her memory. The sight makes me smile. This is all I've ever wanted, but for a long time, I wasn't sure I'd ever see it happen.

"She loves you, y'know," my grandmother says. "And you love her, too. Don't you?" Her smile grows when I nod. "Have you told her?"

"Not yet."

"Well, you better."

"Don't you think it's kind of early for that?"

Grandma Aggie shrugs. "Your grandfather told me two weeks after he met me, and I was head over heels for that man from the first day I laid eyes on him. If you ask me, what's the point in waiting? If you know you feel that way, you should tell her."

It's been a week since I introduced Savannah to my family, and we've been so busy with all things Wrestlefest that we haven't had a chance to catch up on everything that happened last weekend. This is the first time we've shared a hotel room since we started dating two months ago, and word spread like wildfire once someone caught wind of it. I don't know for sure, but I can guess who it was. (Harper.) While we might be sleeping in the same bed this weekend, Savannah and I have barely spoken outside of *Goodnight* and *Good morning*, and sometimes that's only through text message because one of us has to be up before the other—usually me. Today hasn't been any different, filled with a fresh round of joint media first thing this morning, separate signings and photo sessions, then more media, followed by a charity function, and now Legends Night.

The Saturday night before Wrestlefest is always reserved for a special occasion where we gather to honor the veterans of the business and induct them into our Hall of Fame. Tonight marks the first time we're stepping out together not under the guise of a storyline. Legends Night has nothing to do with characters or storylines. Kayfabe is typically shelved because tonight is about those who came before us. Who paved the way. So, tonight it's just us, Savannah Williams and John Brooks. Together.

A flash of black caught my eye when Savannah stepped out of the bathroom earlier, moving across the hall to the floor-length mirror on the wall. A sleeveless black satin dress hung off her shoulders, hugging her curves. Her long brown hair had been pulled into a twisted ponytail updo, her bangs framing her face, leaving her golden skin on full display. A gold choker around her neck, the gold cuff on her left wrist, and the gold chunky statement earrings perfectly matched the hue of her skin.

"You're making it hard to be a respectable man," I whispered, joining her in the mirror. My hands ghosted over her waist, trailing up her sides, her arms, her shoulders, her neck, and finally her chin, pulling her lips to mine. The kiss was a slow, languid dance between us, one that we hadn't shared since Sunday evening when we first arrived in Phoenix. Parting, her answer was a simple smirk, and she helped me finish my tie before she kissed my cheek and walked away.

There had been something different about her since she walked into our room earlier this evening. An air of unease surrounded her as she moved around to gather what she needed, lost in her thoughts, and walked into the bathroom without so much as a word to me. I wondered if it had to do with the fact that we were about to out ourselves in front of the whole company, or if something happened while we were apart, or maybe it was both. I'd had my moments of concern throughout the day, too, but nothing that would make me reconsider. Was she reconsidering this?

"Don't look now, but I think you guys just confirmed the rumors that have been circulating all weekend," Wolf says, interrupting my thoughts and our conversation with Raelynn and Brody.

"And what rumors would those be?" Savannah asks, eyeing the woman at his side.

"Oh, I don't know, the ones that say you guys are *dating*," Wolf emphasizes the final word, brow raised, earning an eye roll from Savannah. "You two show up here *together*, and act like it's nothing! What happened to not wanting to date wrestlers?"

"Who said we are?" I ask.

"Maybe we're just hanging out because we're in a story together," my girlfriend adds.

"Please." Wolf snorts. "You guys have been eye-fucking from the first time you laid eyes on each other at NextGen. It was only a matter of time."

If only he knew.

I catch Brody's stare from the corner of my eye, but ignore him, keeping my focus on Wolf. When I slip my hand into hers, Savannah gives my fingers a small squeeze. We've been under a microscope from the moment we walked in the door, and I was worried it might be too much for her, but she hasn't even flinched. She holds her head high, ignoring the whispers and glares from mostly the other women. "Why her?" I heard someone ask, and I rolled my eyes. "She's nothing special," another one said.

"So what if they *are* dating? What's it to you, Wolfie?"

Raelynn asks with a cocked brow.

"Because she didn't tell me!" Wolf turns back to Savannah. "How could you not tell me? How could *you* not tell me, Brooks?"

"Look to your left," Savannah says, motioning toward Harper. That earns a chuckle from Rae and Brody, but Harper doesn't find it as amusing. "She would have blabbed it to the entire company, just like she did about us sharing a room this weekend."

"I did not!" Harper shouts, granting us a few more stares from the surrounding audience. Harper repeats herself, softer this time, with a hard exhale. "I don't care who you date, Savannah. But I guess dating *Brooks Taylor* has its perks, doesn't it?"

Savannah stiffens beneath my touch, and I tighten my grip on her waist. Wolf turns Harper away, guiding her through the crowd. No one wants a Savannah-Harper confrontation tonight. I press a kiss to the top of my girlfriend's head and whisper against her hair, "Ignore her, Sweetheart. She won't be the only one to have something to say, but none of them matter. Just you and me."

The rest of the night goes by in a blur until we're pulling up to the side entrance of the hotel and dragging our feet inside to get a few hours of sleep before we have to be up again. She sweeps her hair to the side, standing before me, a silent request for help. I drag the zipper down her back, and goosebumps rise across her skin as my fingers trail her spine. I press a long kiss to her bare shoulder, and she inhales before a contented sigh follows. We move around in silence, and I can't shake the feeling that something is bothering her still. I thought she'd be more relaxed following the event, but now that it's over, she seems even more tense than before.

"Everything okay, Sweetheart?" I ask when she climbs into bed, straight into my open arms.

"Fine." She sighs, snuggling further into my side. "Just tired." I don't believe her, but she closes her eyes, ending the conversation before it can begin.

18

Brooks

WRESTLEFEST XXX
SUNDAY, APRIL 22, 2012

PHOENIX,AZ

"That all you got champ?" my opponent, Colin Ryker, taunts after nailing me with a running lariat that sends me flying over the ropes. It's hard to believe *Ryker* is the same kid I saved from hazing when he was called up from NextGen about three months ago. He made his first appearance the same night I won the title from *Grady Chandler* at Capitol Punishment, interrupting the celebration between my character and *Savvy Skye* with a sneak attack.

Tonight is all about putting *Ryker* over, setting up his character to become EWE's new big bad so he can successfully lead the new faction. The faction is meant to include only the wrestlers deemed the most "elite" by none other than Chelsea, and soon her brother Theo when he makes his on-screen return. The wrestlers involved in this faction, named *The Corporation*, will be aligned with the Raffertys ("corporate") and will be deemed part of the show's authority. And tonight, *The Corporation* is adding a new person to their clique. Who is it? I'm not sure, but whoever it is will be coming to *Ryker*'s aid very soon. After *Brooks Taylor* "turned" on *Chelsea* following my win for her against her brother, it was only a matter of time before she came after me. That story was one of the few times I've pushed back on a storyline and won. Amos came to me with the idea for a love interest storyline between *Brooks Taylor* and *Chelsea*, but it wasn't something I felt comfortable with. Want me to be her lackey? Sure. Want me to do her bidding? You got it. But getting involved with the boss's daughter felt like crossing a line, one that I wasn't willing to cross. And now, I'm suffering the consequences.

Ryker rolls out of the ring and throws me into the barricade. My back absorbs most of the shock, but a small twinge shoots through my shoulder where I land on it. The crowd explodes when he looks to them for approval, and I struggle to get back to my feet. We've always had a love-hate relationship, the fans and I, but when the time comes for them to be on my side, they never disappoint. Besides, sometimes it's fun being the guy they love to hate, even if I'm not a heel.

Colin lifts the apron that covers the belly of the ring. Under the ring is where you'll find an array of different treasures—tables, ladders, chairs, Kendo sticks, maybe even one of the production crew members—all at our disposal. From my spot against the barricade, I see him pull out a Kendo stick.

Fuck, I groan.

Kendo sticks are hollow bamboo shoots taped together at each end. The tape allows them to spread apart when smashed against your opponent, and the impact hurts like hell. Using the barricade, I pull myself up, only to fall back to one knee when *Ryker* strikes the stick across my back.

"*Oh, that's gotta hurt,*" I overhear *Scott Harrington* say from behind the announcer's desk.

You fucking think, Scott?

"*I thought you were the champ,*" *Colin* says, and another

strike follows. *"Look more like a chump to me."* He goes for another swing, but this time, I catch the stick in the palm of my hand, and his eyes widen.

I rip the stick from his hands and toss it behind me, but *Ryker* takes off around the ring. And as much as I don't want to follow, I do, only to be met with a "surprise" boot to the face. The impact sends me back down to the floor and puts my opponent back in control of the match. I watch him dig through the underpart of the ring again, this time pulling out two steel chairs. He tosses them over the ropes and into the ring before he turns back to me. I give him an inconspicuous nod, and he reaches down, hauling me to my feet and pushing me under the bottom rope.

Ryker slides into the ring and picks up one of the chairs. He waits until I'm about halfway up before he swings. The strike doesn't land flat like it should. Instead, it's turned slightly on impact, and I feel the metal edge scratch the side of my head. The sound it makes is sickening, and the crowd gasps when I fall to one knee. My hand instinctively reaches up when I feel the first bead down the side of my face—blood. *Shit.*

Savannah's backstage watching, and she's not going to be happy when she sees this. She warned me about working with Colin—told me how he used to get a little rough in the ring while they were in NextGen. He liked to do things like rip the padding of the turnbuckle or undo the tape on the ropes before throwing his opponent into it without much warning. *Colin Ryker* is a heel through and through, no doubt about that, and he knows putting a beatdown on someone like me is one of the best ways to make a name for himself. But that's part of what we do; sometimes we work with people who aren't as fluid—aren't as nuanced—and that's okay. We make it work. We help them become better. That's the name of the game, and it's always a risk when you step foot in the squared circle.

It's not a lot of blood, but enough to elicit a reaction from Mike, the referee. "You good?"

I nod, waving him off. This is nothing. I've competed with blood pouring down my face before. I've competed with a torn muscle. I can handle a little scrape. Wiping my hand on my pants, I don't have to look to know *Ryker* is standing behind me, teeth bared, poised to strike again, but then everything comes to a halt.

The crowd erupts when *Savvy Skye's* music follows her down the ramp as she seemingly comes to my aid. What is she doing? She's supposed to be banned from ringside. Everyone is banned, except...

Oh, you've got to be fucking kidding me.

"*Get out of here, Skye!*" the referee yells, but she steps through the ropes anyway, as if she doesn't hear him.

She comes to stand in front of me, eyes locked on *Colin Ryker*, daring my opponent to take a step forward, until I watch her face slowly morph into something more sinister on the big screen. *Brooks Taylor* can't react, though. So, I'm forced to play along. Pretend I haven't noticed.

A twisted smile crosses her lips—*fuck, that was kind of hot*—and *Colin* laughs, handing over the chair. The referee tries to interfere, but the look in *Ryker's* eye sends him stumbling back a few paces. It takes a moment for the crowd to catch up to what's happening, and when I finally come to my feet, my opponent nods.

Savvy turns, shoving the edge of the chair into my gut before hitting me over the head. When I fall to the mat, she smashes the steel across my back—once, twice, three times. Damage done, she drops the chair beside me, and through the slits of my eyes, I watch her slowly back herself into the corner.

"*What is she doing?*" I can hear *Jude Paul's* voice from the commentator's table, along with so many others in the crowd.

"Savvy Skye has just turned against Brooks Taylor."

Savvy silently sits on the top turnbuckle, watching as *Colin* finishes the match. He spears me when I stagger to my feet, then rolls me onto my back, hooking my leg for the pin. The referee refuses to start the count. This is exactly how *Ryker* and I planned it. Well, how the writers planned it, except for the part where they forgot to mention it was my girlfriend who would interfere.

Any second now, we'll be joined by—

"What are you waiting for?" *Chelsea*'s scratchy female voice comes over the speakers. She walks out from backstage, standing at the top of the ramp. *"Count! Now!"*

The referee looks between the four of us, and with a heavy sigh, he falls to the mat. His hand comes down three times, declaring *Colin Ryker* the winner.

Still perched on the rope, *Savvy* doesn't even look at the man she just aided in my demise; instead, her gaze is locked on me. Her walls are up, keeping her personal feelings about this locked away, not even allowing me to penetrate them. Finally, she rips her gaze from mine, jumping down and ripping the belt from the referee's hands as soon as he collects it. She gives it to *Colin* and raises his hand in victory. She bites down on her bottom lip, beaming up at him, but looks away when he tries to lean down for a kiss.

At least I didn't have to watch *that*.

He leans down again, this time whispering something in her ear before she nods. *Savvy* picks up the chair again, running her fingers over the edges of the slick metal. She glances at me, unfolding and sitting it on top of my chest, pinning me for the second time tonight. The pressure is instantaneous, knocking the air out of my lungs, and I remind myself to breathe. This is Savannah. My girlfriend. While she might be working a storyline, she isn't going to do anything that will actually hurt me. She hasn't remotely put any weight on the seat. I can't see, but I can guess she's hovering above it, only making it appear like she's sitting down. Still, I struggle beneath her, selling the moment.

Savvy sits backwards, showing no remorse for what she just did. She stares down at me over the back of the chair, straight into my eyes, as she speaks. "*You never saw it coming, did you, baby*?" Her voice is sickeningly sweet before she scoffs. "*You were so busy playing the hero, you didn't see what was happening right under your nose. They saw me for what I really am, but you, Brooks Taylor...you thought I was just here to be your cheerleader. To stand on the sidelines and help you shine. I'm not here for you. I was never here for you. I'm here for me.*"

When she stands, I push the chair off my chest and take in a large gulp of air. *Savvy* pauses at the ropes, meeting my gaze over her shoulder one last time, and for a brief moment, I'm looking at Savannah, not *Savvy Skye*. The hint of a smile, almost remorseful, tugs at her lips.

"*Let's go, Skye!*" *Chelsea*'s voice echoes down the ramp. I shake my head, pleading with her to stay, because that's what *Brooks Taylor* would do. And that's who I'm supposed to be right now, not John Brooks. *Savvy* takes the final step out of the ring and jumps down from the apron. She walks backwards up the ramp to a chorus of boos, watching the officials surround the ring to check on me, but I shoo them away. I don't need their help. I pull myself up using the ropes and watch as *Chelsea* grabs hold of *Savvy*'s wrist and lifts her hand into the air.

That wasn't part of the plan—at least not the one I was

prepared for. Was I aware that Colin was going to win with some assistance? Yes. Was I aware this was setting up for a new storyline that included me and the impending corporate faction? Also yes. I never would've imagined they'd pit Savannah against me, but I should've known. I'm sure the idea spawned in Amos's head the moment he found out we were dating. Honestly, I could've accepted it if someone had warned me...Come to think of it, why didn't *she* warn me?

I push through the curtain and immediately scan gorilla, but she's nowhere to be seen. The least she could've done is wait for me here and look me in the face as I came back from getting my ass handed to me by none other than her. I had no idea what was coming—or who—just that someone would come out about thirty-five minutes into the match and lay me out. I was supposed to be ready for anything—chair, ladder, table, brass knuckles, whatever they had up their sleeve.

Amos waves to me from the corner, offering a thumbs-up when I finally look at him. *At least someone is fucking happy.* I shake my head and walk past him even though he beckons me his way, and truthfully, I'm just as shocked as he is. I can't remember the last time, if ever, that I've walked right by him after a match like this. Amos wanting to talk for a second after a Wrestlefest match is normal, but he doesn't want to know what I think about this. Not right now, anyway. Not before I've cooled off.

Every eye in my path avoids my glare, only stopping to look once I've passed them, matching the whispers of "Did you see what happened?" and "I thought they were together." The only people who don't avoid me are Wolf and Brody. They're perched by a pile of black equipment boxes, talking in hushed tones that become even quieter when they see me, stopping completely once I reach them.

"Hey, man. Good match," Wolf says, and I scoff in return.

"You wouldn't happen to know where my girlfriend is,

would you? She wasn't in gorilla," I say, rolling my eyes when they share a look. "What?"

"We were just discussing if you knew that was coming or not, and from your demeanor, I'm guessing not," Brody says. "Why didn't she tell you?"

I scrub a rough hand down my face before letting my fingers card through my hair. "That's what I'm trying to figure out."

"Well, have you told her about—"

"No." My jaw clenches so tight it could turn carbon into a fucking diamond. "And I don't plan to."

Brody scoffs, shaking his head. "That's a bad idea, Brooks."

"Why do I get the feeling I'm missing something here?" Wolf asks, his eyes flickering between the two of us.

"Don't worry about it, kid," Brody says, planting a hand on his shoulder. "We'll tell you when you're older."

"Assholes." Wolf rolls his eyes, earning an amused chuckle from our friend. I can't trust Wolf with the truth about the bet. He'd tell Savannah and not even mean to. It would just slip out, and that isn't a mess I want to clean up.

"Have you seen her or not?" I ask.

"Sorry, man. We were all watching back in catering, and she snuck off about twenty-five minutes in. Haven't seen her since. I just assumed she was waiting for you in gorilla."

"What about Rae?" I ask Brody.

"Rae and Jo already left," he says, shoulders lifting in a small shrug.

Breathing out in frustration, I turn on my heel to head for the locker room. If she wasn't in gorilla and she's not with our friends…she must have left for the hotel already. There's probably a text waiting on my phone. I need to get my head checked by Doc first, and then I can change and worry about why my girlfriend didn't tell me this was coming. I turn the last corner and see her standing outside Doc's office.

She's braced against the wall, arms crossed, and her eyes lift from the floor when she hears my footsteps. Her narrowed gaze travels over the line of blood on the side of my face and each red mark that litters my body before meeting mine. Her hands ball into fists in the crooks of her arms, like she's trying to keep herself from reaching out to me. She doesn't know how I'm going to react, and because of that, she keeps her distance.

"What in the hell was that?" I ask, not meaning to sound so harsh, but the longer my search for her went on, the more irritated I became. On the flip side, the longer it went on, the more I thought about *why* I was so irritated in the first place. If she had been honest with me, if she had told me this was happening, I wouldn't have cared. It was the element of surprise, doing it without warning, that pissed me off.

Savannah's only response is silence. She rolls her lips together and looks away.

"You didn't even try to tell me, Sav. You just...did it. Just like that."

She sighs, rubbing her face. "I couldn't tell you, John."

"You couldn't?" I practically spit the words. "Savannah, I'm your boyfriend! A little warning that you're going to turn on me would have been nice. And not just turn on me, you attacked me with a chair and then sat on me in said chair."

"And as my boyfriend, who is also in this industry, you *know* the rules. You know that if they tell me not to say something, I can't."

"There are certain times that doesn't fucking matter, Savannah."

Savannah exhales. "It's just business, *Brooks*."

Brooks? I scoff. She doesn't call me Brooks outside of the ring. "Just business?"

"Yes!" Savannah yells. "I wanted to tell you. I did. But Amos made it clear. No one was supposed to know. No one, but especially not you." She shakes her head. "They wanted you to be surprised. They wanted it to be realistic. You knew this was coming, Brooks. You knew everything—"

"Except *who* it was!"

Savannah pushes off the wall, stepping closer to me, but doesn't close the distance. "I did what I had to do, and it was just business. I thought you, of all people, would understand that."

My hands clench at my sides. Even though I know she's right, I need a few more minutes to cool off. I don't want to say something that will make things worse.

"I'll go," she says. "I'll let you get dressed, cool off a little, and we can talk more later...I wanted to check on you before I left." Finally, she closes the distance between us, kissing my cheek, and I relish in the feeling of her lips on my burning skin. When she pulls away, her fingers glide over my skin, pushing away the hair from my forehead to examine the cut before her gaze meets mine briefly. The whole interaction lasts less than ten seconds, and it leaves me wanting more when she steps away.

One final question pops into my head, and I have to ask before she's gone. Savannah looks over her shoulder when I call out to her. "Did you always know?"

"They told me yesterday, but Tim said it was always part of their plan." She shrugs, a soft smile gracing her lips before she leaves.

I slam my palm into the concrete wall at my side and immediately regret it as a sharp pain shoots up my arm. "Fuck!"

"That looked like it hurt," a voice says from behind me.

A humorless chuckle passes through me as I try to rub out the pain in my wrist. *You've got to be kidding me. This is the last fucking thing I need.*

"That's gotta sting, huh?" he continues.

"What do you want, Drake?" I ask between clenched teeth.

"You and I have a debt to settle, or did you forget?"

I kick off my shoes, leaving them by the door, when I walk into our room over an hour later. The air smells like vanilla and coconut with a hint of warm wood. It's thick and humid, even out here in the living space, from the hot shower she must have taken when she got back. I find her in bed with a book in her right hand. Her left toys with the end of the damp braid hanging over her shoulder. I drop my bag on the oversized armchair in the corner and sit on the edge of the bed. Warm, chocolate eyes lift from the page, and when we make eye contact, the book closes instantly.

"I'm sorry," I say quickly, and she looks taken aback. "I shouldn't...I know how this works, Sav, probably better than most. But in that moment...being in the middle of that ring, being on the receiving end of your attack, I forgot, and I took it out on you." I cautiously reach out to her, and a wave of relief washes over me when she doesn't pull away. "I'm sorry," I say, pressing a long kiss to the warm skin of her hand. "You are the most important thing to me, Savannah. You and you alone. Fuck the belt. Fuck the titles, the notoriety...Fuck it all. If I don't have you, then it doesn't mean anything."

"John, you don't mean that."

"Yes, I do. I love you, Savannah. I know we haven't been together that long, but I don't know how else to describe it."

"You love me?"

"I think I loved you since the moment I met you."

"Okay, now you're just sucking up," she says, and her laughter strikes a chord in my chest, making me smile.

There's no other way to describe the way I feel about her, and it's incredible, but also absolutely terrifying. There have been only a few women in my life I've loved, but getting to know Savannah has made me realize none of them ever came close to this.

"I love you, too, John."

The words draw my gaze up, and I don't waste another minute, pressing my lips to hers in soft, gentle pecks that are soon not enough. She must think the same because Savannah pulls my mouth to hers, and I push her back onto the mattress. I reach behind my back, fisting the fabric of my shirt and pulling it over my head. Her fingers ghost up my sides, sending a shiver down my spine, tracing over the black ink on my side.

"What is your tattoo for?"

"That's a loaded question," I say with a small huff, but it doesn't seem to faze her. Rolling to her side, I prop my head up on my elbow, and Savannah's left hand comes back to trace over the skin again, where the three railroad spikes form a cross. "It's part faith, but also part...survival. I've told you about my father. A good and faithful Christian on Sunday mornings, but the rest of the week, you never knew which version you were going to get. Watching him play the role, but not live the life, turned me away from my faith for a long time. When he kicked me out, I didn't understand how someone—how a father—could do that. And he told all of my friends' parents not to help me, made up some bullshit excuse to persuade them. It was one thing after another, and it made me hate him. Made me hate God. But then I worked my way across the country to Texas, got a job, found a wrestling promotion that would take me, and the rest, as they say, is history. As I got older—met more people—I realized sitting in a pew on Sunday morning, pretending to be someone else one day a week, isn't what faith is about. And while I've forgiven my father for everything that has happened, I'll never forget it."

"I'm sorry," she whispers.

"Don't be, Sweetheart. We all have crosses to bear. This just happens to be one of mine. Maybe one day, I'll get closure on everything, or maybe I won't. Who knows?"

"Well, when that day comes, if it comes, I'll be right there to help you through it."

Savannah cradles my face in her hands and presses a gentle kiss to my lips that turns hungry when she opens her mouth in invitation. I oblige, letting my tongue slip inside to tangle with hers in a desperate embrace. I hook my fingers into the waistband of her sweats and pull them down her legs. She gasps when I glide my finger over her slit.

"Shit," I hum, and part her with my fingers, watching her eyes roll into the back of her head. "You're so fucking wet already, Sav."

"Stop teasing," she demands. "I've waited long enough."

I stand at the edge of the bed, shoving my jeans down my legs, and her eyes lock in on my already hardened cock. "How do you want me to fuck you, baby?" I ask, stroking the head.

Savannah smirks. "Dealer's choice."

I wrap my arm around her waist when I climb back onto the bed, pulling her to straddle my hips. Savannah whimpers as the head teases her entrance and rocks her hips against mine. Bracing her palms on my chest, she digs her fingers into my pecs and leans down to kiss me. I bite down on her bottom lip and center my cock, pushing inside her. The anticipation is fucking brutal—it's been entirely too long since the last time I got lost inside her.

"You okay, Sweetheart?" I ask, but she doesn't answer verbally; instead, she slowly lowers herself until she is fully seated. She doesn't move for a few heartbeats, adjusting to the newfound fullness.

Savannah's body begins to move in slow waves, swallowing

my dick whole with each complete cycle, and it's heavenly. My hands find her hips, digging into the flesh but not forcing her to move any faster. I let her set the rhythm, set the pace, as she rocks against me. Her back curves, her hands grasping onto my legs, and her head falls back, the ends of her long braid tickling the tops of my thighs.

"Fuck. Just like that." I can't contain a soft whimper from the intense pleasure when she moves at this new angle. The view is breathtaking. She is breathtaking. I wish this could last forever. She sits up taller, her left hand coming up to squeeze her breast. Delicate fingers tweak and pinch her nipple, and all I can think about is doing the same damn thing.

Her hands fall to the comforter on either side of my head when she leans forward. The gentle brush of her nipples against my chest drives me fucking mad. I squeeze the doughy flesh of her left breast, kneading it before lifting it to my mouth. My tongue swirls over the pebbled bud of her nipple. A soft moan ripples through her when my teeth graze it, and then I soothe it with my tongue again. Over and over again, I draw out delicious sounds from her as she rides me.

My free hand roams her body, relearning every inch of the naturally tanned flesh I can touch, before I reach down to cup her ass.

Gripping her sides, I force her movements to quicken, force her pussy to slide up and down my dick at a brutal pace, taking in every last inch before I pull almost completely out again. She's close—I can feel it in the way she tightens around me.

I wrap my right hand around her throat, giving it a gentle squeeze. Nothing too hard, but enough pressure to hold her still. Our lips brush, but I never allow them to close the gap, and her breath comes out in heavy gasps.

"You feel so fucking good. So perfect. Like you were made just for me." She whimpers as I whisper the words. And the more praise I feed into her ear, the wetter she gets, her arousal dripping down between us. "You want to come on my cock, Savannah?" She nods, and I release her. "Then show me how bad you want it."

Savannah sits up, but instead of intensifying her movements, it feels like she slows down. Each roll of her body strokes every inch of my cock, and it drives me fucking wild. She slowly guides her hand down her abdomen, reaching between her legs to finger her clit, and the response from her body is immediate.

My name falls past her lips in a soft gasp, her movements stuttering. My fingers dig into the flesh of her sides, driving her forward through her orgasm. Her walls tighten around my cock as she comes undone above me.

Wrapping my arm around her waist, I roll us so I'm on top, and Savannah gasps when I push back inside her, hooking her ankles around my back. My nerves are on fire as she moves with me, matching each thrust with her own. "I'm close, Sweetheart," I whisper, and she whispers the same. Unbridled heat and ecstasy fill my veins when I pump into her one final time and crest the wave of my own orgasm. Her head falls back, mouth open in a voiceless moan as I come inside her. Her nails dig deeper into the skin of my shoulders, and I feel her walls clench around me at the start of another orgasm.

The feeling that follows is one that no word can truly express—euphoria, maybe? I collapse beside her, and she leans over to kiss me, soft and leisurely. Our mouths molding together, tongues tangled in a slow embrace meant to relish the moment, not rush it. Her nails scrape gently across my scalp as we lie like that for a while, catching our breath and enjoying the high.

I meet her contented stare when we part, and I beg, "Say it again."

Savannah's thumb grazes across my lips, then traces the

line of my jaw with her finger, touch as light as a feather. When she looks up to meet my gaze once again, she whispers, "I love you, John."

The words clench my heart. That's all I've wanted to hear from the moment I saw her in NextGen two years ago. Gathering her fingers in my hand, I bring the tip of each one to my lips before planting a brief kiss on her lips. "I am so glad you decided to break that rule."

19

Savannah

TUESDAY, APRIL 14, 2015
TAMPA, FL

The humid Florida air smacks me in the face the moment I step out of the Tampa airport. It's thick and heavy, already coating my skin in a thin layer of perspiration, a stark contrast to the bitter cold I left behind in Salt Lake City. I hoped it would be a little cooler here, considering it's still early—hardly eight in the morning—but no such luck. Raelynn gave me a ride to the airport on Sunday, which means I have to take a cab home unless I want to walk. Rae hadn't anticipated Brody asking her on a date last night, or I would've never ridden with her, but who was I to stand in the way of their long-anticipated shot at love? It's only taken five years and three failed relationships between the two of them, including Rae and Nash, who broke up almost five months ago. She and my brother started dating at the end of 2012, despite my warnings to him that it would be hard, considering our schedules. They were good together, but I think she and Brody are better suited.

I glance at the cab station, where there are zero cabs. *Fantastic.* Of course, there wouldn't be any cabs the one time I need one. I'm tired, I'm starving, and I'm in desperate need of a coffee. I wonder if I can convince whatever cabbie picks me up to stop for one. I'll even buy him one. Yes, I could walk back into the airport and get one, overpriced chain coffee where they burn the beans. I want an iced coffee, medium ice, with a thin layer of vanilla cold foam, and the best place to get that is at Cream & Sugar, the coffee shop four minutes and thirty-seven seconds from our house. I discovered it accidentally a few months after I moved into John's house, not long after Wrestlefest XXX, and now I go almost every day we're home.

"Looks like you need a ride." Normally, a random man shouting something like this at me wouldn't end well... for him, but the sound of *his* voice stops me in my tracks. I must be dreaming because he's not supposed to be here. He's supposed to be in Canada, but the bite from my nails embedded into my palms tells me this isn't a dream.

My heart skips a beat when I turn on my heel and see him standing there. Dropping my bags, I sprint straight into his arms, wrapping my arms and legs securely around him. A deep inhale fills my lungs with the warm scent of him— earthy scents of blue cypress and vetiver—and he chuckles when I tighten my grip.

"I missed you, too, Sweetheart." John kisses me, and I can't hold back a hum of sweet satisfaction, feeling his lips on mine. It's been two weeks since I last saw him. Two weeks since I dropped him off at this exact airport to fly north of the border for a guest role on some television show that neither of us watches, but that sounded like fun, regardless. He wasn't scheduled to come home until Thursday. What is he doing here?

"What are you doing here?" I ask, pulling back to look in his eyes. His hair is slightly longer than when he left, and there's scruff on his chin. "I thought you weren't coming back until—"

"They didn't need me as long as they thought," he says with a soft smile. "I got in a couple of hours ago. Brody mentioned he and Rae were sticking around Salt Lake, so I thought I'd surprise you." Instead of answering, I embrace him again, burying myself in the crook of his neck. "I brought coffee."

My grip immediately loosens, and my feet fall to the pavement, walking toward the Jeep of their own accord. I hear him chuckle behind me before he opens the door, revealing the same iced coffee I'd been dreaming of not two minutes ago. "God, I love you," I say before taking a long sip.

We've been together for over three years, and every day I fall more in love with this man than I was the day before—even days he makes me so mad I could cuss him up one side and down the other. But I don't...Usually.

"Ready to go home?" John asks. His fingers thread through the belt loops of my jeans, tugging me into him again.

"Only if that means you'll scratch this itch I've had for the last two weeks."

His brows shoot up, and the twinkle in his eye makes me giggle. "You didn't even have to ask."

"What are you doing?" Warm hands fall on my shoulders, and he kisses the top of my head. We spent all of yesterday wrapped in each other, making up for the time we'd spent apart, but that meant I had work to do when I woke up this morning. I left him wrapped in the sheets to get some work done in preparation for Wrestlefest next week. This year, I'll be facing *Lyla Santiago*, the former female commentator who recently returned to the company while Scott Harrington was on a short leave of absence. This will be the first of two big matches between us. The story is dumb, revolving around me confronting *Lyla* for saying some not-so-nice things about me on air, but it keeps me on television, and that's all I care about at the moment. Was it common for commentators to get involved in a storyline? No, but they wanted to do something drastic in welcoming her back to the company.

Not long after I joined the corporate faction—*The Corporation*—three years ago, alongside *Chelsea, Colin, Nohea Nokoa, Asher Slade,* and later *Theo*, I won the women's title for a second time. What can I say? Going along with their ideas had some perks, including becoming the longest-reigning EWE Women's Champion. Two years ago, I surpassed Juliet's record of two hundred and seventy-three days, and moments before I was set to break the record, *Moxie* returned to answer my challenge, ready to dethrone me seconds before I could make history. I retained my title and cemented my name in the history books. Almost two months later, at the June premiere event, High Voltage, I lost the title to *Cali "The Diamond" Kennedy*—or Callista Kennedy, daughter of Clarence Kennedy and Holly Graham, two EWE legends. Since then, it's been random matches here and there, but no big storylines, so when they presented the one with Lyla, I latched onto it.

"Going over some stuff for next weekend," I say, craning my neck to look up at my boyfriend. John stares at the screen where I've been watching some of Harper's old matches, since she will be ringside to aid Lyla. "I'm glad you're here, though, because we need to talk about *this* weekend."

"This weekend?"

A week from today marks the fifth year since my debut, but that's not what we're meant to be celebrating. No, this weekend, we're celebrating John's decade-long tenure with the company. He made his official debut on April 4, 2005, against none other than *"The Great" Fata*, and while John wasn't exactly a fan favorite in the beginning, I think it's safe to say that's no longer true. He was out of town on the actual anniversary, so the plan is to celebrate when everyone is home, but it's been like pulling teeth to get him to sit down and talk to me about it.

"Is this about my tenth? Savannah, I told you—"

"John, this is a big deal. It's your tenth anniversary with the company! Why don't you want to celebrate that?"

"I don't need some big, elaborate party or whatever. I'd be happy with just you, me, and a nice dinner." He plants a quick peck on my lips and smiles at me, but it doesn't reach his eyes. Something is bothering him, and it's not just this anniversary discussion. I noticed it yesterday, too. The distant look in his eyes when he thought I wasn't looking. The way his smile barely lifted the corners of his lips before he forced it to. "Hell, we can even make dinner here. I'd be perfectly fine with that, too."

"What if we do dinner here and we invite—"

"I don't want to, Savannah!" The outburst shocks me, and I swallow back the rest of my sentence. John deflates, his shoulders falling with a heavy sigh, and he pinches the bridge of his nose. "I don't want any of it, Sav. I just...Just let it go." His eyes meet mine from across the room. "Please."

"Okay, if that's really what you want...I'll let it go," I say, forcing my jaw to unclench. I don't want to make this a bigger fight than it is. I don't need to. It's not my party, it's not my anniversary, it's his. And if he really doesn't want to do something, then we won't. "But if you'll excuse me, I have work to do."

John stares at me for a moment longer, and without another word, he exhales and walks out of my office.

I heave the brown paper bag onto the island and pull a wine bottle from the wine cooler John had installed in the island base not long after I moved in. Was it completely necessary? No. Am I a fan, regardless? Yes, yes, I am.

I spent more time than I anticipated working before Rae called to ask if I wanted to meet for some ring time. She returned from Salt Lake City last night, and I knew she was dying to share all the details. While I wanted to hear everything, I also knew getting in the ring would be a good way to rid the leftover tension I felt after whatever that was this morning.

Something is bothering John. That much is obvious, but for the life of me, I can't figure out what. There's no way the idea of having a small get-together with our friends elicited that kind of response. Something else is going on, and I have every intention of figuring out what...starting with take-out from his favorite restaurant.

The front door opens and closes in the distance. His footsteps echo through the quiet house as I pop the cork from the bottle. Filling only the bottom of the glass, I lightly grip the base and move it in slow, circular motions. The dark ruby liquid swirls, and the legs bleed down until the puddle forms again. I inhale the aromas of black cherry, vanilla, and oak before taking a small sip. He shuffles into the kitchen, still dressed in his gym clothes, but doesn't say anything as I pour a generous amount into two glasses. Lifting mine to my lips, I stare at him over the rim and wait.

Downcast eyes finally meet mine, and the moisture behind them almost breaks my resolve. He blinks it away and swallows the tension in his throat before he takes a breath and steps up to the island. "I'm sorry." I don't say anything in return. I've learned that it's best to let him get it all out before I jump in. "I shouldn't have snapped at you earlier. You—You're just trying to do something nice, and I—I know I was being an asshole. You're right, it is a big deal, and I didn't mean to belittle that, or make you think I was belittling it. I'm not, I'm ecstatic about it. I'm grateful for it, but I'm just not in the mood to celebrate...Not right now."

"We don't have to do anything outside of dinner tonight if you don't want to," I say.

"But you—"

"I want to do what *you* want, John." With a cautious step forward, I leave a small space between us, but he takes my hand, pulling me the rest of the way. "This is your anniversary, not mine. And if this is all you want, that's fine with me. I'm sorry for being pushy." I smile, letting my fingers caress the side of his face, and catch his eye. "However," I draw out. "I want you to tell me what's bothering you."

His blue eyes widen. "What?"

"John, something is bothering you. Try as you might, you're not very good at hiding it," I say.

He takes a step back, just out of my reach, and scrubs a hand down his face. "I, uh...I got a call from Ari." That doesn't sound so bad. "Yesterday, right before I picked you up, she called to tell me that our father asked about me." *Their father...What the hell*? The question must be written clearly on my face because John scoffs, nodding. "I guess...I guess she's been meeting up with him recently. The most recent time was Sunday, and he asked about me. Asked her if I'd be open to meeting with him. I don't...This man kicked me out at seventeen and told me not to come back if I couldn't man up and stop chasing stars. He's the same one who packed up and left the day my sister turned eighteen. Now, he wants to try to mend fences out of the blue."

"Why didn't he reach out to you himself?" I ask.

"He doesn't have any way to contact me. That's why Ari told me, because he asked for my number, but she wouldn't give it to him without talking to me first."

"What do you want to do?" I ask after a moment.

"I don't know. And I feel terrible that I took this out on you, because you don't deserve that, Sweetheart. You were trying to do something nice, and I—I was an asshole. I had just gotten home, just gotten you back, and the last thing I wanted to think about was Leeland Cabot. I planned on telling you this morning, but then—"

"We started talking about the anniversary." I sigh and close the space between us, draping my arms over his shoulders, loosely threading my fingers together. "I think you should go meet him." John's gaze snaps up from the floor, brow furrowed. He starts to argue, but I interrupt him. "You've never gotten closure, John. Everything that happened between you and your dad is still an open wound. I'm not saying you have to forgive him or even be okay with his reasoning, but at least you can close the door on this once and for all. You can try to move on."

"I have moved on."

"Your reaction to this news says otherwise."

A deep inhale matches the heavy exhale that follows, and I wait for his rebuttal—some reason why meeting with his father is a bad idea, despite it being the only way he'll be able to move on. I'm shocked when a small smile crosses his lips. Not exactly how I imagined this going, but let's see how it plays out. He leans down to kiss me and says, "You're right. I know you're right, and I think that's what has been the hardest part of this. I'll never get over it without confronting him."

"Did she say when he wanted to meet?"

"Saturday." John chuckles when my eyes grow at least three times their size. His father wants to meet on *Saturday*? That's in three days, and just so happens to be the same day I had planned to host the anniversary dinner. Then we have to be in Boston on Sunday night or early Monday morning at the latest. That's not a lot of time. "Ari has been texting me all day asking if I changed my mind."

"I think you should go."

"Savannah—"

"If you don't, it will be on your mind all week leading into Wrestlefest. You don't need this kind of distraction with your match next week. Call Ari back and tell her you'll meet him on Saturday."

John sighs, but nods. He doesn't have a choice. The last thing he needs is something like this weighing him down when he has a cage match against *Nohea Nakoa* and *Colin Ryker* next Sunday. It's his first title shot in two years, and the last thing I want is for it to be messed up because of his father. "What would I do without you?"

A quiet hum escapes me before I smile. "Crash and burn."

John searches the parking lot until he finds the furthest space from the front door. The address Ari sent three days ago led us to a luxury residential community and country club in a northern suburb of Indianapolis. When we pulled up to the front gate, it reminded me of our neighborhood in Crystal Bay, except Sycamore Farms is surrounded by an expansive rolling countryside, farmland, and built-to-last homesteads. After he came clean about his father's request, my boyfriend returned to his normal self. We spent our days off lounging by the pool, having dinner at our favorite restaurants, and enjoying morning strolls to Cream & Sugar. Until this morning...John hasn't been himself from the moment he woke up, and I'm starting to worry that maybe I shouldn't have pushed him to do this.

John doesn't turn off the car, and his hands grip the

steering wheel so tightly that his knuckles turn white. His eyes are glued to the double doors of the red brick building at the other end of the parking lot.

"You don't have to do this," I say

"But you think I should."

I reach over to gently pull his gaze away from the door to meet mine. He leans into my touch, even briefly returning a small smile. "Do I think this will give you the closure you need? Yes, I do. But it's not my decision, John. You need to do what's best for you, and if that means getting on a plane and flying to Boston without so much as a word to Leeland Cabot...then, so be it."

Gnawing on his bottom lip, his blue eyes search my cheeks before his breath fans across my face in a deep sigh. John sits back in the driver's seat and runs a hand through his hair. He clutches the key for a brief moment, long enough to count five Mississippis before he kills the engine.

When we walk through the front door of the clubhouse, I feel like I'm backstage, watching him transform from John Brooks to *Brooks Taylor*. His shoulders push back a little further, as if attached to a string pulled taut, almost at its breaking point. His face falls into a thin line, and his eyes scan every inch of the hallway we walk down, ignoring the patrons who stop and stare. Wide gazes reveal what's going through their minds before they recompose themselves.

"Should we come up with a safe word?" I ask.

"What did you have in mind?" His words are tense, eyes now fixated on the French doors that showcase the foyer of the restaurant. A shiplap white desk sits before a wall of faux greenery, and blue-gray drapes hang on the back side of either door. *Fuzzy's on 18th* hangs over the door's blue-gray painted doorframe in gold script.

"I'm thinking kumquat."

John laughs—a real laugh—and halts our steps mere feet

from the entrance. When he looks down at me, I get a glimpse of the man behind the mask. "Kumquat, huh?"

"It's just different enough not to come up in conversation, but not too odd that it would seem weird if we say it."

John breathes out another soft laugh before he leans down to kiss me. "Kumquat it is, then."

"You ready?"

"I'm ready to be done with this," he says, resting his hand on my lower back.

The host offers us a tight smile and asks for the member's name when we walk inside. He leads us through a maze of tables, past the bar, and into a separate room that overlooks the golf course. The windows along the back wall are open, letting in the beautiful spring day before the rain showers that are supposed to roll in this evening. Every table along the windows is filled, but even from here, I know which one we're headed for.

A man occupies the table at the far left end. He's pressed his back far into the corner of the room, but leaves enough space to get a full view of the outside. His eyes scan across the newspaper in his hands, but even from here, I know they are a similar color to those of the man at my side. Actually, there are a lot of similarities between the two men—their broad, square jawlines, prominent chins, bushy eyebrows, and slightly bulbous noses.

"Mr. Cabot," the host says, catching his attention. "Your guests have arrived."

Leeland folds the paper in half three times before slapping it down on the table and standing. "Well, I'll be damned. You really showed up." A wide smile spreads across his thin lips, and he juts out his hand toward John, who doesn't so much as look at it. "Oh, c'mon, boy. Shake your ol' man's hand. That's one of the first things they teach you in that circus you call a job, isn't it?"

Shit. I sigh. We didn't even make it five minutes.

"You must be Sarah," Leeland says, turning his attention to me when John still refuses to shake his hand.

"It's *Savannah*," John answers for me.

"Oh, right. Savannah. You're a pretty thing, aren't you? Remind me of my last ex-wife, Holly."

Is that supposed to be a compliment? And, who's Holly? John never mentioned her. How many ex-wives does this man have?

"Sit, please. Make yourselves comfortable," Leeland says and motions at the table.

I count to three before John finally relents. He pulls out the chair between them, allowing me to sit, before he chooses the one to my right, giving him an open view of the entire space. I reach my hand out to him, and he takes it, bringing my knuckles to his lips.

"I have to be honest, I wasn't sure you were going to show," his father says, bringing the white coffee mug to his lips. "Ariana said you agreed to meet, but I had my doubts."

"I highly considered asking the pilot to turn around well before we landed." John looks bored, but his grip on my hand tells a different story.

"There's that famous John sense of humor I've missed all these years."

"Don't call me that," John says.

His scoffs. "That is your name, isn't it?"

"The only person allowed to call me by that name is the woman sitting next to me."

Leeland stares at his son through the narrowed slits of his eyes, biting down on his bottom lip, and slowly, a smile lifts the corners of his mouth. I've seen that look before. It's the same one *Brooks Taylor* displays when he's challenged by an opponent. After a moment, Leeland blinks his gaze away from John toward me. "Are you hungry, Savannah? The special today is delicious, one of my favorites—a kumquat chicken dish with a special kumquat hoisin sauce over rice."

John's hand stiffens in mine. I clench my jaw to keep from laughing, refusing to meet his stare that burns into the side of my face. You've got to be kidding. Of all the things...Fucking *kumquat* chicken.

"No, thank you, Mr. Brooks," I say, clearing my throat.

"Leeland, please," he says, briefly glancing at our joined hands now on the table. "So, how did you two meet?"

"I'm sure Ariana already filled you in," John answers a little too quickly. "Not that it's any of your business."

"If you're going to be this difficult, you can just leave now."

My heart drops, and a frost coats my insides like a winter's morning on the farm.

John scoffs. "You haven't changed a damn bit."

"On the contrary, John. I have changed, it's you who still hasn't grown up. You're the same, whiny little shit you've always been. I'm sure you told her"—Leeland motions toward me—"all about how mean and nasty I was, leaving out what an absolute nightmare you were to raise."

I can't contain my gasp.

"You were an insolent child who always had to have the last word, and I couldn't stand you. You thought you knew better than everyone, and your grandmother only made it worse because she coddled you and your sister. But I made sure there was food on the table, a roof over your head, and clothes on your back. You had the world at your fingertips. You could have done anything, been *anything*, and you chose to run around in tights for the rest of your life. What kind of a man does that?"

John's head bobs as he skates his tongue across his front teeth before rolling his lips between them. "Are you done?"

The server appears with a fresh glass of what I assume is whiskey, based on the sweet aroma mixed with a hint of cinnamon, setting it before Leeland. *Glad to see we're starting early*. He flips open a padded black notebook and clicks his pen, as if blind to the heightened tension radiating off the table in seismic waves. His mouth opens, ready to begin his spiel, but I interrupt him, "Can you give us a few minutes?" His brow furrows, but he stuffs the notebook into his cream-colored apron with an eye roll.

John waits until the kid is gone to say, "You may have provided monetarily, but you were never a father. None of what you just said makes up for the shit you put us through. You weren't the one taking care of Ariana. You weren't the one making sure Mom got out of bed and ate every day. You weren't the one picking up the pieces of our shattered lives every time you and Mom got into an argument because you refused to leave. We would've been better off without you."

"Better off? That's funny, because from what I hear, your mother still doesn't have a job. She freeloads off of you and Grandma Aggie. If it weren't for the two of you, she'd be on the damn street. Just like you would've been had I left."

"Whatever helps you sleep at night, Leeland."

"You are just like your mother," John's father says. "At least Ariana has the decency to show me some respect." That earns a scoff from his son. "There was a time when we were close, John."

"That was before I learned what a narcissist you are."

"I'm the narcissist? You're the one who went into show business." Leeland chuckles, folding his arms, the white knit polo tight across his chest. "And from what I hear, you were more than happy to step on anyone who got in your way to the top. You didn't care who you hurt as long as it ended with your name in lights. Heard you fucked the boss's daughter, too."

"There are a lot of things that I did in the beginning of my career that I regret, but the one thing I can say that I never did is sleep with Chelsea Rafferty."

"Oh, that's right, I forgot. You prefer fresh meat," Leeland says, and turns his gaze on me. "Or is it the other way around? Are you using him to get what you want?"

John's hand slams down on the table, rattling the table settings. "Don't you fucking talk to her like that. Savannah and I knew each other well before she came to EWE, and I'll be damned—"

"Down, boy. I'm just curious what the dynamic is here. She's obviously younger than you and newer to the business. Sleeping with the face of the company has its perks, I'm sure."

"I didn't need his star power to become one," I say, and from the corner of my eye, I see John's mouth lift.

"What do you want, Leeland?" John asks after a moment, sounding more confident than he did before. "Because from where I'm sitting, this feels more like a setup than an apology."

His father chuckles, unwinding his arms to fold his hands together on the table as he leans in. "And what am I supposed to be apologizing for?"

20

Savannah

TUESDAY, NOVEMBER 22, 2016

CELESTIA, TX

Frost-tipped blades crunch beneath my feet as I walk the distance between the main house and the chicken coop. The sun barely peeks over the distant hills, turning the sky into a watercolor canvas of orange, red, and yellow. I tug my oversized flannel coat tighter around my frame as the wind whips across the open field. The air has a slight bite to it this morning, and it isn't supposed to get much warmer, according to the weatherman, but I don't care. The cold is a welcome friend compared to the weather we've been traveling in recently, making it officially feel like fall.

I've missed this. I never thought I'd say that, but I've missed the simplicity of this life. Not enough to give up what I have now, but enough to admit it—if only to myself.

Mere feet from the coop, a flame spreads across my skin when fingers wrap around my hand and thread through mine. He pulls me back two steps and stoops down to press a gentle kiss against my lips. "Good morning, Sweetheart," he murmurs against me, and I hum in response. "You're up early."

"Wanted to grab breakfast with Papá," I say. "You were knocked out, so I let you sleep."

John is dressed in the same black sweatpants that hung low on his hips last night before he lured me into bed. He barely moved this morning, only stirring slightly when I lifted his arm from around my waist.

"There's coffee inside, and I'm sure Mamá has started making breakfast for you before we have to leave to pick up Ari and Sam from the airport."

"I'll join her inside, then," he says, pulling me in for another kiss. This time, however, he pulls my chest against his and slips his left arm around my waist. His other hand cradles mine against his heart. Before I know it, we're moving in a slow circle across the frozen ground. Questions fill my mind, starting with *What in the hell are we doing*? But I can't voice them. I'm too captivated by the blue eyes staring down at me and the way the sun casts a warm glow on his face, highlighting the dusted freckles across his nose. The same ones that typically blend in with his skin, only standing out when you're right in front of him.

I laugh when he spins me out and then pulls me back in, and his warm breath tickles the side of my face. We gently sway, still wrapped in each other, as the sun now crests the hills and trees.

"What would you say if I asked you to marry me?" There's no hesitation in his voice, only soft intrigue.

"Well, that depends," I say, leaning a little further into his embrace. "Are you asking?"

"As tempting as going to the courthouse sounds...I think I'd rather do it the right way."

"A courthouse wedding isn't the right way?"

"Yes, it is," John says, before kissing my temple. "But I want to do this whole thing the right way. I want to give you the wedding you deserve. One day, Savannah, I'm going to ask you to marry me, maybe today,"—he squeezes me gently—"maybe tomorrow, or maybe in a month from now. And—"

"So, let's do it, John. Let's get married tomorrow when your mom and Grandma Aggie get here. It would be simple and easy—"

"The complete opposite of our everyday lives."

"That's why it's perfect."

He chuckles. "We could get married in a back alley somewhere dressed in brown paper bags for all I care, but it's not what you want, Sav."

"All I need is you."

His chest rises and falls against my back with a heavy breath before he turns me around to face him. "I want to give you everything you want, whether it's a full wedding or the—"

"And what about what *you* want? What about what you've always dreamed of?"

"I'm looking at it," he says, and I can't help but roll my eyes playfully.

"You are so corny."

"My only request is that you're the one walking down the aisle that day." John brings my knuckles to his lips. "I want to do it all, Sweetheart. Pick the perfect shade of maroon from thirty different shades, because it will obviously be a fall wedding; decide which linens have just the right pattern and texture; stress about the seating chart, because it would be a disaster if my cousin Tommy ends up anywhere near the Raffertys; hand-select the perfect invitation design; and taste a million different cakes until we're sick to our stomachs. I want it to be everything you've ever dreamed of—"

"It sounds like torture," I say, with a soft laugh.

"Hey, at least we don't have to scout locations. We have the perfect one right in front of us. It's where you've always wanted to get married. Right here, at Willow Pond."

Tears prick the corner of my eyes. He remembers that?

I think I've only mentioned that once. Somewhere between our third and fourth dance at Moxie's wedding—a beautiful ceremony on the cliffs of New England between her and Nic Swanson, her long-time boyfriend and a former wrestler who retired after a career-ending neck injury—John asked me where I wanted to get married. I told him Willow Pond Farm was the only backdrop I'd ever imagined. But that was...That was four years ago.

"Let me do this for you, Sweetheart," John says.

"You do more for me than I've ever done for you."

"That's not true." A breathy laugh fills the space between us in a warm, misty cloud. He tucks a few loose strands from my braid behind my ear before his fingers trail down my jaw. "I don't need a piece of paper to know how much you love me or how much I love you, but I want it. And one day, Savannah, I am going to ask you to marry me."

"Guess I'll just have to keep waiting, then," I say, with an exaggerated sigh.

He rolls his eyes and leans in for a kiss. Our lips brush just as a loud rooster's crow sounds behind us. John sighs. "That damn chicken."

"Oh, don't be like that, Buddy loves you." I try to bite back a giggle, only to fail as his brow rises to meet his hairline.

Buddy the Chicken is the oldest chicken we've ever had at the farm, and by far the nosiest. Over the years, he's had a knack for perfectly timed interruptions, especially when it comes to me and John.

Untangling myself from our embrace, I stuff my hands into my coat pockets, walking backward to the coop to collect eggs and clean it out. "Better get inside, Mamá has missed your mornings filled with coffee and contemplation."

"Are you done?" John asks, bringing the conversation to a halt. He glares over the table as one server clears away the dirtied plates and silverware while another sets the black checkbook in front of him. "Because I am."

We just spent two whole hours listening to his sister tell us—in excruciating detail—about the vacation she and her fiancé had taken with none other than Leeland Cabot. That's right, she and Samuel are joining us straight off the plane from Cabo, Mexico, where they just spent a week with John's father and his girlfriend. Sorry, his *fiancée*—I always forget that.

Leeland invited us, too, but my boyfriend sent a simple *No, thanks. We're good* in reply to the group text. John and I had work, and I knew better than to push him when he told me about it over dinner later that night. Over the last month, Ari has called more times than I can count—at least once a day—up until the day she left, begging him to reconsider. And now, that same energy is being used to try and convince her big brother to attend their father's wedding...on New Year's Eve...in Hawaii. After our luncheon with Leeland last April, John made it clear that he had no desire to see his father again. However, his sister has yet to receive the message.

"Ari, let me say this as simply as I can...I don't care."

"Brooks—"

"I *don't* care," he says, interrupting her. "And I hope you got it out of your system because I don't want to hear about Cabo or Leeland or the wedding again. We're not going, just like we didn't go to Cabo. I want nothing to do with him."

I slide my hand across the white linen and retrieve the checkbook, slipping our joint credit card inside and handing it to the server with an apologetic smile.

"Does Mom know you went on this trip?"

Samuel scoffs, earning a glare from Ari. "Don't look at me like that," her fiancé says. "I told you this was gonna come back and bite you in the ass."

"Where does she think you've been the last week?" John asks.

"With Samuel's family," Ari says.

The server returns the bill to me and I sign it, keeping a close eye on my boyfriend as he simmers. I'm shocked he let her go on as long as he did, but it was better she get it out now before Debra and Grandma Aggie arrive. Speaking of... we need to get a move on if we're going to be at the airport on time.

John rolls his lips between his teeth, glare narrowing on his sister. "Ari, I'm warning you. Do not bring this up again, but especially not around Mom."

Ari huffs, straightening in her chair. "Fine, but only if you promise to consider going to the wedding."

"Not gonna happen."

"C'mon, Dad really wants you there."

"I don't care what he wants."

"Careful, big brother," Ari says, tossing her napkin on the table. "You're starting to sound just like him."

I gasp as she leaves without another word, and Sam sighs before pushing up from the table to follow her. John's gaze is fixated on her retreating figure, but the emotion from moments ago has been completely replaced by something far more dangerous: betrayal.

"Good morning, Debra," I say, joining her on the porch with two steaming mugs of coffee. She glances up from her book, eyes narrowed behind tortoise-shell eyeglasses. She's been out here almost all morning. I first noticed her on my way in from the barn with Papá earlier. We got up earlier than usual to finish daily chores before Thanksgiving dinner preparations. That was two hours ago.

Our families aren't exactly…cohesive. No, I take that back; John's mother isn't cohesive with *my* family. Or me.

When John called to invite her to Celestia for the holiday, she was quick to make an excuse for her planned absence. "Your grandmother can't make the trip," she said, but unfortunately for his mom, he'd already called Grandma Aggie, and she was over the moon.

I think Debra's issue is me, but she'd never admit it. Or maybe she's so engrossed in her tormented past that she fears her children might go through the same thing she did—a loveless marriage with a partner who held her hostage for over half her life—and she doesn't want to get attached. Or maybe her concern for her elderly mother *is* the reason she didn't want to travel. Whatever it was, she always prefers to stay home, and anytime she's forced to join us, she spends the majority of the time in quiet solitude.

"I figured you could use some fresh coffee, and my mother set aside a plate for you," I say, extending the mug to her. Her only response is a curt smile. I sigh, placing the mug on the handcrafted table next to her, preparing to leave, but I don't even make it two steps before the filter between my brain and my mouth disappears. "Do you hate me?"

Okay, maybe hate is a little extreme, but what other word should I use?

Debra glances up, looking even more annoyed than she did a moment ago, if that's possible. When I don't back down, she closes her book with a small huff and her long, bony fingers thread together in a tight knot on top of its deep turquoise-colored cover. "I don't *hate* you, Savannah."

"But you don't like me."

She sighs, briefly glancing down at her hands. "I think

you're just like the others. Only you've managed to stick around longer than they did." What is that supposed to mean? "And you know, I find it peculiar, Savannah. You don't have a ring on your finger, but—"

"Excuse me?"

"Remind me. How many years have you been dating my son? Four? And still nothing." Debra rises from the couch, her arms crossing tightly over her chest. Her brown eyes flicker down to my hands that clutch the now lukewarm mug. "And truthfully, I think that makes you...lucky."

Lucky?

"You still have time to get out before it's too late. Marriage is not everything it's cracked up to be. It only brings out the worst in you...and your partner. It forces women to bend until they break, because that's what society expects out of us. Men are nothing but liars and cheats, all of them."

"Maybe in your experience, but not mine," I say.

"Oh, that's right, I forgot. Your parents are living the perfect fairytale," Debra says, with a slight scoff. "They've truly set you up to fail."

"You know nothing about my family, and you don't know your son. John is nothing like this father—"

"Wrong. He is exactly like his father."

"Your son has done nothing but love and care for you. He's made sure you have everything you need, everything you want. And you treat him like it's his fault you're in this situation. The only person to blame for your unhappiness, Debra, is you."

Her laugh catches me off guard. "He really has his hooks in you so deep that you can't see the truth. Or you refuse to. He's controlling you, Savannah. He controls everything about you and your life. Mark my words, one day, you're going to wake up and realize you're trapped with no way out, not until he's done with you."

"Careful, Debra," I say, with a tight smile. "Someone might think you're jealous, maybe even a little worried that when he does put a ring on my finger, I'll put a stop to the exploitation of your son." Her eyes narrow into slits. "John is *nothing* like his father, and you might know that if you took the time to get to know him, instead of pretending like every man is just another Leeland Cabot. Did you ever stop to consider that maybe you're the problem?"

A soft gasp echoes the way her eyes widen.

Did I take it too far? Maybe, but that didn't make it any less true.

"Now, if you'll excuse me, they need help preparing dinner. You're welcome to join us, but I know being pleasant and present isn't your strong suit. So, by all means, enjoy your solitude."

Turning on my heel, I head back for the door because my mother, Grandma Aggie, and Ari are waiting for me. John joined Nash on a ride out to check on the cattle so my oldest brother could go pick up his girlfriend and former high school sweetheart, Amara. This will be her first official Williams family holiday since they started dating again before she and Crew join her family later. My father is out near the garage with the twins and Samuel, trying their hands at deep-frying turkeys. There is a lot to do if we want to eat before nine o'clock. I don't have time for Debra's pity party. If she wants to continue to confine herself to the corners of every room she's in, trapped in her grief and despair, fine. But I'll be damned if she's going to drag her son down with her.

"Savannah." Debra's voice stills my hand as I grasp the doorknob. "For your sake, I hope you're right about him."

"Bird looks good, Pa," Crew says, carrying in a large bowl filled to the brim with mashed potatoes—not the kind you get out of a bag, either, these are the real thing—and the matching gravy boat. The twins follow suit with dishes full of fresh brussels sprouts, squash, asparagus, and green bean casserole. Amara carries the macaroni and cheese she helped me make—her first attempt at making it from scratch. Nash holds the overflowing plate of stuffing—which might be the only thing prepared from a box—and the adjoining kitchen door for John. He brings the ham my mother made for Debra, since she doesn't like turkey, along with cranberries, cranberry sauce, and candied yams to the table. Hot on his heels, Ariana tries to talk to her brother, but he ignores her the whole way, and her fiancé follows with the salad bowl and an eye roll.

John gives me a grateful smile when I lift the cranberries from his forearm. After he unloads the rest onto the table, he wraps his fingers around the base of my neck, pulling me in for a long kiss on my temple. "I love you," he whispers.

"Brooks," Ari says, interrupting us, and my boyfriend sighs. "Why won't you—"

"Ariana," he snaps, pulling away from me.

Nash meets my gaze across the table, slowly setting down the dish in his hands. My brother glances briefly at John, then back at me, and I shake my head.

Stay out of it, Nash.

"I told you yesterday, I am *done* discussing this. It doesn't matter how many times you ask, my answer isn't going to change," John says.

"Why can't you just do this for me?" Ari pleads, her voice morphing into a whine.

"Because just like you, Ariana, I can make my own decisions. And it's my choice not to be around him. You want to put yourself in the position to get your heart broken again?

Be my guest. But don't say I didn't warn you."

"He's different—"

"Enough," John hisses. He takes a deep breath, pinching the bridge of his nose as he tries to collect himself. "This is not the time or the place for this conversation."

There's no room for more debate when the others reemerge from the kitchen, including his mother and grandmother.

Aside from the cold shoulder John gives his sister—especially when she almost slips about Cabo—and the strained answers from Debra whenever my parents attempt to draw her into the conversation, dinner goes by without a hitch. We learned that Blake recently passed his journeyman exam to become an electrician, and he started dating a girl named Sarah. Bodhi broke up with his girlfriend (Laura, I think?) last week, and law school has taken up the majority of his life, much to his dismay. As for the other Williams children? Not much has changed.

"Savannah," Papá says, catching my attention at the head of the table. "Did you decide if you're going to re-sign with EWE, yet?"

Except that.

"We're working a few things out," I say.

My contract is set to expire at the beginning of next month—December 5th, to be exact. The day after Wreck the Halls, the December premiere live event, before we head to Europe for two weeks. The company and I have been negotiating for at least a month now, mostly about salary. I'd be more willing to bend on the other things if they'd compromise on the financial side. When I initially received my new contract, I was surprised by how much they were trying to lowball me. Even before I discussed it with John, I decided to attempt renegotiations.

"Getting close?" My father asks.

"Maybe."

"You're one of their biggest draws. Why wouldn't they want to pay you more?" Nash asks.

"Not to mention, you're basically married to the face of the company," Blake adds, and I roll my eyes. "Isn't there something he can do? Is there something you can do?"

"We don't—"

"Savannah and I try to keep our business lives separate," John says, answering for me. Why did he interrupt me? I was about to say the same thing.

"Not to mention—"

"Not to mention, Amos will ultimately give her whatever she wants. He loves her, and there isn't a chance in hell that he'll ever let her walk away."

"Add a private jet to the list of demands, SJ," my oldest brother says, earning a chuckle from the table.

I can only offer him a tight smile before I catch Debra's gaze from across the table. Her raised brow over the rim of her wine glass tells me exactly what she's thinking. I tear my gaze from hers to look at John, who also noticed her suspicious glance.

"Who's ready for dessert?" Mamá asks. "We have flan, pumpkin pie, apple pie..." She continues naming other options, and slowly the table empties as everyone carries their plates to the sink before choosing a dessert.

John gathers my dishes, leaning down to plant a kiss on top of my head before he disappears into the kitchen, Samuel following suit. That leaves only me, Ari, and Amara at the table.

"Did I hear you say something about Cabo earlier?" Amara asks.

A ball forms in the pit of my stomach, but Ari's brown eyes light up like the Fourth of July. Any minute, her brother is going to walk back through that door. Her mother, too. The last thing I need is for one of them to walk in while she's talking about the vacation she just took with her father.

"Yes! Samuel and I—"

"Ari," I cut her off. "Not right now."

"Oh, come on, Savannah. Not you, too."

"Yes, me too. This is not the time or place. Unless you're ready to tell your mom the truth, I'd zip it."

Ariana rolls her eyes and sits back in her chair with a huff, looking more like a toddler than a woman in her late twenties.

"I'm sorry," Amara says hesitantly, trying to gauge what kind of landmine she just stepped on. "I didn't realize it was a secret."

"It's not your fault, it's theirs," Ari says, using two fingers to point at me and her brother as he returns from the kitchen.

"What'd I miss?" John asks, sitting beside me with two plates full of an array of sweets.

"Oh, nothing. I was telling Amara how unfortunate it is that I can't tell her more about my trip to Cabo because you're a stubborn ass."

You've got to be fucking kidding me.

John sets his fork on the table, not even getting the chance to cut into the first piece of pie. "Ariana, I've had enough of your shit. You're acting like a spoiled little brat, and—"

"And you're a self-righteous asshole! You're being selfish and rude," she quips. With each word, John's jaw clenches a little tighter. I reach down into his lap, taking his hand in mine and giving it a gentle squeeze. "Dad apologized. He wants to make up for what he did, but you won't let him. Why can't you just let it go?"

A sharp, high-pitched crash echoes, and all heads turn toward the door where Debra stands, her hands frozen in front of her, the plate she'd been carrying now in pieces at her feet. Her children jump to their feet, but she flinches away from them. "What did you just say, Ariana?" Debra's tone matches the blazing fury in her eyes. "You've been seeing your father?"

Ari gnaws on her bottom lip, hands folded in front of her, with her eyes glued to the floor.

"And you knew about this?" Debra turns to John.

"Mom, this isn't his fault," Ari defends. "He only went the one time because I—"

Debra scoffs, looking between them in disbelief. "You've been in touch with him? Well, I must say, that might be the hardest part to believe. After everything he put you through, John Brooks. You would dare give him the time of day? I bet it was *her* idea, wasn't it?"

"Don't do that." John steps in front of me, blocking his mother's glare. I watch the muscles in his back tighten beneath his Henley, and the muscles in his neck strain. "Don't you dare drag her into this. You want to be mad at someone? Be mad at me. I don't care. But you will not take this out on Savannah or her family, for that matter. They've been nothing but kind to you and—"

"Watch your tone, boy!"

"Whoa! What's going on in here?" I hear my father's voice, but John's massive form still blocks my view of the scene.

"Oh my word, is everyone okay?" Mamá is next. No doubt she's seen the shattered plate on the floor and is worried someone got hurt.

Finally, I glance around my boyfriend as Grandma Aggie walks in, clutching onto Crew's arm. Her eyes dart around the room to each member of the Cabot family before settling on John. "Does someone want to tell me what's going on?"

After a brief moment of silence, Debra looks at John, then Ari, and finally me. She chuckles softly, shaking her head, and says, "It would appear that my children inherited more than a last name from their father, after all."

21

Savannah

FRIDAY, DECEMBER 2, 2016

CRYSTAL BAY, FL

"Thanks, Noah," I say, my thumb hovering over the red circle on the bottom of the phone screen.

Noah Callahan, the former show producer who caught the attention of Chelsea Rafferty and swept the Darling of Wrestling off her feet, was promoted to Chief Content Officer at the beginning of this year. I'm surprised they waited that long. Everyone was sure he'd move up the ladder not long after he and Chelsea got married two years ago, but he remained only a producer until recently. Not that it wasn't deserved. Noah has been an integral part of some of the changes backstage and on screen, which have resulted in an uptick in views over the last six months. Needless to say, things are looking good for Noah Callahan, and I'm lucky enough to be on his radar when it comes to stacking the women's division.

"This will be better," he says, and I can imagine the way he's nodding his head on the other side of the phone. Who he's trying harder to convince right now, I'm not sure.

"Yeah, you're right, this is *much* better." A soft chuckle is his only reply. "I'll see you on Sunday."

"Sunday," he agrees. "Oh, and Savannah? I really need you to sign that contract before then. Don't forget."

I toss my phone on the island and let my head fall into my hands. I can't help but laugh at the absurdity of the phone call I just had. Did he think I wouldn't find out? Or at least put the pieces together? As soon as Noah told me Creative had decided to go a different direction with my upcoming storyline, I knew exactly what had transpired in the last forty-eight hours.

I had received two different calls on Wednesday morning—two days ago—following our return from Thanksgiving, where things hadn't exactly gone to plan...Thank you, Debra.

I digress. John's mother is just another thing to add to the list of things that have irritated me lately.

The first call I got on Wednesday morning was from Noah. He wanted to know if I had given any more thought to my future with the company. My contract was set to expire at the beginning of December—this coming Monday, actually. We'd been going back and forth for the last month, renegotiating, and it seemed that an agreement had finally been reached. I told him to send it over, and I'd take one final look at it before signing. It's been sitting in my email ever since. The second call was from Brian, the new head of our Creative team, and Xander Collins, the head of Talent Relations. With confirmation from Noah that I'd be re-signing, they wanted to discuss a new storyline—a *love* storyline—and with it came a new title opportunity.

"They want to put me back in the title picture," I said, walking into the gym after the phone call.

"That's great," John said, straddling the weight bench, but his eyes were locked on whatever message he typed on his phone. I leaned against the wall, deciding how to approach the second part of the conversation. John wasn't going to be happy, I knew that, but this was business, and if this was my chance to win another title, I was going to take it. "That's all they had to say?" he asked, but still didn't look up from his phone.

I took a deep breath. "No...They, uh, they want to put me in a new storyline...with Drake."

John's fingers froze, and finally, he looked up with a furrowed brow. "A storyline with Drake?" I nodded. "As in a love storyline?" Another nod. "You're fucking kidding me. Savannah, you can't—"

"John, I know you don't like him, but I don't have a choice."

"Don't have a choice? You always have a choice. Why in the hell would they put you in a storyline with *him*, of all people?"

"He just came back, they want to give him a push, and—"

"There are plenty of other women they can throw at him. Plenty who'd be more than willing to throw themselves at him. They can get one of them to do it, because I'll be damned if my girlfriend is going to be on the arm of *Damian-fucking-Drake*."

I rolled my eyes. "It's just a story. You know it doesn't mean anything."

"Savannah, this isn't up for debate. You're not doing the story." John planted his hands on his hips, face pulled into a thin line, and his jaw clenched so tightly that I swore he was going to chip a tooth.

Who in the hell was he to tell me what I could and couldn't do?

"In case you've forgotten, I already have a father, I don't need another one," I said, pushing off the wall. "You don't get to tell me what I can and cannot do. This is my job, and if anyone should understand that, it's you, *Brooks*."

His jaw clenched even tighter.

"I have to go meet Rae. She wants to try out some new stuff before Sunday." I wanted him to say something—anything—

that would prove he was going to let it go, that he wasn't going to hold onto this, but he didn't. With a slight scoff, I shook my head. "I didn't come here to ask for your permission, John. I just wanted you to hear it from me, before Drake tried to start shit with you," I said, and walked out the door.

I don't know why his reaction irked me so much, because I knew it was coming. The problem wasn't that they wanted to put me in a "romantic" storyline with someone else; the problem was *who* the story was with. It's no secret that he and Drake dislike each other—and that's a nice way to put it. Sure, they can do what they have to for work, but you'll never catch them pretending to get along, even for the sake of a match. They'd rather call everything in the ring. Maybe they'll set up a few spots ahead of time, but for the most part, they ignore each other until they have no choice. And I've always believed that's why they have some of the best matches of any duo on the roster.

We haven't talked much since I left the gym that afternoon—John having multiple media days in a row didn't help, either—but this morning he walked into the kitchen with a new lease on life and a thousand-watt smile. John wrapped his arms around my waist and pressed a long kiss to my temple. "I'm sorry for being an ass," he whispered. "I know I have a lot of making up to do. Let me take you to dinner tonight and then bring you home so I can *show* you how sorry I am. Please?"

It wasn't the apology I wanted, but it was enough. And I got at least two more as the day progressed. This wasn't normal. We didn't fight like this, and I was ready to put it behind us until I saw Noah Callahan's name appear on my phone twenty minutes before my boyfriend was supposed to be home from his workout with Brody.

Now, the garage door opens from the other end of the house, and I take a deep breath, trying to steady the growing fire rising in my veins. *Don't freak out. Just talk to him about it…Maybe it wasn't even him. Maybe it was their idea to change it.*

"Hi, there." His voice is warm as he walks into the kitchen. "Did you decide where—"

"John, I need to ask you something, and I need you to be honest with me," I interrupt, looking up from my fingers on the marbled countertop. He approaches with more hesitation than he had moments ago, but nods anyway. "Did you call and ask them to change my storyline?"

He doesn't even flinch. Doesn't say anything or look away; he just stands there.

"Did you—"

"I don't trust him, Savannah."

Words escape me when he admits to it. He doesn't even try to deny it—no excuse, nothing. Everything I just thought in the minutes before he walked through the door turns to ash in the fire that consumes me. How could he do this? How could he get involved in my job, in my business? He could have gotten me fired for something so unprofessional. My mouth opens and closes too many times to count as I search for the words to respond, but nothing seems appropriate.

"Sweetheart, I-I know it was wrong, but I couldn't sit back and watch you—"

"I cannot believe you! Whatever issues you two have shouldn't impact my career, John," I say, taking a step back when he moves closer. "You don't trust him? Fine. Trust me. Have faith in *me*. But obviously you lack both."

"That's not true."

"We have always kept things separate. *Always.*" I shake my head, still in disbelief. I wanted to believe he didn't do this, but deep down, I knew there was no other explanation. "You had no right to get involved. No right to stick your nose in my story. What if I had done the same to you?" He rips his gaze from my own. "You would be livid, and you know it."

"I apologize for making you feel this way, but I'm not sorry for doing it. You don't know him, Savannah. He is not a good person. This has nothing to do with my feelings about Miles Drake. This is about keeping you safe."

"Safe from what, John?"

"Just because you're secure in our relationship doesn't mean he won't try something, and the second he tries something with you, I'm going to jail." John takes another step closer, and this time, I let him. He leaves a small gap to give me the choice of what to do next. I want to be mad, and I am, but I want to be madder. Against my wishes, the blaze inside my chest begins to fade.

"I'm still upset with you," I say, because, despite my disappointment, I don't want to fight anymore, not after the last few weeks.

"I know." His hands flex at his sides, like he wants to reach out, but restrains himself. "And I promise that I won't ever do it again, unless it comes to him."

A heavy exhale passes through my lips, and I take the final step forward, draping my arms over his shoulders.

"Forgive me?" John asks, letting his hands come to rest on my hips.

"You're on probation."

"I'll take it." A soft smile lifts his cheeks before he leans in, covering my mouth with his own. The kiss is soft, timid, testing the waters to see how much I'm willing to give. When he pulls back, he tucks a stray piece of hair behind my ear. His gaze falls to my lips briefly, asking for permission, and when I nod, he wastes no more time, molding his mouth to mine. John sighs when I part my lips, opening myself even further to him. With every pass of his tongue, my need for him grows stronger. In one swift motion, he lifts me off my feet, setting me on the counter as a laugh spills from me.

John smiles, leaning in to kiss me again. A deep, slow kiss that makes me squirm. He pulls down the top of my sundress, exposing my braless chest, and draws a line with the tip of his tongue up the valley of my breasts. My head falls back when his mouth finds the column of my throat. He inhales deeply before pressing his lips to the same spot. Goosebumps erupt over my skin.

"I thought you wanted to get dinner," I say with a breathy chuckle, pushing my fingers through the length of his hair.

"We will." His words are warm against my skin. Fingers bunch the fabric of my dress, shoving it up my legs, the air ice-cold against my skin. "But you know I'm a dessert before dinner kind of guy."

He drags my ass to the edge of the counter, and he never breaks eye contact as he pulls my underwear down my legs and kneels before me. *Holy fuck.* The sight is one that I'll never forget. The look in his eyes…Want—no need—and it's all because of me. I can't say this is the first time we've christened the kitchen, but it's the first time he has chosen this particular spot for this particular activity.

John kisses my ankle, a lingering kiss that lights my skin on fire where his lips touch, and a rush of warmth spreads throughout my body when his tongue draws a line from my ankle to my thigh. He spreads my legs farther apart, lifting one of my feet to the counter and the other to rest on the handles, exposing me to him completely. His eyes practically roll into the back of his head when he looks at me, left wholly open to him. I've never been with someone who enjoyed eating pussy as much as John. The first time he tried, I was self-conscious because neither of my exes had been interested in it. Did they love getting their dick sucked? Absolutely. But they had no interest in returning the favor.

"Fuck, Sweetheart." John's voice is soft but thick with desire as his fingers ghost between my legs. My body clenches when he dips inside me, and I moan at the loss when he pulls back out. He brings his fingers to his mouth, sucking them clean. Blue eyes meet mine when they open again, and he smiles, but doesn't waste another minute, burying his face between my legs.

I cry out, my back bowing, fingers white against the edge of the marble. Soft grunts of satisfaction fall past his lips as his tongue strokes up and down and then flattens against my clit, dragging over the sensitive bud at a brutally slow pace before returning to my center. His tongue soon is replaced by his fingers, pushing inside me.

My nipples ache, desperate for attention, but I'm so close to the edge of the counter, I'm sure I'll fall if I let go. The only thing keeping me steady is his arm and my hands. Testing my theory, I brace myself with my right hand and let my left slide up my side to my chest, squeezing my breast. I lightly pinch and roll my nipple, and a soft whimper of pleasure falls past my lips.

"That's my girl," he murmurs against me. "Do whatever you want. I want you to feel good, Sweetheart." His tongue makes long strokes over my center, and then the tip of it slips past my folds, a pattern that makes my body tense as I climb higher. I breathe out an *Oh, fuck* under my breath when he suckles my clit between his lips. My breathing turns labored as he continues to flick against the sensitive bud, long fingers curling inside me. I trust his strength, letting one hand tangle in his hair, and the other falls against the counter behind me as my orgasm builds to its peak. My body tingles, and a wave of heat radiates from my core.

He continues to push thick fingers inside me as I ride the waves of my orgasm. Lapping up the remainder of my release, John hums in satisfaction before his tongue drags one final stroke up my center and clit.

I stay there, eyes closed, head back, completely open to

him, soaking in the high for a moment longer. John pulls himself up from the floor, and I begin to step down so we can clean up before dinner, not anticipating the sudden fullness as he slips his cock into me with one solid thrust. My eyes open to find his staring straight into mine as he rocks into me. This time, though, there's something else hidden in his eyes. Behind all the want and desire, there's something I haven't seen in a long time. An uncertainty—or fear, maybe. I can't quite describe it. Whatever it is, it draws me closer to him.

I press my forehead against his and kiss him. His tongue darts into my mouth, opening me wide to him as we move in a familiar rhythm.

"Come for me, Sav," he begs. "Come on my dick."

The words draw me closer to the edge once again. "I'm close," I whisper.

"I know, baby. You come when you want, I'm right behind you."

My hand falls between us, circling the already sensitive bud, and before I know it, another orgasm rushes through me. He continues to fuck me through it, spilling inside me as we come together.

John lifts my gaze back to his and kisses me again. I sigh into the kiss and can feel the weight of the last few days begin to settle on my shoulders again. Tears sting my eyes as they form, and one slips down my cheek despite me trying to suck them back down. "Hey, what's wrong?"

"Nothing," I lie.

"Don't do that, Sweetheart." John pushes a strand of hair behind my ear, letting his eyes roam across my face for a brief moment. "I know that I haven't made this easy on you. I'm sorry. I do trust you, Savannah. I trust you with my whole heart, but it's him I don't trust. And I'm just sorry you got caught in the crossfire."

"Is there something else going on?" I ask, remembering

the strange look in his eyes moments ago. He sighs, biting down on his lip before shaking his head. "John, you can tell me—"

"No, Sav. It's nothing like that. I just...I feel bad for how I acted and how I've treated you over the last few days. I want to do everything I can to make this up to you."

"Well," I say with a small smile, and wrap my legs around his waist. "This was a pretty good start."

John chuckles softly, pressing a quick kiss against my lips, and helps me stand off the counter, adjusting my dress. I watch him disappear into our bedroom at the other end of the living room before I finally let my smile fall. Sex and a few "I love you's" aren't going to fix what happened, but like I said, it's a start. However, I'm fully convinced there's more to this story. This is more than John's dislike for Drake; his distrust of Drake. The nagging feeling in the pit of my stomach that refuses to go away only confirms it. However, figuring out what it is will have to wait until tomorrow, because tonight I'm not in the mood.

It's been two days since I confronted John about Noah's phone call, and every time I start to get past what happened—to let it go once and for all—it creeps its way in again. I have to remind myself that John only got involved for my benefit...He isn't trying to dictate my life or career. He doesn't trust Drake (granted, neither do I after hearing all of the stories about him), but that's not a good reason to meddle in my fucking career and my—*Breathe.*

Everything is going to be fine. Everything *is* fine. The conversation is over, we've worked things out, and there's no reason to continue rehashing it. John knows how I feel; he won't do it again. And if he does...

If he does, I don't know what I'll do.

We've never—*never*—gotten involved in one another's professional lives. We have always been able to separate and maintain that boundary. Why was this any different? After my character turned on him four years ago, we both agreed that whatever happens on the mat stays on the mat. Storylines are nothing more than that, and if we got placed into a love angle, it was just part of the job. I've never been jealous or worried about him working with the other girls, because I trust him, but I still don't know if I can say the same for John...I still can't figure out why he is so worried about me working with Drake. He's the furthest thing from my type, not to mention his self-absorbed, holier-than-thou tendencies were enough to turn me off as soon as I met him.

The squeal of metal hinges echoes through the empty gym. I've been the only person in the local gym for two hours now. After tossing and turning most of the night, I got out of bed two hours early so I could have some alone time and try to work through my annoyance, which had only seemed to grow since we got to Orlando last night. Whoever else decides to show up before the rush that will arrive around seven can have the other half of the gym, far away from me.

Tonight is Wreck the Halls, a Christmas-themed premiere event before we leave for a two-week European tour. Tomorrow is the last day of my current EWE contract, and I still haven't signed the document in my inbox. I'm supposed to have it to Noah by eight o'clock tonight, but every time I look at it, I can't bring myself to sign the dotted line. Since Thanksgiving, everything has felt off. Now with this storyline fiasco...How can I be sure this is the right thing to do?

My heart leaps out of my chest when I turn away from the weight rack and straight into a person standing less than a foot behind me. Ripping my headphones out of my ears, I take a deep breath, trying to regain my composure.

"What the fuck is wrong with you?"

"Where do you want to start?" Drake laughs, his tongue poking to play with the silver hoop that hugs his bottom lip. "Sorry, didn't mean to scare you, Sav."

"What do you want?"

"I hear we won't have the pleasure of working together after all," he says, and juts out his bottom lip in a frown. "Is it true that it was Brooks? That he's the one who put a stop to it, I mean." I roll my eyes, heading toward the treadmill without an answer, but he follows. "I'll take that eye roll as a yes. What's his deal?"

"He doesn't like you," I say, about to step up on the machine.

"The feeling is mutual."

When I turn back around, I almost run straight into his chest from how closely he follows. Taking a step back, I plant my hands on my hips, asking, "What is it with you two?"

"What do you mean?"

"Well, you guys seem to really hate each other, but I can't think of a single reason why."

"Oh, come on, Savannah. Don't tell me he has you fooled into thinking he's some good guy."

"I have a feeling I'm going to regret this," I say, crossing my arms. "But what are you talking about?"

"It's none of my business what he does or doesn't tell you—his *girlfriend* of how many years? Four? Wow, you'd think you'd have a ring on your finger by now. That's a long time without that kind of commitment."

"Don't patronize me, Drake."

I know exactly what he's doing, and it's not going to work. Little does he know—or anyone else, for that matter—that John and I have been talking about our next steps. Hell, we've even talked about eloping. It would make it a lot easier, but I know he wants to do the whole thing—a church ceremony, dinner, and a party. The whole shebang. Who am I kidding? So do I.

The ring comment isn't what bothers me most. What does he mean by what John does or doesn't tell me?

"What are you talking about?" I ask again.

"Did you ever wonder *why* Brooks was interested in you all of a sudden?" What does that mean? John and I have a history that the majority of the world knows nothing about. And when the gossipmongers backstage started questioning how our relationship came to be, especially when everyone believed I was dead set on *not* dating a coworker, we simply said things just happened.

It wasn't a total lie, and we had been working on a storyline together, so it was easy to believe. However, this feels like Drake is insinuating something different.

"Ever wonder what made him decide to ask you out?" The smirk that crosses his face makes me sick. I know better than to feed into this. I should be telling him to take his game of twenty questions and shove it where the sun doesn't shine, but unfortunately, I'm too curious. "Ever wonder—"

"Get to the damn point, Drake."

"Brooks is not the man you think he is, Savannah. You see, the real reason John Brooks asked you out all those years ago is because I made a bet with him."

My first instinct is to laugh, but every word he speaks twists my stomach tighter and tighter until I feel like I'm going to throw up. What does he mean by a bet? John was involved in a *wager* to ask me out on a date. You've got to be fucking kidding me. Surely, he's joking. He has to be...right?

"What are you talking about?" I ask, trying to hide the desperation creeping up in my voice.

"Right after you lost your first title," he says, propping

himself up on the leg machine beside him, settling in for whatever story he's about to share. "Brooks and Brody came down to the bar, and they were hanging out with some of us guys. I'm not proud of it—boys will be boys, and all that—but we all got to talking about how someone should step in, give you a shoulder to cry on, help make you feel better—"

"You're disgusting."

Drake shrugs with a devilish grin. "Yes, I am, but that's beside the point."

"Which is?"

"Brooks offered himself up to be that person."

A deep pit fills my stomach, and the breath escapes my lungs. He's lying. He has to be lying. John wouldn't...He would never do that.

The smile that Drake wears slips into something more sympathetic when I meet his eyes. "And I made a little wager with him to get you in bed before Wrestlefest. Obviously, I lost in one aspect, but I made $2,400, so I guess I can't complain. But hey, everything worked out for the best, right?"

"Tell me you're lying, Miles."

"No can do." He shrugs. "I tried to warn you, Sav. John Brooks just isn't the man you thought he was."

WRECK THE HALLS
Live Broadcast

DECEMBER 4, 2016
ORLANDO, FL

"Well, Damian Drake is not wasting any time getting this match going," Jude Paul says when the bell rings and Drake runs toward his opponent with a sharp right hook. Brooks Taylor ducks under the swing when he charges again, swinging his bicep into Drake's neck. "Clothesline by Brooks, quickly taking control of this match."

Brooks grasps Drake's legs, creating a figure-four hold, and lifts Drake onto his shoulders before turning Drake onto his stomach. "Texas Cloverleaf," Scott Harrington practically yells into his headset. "When's the last time you saw Brooks Taylor do something like that? He didn't come to play tonight."

"Well, this is a Last Man Standing match for the title, Scott. It's going to take a lot to keep both of these men down for a ten count, and I think Brooks Taylor knows that. He's going to pull all the tricks out tonight."

"We see Drake clawing his way to that bottom rope to break the hold, but...No! Brooks drags him back to the center of the ring."

Drake swings his leg up and kicks Taylor in the face when

he attempts to reapply the Cloverleaf. The impact stuns Brooks, and it gives Drake time to scramble up to his feet. He nails his opponent with a running lariat—using his forearm, he delivers a power strike to his opponent's neck that sends him over the top rope.

"That's all you got, Brooks?" Drake taunts from inside the ring. "I thought you were going to put up a fight tonight, Taylor!"

Drake climbs out of the ring, jumping down to the ground where Brooks has come to his knees. Gripping the ends of his opponent's hair, Drake slams his opponent face-first into the barricade repeatedly. It's brutal and relentless. Satisfied with the attack, he sends Brooks headfirst into the steel steps.

"Brooks goes headfirst into the steel steps!" Jude says. "And the referee begins the count."

1...2...3...

The referee stops once Brooks makes it back to his feet, much to his opponent's dismay.

Drake doesn't waste time. He immediately throws rapid-fire punches, but Brooks counters, blocking each one. A hard kick to the chest sends Drake sailing into the barricade, and with a running forearm, Brooks sends them both sailing over the barricade into the front row. The impact knocks the wind out of both men, but Brooks Taylor manages to pull himself back up first. He grabs one of the folding chairs from the cleared seating area and swings, striking his opponent's back. Drake screams, falling back to the ground. Another blow to the shoulder, but the next swing lands on the concrete floor when he rolls out of the way, echoing through the air.

The men trade punches, fighting through the crowd and up the stairs of the arena between sections. Fans on either side are spurring on the insanity with thunderous cheers that surge with each strike. Reaching the top of the steps, Drake hits a stiff European uppercut, throwing his forearm upwards into

Brooks Taylor's chin. It sends the champ stumbling backward. One wrong move and he'll go tumbling back down the stairs.

Drake whips Brooks away from the stairs, slingshotting him into the concrete wall instead.

"Taylor goes headfirst into the wall, and I don't know if he'll be able to recoup from that, Scott," Jude Paul says as the referee begins another count.

1…2…3…

Scott agrees. "I'm not seeing any movement right now. The referee is already at the five count."

Finally, Brooks stirs, but before he can fully come to his feet, Drake drags him into the hallway by the hair.

"Stay," Drake commands when he props Brooks against the wall. He swipes his arms, clearing a table full of merchandise, but when he turns to retrieve his opponent, Drake is met with a boot to the face.

The crowd around them cheers, egging on Brooks as he climbs on the table. Leaping from the table, he drives his elbow into Drake's chest, and it sends them both to the ground. Fans gasp upon impact with the solid ground, and both men lie sprawled out on the concrete floor.

Again, Brooks stirs first, and he leans back against the wall as the referee counts, already at four. He makes it to eight before Drake finally stumbles to his feet, but Brooks is there, waiting with a flurry of punches. The assault continues through a different hallway than the one they entered and down the stairs. Reaching the lower level once again, Drake grabs one of the large trash cans and tosses it at his opponent, who catches it.

A deadpan expression crosses Brooks Taylor's face as he throws it off to the side. Drake takes off, sprinting through the crowd, but Brooks catches up to him when he reaches a set of steel barriers that block off backstage.

"Oh! Brooks Taylor with a barrier to the face," Scott

Harrington says, when Brooks grabs Drake by the back of the head and smashes his face into the top of the barrier. Drake stumbles backward, trying to regain his composure as the champion sets up another devastating attack. "Now, what is he doing?"

"It looks like Taylor is setting the barrier up against the side of the stage to create a ramp, of sorts," Jude says. "These men are using anything as a weapon to wear down their opponent."

Satisfied with the setup, Brooks kicks Drake in the midsection and forces him into a standing headlock. Bending at the knees, he lifts the challenger off his feet and tosses him backward.

"Suplex by Taylor!" Jude Paul yells. "He just suplexed Damian Drake into the steel."

"No give whatsoever," Scott adds, as both men lie on the ground, trying to recoup.

It takes until the count of six for Brooks to climb to his feet, granted a little unsteady, and he forces Drake to do the same. They trade blows to the head as they make their way through the crowd once more and finally back inside the ring.

"Wait, what's this?" Scott Harrington asks when someone walks out from backstage. There's no music, no backdrop, nothing. "What is Savvy Skye doing out here?"

The three-time women's champion doesn't pay much attention to the crowd, not even stopping to offer a quick smile or high-five like usual. Her focus is solely on the two men who are finally back in the ring. She stands at the bottom of the ramp, arms crossed, watching Brooks Taylor dominate his opponent. After a few moments, she slowly begins to make her way around the side of the ring.

"What are you doing out here?" Jude Paul yells outside of his headset when she gets close enough. Savvy looks over her shoulder, and a smile slowly spreads across her red-painted lips before she turns back. "You know something, Scott? I don't *like the look of that."*

"Me either."

"This is a Last Man Standing match, so anything goes. No disqualifications, no pinfalls, and the only way to win is by beating your opponent so bad they won't get back up. That means she can be out here and interfere without costing Brooks Taylor the match."

"You assume she's here to help Brooks," Scott says. "But they haven't been together in a long time, Jude. She might be out here to join forces with his archrival, Damian Drake."

Brooks whips Drake into the ropes and hits him with a hard clothesline, sending him down to the mat. The champ wastes no time, putting his opponent into a figure-four leg lock, but this time, instead of twisting Drake onto his stomach for the cloverleaf, Brooks drops to the mat upon rebound, falling backwards to apply pressure to Drake's legs.

"Brooks can't win via submission, but he can win if Drake passes out from the pain, or if he does enough damage that Damian Drake cannot get back to his feet," Jude explains.

"I hate this hold. It's the most painful one to be put in," Scott says.

Drake attempts to lift the foot of his opponent and escape, but Brooks pounds his fist down onto Drake's ankle.

"If Drake can counter the attack, somehow rolling onto his belly, that would take the pressure off his leg and apply it all on Brooks."

"That looks to be what he's trying to do," Jude says.

Slowly, Drake twists his upper body, and his lower body soon follows until both men are face down on the mat. Brooks screams out in pain as the pressure Drake had been feeling is now applied to his own leg. Drake can only maintain the hold for a moment before his legs give out. Both men lie in a tangled mess of limbs as the referee begins the count.

Rousing first, Damian Drake slides out of the ring, trying

to regain his bearings. That's when he finally notices the new person standing outside the ring.

She watches him, but doesn't attack. Instead, she slinks into the ring and watches Brooks slowly climb to his feet. Without warning, Savvy sweeps his leg, sending him back down to the mat with a sickening thud. She stands over him, staring out at the crowd, and their cheers only egg her on. She snakes her arm around his neck, forcing him up into a bridged position. The soles of his shoes dig into the canvas, and she drives her knee into his exposed spine. She does it three more times, and while normally she'd drop to her knees, she stands tall, slamming her forearm down hard on his chest. She does it two more times, knocking him back onto the mat with the third blow.

"Heartbreaker! Savvy Skye just performed her finishing move on Brooks Taylor," Jude says as a chorus of "Holy shit" rings out from the crowd. "The champ is down, and I'm not sure he's getting back up."

"That was one of the most brutal Heartbreaks I've ever seen!" Scott's excitement and confusion blend in with the crowd.

Savvy looks around the arena, meeting the eyes of every fan seated along the barricade. She bites down on her lower lip with a grin before she meets the bulging eyes of the other man in this match as he watches the scene unfold.

"What in the hell just happened?" Jude asks when she steps through the middle ropes and walks down the steel stairs without a word.

The referee has already reached the count of five as she begins her ascent up the ramp, walking backwards so she can continue to watch the aftermath of her interference. Brooks never gets back up, and the referee finally reaches ten.

"That's it, that's ten! Damian Drake has won the title."

"Yeah, thanks to Savvy Skye," Scott says with a soft chuckle. "Something tells me this was meant to send a message, Jude.

One question remains—why Brooks Taylor?"

22

SUNDAY, DECEMBER 4, 2016

ORLANDO, FL

"Where do you think you're going?" I ask when the tour bus door opens and my girlfriend heaves one bag over her shoulder, then sets a suitcase on the ground.

"I'm leaving."

"Leaving?" I scoff. If she thinks she is going to walk away without explaining what just happened, she has another thing coming. That was not part of the plan. Hell, she wasn't even supposed to be out there tonight. It was supposed to be a normal match between me and Drake, and I was supposed to retain the fucking title. But that didn't happen because she turned on me *again*. And when I asked Noah about it, he shook his head and said I needed to talk to Savannah. "Can't we talk about this first?"

She doesn't answer, but she doesn't make a move to leave, either.

"I am so confused, and rightfully so, don't you think? You just cost me my match, Savannah. Without warning. Please, can we go inside and talk?"

She still doesn't move, but after a moment, I urge her back

inside, and she gives in.

I close the door and take a deep breath before facing her. Normally, this is when we'd share a quick meal, then shower, and afterwards get lost in the sheets. Instead, Savannah stands in front of the sink in the dimly lit kitchen, arms crossed over her chest. She's changed from the white cropped shirt she wore in the arena into a vintage *Brooks Taylor* shirt—black with a white design of an eagle and *Built for this* written beneath it—and it makes me think that, despite whatever this is about, there's still hope. My gaze travels over the interior of the bus, and everything looks in place, except it doesn't at the same time.

Wait, where is that stack of books that was on the table earlier?

She packed all of her shit and was really about to leave without saying a damn word. What is going on?

"Were you going to leave without saying something?" I ask. "If you want to end things, Savannah, you're going to do it to my fucking face."

Her eyes lift from the floor, slightly narrowed.

"You've barely spoken to me all week. Barely looked at me. I knew something was wrong, but I guess I assumed you were trying to get over the shit with the Drake story. So, I let it go, but now I realize maybe letting you cool off on your own was a mistake. Then you come out there and do that, and now..." I scoff. "Now, I come out here to talk about all of this, and I find you leaving?"

She doesn't say anything.

"Savannah, please talk to me!" I step forward, grasping her arms, pleading with her.

She takes a deep breath and a small step back. "Why did you want to be with me, John?"

The question takes me aback. "What do you mean? I-I've always wanted to be with you. We—"

"But why?" If she asked me this question any other time, I could give her a million reasons, but right now, my mind goes blank.

"You were—are—different. You're *you*. I don't—I don't know what you want me to say here, Sav. If I'm being honest, I'm a little caught off guard."

"The truth."

"That is the truth!"

"It wasn't because of a bet?" Savannah asks.

It feels like a black hole opens inside my chest. The emptiness grows, threatening to swallow me whole, as her expression morphs in the moments that follow. Her mask of indifference falls, and I can see the hurt behind her eyes. Not just hurt...there's anger, too. So much anger. I wonder how long she has been holding onto this.

"When you asked me on a date four years ago, was it because you wanted to or because you *had* to?"

"I wanted to." The answer comes instantly. Of course, I wanted to ask her. I wanted to date her from the second I saw her again at NextGen.

"Not because you had to?" she asks again, but the more I think about it, I'm not sure I can rightfully deny it. Not when the push to do it had come from some connived version of chivalry to protect her from the assholes we work with. "Answer the question, John."

"Yes." I sigh, and my tongue pokes out to wet dry lips. "There was a bet that Drake made, but Sweetheart—"

Savannah scoffs. "Unbelievable."

"Savannah, it's not like that!" I grasp for her when she tries to push by me. "I wanted to, and I would have regardless of that damn bet—"

"When?"

"Eventually!"

"Eventually." She repeats it with such utter disbelief and

disgust, shaking her head. "I can't believe this."

"It was me or them, Sav," I say. That doesn't make it right, but that doesn't make it any less true. "I didn't want you to get hurt. None of them cared about you. They were talking like you were some doll to be passed around. I couldn't just sit by and—"

"You should've told me!"

"Told you what? 'Hey, Sav, just so you know, Drake just made an outrageous bet, and I have to get in your pants before Wrestlefest to win. You want to go on a date?'"

"You're disgusting." Her beautiful face contorts, and the look in her eyes is one I've never seen before. One I never want to see again.

"That's not what happened, though, is it?" I don't mean to yell, and I take a deep breath to try to calm myself before I speak again. "Did it ever occur to you, when Drake—I assume, it was Drake who told you this, right?" She doesn't answer. "Did it occur to you when he was telling you all of this that maybe, just maybe, I was looking out for you?" I ask, and after a moment, Savannah rolls her lips between her teeth, looking away from me. Something in her refusal to answer tells me that she had considered it, so why wasn't she willing to accept it? "Tell me something, Savannah, did we sleep together before Wrestlefest?"

Her gaze rises to meet mine again, but she refuses to answer, crossing her arms again.

"No," I say. "We didn't. You want to know why? Because despite how desperate I was for you, how badly I wanted you...I wasn't going to let him win. I wasn't going to let that be the reason I got to be intimate with you again. And sure, I could've told him we didn't, even if we did, but I never wanted him to have that over me."

"I'm supposed to just be okay with this? Because you were 'doing it for me?'" Savannah adds air quotes to the words for emphasis.

"No! I'm not saying that. Be mad. Be upset. Be whatever you need to be, but don't just leave."

Her face falls, and she lets her tongue run over her lips. I notice a wetness coating her eyes. "You paid him, John. You fucking paid—"

"Because I had to, Savannah. If I hadn't, it never would've stopped. He would've never stopped. I did what I had to do to put a stop to things once and for all."

"You should've told me!"

"Would you have agreed to go on that date?"

"I-I don't know," Savannah stutters. "Can you say that it's not the only reason you finally chose to ask me?"

"You didn't want me to, Sav." For so long, she stuck to her guns about not dating a coworker, even me. I never knew when the right time would be without seeming pushy. "You didn't want anyone to. You said—"

"And yet, I said yes to you!" Savannah scoffs. "You want to know why? Because I realized that I would always want more, John. There would always *be* more—always be some new opportunity, some title to chase—but I realized I didn't have to do it alone. I didn't want to do it alone; I wanted to do it with you. And I thought that's what you wanted, too, but y-you didn't want that, you didn't even want to ask me out—"

"I love you, Savannah," I say, taking a step closer to her. Wiping away one of the tears in the corner of her eye, I fight the urge to kiss her. "I am in love with you and despite what you might think—"

"Don't say that." Savannah shakes her head, stepping back. "Don't you dare say that." She rakes a hand through her long hair as she paces. "You don't love me. That's not love, John. You don't do this to someone you love. You don't *lie* to them for years. You don't hide things. I thought I knew you, but it's obvious I don't know you at all." She pulls back when I reach for her. "First, you don't even trust me to be in a simple storyline—"

"I don't trust him, Savannah. Look what he's done already."

"What he's done?" She scoffs. "You interfered in my business, in my work. I've never done that to you. No matter what it was. I always let you do what needed to be done."

I knew it was wrong, but the thought of them working together didn't sit right with me. Or maybe it was my self-consciousness—fear that if they worked together, what was happening right now would have happened. Guess that didn't work out so well, huh?

"You want to know something, Brooks?" Savannah asks, and the use of *Brooks* cuts me to my core. "I could've lived with that…With you getting involved and sticking your nose in my business. I could have gotten past it, but what I can't get past is learning the only reason you ever gave a damn about me is because of some bet."

There are so many things I want to say, but I can't get the words to come out.

"I'm going home. I need some time…to think."

"Savannah—" I reach for her, but she pulls away and pushes out the door without another word.

It's been two days since Savannah walked off the bus. I'm supposed to be on a plane to Europe for the holiday tour overseas, but so is she. After she rejected my phone calls yesterday and ignored all my text messages, I decided to put some distance between myself and the Orlando airport…on a plane in the opposite direction I should be heading.

The first thing I notice when I pull into the driveway of our

Crystal Bay home is the moving truck, and the second is her car with the keys in the ignition, as if she was about to leave, but ran back inside because she forgot something. This is not what I expected to find, but part of me questions whether I'm actually surprised. She was going to leave Orlando without saying goodbye; why wouldn't she do the same now?

I search downstairs, but she's nowhere to be found, and there's no response when I call her name—not until I'm halfway up the staircase and she appears at the end of the hallway, carrying a box.

"You're supposed to be on a plane," she says.

"So are you," I say, taking the final steps up to the second floor. "Savannah, don't do this. I love you. I'm sorry—"

"You don't even know what that means!" Her voice carries through the house that suddenly feels empty, the way it used to, before her. "You don't love me."

Her words hit me like a brick wall. How can she say that?

"You love the idea of me, Brooks, but that's not…that's not enough for me, and it shouldn't be enough for you."

"That's not true, Sav. I love *you*, not some idea. You, and only you."

Wetness coats her brown eyes. I want to reach out and comfort her, but I can't stand the thought of her pulling away from me one more time. "I wish I could believe that, but I don't feel like I even know you. How can I?"

"You do know me, Sweetheart. You knew me well before all of this. Before EWE. Don't let him get in your head, Savannah. Please."

"I haven't known you from the moment I met you," she says, swallowing back her tears, but those ten words break my heart. "How do I know what was real and what wasn't?"

"It was real. All of this was real, Sav! Every bit of it. I may not have told you about that stupid fucking bet, but I never lied to you." Relief floods my system when she doesn't retract from my touch against her cheek. "I can't lose you, Savannah."

"You can't lose something you never had."

"I love you, Savannah," I say, because it's the only thing that feels right. "Despite whatever you think—"

"You don't lie and manipulate someone you *love*, John. You don't keep things from them or pretend—"

"I didn't lie!"

Savannah scoffs. "You didn't lie? What do you call taking a wager to start dating your girlfriend, then? You've been in control this whole time, pulling the strings of our relationship, telling me—"

"What are you talking about? I did it to protect you! I told you. It was me or them. Drake and his merry band of idiots were going on and on, so I told them to back off, and it turned into this. I know it's fucked up, I know it was stupid, but I couldn't sit by and let them talk about you like that, Sav. I didn't want you to get hurt."

"And look where that's gotten us, Brooks."

"This…Us. It was all real. My feelings, my love for you—"

"No, it wasn't," she says. "You manipulated me, used me… and for what?" Her eyes pierce mine, and her words echo what she said moments ago.

You've been in control this whole time.

Shit, is she right?

"What did you get out of the bet?"

"This wasn't about winning or losing for me, Savannah. This was about protecting the woman I love." I take her face in my hands. "I don't care how many times I have to say it before you believe me, but I love you. This wasn't just about a bet."

After a heartbeat of silence, she takes a deep breath and steps back out of my grasp. She wets her lips, her gaze never leaving mine. "I can't love someone I don't know."

Did she just say she can't…she can't love me? No. That's not possible. She wouldn't…She couldn't…Her gaze never wavers, and the words begin to swirl around my mind in a never-ending echo. *I can't love someone I don't know.*

"You don't—You don't love me?" I ask.

For the first time, she breaks her stare, glancing down at her feet. "I don't—I don't know, Brooks. I don't know what I'm feeling right now. There's too much to process, too much to try and understand. I just...I need some time."

"Say it, Savannah." I want her to say the words, not skirt around them. I need to know if she means it. If she really doesn't think she can love me. If she won't say them, then I know she doesn't believe that. "Tell me you don't love me, and I'll let you walk out that door, but until you say those words... until you say that you don't love me anymore, I'm not going to stop fighting for you. Fighting to make you see that I do love you. I'm in love with you, and—"

"Savannah?" a deep voice calls up from the foyer. I recognize it instantly.

You've got to be kidding me. She called her brother? And not just any of her brothers—she called Crew. I can only imagine how pissed he was when he got that call. Fuck, did she tell him about the shit with Drake? She would have to, otherwise he would never understand why she was leaving so suddenly. I am so fucked. If he knows the truth...there's no stopping what comes next.

"Y-yeah," Savannah calls. Her voice breaks. "I'm coming!"

"I saw the truck, and—"

"Crew, I said I'm coming!"

"Is he up there with you?" I can imagine Crew's chest puffing up; all it would take is one word from her to send him up the stairs to start a fight I don't want.

"Just go outside," Savannah demands, and I hear Crew grumble under his breath before his footsteps retreat out the front door. Savannah closes her eyes, taking a deep breath.

"Do you love me, Savannah?" I ask the question I'm most

scared to know the answer to. But I have no choice. I have to know what she wants. It was never my intention, but if she truly feels like I've been controlling her, controlling our relationship, then I'll do the right thing. I'll let her go. I won't keep her trapped in a relationship she doesn't want...even if it will kill me to watch her walk out that door. "Yes or no?"

There's a small beat of silence before she opens her eyes, tears welling as she looks straight at me. "I don't love you." Savannah shrugs. "I can't."

A harsh sting immediately floods my vision, and nausea claws at my throat, but I refuse to let the emotion overtake me. I know she doesn't mean it—she can't mean it—but she said it. She said what I needed to hear to let her go, and that's what I'm going to do.

"You don't love me? Fine, then get out."

Savannah gasps. Her mask falls, deepening the crack in my heart. Normally, I'd reach out and pull her into my arms, tell her everything will be okay. We'll make it through whatever is going on.

Not this time.

I stand here, arms glued to my sides, and watch as she takes a shaky breath and picks up the box she'd been carrying. With one final glance, she walks away.

The front door slams moments later, and my entire being jolts as if struck by lightning. Whether it's from the impact or the adrenaline pumping through my veins, I can't say. Everything in me screams to run after her. To stop her. To not let her leave, not like this, not at all...This is not how our story ends.

It's better than coming home to an empty house.

How could she pick up and leave as if the last four and a half years meant nothing?

Hell, longer than that.

The thought brings a wave of anger over me. How could

she do this? How could I?

Part of me hopes—prays—that I'll hear the door open. That she'll walk back in, saying she didn't mean it, saying she still loves me. But a bigger part of me knows she won't.

Savannah was right. I *was* controlling everything—the man behind the curtain of our entire relationship—right up until the very end.

I pick up the nearest object—a picture frame with a photo of us from a trip to Asheville two years ago—and throw it at the wall. The glass shatters into pieces. The frame splits apart at the seams. Should I have done it? No, but it was the only way I could think to relieve the mounting pressure building inside of me before I explode.

PART TWO

23

Savannah

SUNDAY, MARCH 26, 2017

CELESTIA, TX

One hundred and ten. That's how many days it's been since I told John I didn't love him. One hundred and nine since I showed up on my parents' lawn, asking if I could stay for a while. One hundred and eight since Mamá begged me to know what happened, and I lied. Ninety-five since I told Raelynn the truth. And eighty-five since the last time I almost got on a plane and flew home to him. One hundred and ten days of withdrawals and waking up to reach across the bed for someone who isn't there. One hundred and ten days without him, and each one is just as hard as the last.

I've been occupying one of the bedrooms in the guest house since I moved back to the farm. I could have easily taken up residence in my old bedroom in the main house, but I knew the guest house would give me more of the privacy I needed. In hindsight, I could've just gotten my own apartment, a short-term thing, but I wasn't sure exactly how long this was going to last. Besides, when I was packing everything up, calling Crew and deciding to come home to Willow Pond Farm felt like the safe choice.

Crew moved out of the guest house almost two years ago after our parents gifted him a few acres on the outskirts of the ranch, where he built a small bungalow. He told me last Thanksgiving that he'd already started working on the plans for the house he wanted to build for Amara. But Nash still lives in the other room, and our schedules vary enough that it's like having my own place most of the time.

I've kept myself busy. Every morning, I get up with Papá and Crew. I've been helping Mamá put together recipes and a business plan for the restaurant she wants to open. I've spent more time with Cassandra and Kingsley than I have in years. But it's still not enough to take my mind completely off things. I miss him. I miss my life. I miss EWE and the ring. Hell, I even kind of miss Harper's annoying ass. When she didn't tag along with Wolf for the annual New Year's trip, I found myself both relieved and disappointed (the others were just relieved).

My triceps quake as I lower the barbell to my chest, hovering for just a second before forcing it back up. This is my second time in the gym today; the three straight days of rain have made it nearly impossible to go for a run outside, but it's supposed to clear up tomorrow. So, maybe I'll get some fresh air without the added farm scents.

A low, continuous whirr catches my attention. What the hell? That's the third call in two minutes. *Shit, that's the third call in two minutes.* What time is it?

I re-rack my weights, sitting straight up from the flat bench to read the clock on the wall: *10:13 p.m.* That's 11:13 p.m. Charlotte time.

Shit.

Shit, shit, shit, shit.

When Rae called earlier, she reminded me that tonight was Elite Wrestling Entertainment's March premiere event: Mayhem. She had a triple-threat tables match versus *Kerrigan*

Tate and *Roxanne*. Bennett would be facing *Ego Wandell* in a singles match to end their four-month-long feud before *Noeha Nakoa* would interfere to challenge *Wolf Bennett*'s honor, something "*The Gladiator*" hates. She's kept me updated on what the two of them have been doing. Occasionally, Brody, but never *him*. Sometimes, she slips—they all do—and starts to tell me about him, but she always catches herself.

Despite the name of the event, though, there shouldn't have been anything too crazy going on at the show.

A call right now is too late for it to be about Raelynn or Bennett, and Brody didn't have a match tonight, which means...My heart sinks. There's only one person it could be about.

The buzzing ceases, only to start again almost immediately. I swipe my phone from the floor and answer without looking. "What happened?"

"What took you so long?" My best friend sounds out of breath, like she's either just run a marathon or is pacing the length of the bus she shares with Brody.

"Raelynn—"

"Sav, it's not good."

"Rae, *what happened*?"

"I don't—I don't know." I can imagine her pushing a hand through her long black hair, tugging at the roots. She'll take the thirty steps from the front of the bus to the back, and then do it again. "Brody said it was supposed to be a clinic, nothing major, nothing that would cause any issues, but Drake fucked up. He dropped Brooks...They were doing a spot at the announcer's table, and it looked like he landed wrong. He couldn't put much weight on his left arm when he got back up, but they kept going."

Of course, they did. Of course, *he* did.

"The left side of his chest was starting to discolor by the end of it. Mike couldn't even lift his arm for the win."

This is bad. This is really bad. He probably tore something, and what could have been only a few months out has turned into possibly a year or more, because he wouldn't stop the fucking match.

"Brody's inside trying to find out what's going on, but there isn't much Doc is going to be able to do here. They'll probably send him to the hospital."

And he's going to hate that.

"I'll call you back." I end the call without waiting for a goodbye.

My feet move on their own, carrying me out of the gym, down the stairs, to the bottom floor of the barn. My finger hovers over the name, but a commotion from the other end of the hall catches my attention. I come face-to-face with my second-oldest brother. Nash stands at the end of the hall, panting. His hair sticks to his face, clothes like another layer of skin, water pooling beneath him with every step he takes. Clearly, he just ran through the early spring storm outside.

"Savannah." Breath. "There you...are." Breath. "Fuck, I've been looking for you." Breath. "SJ, it's Brooks, he's—"

"Injured, I know."

In my attempt to move past my brother, he catches my arm. "Where are you going? I just said—"

"To pack a fucking bag, Nash!" My chest heaves with each breath, trying to hold it together a little longer.

His grip loosens. "You're going?"

"Of course, I'm fucking going. John is hurt and..." I notice a slow smile spread across his lips, and it infuriates me. "What are you smiling about?"

The empty suitcase on my bed stares back at me with a knowing grin. The same one my brother had when he said, "I knew you still loved him." Everything in me screams to pack the bag and run, but Nash's words hit me like a damn freight train. *I knew you still loved him.*

"I thought you'd be gone by now," Papá says from the doorway. His arms are crossed over his broad chest, one brow raised. "You shouldn't be driving in this. It's only getting worse. Get your stuff together, and I'll drive you down to the airport. You goin' to Austin or is he sending the—"

"I-I'm not going."

My words shock me, but they seem to shock my father even more. The space between his brow crinkles, and his stare forces me to look away.

"You're not going?" he asks.

I close my eyes to fight back the tears that have started to gather and swallow the lump in my throat. "I can't, Pa."

"Ten minutes ago, you were rushing out the door, and now you *can't?*"

"If I go—if I see him—I know I'll never be able to walk away again."

"Who says you have to?" Papá takes a cautious step inside.

"You wouldn't understand."

"You're right, I don't understand. I still don't even know why you left in the first place. None of this makes any sense, Savannah. One minute, you're both happy, and the next, you show up here with all your stuff, asking if you can move in here. If you ask me, it sure sounds to me like you're runnin' from something."

"I'm not running! Things just got...complicated, and I had to leave. I had to."

"Do you or do you not love that man?" he asks. I take a deep breath, but don't answer. "Savannah Josephine, you need to decide what you want. What you really want. You're messin' with real people and real feelings. That comes with real consequences. You don't get to choose to love him one second and not the next."

"That's not what happened."

"I wouldn't know, because you refuse to talk to me." Papá scoffs, shaking his head. "You don't wanna talk? Fine. Don't talk. But the way you've reacted tonight tells me you still love him, and you've been given the chance to work this out. You just have to make the choice, SJ. You either pack that bag and get on the plane, and you don't look back, or..."

I bite down on my bottom lip, tears brimming in my eyes. I've never hid things from my family, unless you want to count Crew's late-night escapades, but those weren't my stories to tell. Eventually, any secret we had always came out. The Williams family has always been an open book, sometimes a little too open, lacking the boundaries that most people have. Major things become lessons for everyone, minor things become dinner conversation, and for once, I don't want to be part of the discussion.

"Or you let him go."

24

Brooks

MONDAY, DECEMBER 4, 2017

RAVENSWOOD, IN

White siding that could use a good power wash covers the exterior of the fourteen-hundred-square-foot farmhouse at the end of the snow-covered drive. I make a mental note to remind her to schedule that for the spring—not that she'll remember. Her memory has gotten worse over the last year, no matter how much she or my mother wants to deny it. My grandmother was diagnosed with early-stage dementia two years ago, and the disease has not only taken a toll on her, but on us. She refuses to move in with Mom, and Mom refuses to move in with her. With neither willing to bend, I had no choice but to intervene and hire home health care for my ninety-two-year-old grandmother.

This little white house has been a sanctuary in my chaos for as long as I can remember. I've taken this route too many times to count in thirty-seven years, but I've never dreaded it quite like today.

The front porch steps are semi-cleared of snow, and a thin layer of ice makes the wood slick beneath my boots—nothing like a half-assed attempt. Guess I'll have to make sure that gets done, too. The wind whips through the open porch, smacking my exposed neck and cheeks with tiny pinpricks of moisture. My only resistance against the single-digit temperature is the thick sweater I threw on this morning before leaving for the airport. I didn't think it would be *this* cold this early in the season, so I left my winter coat back in Florida, where it's currently seventy-eight degrees.

You know it's winter, right? Her voice rings through my ears as if she were standing beside me, and it stops me dead in my tracks, just like it always does. Taking a deep breath, I push all thoughts of her to the back of my mind. Now is not the time...but after my sister's admission yesterday, all mental barriers I had came crashing down.

"What's the verdict?" Ari's voice rang out from the kitchen the moment I stepped off the elevator. She appeared in the double doors of my condo entryway with a half-eaten sandwich in hand. She was dressed in athleisure wear, but we both knew the most activity she'd be doing was running her damn mouth. My sister was in town for work, her new job requiring her to travel between Indianapolis and Florida at least once a month. We finally sat down and talked about Thanksgiving when I got home from Europe last December, but that was the easy part of the conversation. The hard part came after, when I had to tell her what happened after everyone left Celestia.

"They think I could be cleared as early as next month," I said.

"That's great news!" she said with a mouthful. "Why don't you seem more excited? I thought you'd be bursting at the seams to get back into the ring."

"I don't know, Ari," I said. "It's not...It's not the same."

Nothing was the same. Being backstage felt like being in a foreign country. I had become so accustomed to having her around, knowing she was there, that being there without her didn't feel right. I told myself I just had to get through Wrestlefest, and then I would take a small break. If I could make it to the end of April, then I'd take the time to go through the motions and process everything properly, but life had other plans.

Nine months ago, I suffered an injury that almost took me out of the ring for good. I don't blame Drake, even if I'd like to. Every wrestler knows the risk when we step into the ring, and even the simplest of moves can lead to injury if you're not careful. That hasn't stopped the rest of the locker room, and even a few sports talk shows, from giving Drake flak. So, I don't feel the need to add on to the mountain of criticism he's faced—first, for my injury, and later the accusations that came out about his escapades outside the ring. He was finally getting exactly what he deserved.

The discoloration on my skin and the inability to move my left arm at Mayhem that night sent everyone into an absolute frenzy. I told them I'd be fine until I got home, where I could consult my own doctor, but Amos refused to let me leave without Doc checking on me first. Doc wanted me to go to the hospital in Charlotte, but I wasn't going to an emergency room eight hours from home if I wasn't dying...That stunt, as my doctor called it the next morning, resulted in a stern talking-to before I was scheduled for an OR time of six o'clock the next morning.

One week after my surgery, I put the house up for sale and bought a condo on Longboat Key, a beach community about an hour and a half from Crystal Bay. I couldn't stand being in the same five-thousand-square-feet she haunted. Everywhere I looked, she was there—some memory or thing she left behind. And not even the pain of a ruptured deltoid paired with a dislocated shoulder and Grade II strained pectoral muscle—oh, and let's not forget the rotator cuff discomfort I'd been putting off, which could be why the deltoid rupture happened in the first place…None of that compared to the pain of her absence. It had been almost four months since she walked out the door, and I thought that maybe, just maybe, she'd still care enough to at least call or text, but she never did. Every time I was there, I waited for her to walk through the door—hell, I still do some days—and say she didn't mean it, because I know she didn't. But that day has never come.

"You mean because Savannah isn't—"

"Don't say her name." The outburst surprised both of us. I don't know where it came from, and the words came out harsher than necessary. But I didn't apologize. I wasn't in the mood to have that conversation with my sister, and I was going to do whatever it took to make it stop immediately. I took a deep breath before starting over. "She doesn't care, Ariana. It's been a whole year and—"

Ari sighed. "Brooks, it's not that she doesn't care. She does. More than she would like to admit, if I'm honest."

"What are you talking about?"

"She's going to kill me for this," Ari said under her breath, rubbing her temples. "Savannah has called and checked on you every week since you got hurt. She pretends like it's just to chat, to see how the new job is going or how life is going, and I know part of that's true, but I'm not the true reason."

What the fuck?

"She called the night you got hurt."

Again, *what the fuck*?

"She was worried sick about you. I begged her to meet us back here, but—"

"So, she can call you to check on me, but she can't pick up the phone and call me herself?"

"She's trying to let you go."

"Trying? She's fucking *trying*? She's the one who walked out that fucking door, Ariana. She wouldn't have to try if—"

"John." My sister interrupted me. "I know you don't want

to hear this, and I don't want to be the one to tell you, either, but I think you need this time apart. You both have some healing to do, some stuff to figure out, and maybe...Maybe one day, you'll find your way back to each other."

And that's how I found myself here, standing on my grandmother's porch in the middle of an early December snowstorm. To officially start healing.

The other side of the door is quiet for a while after I knock, but finally it swings open to reveal Grandma Aggie. Her brown eyes widen, whether in surprise or fear, I'm not sure. To her, I could either be her grandson or a "strange" man. You never really know what version you're going to get.

John!" Her voice is raspy, matching the new frailness of her appearance. "This is a surprise. What are you doing here?"

I lean down to kiss her cheek, and she wraps her bony arms around me the best she can. "Is Mom here?"

"Yes, yes, come in. She's in the kitchen." My grandmother takes two small steps to the side and ushers me in. I kick my shoes off on the black mat where I recognize two pairs of snow boots, alongside an unknown third. They're bright pink with white fur around the top and white pom poms dangling from the strings. Good thing Amos never saw those, or they definitely would've made their way down to the ring when *Savvy Skye* was still in her peppy cheerleader gimmick.

Mom's voice rings out from deeper inside the house, a hint of worry tacked on the end as she calls out for her own mother. Seconds later, she appears in the hallway from the direction leading to the kitchen. "There you are, what are you—Oh, Brooks." Her eyes narrow, looking between us. "What are you doing here?"

"Don't take that tone with him, Debbie. If my grandson wants to stop by, he's more than welcome." Grandma Aggie pats my arm. "Hush," she snaps when Mom begins to argue, turning back to me. "Now, sweetie, to what do we owe the pleasure?"

"I need to speak with Mom," I say, and her glare softens slightly. "It shouldn't be too long. I have to get back home for a meeting with Xander at the training center." That and I don't plan on being here any longer than necessary, especially after this conversation.

My grandmother looks between us before a smile creeps up on her face. "How about I make some tea?" Before I can decline the offer, Mom does it for me. No doubt she's worried about my grandmother handling it alone, not that I blame her. Ari told me Grandma Aggie forgot she was cooking a few weeks ago and left the stove unattended for God knows how long before the in-home assistant woke up. "I'll have Anna help me," Grandma Aggie says, waving us off as she rounds the corner.

It's quiet for longer than is comfortable. The only sound is the *tick-tick-tick* of the clock on the brown paneled wall, and Grandma Aggie shuffling around the kitchen. Mom still stands in the hallway, arms folded tightly over her chest. "What is this about, Brooks?"

"I, uh…I think it's time we have a conversation about everything."

"I'm not sure I know what *everything* is, but if this is about Thanksgiving and you blaming me for Savannah leaving—"

"Don't," I say, and force my jaw to unclench. "Don't bring her into this. I know you had your issues with her, for whatever reason, but that's a conversation for another time. This isn't about her. This is about you and me."

25

Savannah

THURSDAY, FEBRUARY 7, 2019

CELESTIA, TX

"Hannah!" My voice carries across the open field, bringing a sudden halt to everything. All eyes turn my way as I walk onto the field from the parking lot. I'd been running ten minutes late and asked Jana to start practice, but from the looks of it, my assistant coach was too busy gossiping with two of the high school girls to do so properly. I'm not sure what a twenty-something woman has in common with high schoolers, but apparently, today that commonality was more important than watching my fucking practice.

Hannah—a senior and veteran of the squad who thinks she's God's gift to cheerleading—stands front and center, chin held high. She's putting up a front for the others, but I've seen the look in her eyes enough times in and out of the ring to know that she *knows* she just came within inches of a career-ending injury.

"I have half a mind to kick you off the damn squad right now," I say.

Hannah is someone who likes to push the limits, to see just how far she can go, and then reel back at the very last minute. But she's never done anything *this* stupid—not in front of me, anyway. Despite some of the other squad members expressing their concerns, I've never caught her acting up, and supposedly neither had Jana. Now I'm starting to wonder if that was a lack of attempt on Hannah's part or a lack of attention on Jana's when I wasn't around. There's been a handful of complaints brought to my attention over the last month, insinuating that Hannah has been wobbling her ankle on purpose in the middle of a liberty, over-exaggerating her movements when setting up stunts, and pretending to fall too early to mess with her bases...to name a few.

But today I finally witnessed it myself.

As she prepared to dismount, I watched as she twisted mid-air when she should've fallen back into a basic cradle, and her bases weren't prepared. The group landed in a twisted mess of limbs, and she came within inches of landing neck-first into the turf. Thus, the reason for the scared look in her eyes.

"I was just messing around. It's not that serious." Hannah scoffs, trying to maintain some dignity.

"Not that serious?" A fire flares in my chest. "You almost broke your damn neck. You think that because you're the captain and one of the more experienced girls, that means you can do whatever you want. Trust me, Hannah, even the best get injured. I've seen it happen more times than you can count, and not everyone is lucky enough to come back."

"Oh, you mean like your ex-boyfriend?" the blonde teenager quips, rolling her eyes, and I hear more than a few gasps from behind her.

Hannah and I have had a complicated relationship since I took over as head cheerleading coach at the high school my first summer back home. Hannah was moving from her sophomore to junior year and was most likely to be voted captain, which gave her a big head. I wasn't impressed with the teacher's pet act, and when she realized sucking up wasn't going to get her anywhere—with me, at least—her attitude did a complete one-eighty.

"That's it, you're suspended," I say.

"What?" Her face falls. "Coach, you can't do that!"

"I just did."

Hannah looks around at her squad, but every single one of them avoids eye contact. "Jana," she pleads, but my assistant coach shrugs. "This is bullshit. I'm going to make sure that my father hears about this."

"Great. Have him give me a call, and we'll discuss how I kept his daughter from ending up in a wheelchair."

"I am so sorry," Jana says.

Hannah storms past us, mumbling under her breath. Something along the lines of: *I'll have your job for this.* I roll my eyes. One day she'll thank me for this. Maybe.

"The girls had asked me a question about tryouts for next year, and I got distracted. I know it's not an excuse. I'm sorry."

"Jana, the next time I ask you to lead practice," I say, and turn to look her dead in the eye. "I expect you to *lead*, not hand it off to a teenage girl with an attitude problem and an ego the size of Texas." I don't wait for her response, turning back to the rest of the squad members, who have a new pep in their step as they form a half circle in front of me. "If anyone else here thinks they are bigger than this squad or thinks they can perform stupid stunts without consequences, now is the time to leave. I will not have any of you getting hurt on my watch because you think it won't happen to you. It can, it will, and it has. I've seen it happen, and I don't want that for any of you. Are we clear?"

"Yes, Coach," they say in unison.

"Okay, from the top then. Casey, fill Hannah's spot for now."

I adjust my baseball cap further over my eyes and shove

my hands into my windbreaker, taking a step back to watch the routine. How in the hell did I get here? I went from main-eventing the biggest nights in sports entertainment to...this. Most days, I wonder if it's worth babysitting high schoolers so I don't have to face what I left behind. Because if I ever want to step foot in the world of Elite Wrestling Entertainment again, I *will* have to face it...Face *him*. It's been over two years. You would think I'd be able to move past it by now, but...I'm not sure I ever will. Some days are easier than others. I won't think about him at all, and then something will happen, and like a tidal wave, everything comes crashing down, sweeping me away in a sea of memories.

I've kept my distance from most things EWE, but I know it will never leave my life completely. Not only is my best friend still an active member of the roster, but the Williams boys have continued to get together on Monday nights and every other Thursday to watch. They tried to hide it from me, moving their viewing parties from our parents' house to Crew's house. I guess they didn't think I'd notice when everyone went missing twice a week. About a month after I moved back home, I walked in on them watching Battle of Champions, and all five of them—my brothers and Papá—froze like a deer in the headlights.

"You don't have to hide this from me," I said. "Just because I left doesn't mean I don't want you to watch. I just...I need some time before I watch again."

After that, they returned to their regularly scheduled get together centered around our childhood living room, despite Mamá's protests that it was insensitive to me. But I truly didn't care. They could watch if they wanted to, and after a while, I started to join them on occasion. I wanted to know what everyone was up to, but every time, I would find myself missing the ring...the people...him. So, I stopped because it was the only way to (somewhat) ease the ache in my heart. To fight the call in every fiber of my being to return to the ring.

However, it was hard not to watch when I walked into my parents' house three nights ago. My brothers were watching the end of *Monday Night Rage*, and they were pissed. They just *knew* they were about to witness *Brody Wilder* and *Brooks Taylor* get screwed out of the EWE World title. *Austin Spencer* had inserted himself into their match, making it now a triple-threat match at Capitol Punishment scheduled to take place later in the month. From what my brothers said, *Spencer* had been getting in the middle of *Brooks*'s shit for a while now, and the writing was on the wall.

They're going to get Viviana involved next, was the first thing that came to mind, followed by: *She's lucky I'm not there.*

"Heads up!" A voice rings out, catching my attention right before I'm nailed in the head by an oncoming soccer ball. I stick my arm out, deflecting the rogue ball, and send it soaring off the field. When I glance down the field, a boy stands near the goal with a sheepish grin. "Sorry, Coach Skye," he yells. Coach Skye, not Coach Williams, because on my first day, some of the girls had been a little too excited that *Savvy Skye* was going to be their new cheerleading coach. And I didn't have the heart to tell them no when they asked if they could call me by my ring name when they seemed so excited. Gathering the ball, I drop-kick it back down the field and wipe my hands on my thighs.

A soccer ball to the face is the last thing I need right now. This weekend is Crew's wedding, and Amara is already freaking out. I don't need to add a bruised bridesmaid to the list. Speaking of, I'm surprised I haven't heard from anyone in the last twenty minutes. That's why I was late to begin with, helping Mamá and Amara with some last-minute wedding errands. Today might be the only day since my first month of coaching that I was happy to leave for practice.

You've got to be kidding, I think when my phone begins to

vibrate inside my jacket pocket. *Jinxed myself.* Digging it out of my pocket, I almost drop it when I see the name on the screen.

When I call out to my assistant coach, she perks up immediately. "I, uh...I need to take this. Can you handle this for a minute?"

Jana laughs. "Wedding crisis?"

"Something like that," I say, picking up my pace to get away from the chaos on the field. I take another look at the name just to be sure I'm not imagining things. I could let it go to voicemail, but knowing him, he wouldn't bother to leave one. He'd call me back in a day or two, instead, or not at all. But after what I saw a few days ago, I'm too curious not to answer. "Hello?"

"Savannah!" His gruff voice rings out. "It's Amos Rafferty. How are you?" He introduces himself as if I don't already know.

"Amos," I breathed, still wondering if I'm imagining the whole thing. It's good to hear his voice again. "I-I'm good. How are you?"

"Great, great. I hear your brother is getting married this weekend."

How does he know about that?

"Yeah, he is. High school sweetheart."

"That's great. I'm sure it will be a beautiful day. Give them my best, will you? Hey, listen, I was hoping to catch up before the festivities begin. Do you have a minute?"

My stomach tightens. It can't be this simple, can it? "Sure."

"Look, Savannah, I'm just going to cut to the chase. We want you back." Hearing the words, my already racing heart leaps out of my chest. "I know things were a bit...tense when you left, but I think it's the perfect time to bring you back. You've been gone long enough to reset and recharge, to let things go and—"

"You want me to come back?"

"Yes," he says immediately. "We want to re-sign you for at least two years, if not—"

"Amos—"

"You don't have to give me an answer right now. But if you're at least open to the idea, I'd like you to come sit down with me, Noah, and Brian on Monday."

He wants me to come back. Every fiber in my being screams out *yes*, but there is still a small sliver of doubt in the back of my mind. What am I going to do about *him*?

26

Brooks

"Knock, knock," a deep voice rings out, following the arrival *ding* of the elevator. I knew I should've gotten that damn key back. What in the hell is he doing here? This is the first Thursday I've been off since my return late last April, and of course, my best friend would decide he wants to spend it with me, because apparently, we don't see enough of each other at work. He should be taking his better half out to dinner, not showing up unannounced at my condo. "Yoohoo, Brooksy, you home? We come bearing gifts."

We? Who in the hell is *we*?

With a sigh, I twist the knobs of the grill, extinguishing the flames, and walk back inside to find Wolf in the kitchen leaning over the breakfast bar. He doesn't seem to notice me, eyes glued to the stone countertop, his mind a thousand miles away. That's how it's been with him lately; he might physically be present, but his head is somewhere else. I feel bad for the kid. Granted, I don't think anyone, except for him, is surprised by what happened. He never wanted to hear what we had to say about Harper, and eventually, that refusal came back to bite him in the ass. They got married last January on a secluded beach in Hawaii, with only their immediate family present, and planned to host a big shindig after Wrestlefest for the rest of us. But two months after saying "I do," he found her in bed with another man. Not just any man. Our coworker Grady Chandler. And now, Wolf has to see her sucking face with him every day at work.

"There you are!" Brody struts down the hallway from the master bedroom. "I was starting to think maybe you'd gone out tonight."

My brow cocks, and I ask, "Who would I be going out with?"

"I don't know. Maybe you have some secret girlfriend or something that we don't know about."

A laugh sounds from the other man in the room, and he finally lifts his head to look at us. "Good one, Brody. But we all know he's still hung up on Savannah. No chance in hell he's taking some other girl out, especially on Valentine's Day."

My chest tightens at the sound of her name. Fuck, why am I like this? It's been two fucking years, I should be over it by now. Over her. But every time I hear her name, the walls fall faster than Jericho.

"What are you guys even doing here?" I snap, regretting it almost immediately because it only confirms what Wolf just said. I fold my arms over my chest, readjusting my stance. "Shouldn't you be out with your fiancée?"

"She's sulking at home. Told me to round up you two sorry fuckers and have a guys' night. I'll take her out tomorrow or Saturday when she's in the mood to be bothered," Brody says.

"Why is she sulking?"

"Beats me."

"You're lying," I say. "Now, tell me what you're really doing here."

Brody joins Wolf in the kitchen, draping an arm over his

shoulder to pull him in close. "Can't a guy just want to hang out with his two best friends?" When neither of us answers, Brody sighs. "Look, you are my best friends, and I hate seeing you both in such sour moods all the damn time. I figured we got tonight off, and Rae wanted her space, so we should make the most of it. When's the last time we had a guys' night, anyway?"

"Before you started dating Rae. At least Savannah let us come hang out on our days off while they were together," Wolf says without hesitation. He holds Brody's stare for a moment, then mine, before pulling out of the one-armed embrace and retreating to the wet bar in the corner of the living space. He's not going to be happy when he realizes the good bottle of whiskey is gone. I only bring it out for special occasions...or nights like this.

"What's going on with Raelynn?" I ask, trying to change the subject. It feels like the safest option, allowing Brody to take over the conversation again while I try to ease the unrelenting tightness in my chest.

"She's just in one of her moods," he says, letting his head fall. "And..." He glances around the corner when a cabinet door slams. Wolf opens and closes the different cabinets, mumbling to himself. Brody shakes his head and turns back to me. "And despite how many times I tried to convince her that getting some fresh air and good food would help her mood, she refused. Said she didn't feel like it, all she wanted to do was soak in a hot bath with her new book and eat ice cream while watching some chick flick."

"Where are the gifts you mentioned?" I say, remembering what he'd say when they walked in.

Brody rolls his eyes, slipping his hand into his jacket and pulling out three cigars. "Figured this would keep you from kicking us out immediately."

"Yeah, I guess you can stay. I was about to make—"

"Brooks, you asshole!" Wolf's voice rings out. Looks like he figured it out. "You drank the good shit."

"Well, if you'd leave your house every once in a while, maybe you could've helped me polish off the bottle," I say.

He's become quite the hermit since the divorce, barely leaving home unless it's a work-related event. I was surprised when Brody told me he joined them in Celestia for Crew's wedding last week. The wedding Brody didn't even want to tell me about, but I'd known about it since the oldest Williams popped the question because Ari let it slip. She had been invited, and she almost considered not going until I told her she should. She was friends with the Williams family, too, and I knew she'd kept in touch with Savannah more than she originally said after our breakup. I'd seen Savannah's name appear on my sister's phone more than once. If the Williamses were going to continue to welcome her—especially after the Thanksgiving fiasco—who was I to put a stop to it?

Ari took a small gift from me, and much to my surprise, I got a text from Crew the day after. It was short—simple—but I knew it was a lot for him to send me anything besides "*Fuck you*."

Without missing a beat, Wolf counters, "Well, maybe if you would leave *your* house, you wouldn't freak out every time you hear Savannah's name." He untwists the cap of the only whiskey bottle I have in stock and empties half the remainder into the six shot glasses he'd lined up along the counter.

I look over at Brody with a cocked brow. *When did Wolf get so brave*?

Brody rubs the space between his brows with a heavy sigh. This is not how he wanted tonight to go, but I can't say I'm surprised. This is the first time it's been just the three of us in a while. Brody has been busy with Raelynn, Wolf has been busy sulking, and I've been busy rebuilding my life, or trying to.

"I don't freak out every time I hear Savannah's name," I say.

Wolf gathers the shots in his hands, moving them to the breakfast bar. He pushes two toward Brody and hands two to me. "Your stress lines say otherwise."

"I don't freak out when I hear her name. You guys don't have to walk on eggshells around me when it comes to her. It's been two years, and—"

"And you still love her."

"And as long as she's happy, then I'm happy," I say, but the look they share mirrors the thoughts in my head.

"Don't bullshit a bullshitter, Brooks," Wolf says.

He's the first person who hasn't handled me with kid gloves since the breakup. Everyone, including Brody, has tiptoed around me and anything that might bring her up, and I fucking hate it. It's only made it harder to move on because it feels like I'm supposed to be holding onto something that isn't here. This is not how I thought my life would turn out, but I don't blame Savannah. She only did what she thought was best.

I was wrong, I know that. I should've told her the truth, but she never would've said yes to a date if she knew about Drake's wager. And the deeper we got into our relationship, the more time that passed, I knew I couldn't tell her. Because, despite my hope that she would understand and we could work through it, part of me was scared of exactly what happened.

"Am I still working through some things? Yes, but that doesn't mean you guys can't bring her up. You are friends with her and her family, and I can't pretend that she doesn't exist or expect you to do the same. Our lives are intertwined, and we're all learning how to navigate the new waters."

"Sounds like something my therapist would say," Wolf says with a small laugh. He picks up both of the shots in front of him and raises them in the air. "To us, a bunch of sorry fuckers who are in a sour mood all the damn time."

Brody rolls his eyes in reply to Wolf's jab at his earlier words, but lifts one of his own glasses in the air. "To you, sorry fuckers."

I do the same, but don't add anything, bringing the rim to my lips and letting the liquid slide down my throat in one gulp. It burns a path down my throat into my stomach, warming my insides immediately.

"How was the wedding?" I ask, handing both of them a fresh beer when I return to the balcony. Neither of them answers. "C'mon, tell me. How was it?"

Brody sighs. "Brooks—"

"No, Brod, it's okay. I want to know."

Wolf shrugs, taking a sip of his beer. "Nothing out of the ordinary. Got to meet Bodhi's new girlfriend, though, some hotshot lawyer down in Austin from the firm he left last year. And Nash was so nervous during his speech that he kept messing up."

"The shots race you two were doing didn't help," Brody says.

"Gave everyone a good laugh, though," Wolf says with a chuckle. Brody rolls his eyes, but can't fight his own small laugh, no doubt remembering that night. After a moment, Wolf clears his throat and turns to look at us. "Can I say something and it won't be weird?"

"I'm scared to say yes, but yes," Brody answers, staring into the black abyss before us.

The condo overlooks the Gulf, the balcony walls made of

glass, giving unimpeded floor-to-ceiling views of the striking blue waters from inside. But right now, the only thing you can see for miles is the inky night sky.

"The whole thing felt off..." Wolf meets my gaze, and a pit forms in my stomach, threatening to swallow me whole. I'm not sure that I want to know what comes next. "Without you there. Don't get me wrong, it was a good time. Crew and Amara were happy, and it was everything they wanted, but it still felt like something was missing."

That's not what I was expecting, but I'm not sure it makes me feel any better, either. Brody avoids my stare, his own falling from the waves sixty feet below to the bottle in his hands. He picks at the label with his thumbnail. Did something happen at the wedding? No, because Ari would've told me if it did... right?

I don't know what I'm supposed to say next, if I'm supposed to say anything at all. Do I admit that I wished I had been there, too? Or do I ask if Savannah said something to make him feel that way? No, I have to do something to ease the tension and circle back to the lighthearted conversation we've enjoyed most of the night. It won't be long before they have to leave, and I don't want it to end on a sour note.

"You said you weren't going to make it weird," I say, taking a sip of my beer. That does the trick, making Brody laugh, followed by Wolf.

"Hey," Brody starts. "I meant to ask you earlier...how'd that session go with your mom and Ari?"

Wolf all but chokes on the sip of beer he'd just taken. "I'm sorry, you went to therapy with your *mom*?"

"She was a bit reluctant, but ultimately decided to give it a try," I say, taking a long drag of my beer.

"And?" Brody pushes.

I shrug. "And we're working on things. She has to work on herself before we can truly talk and move past everything."

"Do you blame her for Savannah leaving?" Wolf asks. Damn, he's really hitting me with the hard shit tonight, isn't he?

It's my turn to pick at the bottle label, avoiding both of their stares. I told Brody about the conversation I had with Mom the December before last, about how reluctant she was to hear what I had to say. Then, a month later, my grandmother called to tell me Mom had decided to go to therapy, and about how the therapist wanted me and my sister to sit in on a few sessions. But that was as much detail as I'd ever given him.

I don't blame my mother for Savannah leaving. Okay, maybe I blame her a little. She was never very welcoming, constantly nitpicking and complaining, but it wasn't anything Savannah couldn't look past. She was willing to put up with it—with her—because she loved me and my family. It wasn't until that day in therapy that I found out about some of the altercations between them because Savannah had never told me. I hated that she felt like she couldn't tell me. But despite their differences, I know that ultimately, Mom wasn't the reason Savannah decided to leave.

"No." I sigh, lifting my gaze. "That's all me."

Wolf clears his throat. "You don't have to answer this, but what happened? I thought you guys were talking marriage and kids."

"We, uh...We were." I clear my throat. "But things change."

"Not that fast, they don't."

"Wolf—" Brody starts, but I interrupt him.

"Savannah left because she found out about a bet between me and Drake."

It's quiet for a moment, but this time when Wolf speaks, his normal tone is replaced with something far more dangerous. "What do you mean a *bet* between you and Drake?"

Brody shakes his head as I begin the story, filling our friend in on the truth about everything. The whole time, Wolf glares at me from across the table, hands clenched so tight around the beer bottle I'm sure it's going to crack at any moment. I don't think he blinks once, eyes narrowing further into slits with every piece of information he learns.

"You only dated Savannah based on a fucking bet with Miles Drake?" Wolf grits out before he glances over at Brody. "And you knew about this?"

"I was there," Brody says. "Wolf, it's not as bad as it sounds, but—"

"There is no *but*. Savannah was right to leave your ass. What the fuck, Brooks?"

I begin to argue, but I'm grateful when Brody steps in. He explains the full situation, showing it from an outsider's perspective, instead of just my own, and I watch as some of the fire fades from Wolf's eyes. I see the moment he begins to understand why I did it, even if he doesn't agree with my decisions.

"Drake's game is not the only reason I wanted to be with Savannah," I add when Brody is finished. "We knew each other before she ever came to EWE, and—"

"You knew each other?" Wolf interrupts me.

"We met once, at a bar down in Texas. It was well before she ever joined the company. The only reason we never said anything was because she didn't want anyone to think she got handed opportunities because of me."

"And I was dating the one person who would've taken that information and done the most damage," Wolf says, the heat in his tone fading. He sighs, taking a long drag of his beer. "Shit, I'm sorry. I should've listened to you guys, but—"

I shrug. "All good. What's done is done, no taking it back. Now it's time for everyone to pick up and try to move on."

"Can you?" Wolf glances back up at me. "Move on?"

"I don't know," I say, drumming my fingers on the stone tabletop. "I'm working on it, and as long as I know she's doing okay and she's happy, then one day I know I can be, too."

The almost-full moon reflects off the black waters below, the sky around it freckled with white stars. A small cluster catches my eye. Its unique pattern reminds me of one I'd come to know all too well. One that I've traced a thousand times.

I know I shouldn't, but I can't help myself. My eyes trace over the pattern, drawing the invisible lines to connect the dots, and when it's complete, my heart stops as the five-pointed star stares back at me—identical to the one on Savannah's left shoulder.

"John," Brody's voice pulls me back. *John*? He must have been trying to get my attention for a while. Meeting his stare, I notice the concern etched on his face even in the shadows. He's standing now, poised to walk back inside, holding three empty beer bottles between his fingers. "You want another beer?"

I nod. "Y-yeah. Thanks. Grab those cigars, too."

"Hey, what time is it?" Wolf asks.

Flipping over my phone on the table, I tap the screen, and for the second time tonight, I feel my heart stop beating.

12:01 a.m.

PART THREE

27

MONDAY, APRIL 8, 2019

ORLANDO, FL

Bizarre. That's the only word I can use to describe today. Everyone around here seems to be on edge, or maybe it's just me. A heaviness has settled deep within me that radiates from one nerve ending to the next. Matched with a sinking feeling in my gut, it tells me *something* is coming. Something big, and I don't like the anticipation of it one bit. Normally, I could shake it off, put it behind me until I leave the arena, but not this time.

I've been telling myself that it's just because I don't know *who* is going to step out of that curtain tonight, but part of me wonders if it's something more than that...Amos, Noah, and Tim have been extremely secretive about my tag partner. When they first mentioned the idea, they carefully skirted around the topic of a name, saying they had a few ideas, none of which had been solidified. I didn't believe them. The look Amos and Noah shared told me they had already found someone, but they weren't ready to tell me. For some reason, I found that unsettling. Why would they need to keep it a secret?

As time went on, they kept the identity under wraps, only making the three of us—Austin, Viviana, and me—all the more curious…and even more nervous. Who could be so important that they'd need to keep them a secret for over a month now? It had to be a veteran. Someone who could put Viviana's character in her place—someone the fans wouldn't question. A hundred names have run through my mind—*Juliet? Holly? Luna? Moxie?* Any of them would be a good pick. *Cali Kennedy* has been out with a knee injury. Maybe she's making a return…She isn't a vet, but she'd be a good choice nonetheless.

But if it's any of them, why wouldn't Creative tell us?

Trying to find a way to release the nerves, I jump in place, shaking out my hands, ignoring the side glance from Stu, the timekeeper. I plant my feet and stretch my arms over my chest, taking a deep breath as I wait for my cue. Austin has been running his mouth for at least five minutes, but I tuned him out well before he picked up the mic. I haven't been this nervous to step in front of a crowd since my debut match fourteen years ago, and I blame Noah and Amos.

Stu points at me, and my music fills the arena. I take a final breath—cranking my neck from side to side, pushing my shoulders back—and walk out.

Almost like walking through a thin veil between worlds, the nerves melt away when I step in front of the crowd, and *Brooks Taylor* takes his place at the forefront. He stands tall—confident—maintaining the collected nature he prides himself on. This crowd is amped. We're only three weeks away from Wrestlefest, and the closer we get, the rowdier they become.

"*Oh, look who it is,*" *Spencer Austin* scoffs. "*It's like Candyman—say his name too many times and he'll appear.*" *Viviana* snickers at his side, and I roll my eyes.

Each week, the fans have eaten up whatever Austin and I have thrown at them, because while most of the EWE fanbase loves me, a good amount of them hate me almost equally. Whenever they get the chance to see someone knock Brooks Taylor down a few pegs, they enjoy it more than I'd probably like to admit. Everyone knows there isn't anyone who can oust *Brooks Taylor* from the throne of EWE…No one is ready because no one is willing to do what I do for this company. They aren't willing to make the sacrifices it takes to be at the forefront. Not even the man standing in the middle of the ring. And while that same man would like to think he can break me—if only in story form—we both know he can't. *Brooks Taylor* rarely cracks; it's only happened a handful of times, and two of those times were because of *her.*

Savvy Skye. Savannah Williams. The woman I—*No, Brooks. You cannot think of her right now. Focus, just through this segment.*

"*You know, I think it's comical you think you can beat me when you couldn't even beat Vee with a hand tied behind your back,*" *Spencer* says, regaining my attention. He's been going on and on for the last few minutes, but I haven't heard a damn word he said. I hope it's not obvious, or Amos will have my head. "*Should we see a clip? I think we should. Roll the clip!*" His demand is met with a highlight reel from the handicap match between me and *Viviana* two weeks ago.

The chorus of boos that follows the end of the clip surprises me. The crowd has been pro-*Spencer* and *Viviana* almost this entire feud, but this is the first crowd that has mostly been behind me.

"*You didn't even try, Brooks,*" *Spencer* says. "*You could've at least tried to put up a fight, given her something to work with.*"

"*Are you serious, Austin?*" I scoff. "*I wasn't going to fight your wife. Are you insane? Vee is good, but I refuse to do that.*" The nerves creep their way past the veil, and I'm no longer *Brooks Taylor.* I'm John Brooks, and for the briefest moment, *her* name fills my mind again. What if it's her? What if that's why they haven't said anything? It can't be. They wouldn't... Would they? No, she wouldn't, but it's the only real reason I can think of why they'd keep the identity of my partner a secret.

No, Savannah would *never* come back, not for this...Not for me.

A spark ignites in the air following my words. The crowd begins to hum, almost like they know where this is going.

My tongue darts out to wet my lips, and I force the corners of my mouth upward. The chuckle that follows doesn't match the knots in my stomach, but I do my best to conceal how what is going on beneath the surface. *"But I know someone who will."*

Showtime.

The arena goes dark, and for exactly ten seconds, it's deadly silent. I swear the whole place can hear the blood pumping through my system. I don't even realize I'm holding my breath until my lungs scream for air, forcing me to exhale, and the opening riffs of the familiar song consume me. In the blink of an eye, I'm thrust back to a completely different time. One where she was mine and I was happy...

"There's no fucking way," I whisper, but it's lost in the sea of chaos. Screams, cheers, tears, and applause make the building quake beneath my feet. When the chorus finally hits, the lights turn up, and *she* struts out. Savannah Williams. The woman who stole my heart a decade ago. The woman who disappeared from my life over two years ago.

But these people don't know that; all they see is *Savvy Skye*, one of their heroes, returned from the depths.

I force my gaze to remain in front of me, staring down at the couple in the ring, their mouths hang agape. They're allowed to show that response, but I'm not. As far as the crowd knows, I knew it was her the whole time.

Even from this distance, I can see the question in Austin's

eye. He cornered me earlier, tried to pry the name out of me because he didn't believe I had been left in the dark, but I assured him I was just as clueless as he was. He looks between me and Savannah, still questioning how much I knew, before his wife whispers something in his ear.

My breath catches in my throat when I get a glimpse of Savannah in the three-hundred-sixty-degree screen that hangs high above the ring. Her gleaming smile widens as she soaks in every ounce of energy thrown her way. Every time I think the crowd is about to settle, they start again. She looks beautiful, dressed in high-waisted jeans, black heels, and a white, cropped shirt that looks delectable against the warmth of her tanned skin. *No, Brooks, do not say things like that.* Her hair is perfectly curled into waves, much longer than it used to be, hanging well below the under curve of her breasts and grazing the fabric of her jeans below her hips. She looks good—*really good*—like taking the last two and a half years off was the best thing she could've done.

How am I supposed to do this?

When the camera pans out to show the two of us standing side by side, my heart clenches. That's an image I never thought I'd see again.

"*You can't do this*!" *Spencer* shouts over the crowd, getting us back on track, and they finally begin to simmer.

"*It's already done*," *Savvy* says, and the smirk in her voice brings another one to my face. The crowd echoes the sentiment with another cheer. "*You already signed the contract*."

That's right, they did sign the contract before I interrupted them. It had been sitting on the table in the middle of the ring, ready and waiting, signed by me last week while they were gone for their honeymoon. *Theo Rafferty*, once again the "General Manager," made a whole spectacle of it. He made me come down to the ring, sitting across from him, and sign the contract as he *begged* me to tell him who my partner would be.

Brooks Taylor refused to say, and part of me now wonders if Theo was in on this whole thing and last week was his chance to play games with me. Last week, I signed the dotted line on a blank contract; there were no names, no stipulations, nothing...

"*Did you even read that contract before you signed it?*" *Savvy* asks. What is she talking about? There's never anything important on them. Sometimes they're left completely blank, truly all for show, but the look on *Viviana*'s face as she reads over the paper again tells me there's *something* there.

"*Did I read the contract?*" *Spencer* scoffs. "*Of course, I read the—*"

Viviana says something, holding out the contract to her husband, and he snatches the paper from her hands. His eyes scour across it before they lift to stare straight at the woman next to me.

Even from here, I can hear him curse under his breath as he scrubs a hand down his face.

"*Signed. Sealed. And delivered,*" *Savvy* punctuates each word, and I see the smirk on her lips on the screen. "We'll see you in three weeks. Oh, and I hope you're ready because the match...it's going to be No Disqualifications."

What the fuck? is the first thing that comes to mind, and I see Austin and Vee share my sentiment in a quick exchange.

What is going on? No Disqualifications? No one said anything about that. A No DQ match can be like the Wild, Wild West, depending on who you're fighting. There are no rules, except one: pinfall or submission must occur in the ring to win. Why wouldn't Noah warn us? Probably because he knows Austin would've lost his shit.

"*You don't even work here, Skye! Not to mention, the last time you were in the ring with my wife—*"

The last time she was in the ring with his wife, Viviana got injured, but it wasn't Savannah's fault. At Clash of the Titans, the premiere event in November 2016, *Savvy Skye* was facing *Viviana* in a street fight match for the women's title. About halfway through the match, Savannah set up to throw her opponent into the steel steps; however, it didn't go as planned. Instead of going through with the spot, Viviana planted her feet. Her foot went one way, and her knee went another. The official should've called the match right then and there, but Viviana wanted to keep going. A few chair shots and a chain rope to the knee later, *Savvy Skye* picked up the victory to retain her title. Viviana couldn't walk, having to be carried backstage, where Doc could assess the damage done.

"*Scared your wife can't hold her own?*" I ask, and normally, this is where *Savvy* and I should share a look, but we don't.

"*This is between you and me, Taylor,*" *Spencer* shouts, pointing his finger in my direction. "*Leave the women out of this.*" His face now a darker shade of red, bleeding down into his neck and chest. *Viviana* slides her hand into his as the crowd boos in response. "*I'm not putting my wife in a ring with her.*"

"*Your wife would be lucky to step in the same ring as her.*" The words come out harsher and faster than I mean them to. Cool it, I remind myself. Let's try to keep it civil. Austin's brow raises. He's hit a real nerve, and he knows it, but two can play that game. "*Maybe she could learn a thing or two about wrestling.*"

Viviana gasps and looks at her husband, tearfully burying herself into his chest. It's a bit dramatic, if you ask me, but the crowd eats it up. Her character—especially when she was known as *Fortuna*—has always been a little over the top... And while she tries her best, she's a mid-card wrestler at best. Putting her up against Savannah in a No DQ match is almost unfair. *Spencer* wraps his arm around her waist, comforting his wife, and glares up the ramp. "*This isn't over, Taylor!*"

"*You're right. It's not over until I bring the title back where it belongs.*" I drop the mic and motion toward my midsection, using my thumb and index finger on each hand to represent where the belt should hang on my hips. "*We'll see you in three weeks!*"

28

Savannah

TUESDAY, APRIL 9, 2019
TAMPA, FL

"That's it, Sav!" Bennett yells from the outside the ring when I block Raelynn's roundhouse kick. I take hold of her ankle and twist it at the same time I sweep her other leg from under her.

Rae grunts when her back hits the mat, but she resets quickly, climbing back to her feet. Using the ropes to spring forward, I slam my shoulder into hers in a shoulder tackle, sending her back down to the mat. Wasting no time, my fingers tangle into her long black ponytail and lift her into a headlock. With her head underneath my left arm, I fall backwards, letting my feet fall out from underneath me, and drive Rae's face into the mat for a DDT.

Bennett slams his palm on the apron. "Finish her!"

As I untangle from the mess of limbs, the side of my shoe taps Rae's side, and she sells the kick, rolling onto her stomach. I sit on her back and grasp her arms, pulling backward. It bends her back, driving her spine into my knee. Rae cries out when I reach around and wrap my right arm under her neck, further extending her back.

Bennett slides under the bottom rope, climbing to his

knees to be eye level with Raelynn. "What do you say, Rae?"

Rae shakes her head vigorously. "Fuck off, Wolf!"

He asks again when I retighten my grip, and she cries again. "C'mon, what's it gonna be, *Rose*?"

Rae tries to maneuver out of the hold, but she's never been good at getting out of this. Today doesn't seem to be any different. Guess some things never change. Finally, she submits, slapping my thigh.

"That's it, break the hold!" Bennett moves his fingers in a circular motion in the air, as if someone were there to ring the bell. We fall to the mat in opposite directions when I release her.

"I do not miss that," Raelynn groans, rubbing her back.

"Just be glad it wasn't her real finisher," Bennett chuckles.

"Been there, done that. I'm good, thanks." Raelynn and I had spent many long nights together perfecting and planning our finishing moves and submissions, performing them on one another until we got them just right. Needless to say, we spent a lot of time working out the kinks in our muscles for days following those nights.

It feels amazing to be back in the ring, and with someone other than Juliet. Before today, she was the only person outside of Noah, Amos, and Brian who knew about my return. I've been meeting with her almost every day at EWE Headquarters in Houston since I agreed to come back. The first few days were hard. I had to work out the ring rust, and it felt like the first days of training all over again, but it was still the best I'd felt in years.

When Raelynn first pulled into the parking lot of the infamous new EWE training facility earlier, I wasn't impressed. It looked more like a detention center than the old one did, with solid, tan concrete walls and square windows that lined the top just beneath the roofline. Two separate sections formed an "L" shape, meeting in what appeared to be the lobby with two sets of glass double doors and a sign that read *Elite Wrestling Entertainment Training Center*, the only indication that this building isn't a prison. However, what the outside lacked in curb appeal, the inside made up for tenfold. The moment I walked in, I found myself jealous that this place wasn't around when I was in NextGen, but I wouldn't give the years we spent in that old warehouse for anything.

I had been invited to the grand opening in the autumn after I left the company, but declined. I wasn't anywhere near ready to be back; hell, I'm still not sure I am. Then I heard through the grapevine (aka my brothers) that it had finally opened with John standing beside Amos as he cut the ribbon.

"C'mon, Sav, my turn," Bennett says, catching my attention. He coaxes me back into the center of the ring after a quick water break. "Rae went easy on you, but I'm not going to be as nice."

Raelynn laughs from the corner of the ring. "You talk a lot of trash for someone who got swept by both of us the first time we got in the ring with you."

He throws her a sour look over his shoulder, and I sweep his legs out from under him. Raelynn howls with laughter, and I stand over him with a cocked brow.

"That doesn't count! I wasn't ready!"

"Well, then get ready," I say, chuckling to myself.

Bennett groans, taking his sweet time to push up from the mat, and I hear the lobby doors open and close. My two friends look that way, but I have a feeling I know who it is, especially after the phone call I got earlier. "C'mon, while I'm still young."

"I miss the days when you weren't so demanding," Bennett says, bringing his attention back to our fight. We circle, sizing each other up.

"Oh, really? When was that?" I ask, and we lunge at the same time.

As we lock into a collar-and-elbow-tie-up with a soft thud—one of my palms on the back of Bennett's neck, the other cradling his elbow—Bennett can't hide that grin that splits his face. "You see who came in?" he asks in a hushed tone, but I ignore him, just like I'm ignoring the person still standing near the door.

I know why he's here. Noah called before Raelynn and I left her apartment, warning me what was coming. Amos wants me to join Brooks in New York, starting tomorrow, for three days of media before we fly to Charleston for an untelevised show on Friday.

With a quick pivot of my hips, I twist my upper body and slide my arm around Bennett's head, pulling him into a side headlock. I tighten my grip just enough to make him work for the escape. He wraps his arms around my waist, shoving me forward into the ropes, and when I turn back around, he's waiting with a clothesline.

"Dammit, Wolf!" I groan as my back hits the mat. Not only did he full stop for extra impact, but his forearm landed in the spot between a perfect landing and the top of my breasts. Women do their best to avoid that area, but the guys...they forget sometimes.

"You good?"

"Just keep going, fucker." With an inhale, I roll to my stomach as he runs the ropes, jumping over me and rebounding off the opposite rope as I jump up. He ducks, missing my swing, and slides behind me.

Arms wrapped securely behind my waist, Bennett lifts me off my feet and over his head, slamming my shoulders into the mat—German Suplex—except he doesn't let go. He rolls through, still holding my waist. I elbow his side, but he only tightens his grip. Adjusting his feet, Bennett tosses me over his head into another suplex, this time letting go.

"You're enjoying this," I say, wiping the corner of my

mouth as I use the rope to stand.

"You've always told me not to hold back," he counters. I shrug with a small smirk before we lock up again. It's true, I never want him to hold back—or anyone for that matter. Bennett glances behind me, and his brow raises. The next time he speaks, his voice is so low I barely hear him. "Don't look now, but if I didn't know any better, I'd say he looks a little jealous."

"Shut the fuck up, Wolf." I kick his gut and shove him away, hitting him with my own clothesline when he charges. Time to end this shit.

When Bennett sits up, I snake my left arm around his neck and sit back on my heels, arching his body into a bow— Seated Dragon Sleeper.

Raelynn snickers from her corner. "Oh shit, you're in deep trouble now, Wolfie."

Bennett tries to kick his legs out from under him, but I tighten my arm on his neck.

"You better tap before she goes for the 'Breaker," Raelynn says.

"What do you want, Wolf?" I ask. "The 'Breaker or a DDT?"

"Do I have a choice?" he asks, his voice strangled.

"I just gave it to you, didn't I?"

"Fuck it," Bennett breathes. "Give me the 'Breaker."

"Good choice." I smirk, coming up onto my feet. Bennett's body hangs almost limp, feet planted on the mat, before I lift my knee and slam into his back. He grunts in pain, and I do it three more times before I drop to my knees. I strike my forearm down onto his chest, and where I'd normally hold onto my opponent, I let Bennett fall to the mat.

"Fuck." He coughs.

"Had enough?" I ask.

"Not even close," Bennett says, groaning as he begins to

roll over onto his stomach. He pushes himself up to his feet.

"Okay! I'm calling time. You two are going to kill each other if I don't," Raelynn says as we circle each other again.

"Who's it gonna be, Rae?" Bennett asks.

"Why do I have to decide?"

"Because you're the one who called it," I say.

Raelynn groans. She hates picking the winner. Bennett and I circle each other four more times, and I'm about to tell her to choose when someone else does for her.

"Wolf," Brooks calls out, his voice closer than I thought.

Without acknowledging him, I lunge forward, but Bennett's foot connects with my gut. He pulls me forward, my head going between his legs, and wraps his arms around my midsection. In one quick motion, Bennett lifts my feet off the mat, my legs landing on his shoulders, before he drops to his ass and my back hits the mat—Powerbomb. Bennett covers, and I think about kicking out just for the hell of it, but I watch as Raelynn's hand slams on the mat—one, two, three.

"I remember your 'Breaker being worse than that," Bennett says, patting my leg before we both sit up, catching our breath.

My brow raises as I look over my shoulder. "Should we try again?"

"No, no." His response is quick. "I'm good." I notice his gaze move outside the ring, and for the first time, I look at the other man who joined us.

John Brooks stands nearby with the same confidence he oozes when he walks down the ramp to face his opponents in the ring, and I wonder if he's putting on the front for little old me. But maybe it's not for me at all. His eyes never leave Bennett, who glances my way with an eye roll and a slight shake of his head. They've remained best friends through the tumultuous ending of our relationship, but I know it's been hard on our mutual friend, who tends to tread lightly on both sides.

"You guys done?" Brooks asks, his eyes still on our friend.

"I don't know about these two, but I'm calling it a night. I gotta get home." Bennett has become somewhat of a homebody when he's not working. I barely convinced him to join us for our annual New Year's Eve trip at my parents' ranch a few months ago. Since his divorce from Harper last year, Raelynn and I have both expressed concern about his level of self-isolation, and I'm starting to think we need to do something. It doesn't help that he has to see her face at work, but rumor has it she won't be re-signing when her contract expires in June.

Rae and I share a look as he climbs out of the ring, patting Brooks on the back. They share a quick word before the latter rolls his eyes and pushes Bennett away, who laughs the whole way to the locker room.

"Should I leave, too?" Raelynn asks without even trying to hide her smirk. She is the only person who knows the truth about what happened. I told her a month or two after I left, and after she heard me out, she told me I was wrong for what I did. She thinks I'm holding on to something I shouldn't be. *It's not like he went through with it*, she said back then. While that might be true, it didn't make the sting hurt any less.

How was I supposed to feel knowing that a stupid bet was the reason he'd gotten off his ass and finally asked me out? Raelynn would remind me of two things: one, I had told Brooks not to ask me out, and two, Brody was part of the whole fiasco, too, but I'd forgiven him. Each time, I'd remind her that Brody wasn't my almost fiancé.

"That's not necessary," Brooks says. "I was just coming to offer Savannah a ride—"

Almost like a moment straight from one of those classic rom-com movies, Raelynn takes a drink of water at the exact moment he says it, practically choking on the sip.

This is going so well. I pinch the bridge of my nose and take a deep breath.

"Sorry, I just—" Raelynn clears her throat. "Water went down the wrong pipe." Her cheeks are redder than a ripe tomato.

"—to New York," Brooks finishes his sentence. His gaze is almost unreadable when it turns back on me, and I know he's putting up the wall to keep things professional and maintain a less-than-comfortable distance between us. It's exactly what I hoped would happen, but now that it's happening...my heart longs for the way he used to look at me.

Raelynn's head whips toward me. "New York?"

"I'm good," I say, ignoring her.

"Sure about that?" Brooks asks.

"Why wouldn't I be?" I'd rather sit in a crowded seat in the back of a plane than be stuck in a claustrophobic tube with no escape next to him.

He chuckles when I don't back down, shaking his head. "Suit yourself, but I'm leaving at six if you change your mind. Rae"—he glances her way—"careful with that water, huh?"

Her brown eyes widen, and the blush returns to her cheeks. She opens and closes her mouth a few times, grasping at straws for a response before she decides on a simple nod.

"Oh, and Savannah." His words pull my attention back to him. "You look good out there, but you watch your bumps. Few of those looked a little rough."

The words bounce around my mind. My breath catches and my stomach drops. *Watch your bumps.* The same thing he'd said after my debut.

"Footwork could use a little work, too."

My jaw sets. Is he really giving me advice? Sure, I've always had a bad habit of using the opposite leading foot, and it's something he worked relentlessly to break me of...I guess that's another thing I lost when I lost him.

The corners of his lips pull up briefly. He *knows* what those words do to me. Without another word, I watch him return the way he came, shoulders pulled taut beneath the blue Henley, maintaining that stereotypical *Brooks Taylor* façade—the one he never put up around me until now.

It's for the best, I remind myself. *You're just here to help finish this story and leave.* That was only partially true; I hadn't decided what I was going to do yet.

"I am so sorry," Raelynn says. "I didn't mean to—He just said, and I-I'm sorry."

When the doors finally close behind him, I glance at her with a raised brow, and it sends us into a fit of giggles. "I cannot believe you did that!"

"He said it!" she argues, still giggling. "Why are they sending you to New York with him, anyway?"

"United front and all that." I shrug, pulling my knees into my chest. While I wasn't looking forward to spending so much alone time with my ex-boyfriend, I knew this was coming.

Amos had made it very clear at our initial meeting what he wanted upon my return. "I don't care what happened all those years ago, Savannah. This is business. I need to know if you can handle this. I can't have you running off halfway through the match," he said that day in his office.

"Have I ever done that, Amos?" I asked, sounding more confident than I felt.

"I just want to make sure. I don't know, and I don't want to know, but what I *need* to know is if you can put your differences aside for the sake of the story. I need the fearsome duo of *Brooks Taylor* and *Savvy Skye* until Wrestlefest."

"And you'll have it."

"How are you feeling about all of this?" Raelynn asks, pulling me out of my thoughts. She crosses her ankles, resting her chin on her knees. "Being back, working with him—"

"I don't know, Rae," I sigh.

I'm surprised she lasted this long before bringing this up. I was pleasantly surprised when she didn't mention this on the drive back from Orlando last night. She and Brody have been generous enough to lend me their guest room during my return. This way, I can get some extra time in at the training facility when we're not on the road.

"Being back, being in the ring, that feels right. It feels good. But being back also means being around him and...I still don't know if I'm ready for that."

"It's been two years, Sav. Don't you think it's time to have a conversation about things?" Raelynn asks. She waits a moment to gauge my response, but when she doesn't get one, she sighs. "Or don't. It's not really any of my business. But either way, I think it's time to let it go." My best friend offers me a lopsided smile. "I get it, why you were upset, but—"

"There is no but, Rae."

"But," she continues, "was it worth it? Leaving...Was it really worth it?"

29

Savannah

WEDNESDAY, APRIL 10, 2019

NEW YORK, NY

"I got it." His voice sounds from the back of the Escalade when the driver opens my door, but I'm already stepping out with the older man's assistance. Brooks offers him a tight but polite smile, coming to stand at my side. His hand hovers centimeters behind my lower back, just like earlier when we stepped off the plane, and I moved closer into his side on pure instinct. It took me by surprise how easily we began to move around each other after that—like we were part of a dance only we knew—especially after the awkwardly silent plane ride. It was like we hadn't missed a beat.

When I arrived at the airport this morning, I rolled my eyes at the look on his face, like he'd won something. The problem was I didn't have a choice—Noah had already told me to meet Brooks at the airport before he showed up at the center last night. I could have told him the truth, but when he walked in with expectations, it pissed me off. It made me wonder why he'd shown up in the first place. Wouldn't Noah have told him I'd be tagging along? Maybe not. Maybe he conveniently left that part out, the same way he and Amos kept my identity a secret for two months.

Brooks and I kept our distance on the plane. It was big enough that he could have the back half while I occupied the front. It wasn't until we got off the plane that he closed the space, reaching for me—the way he used to—as I took the final step onto the tarmac, and I moved closer without a second thought. He pulled away just before his hand landed on my back, and I hate to admit it, but I missed the warmth of his touch, missed the current of electricity that flowed over my skin just having him close.

Now, a crowd congregates near the door of the studio, and before we could get out, they began shouting different variations of our names, chants, and praises. Each one vies for our attention as security leads us toward the door, and despite Brooks urging me forward, I break away to greet the crowd. I do my best to keep up with the onslaught of items thrown my way to sign as I answer all of their questions. Most are about wrestling, but a few about me and Brooks are sprinkled in. It isn't a secret that we dated outside the ring in the past, but the reason for our abrupt end is still something people speculate about. Cassandra and Kingsley love to send me articles, sometimes even video clips, of the times our relationship is brought up on their favorite gossip blogs. And if you're wondering, no, I didn't tell them the truth about why Brooks and I broke up. As far as everyone except Raelynn and Brody knows, we just…grew apart.

"Sav, c'mon," Brooks calls from the door. The familiarity of it tugs at my insides and makes my heart ache.

I force a smile for one final picture and wave goodbye. As I step away from the barricade, my heel catches on the uneven sidewalk, and my misstep sends me stumbling backwards. I squeeze my eyes shut, preparing to either slam into the ground or the steel barricade, but neither happens.

Someone catches me. Not someone—*him*. His fingers

apply a delicious pressure to my waist, pulling me into him. Warmth blooms in my cheeks, spreading down my neck and chest. When I lift my gaze from my hands clutching the fabric of his button-up, the world stills.

The walls have fallen completely, and I see nothing but genuine concern in his deep blue eyes. Everyone around us disappears into the shadows of my peripheral vision, and suddenly it's just the two of us standing in the middle of Manhattan.

"Thanks." The word is nothing more than a whisper.

"You okay?" Brooks asks, hands still firm on my waist.

I nod and start to pull away to steady myself, but when I put weight on my left foot, a twinge radiates through my ankle. "Fuck," I breathe out.

Brooks catches me again. "You can't walk."

"I'm fine," I say, but his hands don't fall from my side. "I'll be fine, Brooks." And I will be. I have to be. It's just a small twinge—nothing I can't handle or work through. Once I get out of these damn heels, it probably won't bother me anymore. I push his hand away from my waist and follow security inside.

Mike Monahan, host of daytime talk show *The Mike Monahan Show*, pulls me in for a tight hug when we walk on stage. He shakes hands with Brooks, who has barely left my side since my little stumble on the sidewalk. Mike motions us to the couch beside his oversized white chair. This is the first time I've realized Brooks and I will be in such close quarters, and we will be for the next three days. The distance we put between us when we sit only lasts a moment before his arm extends along the back of the couch. A spark ignites in the space between my shoulder and his fingertips, but he never closes the gap, letting his fingers dwell in that space, taunting me.

"Well, this is certainly a sight I never thought I'd see again," Mike says, settled into his seat. He looks like a kid in a candy store, staring at us like one of those giant rainbow swirly pops through his eccentric rainbow-rimmed glasses. "*Savvy Skye* and *Brooks Taylor*, together again!" If he only knew. "Sav, tell us, how does it feel to be back after two years? No! Over two years."

"Practically two and a half," Brooks mumbles. His words strike a nerve, but I refuse to let it show—I can't, not right now, not here—and hold onto the smile I painted on this morning.

"Great," I say. "There is nothing in the world like being in the squared circle."

"What have you been doing since you left?" Mike asks. "It's like you disappeared off the face of the earth. No one heard or saw much of you, except the little bit you posted on social media—Oh! Your brother got married recently, right?"

I run through the questions Mike poses before settling on the last one. It seems like the easiest and least loaded question to answer. "Yes, my oldest brother got married in February."

"I think we...have a picture...Ah, yes! Here we go!" A photo appears on the screen nestled between his chair and the couch. The image brings a genuine smile to my face. Crew dips his new bride, Amara, planting a kiss on her lips in front of the newly blended families and wedding party, who throw their hands up with joy. "This is a good-looking group right here."

"It was a perfect day. The weather was beautiful, and it was everything they wanted. I couldn't ask for a better person for my brother."

"It looked like you had a lot of fun that day, too." Mike's brow raises in suspicion, his words locked and loaded, and I get the feeling I'm not going to like what comes next. My suspicions are confirmed when the photo abruptly changes... This one is of me and Jax from the reception. His left hand rests on my waist, pulling me close. We hold drinks in our free hands, laughing at something behind the camera.

My ex-boyfriend and I had been in the middle of a conversation when the photographer asked for a photo. Then she promptly scolded us for not giving her a "real" smile. Nash, Brody, and Samuel heard and started goofing around behind the camera, which sent us into a fit of laughter.

Mike smirks. "You know, I have to ask..."

"I wish you wouldn't." I scoff, still trying to keep it playful.

"Who is this handsome fellow?"

"That is just a friend."

"Just a friend?" Mike's brow raises even higher. "You look awfully cozy for *just* friends."

"We went to high school together, and he's friends with my brother's wife. Nothing more going on there. Trust me."

"Oh, look at that blush! Spill the tea, Sav."

There isn't a blush until he says it. I try to hide the warmth growing in my cheeks, but having so many sets of eyes on me only makes it worse.

Yes, Jaxon and I reconnected at the wedding, but we haven't spoken since. Only minutes before we were interrupted, Jaxon had approached me and said, "Told you he was really into you."

I rolled my eyes.

"So, what happened between you two?"

"That is none of your business, Jax."

"Indulge me, Sav."

I refused, changing the conversation to something less EWE-related and more Jaxon-related. I knew if there was one way to course-correct, it was to get Jaxon Gallagher to talk about himself. The shift in conversation had worked, and after several minutes of listening to him talk about the two (yes, two) girls he'd recently started seeing, I was happy I wouldn't have to do that again for a while.

Mike looks around me to Brooks and says, "Looks like you have a little competition, *Taylor.*"

"He wishes." Brooks laughs but refuses to look at me when I whip around and stare at him. His blue eyes look brighter under the studio lights, and there's a twinkle of mischief in them when he finally looks down at me. His hand grazes the back of my neck before his fingers squeeze gently, possessively. The action throws kindling on the smoldering fire beneath my skin. My body vibrates under his touch, a familiar bloom deep in my core.

"I'm curious," Mike says, pulling his gaze away from mine. "What made you decide to finally pick up the phone and call her? You obviously needed a tag partner, but why *Savvy Skye*?"

"Wouldn't you?" Brooks's confidence is unwavering before they share a laugh.

"Absolutely, but aren't you a little scared she will turn on you again?"

That catches our attention, and the thumb that had been caressing the side of my neck freezes. I glare at the host, who seems to realize he's struck a nerve.

Mike's hands come up in surrender. "I'm just saying, I'd be a little wary, considering your history. But hey, I know we're all interested to see how everything plays out, especially after that match you had with *Viviana, Brooks.*" From the corner of my eye, I see the producer signal for Mike to move along, knowing they've backed themselves into a corner and need to get out of it. "Anyway, *Savvy*, are you back full-time or is this just a quick in-and-out favor for a friend?"

"Guess you'll have to wait and see," I say, replacing my

smile.

"You're such a tease!" Mike giggles.

I laugh along with our host, settling back further into the couch and Brooks. His fingers give my nape another gentle squeeze, and it eases the pit in my stomach. I'm not sure why I worry about what he thought when he saw that photo of me and Jaxon; it shouldn't matter. We weren't together. We aren't together.

"You need to convince her to stay!" Mike says, craning his neck again to look at my counterpart.

"I'm not sure I'm the person to do that," Brooks says evenly. "She might run the other way."

"Oh, pishposh! Something tells me you're the *only* one who can."

30

Brooks

THURSDAY, APRIL 11, 2019

NEW YORK, NY

The elevator ride to the twenty-fourth floor has been excruciatingly silent. Actually, the entire car ride back to the hotel was this way. After our appearance on *The Mike Monahan Show* yesterday, Savannah and I have been dragged all over the city. Appearing in a multitude of shows, radio interviews, podcast interviews, content shoots, and even a magazine interview. Everywhere we go, we've been asked the same questions over and over and over again.

Today at LNX Upfronts was no different. It's the annual event where Live Network Exchange showcases its upcoming programming slated for the new season—entertainment, news, sports, and any other content they plan to have on their broadcast channels. I lost count of the number of times Savannah was asked if her return was a permanent thing or if it meant we were back together. Like *together* together. Each time, she handled it with more grace than I expected, especially after the fiftieth time it was asked, and said, "No, I'm just here to help out an old friend." Then she'd glance my way with a brief smile before turning back to the person standing in front of her. That smile chipped away at my resolve every time I saw it. I hated that her return to the ring was being equated to us getting back together—by interviewers, fans, and coworkers alike. Savannah should be able to come back without it being solely based on me.

Stepping out of the elevator, she picks up her pace down the hallway. Last night I let her get away, but tonight I have questions—a lot of questions. If we're going to work together, we need to be on the same page about some things. Starting with that damn picture of her and Jaxon from Crew's wedding. Okay, maybe that isn't any of my business, it won't hinder us working together, but that doesn't stop me from wanting to know the truth.

I'm shocked when she pauses outside her door after I call out to her. I've tried to start the conversation so many times over the last two days, but every time the words get caught in my throat. And right now it's no different...I think back to last night in the car after the final interview, when I invited her to dinner and she refused. When I tried to persuade her by saying that she *needed* to eat, she said she would eat, just not with me.

Her brow raises, her impatience growing with each passing second that I don't say something. She undoes the straps of her shoes, slipping her right foot out of the black high heel, and then her left. A sharp inhale accompanies a slight grimace when she puts weight on it.

"You should get that looked at," I say, and her eyes snap up to meet mine.

"I told you, I'm fine. I'll be better once I don't have to wear heels for fourteen hours straight. Now what do you want?"

"I-I, uh..." There's so much I want to say, so much I need to say, but nothing comes out. "Never mind. G'night," I say, stuffing my hands into my pockets and walking down the hall.

The entire sixty-second walk to my room, I wrestle with

whether to continue on the path forward or turn around, knock on her door, and just lay it all out. Everything. Past and present. The only thing that stops me is knowing that's not a good idea. When she left two years ago, when I made her go, that was the end of everything—the end of us. We said what we had to say in those final moments, and when she told me she didn't love me, it was her way of saying she was done. She wanted me to let her go...so, I did. Right?

No.

I haven't let her go, not really. Savannah Williams still has a hold on me. She stole my heart years ago and never gave it back, not even the day she walked out that door. And now, seeing her, being forced to stand beside her and pretend like everything is okay, has only intensified the longing I've felt in my heart.

I wave the keycard over the lock, gripping the door handle, but I don't go inside. For one more glance down the hallway, I'm torn between doing what I should do and what I want to do.

I have so many questions—so many things I want to hear about from her and not just from the hushed conversations our friends have when they think I'm not listening...

I heard about how she became the cheer coach at her old high school, how Bodhi graduated from law school two weeks before Blake got married, how Laine opened a restaurant in Celestia, and, of course, all about Crew and Amara's big day. I heard about them all, and every time something came up, I'd quietly send some congratulatory message or gift.

Now, I'm standing outside my hotel room, and all I want is to hear *her* voice. Not the one I've been hearing all day—not Savvy Skye. I want to talk to Savannah.

I turn on my heel, taking the first step back down the hallway, when my phone rings. *Brody.* I stare down at the screen, debating whether or not to answer. Perhaps this is a sign I'm not supposed to turn around, that I should go inside and leave her be.

My shoulders fall with a heavy sigh, and I unlock my hotel room again. I answer the phone, "What?"

"Good to hear your voice, too, Brooksy boy. How's it going?" my best friend asks.

I scrub a hand down my face. "You know how it's going."

"Well." Brody chuckles. "If that Monahan interview is any indication—"

"You didn't tell me about Jaxon." Actually, none of them did. They were all at the wedding, but never told me Jaxon was there. Neither did my sister, but that's a conversation I'll have with her later.

"There was nothing to tell."

"Not from where I was sitting."

"John, nothing happened," Brody says, and his use of *John* shocks me. My best friend never calls me by my first name. "Jaxon was there, she was there. They're friends. They had maybe a five-minute conversation and took a picture. She's allowed to take pictures with her friends." He sighs, and I can practically see him pacing the length of his bus, Rae somewhere in the background, pretending like she isn't listening to the conversation. She's probably even texting Savannah about it as we speak. "Have you guys talked?"

"Not really."

Brody grumbles under his breath. "How do you expect to work together if you can't even speak to one another?"

"What am I supposed to say, Brod?" A humorless laugh escapes me as I sit on the edge of the bed.

"Oh, I don't know. You could probably start with an apology." He cuts me off when I start to ask him what for. "Apologize for telling her to get out—"

"She said she didn't love me."

"Because you told her to."

"Her shit was packed. Crew was there. She was leaving regardless." Brody sighs on the other end of the line, and I do the same. Honestly, I'm not sure who I'm trying to convince more—me or him. "I have to go."

"Brooks, talk to her."

31

Savannah

WEDNESDAY, APRIL 17, 2019

TAMPA, FL

I should be in bed, but instead I'm two hours deep in a workout at the NextGen training center. We have to be in Memphis tomorrow for an untelevised show, and I have to be at the airport first thing in the morning. I probably should've left today with Brody and Rae, but I needed the space, and I think they did, too. The idea of being stuck on a tour bus with them for twelve hours sounds like a nightmare. Don't get me wrong, I love them, and I'm grateful they're letting me take over their guest room, but everyone needs a break sometimes. Not to mention, after the way Raelynn poked and prodded me at the end of our beach day, I definitely wasn't looking forward to being stuck on a bus with her.

"I wish you two would just talk it out," she said, falling into the driver's seat of her Toyota earlier. "Just admit you still have feelings for each other and you want to fix things."

"It's not that easy, Rae," I said.

"Savannah, that man loves you, he always has, and you're just being stubborn. It's been two years. Don't you think it's time to talk about it?" She said the same thing every time John was brought up. Her opinion on the matter hadn't changed, and I knew she'd never let it go until he and I finally sat down and talked. Even if it meant letting go for good.

My conversation with Raelynn isn't the only thing keeping me up tonight. I'm still sore after the shit Viviana pulled on Monday. Was I aware that she and Austin were coming out to "surprise" attack us during the match between Brooks and Wolf? Yes, but I wasn't aware she had intentions of drawing blood. She hit harder than necessary after she baited me out from the commentary table, going straight for my old shoulder injury. Almost like she knew it had been bothering me recently. Part of me wonders if it was revenge for our match years ago when I *unintentionally* busted up her knee in a street fight. A bigger part of me thinks she's mad that I called her a slut on national television without warning. Fair, I suppose, but it isn't the first time any of us have gone off script, and it won't be the last. Sometimes you have to act now and ask for forgiveness later, from both your opponent and corporate.

Everything got a little hazy after I went headfirst into the corner of the steel steps. Viviana had taken advantage of me being stunned and continued her assault when I didn't get back up. I vaguely remember hearing Brooks yell over the roar of the crowd before Viviana was plucked off me by her husband. Finally, I was scooped up into strong arms and carried backstage without a fight.

Brooks stood in the doorway of Doc's office the entire time I was being assessed, chest rising and falling with heavy breaths, his face pulled into a hard line, arms crossed over his bare chest. His skin was an angry red from the strikes of a Kendo stick moments before the match went awry, but that wasn't the only reason. The visible blood should've told me why he reacted the way he did, but it wasn't until I saw the replay and the photos that I truly understood. There was blood *everywhere*—my blood. For a smaller laceration, it looked like a damn crime scene.

Brooks refused to leave my side even after Doc stitched up the side of my head and cleared me. He walked me to the women's locker room and then waited to walk me out to the parking lot, where Raelynn paced outside the bus she shared with Brody. Once she was finished fretting over me, she turned to Brooks, who stood there with my blood still visible on his skin. His hands clenched at his sides before he folded his arms into his chest again. I started to ask if he wanted something to wipe the blood off, but he beat me to it.

"I'll see you Thursday," he said with an even tone, and left. Watching him walk away, I felt the disappointment settle deep in my stomach. I stood there until the arena door closed and my best friend called for me from the bus door.

Raelynn is right. I know she's right. She isn't the only one who thinks so; Brody does, too. Brooks and I need to talk, but I'm scared of what that's going to mean when all is said and done. What if we agree to walk away for good? What if he says he wants to try again? Do I want to try again?

Yes, the word comes to mind without hesitation, and it freezes my movements against the punching bag. I come to a still position upside down. Was that...Is that what I want? I don't...I've never allowed myself to think about it before, or tried not to, pushing any thoughts of him to the back of my mind where they could be stored behind a locked door. I know that wasn't the right or healthy way to deal with things, but it was the only way I knew how to try to move on. To try to get over him. But now...Now, I have no choice but to face it. Face him.

With my back against the vinyl, I take one more deep breath and crunch my abdomen to force myself upward, grabbing the chains. My legs unwind and slide down to the floor before I fall back against the wall.

"You're here late."

My eyes open to meet the blue eyes of the man standing in front of me. When did he get here? I never even heard the door open. Then again, I've been a little preoccupied...with him.

"Couldn't sleep," I say. He nods, now glancing down at his feet. "You?"

"Same," he answers. "That and I wanted to get some ring work in."

I wonder how many times we've just missed each other in our late-night ventures to the training center. I've spent many nights here when I couldn't sleep recently, but I've never run into him. Brody and Rae rely on the training center to work out, which means I do, too, as long as I'm staying with them. Unlike Brooks, I don't have the luxury of a home gym anymore.

My gaze sweeps over his face, and I get the sudden longing to reach out and touch him. To caress the side of his face, to cradle his face in my palm, and feel the warmth of his skin against mine. To graze my thumb over his pink lips before he'd smile and pull me into a long kiss. It would start soft, slow, and careful, but eventually turn into something much more...Well, I'll let you use your imagination.

Oh, for the love of God. I am so fucked. I cannot be thinking about this.

When our eyes meet, the mental wall he's built, the same one he had when I first returned, is firmly in place. He's shutting me out again.

"Well, I'll be out here if you need anything," he says, not waiting for an answer. He leaves, and through the large picture window that overlooks the ring room, I watch him stuff headphones in his ears, and he finishes wrapping his right wrist.

A little over an hour of cardio later, I decide it's time to head back to the condo and finish packing for tomorrow. Maybe I'll even try to get a little bit of sleep, if I can. The ring area is dark; the only light comes from the spotlights over the ring in the center of the room. It casts a pale glow as heavy footsteps against canvas echo through the still air. The sight is entrancing, begging me forward, and I slowly make my way through the maze of six rings to the one he occupies in the center. Brooks runs the ropes—slingshots himself side to side—touching the rope on each side twice before dropping to the mat, doing two quarter rolls and starting over. After three run-throughs, he adds a third touch and a third roll. I know he'll do this until he gets to ten total.

I shouldn't stay, but my feet refuse to listen. I admire the way his massive form moves with such fluidity in such a small space. His determination is one of the things I've always admired most about him, because despite not always being the strongest wrestler, he has character and charisma, and he worked his ass off to become better. He still does. That's what makes him the best. That's why Amos loves him and why he skyrocketed to the top of the company so early in his career.

Brooks stops after five and moves to the center of the ring. This is new. He begins moving his feet through an in-out-in-out-in pattern, as if weaving them through an invisible opponent's feet, almost like a grapevine motion.

"That works better when you have a real opponent there, you know," I say, and it stops him in his tracks.

He looks over his shoulder and chuckles, breathless. "You offering?"

It's my turn to laugh. Was I offering? No, of course, I

wasn't offering...Was I? "I was just about to leave, actually."

Brooks reaches for the towel hanging on the opposite rope and wipes his face. It looks like he's about to start his run-throughs again. I rap my knuckles on the apron and take a deep breath, turning on my heel, but he calls after me. "One match."

"What?"

"One match," Brooks repeats, leaning over the ropes. He stares down at me with a neutral expression. Calm, cool, and collected. "You and me. Right here, right now. And if I win, you and I have dinner on Sunday."

He can't be serious, but there are no signs of backing down. Okay, I'll play along. "And if I win?"

His lips pull into a grin. "If you win, I'll give you what you want the most."

I laugh. "And what's that?"

"I'll leave you alone."

"You're serious?" I ask, and he nods. *Fuck, this is a bad idea.* How are we supposed to maintain our distance and healthy boundaries in a match? That's not possible. But the longer I stand here, trying to talk myself out of it, the more I want to say yes. "I can't believe this...Fine. One match." Dropping my bag on the floor, I climb the stairs and step through the ropes he holds open. "You can wipe that smirk off your face, Brooks."

"Don't hold back, Skye."

"You know who you're talking to, right?"

We circle. No referee, no bell, no crowd. Just the two of us in the stillness of the open gym. The only sounds are the hum of the lights above us, our soft breathing, and the echo of feet.

We step forward at the same time, closing the space, and our hands come up in a draw before I shove him away. We step back, starting the dance again. Two more circles before we lock up, but I slip out of his grasp again, chuckling.

"Tease," he says with a breathy chuckle.

"Look who's talking."

We lock up again, this time keeping the hold. Faces inches apart, breaths mingling, I meet his heavy stare. I tell myself not to glance down at his lips that are *right there*. I beg my mind to forget the feeling of his lips on mine, the feel of his body against mine, but it's getting harder the longer we're in this spot. I have to do something to get out of this lockup. I snake my arm around his neck, tight and fast, forcing us out of the position and putting him into a tight side headlock.

We shift, testing each other's weight, before his hands find my waist. They're light at first, but slowly his grasp becomes firmer, and it brings certain thoughts I shouldn't be having to mind.

Brooks plants his feet, lifting me off my own just enough to stagger my weight. He drops, flipping me backward in a suplex. My back lands on the mat, but I use the momentum to roll through and land in the bottom turnbuckle. The impact forces the breath from my lungs. He pops back up to his feet but doesn't move closer.

I grab the middle rope, hoisting myself up, but Brooks still doesn't approach. His eyes trace every inch of me, studying me, but not like he does one of his normal opponents. This is different. This is...familiar. Remembrance. Like he's looking at a photograph that has captured a certain memory in time. "You just gonna stand there, or are we gonna fight?"

That draws his eyes back to mine, and he offers a brief nod.

Brooks charges forward, but I jump. My feet hit the middle rope, and I moonsault over his head. He crashes chest-first into the turnbuckle. I land on my feet, and if Jude Paul were here, he'd say something like, "*Vintage Skye! Brooks Taylor should've seen that coming.*"

Brooks stumbles out of the corner, and I rise to my full

height. The lights shine off the thin layer of perspiration on his skin, and his chest rises and falls in slow breaths. In the blink of an eye, he takes the few steps forward and moves into my space, closer than an opponent should. The silence thickens when neither of us backs down. There are too many words left unsaid, too many nights spent thinking about one another, pretending we haven't missed each other. How do I know? Because that's exactly what I've been doing over the past two years. I've pretended like I don't yearn for this man. Like I'm not mad at myself for not giving him the chance to explain. Like I don't know the worst thing I could've done was walk out that door—to run.

But now isn't the time to let those emotions get in the way.

I reach up to cradle his cheek, and his eyes flutter closed with a gentle sigh before I slide my fingers through his hair and yank him forward into a knee strike to the gut.

Brooks buckles at my feet, breath stolen from his lungs, dropping to his knees. I shift my neck from side to side and sigh with relief when a crack opens the joints. I reach down to grab a fistful of his shirt and haul him back up to his feet, whipping him into the ropes. He rebounds, but I leap up and wrap my legs tight around his head for a headscissors takedown. He goes headfirst into the mat but tucks and rolls through it.

He lands on his feet, using the ropes to steady himself when he stumbles into the corner. His gaze rises to meet mine, and I shrug with a small smile. He nods, wetting his lips, before we lock up again.

This time, Brooks takes control, snaking his arm around my waist and driving me down onto his knee in a backbreaker. He lets me fall to the mat and circles me for a moment before he grabs my arm and yanks me to my feet. Eyes locked, hearts pounding. If we were in front of a crowd, they would be eating this up, hanging on to every move.

It's his turn to whip me into the ropes.

Rebounding, I lift my leg, ready to connect with his chin, but he ducks to avoid my foot and sweeps my left leg for a takedown. Without missing a beat, Brooks pulls my legs through his and falls to his knees, straddling my waist. *You've got to be kidding me.* Planting my hands on his chest, I try to push him off, but he takes both of mine into his left and pins them above my head.

Shoulders down.

Three seconds from defeat. Three seconds to decide my fate. I know I should (could) kick out, or at least try, but I can't. The fight leaves my body as soon as I hit the mat and he pins me. My body refuses to listen to the instructions my brain gives, instead letting him take the lead, reacting to the way his weight feels on top of me. It's a comforting sensation, one of familiarity, and a rush of anticipation spreads through my limbs. There's a flicker of emotion in his eyes—guilt, ache, maybe even longing. My breath catches when he leans down, his nose brushing against mine.

"One." His breath is hot on my skin as he begins the count.

"Two." Brooks pulls back, and his eyes move across my features, watching, waiting for some indication of what I'm going to do next.

Kick out, I think, but my heart and my body still refuse to listen.

Brooks waits a second longer than he should, but I don't move, and he whispers, "Three."

When we should separate, we don't. His grip tightens on my wrists, and his other hand trails down to my side to my waist, giving it a gentle squeeze as he leans in close again.

"You lose." His words come out breathless, and if one of us moves even the slightest, our lips will touch. We're toeing a dangerous line, and if we're not careful, there will be no going back.

Make the move. Do it.

Before I can, Brooks sits up. The movement flexes his hips, grinding him against me. It draws a moan from deep within me. *Fuck.* That small movement throws jet fuel on the fire.

"John." His name is strangled on my lips as his eyes blaze above me. I'm sure mine mirror the same look of want and need. I wiggle my hands against his grasp, desperate to touch him, but his hold only tightens. He only stares down at me, and just when I think he's going to do what I know we're both craving, he does the opposite.

Without warning, Brooks pushes up from the mat, stumbling back a few steps. I suddenly feel cold from the loss of his warmth.

"Shit," I hear him say under his breath. He scrubs a hand down his face. "Savannah, I'm—I'm sorry. I-I shouldn't have suggested this. I shouldn't..." I watch him begin to unravel before my eyes, and I feel the cracks form in my own armor as it happens. This isn't his fault. I could've said no.

"Brooks," I say, sitting up.

"I'm sorry. You don't have to...We don't have to go to dinner. I—"

"John." I step in front of him, bringing an abrupt halt to his pacing. I take one of his hands in mine. "It's okay. You didn't do anything wrong. We were just...practicing. That's it." I wait another minute before giving his hand a gentle squeeze. "I'm—I'm gonna go. Are you going to be okay?"

He nods, peeling his hands from mine and stepping down on the middle rope. That's his way of telling me to leave. Suddenly, I feel like I'm back in that hallway, and he's telling me the only way he'll let me go is if I tell him I don't love him. I don't move, hoping that this time it will be different. I'm desperate for some connection to him, but he refuses to look at me. His gaze remains glued to the wall on the other side of the gym.

"I'll see you tomorrow?" I ask before I step through the ropes.

He clears his throat, nodding, but still stares into the darkness that surrounds us. "Tomorrow."

32

Savannah

SUNDAY, APRIL 21, 2019
CHICAGO, IL

The clock reads a little after seven o'clock. I tap my phone screen, where two unread messages await a reply, neither from the person I was hoping for.

I haven't seen much of him since our tussle in the ring on Wednesday night. He's had singles matches while I tag-teamed with *Roxanne* all weekend. Not that I minded—she debuted not long before I left, so it's been fun getting to work with her. However, since I wasn't slated to be ringside, Brooks and I had no reason to see each other, and I had no way of talking to him about what transpired a few nights ago. It's become obvious that he's taking full advantage of my scheduled absence. I didn't anticipate feeling so let down by his lack of communication, but it's been bothering me since he turned heel and walked the other way Thursday night when he spotted me from down the hall. I'm not the only one who's noticed. Raelynn mentioned it last night on our drive from St. Louis to Chicago.

And again this afternoon.

"Are you expecting a call or something?" she asked when

I looked at my phone for probably the tenth time since we sat down for lunch. "You've been checking your phone every ten minutes since we woke up this morning."

I brushed her off, trying to change the subject because I wasn't about to tell her what happened the other night. That would lead to a completely different conversation...one where I'd have to admit that maybe, just maybe, I missed him.

I wasn't ready to come to that realization...nor did I want to admit she was right. I *had* been keeping an eye on my phone all day, waiting for the text that I knew wasn't coming. Brooks had quickly dismissed his victory, saying we didn't have to go to dinner, but he'd won, and the terms were clear. I don't think he expected me to let him win.

And I did...Let him win. I'd never let anyone win before, but being there...in that ring...pinned beneath him...I'd never wanted anything more. He'd taken the first step, and I knew letting him win was the only way to start fixing what I'd broken.

"Screw it," I say.

> Gibsons. 8pm.

If he isn't going to break the silence, I will. What do I have to lose? It's not like I can lose him. Less than a minute later, his response appears on the screen.

John Brooks
I told you. We don't have to do this.

> You won.
> And I'm hungry.

He doesn't answer this time, and I have no choice but to take his silence as acceptance. If not, then I guess I'll be taking myself out to dinner.

A large hand wraps around my wrist, pulling me back from the revolving door of the brick building, and the familiar earthy scents of blue cypress and vetiver fill the air around me. Blue and green lights cast a cool glow on his features as we stand beneath the neon sign. His thumb grazes the sensitive skin of my wrist, and the simple action makes my heart race.

"Wasn't sure you were going to show," I say, trying to keep my voice even. Since we met over ten years ago, I have never been nervous around this man. However, being so close to him right now, not knowing where we stand, makes my heart beat at an uneven pace and my head spin.

"Neither was I," Brooks says. He looks handsome, dressed in black slacks and an off-white button-up with the first two buttons undone. I recognize the cufflinks as the ones I bought a few Christmases ago—silver studs with an eagle imprinted in the center. His thumb stills but applies a small pressure to my pulse point. Leaning in to whisper in my ear, "But as you said, I won, and you're hungry."

I laugh, hearing my words from earlier, and for the first time since his arrival, Brooks smiles. Maybe we can do this. Maybe we can move forward.

He motions for me to go ahead, and only when we reach the revolving door does he let go of my arm. His touch is light against my back when he joins me inside, but it disappears just as fast. The host leads us through the maze of tables to a more secluded area in the back of the restaurant.

Within seconds of our arrival, a man dressed in a full suit appears with a thousand-watt smile. His graying hair is combed back into the same sleek style he's always worn. Danny Alcott. "My two favorite people!" He claps his hands together before pressing the back of my hand to his lips. He extends his hand to Brooks and pulls him into an embrace. Danny is one of the managers here—has been for as long as we've been coming—and always finds a spot for us on the books (even when there isn't one).

"Danny, thank you so much for squeezing us in," I say.

"For you, Savannah? Anything. I was hoping you'd come see us while you were in town."

"Wouldn't miss it," Brooks says, taking a step closer.

"How are we feeling about next weekend?" Danny looks between the two of us. "Excited?"

"Extremely," I say, not realizing I'd taken a small step closer to Brooks until his hand lands on my waist. It feels far too familiar for people in our situation, but I can't bring myself to pull away.

The old man's eyes linger on the movement briefly before a knowing smile splits his face. That smile stays in place when he asks, "Pulling out a win, right?"

I smirk. "I have no idea what you're talking about."

"You never do, Sweetie." He chuckles. "Hey, you know I have to ask, but are you sticking around for a while? My girls have missed seeing you."

The grip on my side falters slightly, alongside my smile. This isn't the first—or probably the last—time someone has asked me, and despite the time to make a decision now closer than ever, I don't have an answer. If I'm being honest, I think I've been waiting for a moment like tonight before I make the decision. Maybe it will make it a little easier to see what the right choice is.

I clear my throat. "I, uh...I haven't decided."

"Oh, really?"

"Still have a few things to figure out."

From the corner of my eye, I glance at the man beside me, and when I turn back to Danny, he gives me a somber smile. It's no secret that something happened between me and Brooks, and the majority of people have often speculated what it could have been that led to my sudden departure not only from the company, but from our relationship. The rumors have run rampant—I cheated, he cheated, I was a party girl who couldn't be tamed, I wanted a family and he didn't, I was leaving for another company, and so many others I'd lost count. I can only imagine the rumors that spread around here, picking apart the overheard pieces of our final conversation, the last time we were in town, less than a month before it all went downhill.

"We'll see what happens in a few days."

Danny excuses himself, promising to come back later, and I know he will because he always does, and it's been a long time since our last visit. I don't think Brooks has returned since our last dinner here—at least that's how Danny made it seem when I called earlier.

"What does that mean?" Brooks asks, pulling out my chair. "*You haven't decided.*"

Adjusting my black dress, I sink into the chair and clasp my hands together in my lap. "Amos wanted me to sign a contract right away, but I told him I wanted to see how things go with—"

"With me." His brow cocks as he sits across from me.

"Yes." The word draws out, and I lift my gaze to meet him. "You were part of it, but in general, I wanted to see how things would go."

A soft smile on his lips. "And how are things going?"

"The thought of coming back after two years was terrifying, if I'm honest." I shake my head, scratching at an invisible speck of dirt on the white tablecloth. "But things are fine."

"Only fine?"

"Things are good," I say more confidently, with a smile.

"I assume you heard about Rox," he says, settling back into this chair. Of course, I heard. I was there—he knew that. Current number one contender for the EWE Women's Championship, *Roxanne*, had been injured last night in our tag team match versus *Harper Valentine* and *Elizabeth Petrova*, and she was going to be out of action for the foreseeable future. The big question now remaining is who will take her place against the current champ, *Calla Lily*, at Wrestlefest.

"I did."

"Have they said—"

"Are we really going to talk about work, Brooks?"

He stares at me for a long moment before his gaze falls to the table. "What else do you want to talk about, Savannah?"

"We could start with Wednesday night."

Brooks scoffs, combing his bottom lip between his teeth. He pulls his hands back from the center of the table, but not before I notice the patch of black peeking out from beneath his right shirt cuff.

Is that what I think it is?

It can't be. Surely, he would've gotten rid of it by now. My gaze flickers up to meet his, then back down to his wrist. I know that if you lift that shirt cuff, you'll find a simple black heart with *SJ* in the center. I still remember when he got it years ago. I couldn't believe he'd do something like that. Getting your significant other's name tattooed is supposed to be bad luck, but John Brooks doesn't care for superstitions. Still...why would he keep it?

His voice draws my attention forward again. "I apologized for that. I shouldn't have put you in the situation, and I told you—"

"I-I lost. Fair and square. I—"

"Bullshit." He cuts me off. "That's bullshit, Savannah. You really expect me to believe that? I know better. You could've easily kicked out, and you didn't. You let me win. Why?"

His gaze is as intense as the tone of his voice. Every answer that comes to mind isn't good enough. How do I explain why I let him win in a way that he might understand? I don't understand it myself. I didn't come back to EWE to fix things, but the longer I'm here...that's all I want to do.

"Savannah." Brooks sighs, scrubbing a hand across his stubbled jaw. "I don't—"

"I'm sorry," I say. It's the only thing that seems right in this moment. Blue eyes narrow across the table. "I'm not sorry that I left, but I am sorry for how I did it."

"What does that mean?"

"You hurt me, John. Deeply." His name flows past my lips before I can stop it, and it feels good to call him by his real name, not *Brooks*. If the look on his face is any indication, I would say he feels the same. "I-I was hurt. I was humiliated. I felt like I didn't know you anymore. This person I had spent almost five years with, the man I thought I was going to marry, to spend the rest of my life with...I had just found out you only started dating me because of a damn bet on top of feeling like—"

"That's not true. I've *always* wanted you."

"But you didn't..." I sigh and card a hand through my hair, pushing it off my shoulder. It's suddenly warm in here. "You didn't ask me on your own, Brooks, and—"

"Because you didn't want me to, Savannah! You made that very clear the first New Year's at Willow Pond. You wanted to be left alone."

"No! I wanted you to give me time to find my footing at a company where you were already established. I never expected you to read my mind or know when I'd feel ready, but if you had just..." I take a deep breath and wring my hands together. Closing my eyes, I try to keep my emotions in check. "It shouldn't have taken a bet for—"

"Can we not do this here?" he all but begs from across the

table, rubbing the bridge of his nose. "Please."

"When do you suggest we do it, then?" I don't mean to snap, but the words come out harsh and unforgiving. If not now, when? Maybe we could've talked about this in the last few days if he hadn't been avoiding me.

Before he can respond, the waitress arrives and takes our full order. When she's gone, neither of us tries to continue the conversation. I can hear the sound of his index finger scratching against the white linen before he sighs.

"I don't want to do this in front of an audience," Brooks says. I blink my gaze back to him, but his remains on the table. "Because, despite what you think, Savannah, despite what you believe, I was trying to protect you. I know that's not an excuse. I should've told you, I know that, but I thought I was doing the right thing."

"I know that."

"I don't think you do." The circular motion of his finger stops, and he folds his hands. "And I don't think you realize how hard this—you being back—has been for me. These have been the hardest two weeks of my life, Sav. I never expected you to walk through that curtain. And I never thought you would walk back into my life, but not be part of it. I've been trying to keep you at arm's length, but trying not to be cold to you, and it's been exhausting." His eyes blink closed, and when he opens them again, wetness lines his lashes. He wipes it away. "When you said you didn't love me—"

"Because you told me to!" My outburst clings to the air around us. "You told me to, John. That's what you wanted."

"No! What I wanted was for the woman I love to say it's okay. Yes, you were mad, you were angry, but I wanted you to say you still loved me, and that it was going to be okay. I wanted you to tell me we'd figure it out, Savannah. But instead, you *ran*. You called your brother, packed your shit, and you were going to leave without saying goodbye."

"I wasn't—"

"Yes, you were." His face pulls into a tight line. "After Thanksgiving, you started to shut me out—"

I scoff. "No, I didn't."

"Yes, you did," he says matter-of-factly. "I don't know what happened outside of that tiff with my sister, but you shut me out. Then you found out about Drake, and it hurt you. I get it. But part of me thinks you were just scared. Scared of what came next. Scared of taking those next steps, and—"

"That's not fair."

"Why not? It makes sense when you think about it. You were young when we got together, mid-twenties, and I'm older—"

"That has nothing to do with it. You being seven years older than me isn't—"

"Why else would you jump at the first opportunity to leave?"

The question leaves me speechless.

Without warning, Brooks excuses himself, leaving me with nothing but my thoughts. I watch him disappear the way we came less than thirty minutes ago. His hands shoved deep in the pockets of his slacks give off a calm and collected strut, but his shoulders tell a different story. They carry the weight of our entire conversation. I know I should worry if he'll come back, but I don't, because I know he will. I don't know how I know, but I do.

Is he right?

Was it my fear of the future that made me run so fast? John and I had been talking about marriage for a long time before everything happened. Hell, we'd even joked about going to the courthouse at Thanksgiving...Or was it feeling like I wasn't in control of my own life after my conversation with Debra? That I was trapped and he was controlling me. When in reality, John was the furthest thing from controlling.

He'd always been protective—of me, his sister, his mother—sometimes to a fault, and he liked to make sure everyone had what they wanted, not just what they needed, but he'd been truly never controlling.

Was it nerves? Fear of the unknown? Every time I think back to that week when things finally went south—first with the storyline fiasco and then finding out about the bet, on top of the Thanksgiving drama—I think maybe I did overreact. But I suppose my pride hasn't allowed me to admit that to anyone else.

I've been too hurt, too prideful, to want to admit it, and even if I had, the damage was already done...I'd done the one thing he asked. I had to, or I never would've walked out the door. I did what I had to because I needed space. I needed time. And I said things that I didn't mean...Like that I didn't love him.

Maybe it was true.

Maybe I had subconsciously sabotaged everything I'd ever wanted with the man who loved me almost unconditionally because of a brief moment of anxiety and fear, without even truly realizing it.

Brooks reemerges almost ten minutes later, hands still shoved deep in his pockets as he moves through the restaurant with more grace than you'd expect from someone his size. He pulls out his chair and resituates himself at the table, taking a long sip of the whiskey the waitress had dropped off not long after he left. He lets the glass fall back to the table, his gaze lifting to meet mine.

"I'm sorry," I say before he can. "For everything."

"I know that." His voice remains even—monotone almost.

"I don't want to make this harder than it has to be. I don't. Brooks, I care about you. I always will."

"And I..." Brooks pauses, swiping his tongue over his lips before he expels a soft breath. "...Care about you."

That's not what he was going to say, and I can almost guarantee I know what he was going to say, but I won't push him. Not tonight. I reach across the table and cover his hand with mine, giving it a small squeeze. "Friends?"

Brooks hesitates, but nods. "Friends."

"And friends can enjoy a nice dinner together and catch up, right?" The corners of my mouth lift in an encouraging smile. I watch him try to fight it, but he can't, and finally, his mouth lifts in return.

Strong hands guide me out of the restaurant and toward the street, where we can hail a cab. In another lifetime, we'd walk the city streets wrapped in each other before he'd pull me in for a kiss and call a cab to take us back to our hotel, where we could properly end the night. Instead, his chest is pressed firmly against my back as he reaches around to open the yellow door. He steps off the curb, gripping the top edge of the doorframe while the other rests on my hip. He gives it an affectionate squeeze when I turn around to face him.

"Thanks for coming with me," I say.

"Thanks for letting me win."

A warmth blooms in my cheeks, and I bite back a smile.

"Good night, Savannah," Brooks says. He urges me toward the open taxi cab, but my feet remain planted, and it only brings us closer. So close that I can smell the pungent aroma of the one whiskey he had at dinner on his breath.

What am I doing? This goes well beyond the bounds of friendship we set not even three hours ago. This comes dangerously close to crossing the line we were supposed to be staying away from, but I can't seem to step back.

"Sweetheart," he breathes out, and his face is dangerously close to mine.

"John."

Our lips barely brush, and I feel his body turn to stone. Eyes closed, he white-knuckles the doorframe. When he speaks, his voice drips with an aching need so heavy, I feel it in my bones. "You'll regret it in the morning."

"No, I won't."

A soft exhale tickles my skin as he breathes. "You will."

I can feel the corner of his mouth lift before I step forward, closing the gap. His hand tangles in my hair, and the other digs into the fabric at my waist, pulling me even further into him. This kiss is desperate and punishing—it's all teeth and tongue. It's everything we've been needing. Everything we've wanted since I walked out on that stage. Since I walked out that door two years ago. Being this close to him feels right— feels whole. It feels like home. And I never want to leave again. This is where I belong.

Parting from me, Brooks rests his forehead against mine. His hands lift to cradle my cheeks, and he presses a single kiss against my lips. When I try to pull him into the cab, he resists.

"Not like this, Sweetheart." He shakes his head with a sad smile. "You have no fucking clue how badly I want to get in that car right now." A breathy chuckle follows that statement, and for a moment, I see the man I met in that college dive bar almost eleven years ago. The man I never thought I'd see again after that night, but who had captured my heart well before he even knew it, and has never given it back. "But you *will* regret this in the morning." His thumb skates over my lips, eyes searching my face before he speaks again. "I want this, Savannah. I want you. But I don't want you to want this because you're caught up in some kind of nostalgia. I want you to want it because you want me. Want us. I don't want you to wake up in the morning and regret this—regret me.

Because I can't live in a world where you regret me."

Warmth builds in my eyes. The confession sobers me up from the high I was riding moments ago.

"I love you, Savannah Williams." John presses one final kiss against my lips before he takes a few steps back. "I never stopped, but I think—I think we should keep our distance."

33

Savannah

THURSDAY NIGHT COMMOTION
THURSDAY, APRIL 25, 2019
INDIANAPOLIS, IN

I don't have to be in here. I could have just as easily watched this from one of the monitors in the back with Rae and Bennett, but I hoped I'd be able to catch Brooks on his way back after this segment. We're about to spend an entire weekend side by side, and I don't feel like being ignored in the name of "keeping our distance."

That's what we've been doing all week, unless it has to do with work, just like he wanted, and I have to admit I've found myself missing him. Am I even allowed to say that? I don't know. I don't think so. It's not like I have a reason to miss him, we're not together—haven't been together—and I'm pretty sure the whole "friends" thing went out the window after dinner on Sunday.

I thought we had finally found some common ground where we could let the walls down a little, and then I went and screwed it up in a moment of what...Nostalgia? Longing for something that no longer exists? I've spent the last four days dissecting every little thing that has happened over the past two and a half weeks, and every time it comes back to his confession on the street in the middle of downtown Chicago.

He still loves me. I've asked myself if I feel the same countless times, and each time, the immediate answer is…yes. The more I think about it, the more I think that's the reason I've continued to push him away. It doesn't make sense, but at the same time, it makes complete sense. I am scared. Scared to get hurt again. Scared to let him in again. But I'm even more scared of living a life without John Brooks in it…

"Brooks Taylor is jealous!" Spencer Austin yells, drawing my attention back to the screen in the corner. The three of them—*Spencer, Viviana, and Brooks* stand in the middle of the ring for an "interview" with Jude Paul.

I'm not slated to join them; my only contribution to tonight's show was joining the battle royale for the number one contender's spot to face *Calla Lily* at Wrestlefest. And while I knew I wasn't going to win, it had been nice to get in the ring with all the girls. *Kerrigan Tate* won the royale, and from what I've seen of her in my short time back, that match is going to be one to watch.

"That's right, I said it. You're jealous of me."

Brooks chuckles. *Jealous?* he mouths, and points at *Austin.*

"When you came back last year, you weren't the guy anymore, Brooks. You come out here and play the character of Brooks Taylor, but you're not even him anymore. You're just the washed-up, has-been version of your former self."

The crowd begins a divided chant of their names, "Austin" and "Brooks," and I hate to say that I think the *Austin* side is louder. *Brooks* shrugs, a smirk on his lips.

"Half of this crowd cannot stand you, and the other half just refuses to admit that you're not the great Brooks Taylor you once were. But this isn't why we're here."

"You mean the last five minutes of your whining and

complaining isn't why I'm here?" Brooks asks, and *Spencer's* face falls. *"Oh, I'm sorry, please continue."* He tries to hide his laughter, biting down on the inside of his cheek, before he motions for *Spencer* to continue.

"We're here because it's time someone put you in your place, Brooks. I'm tired of you and your arrogant ways. You walk around here like you own the place, but you're no better than the dirt beneath my shoe." Spencer white-knuckles the microphone, spitting the words. *"You've been handed opportunity after opportunity, while the rest of us have to claw and fight to get a crumb, a morsel of a chance...People like me, Ryker, Drake. You step on us, on all of us, to put yourself at the top, and you can't even wrestle!"*

Seriously? We're going back to that? Come on, Austin, you can do better than that.

Claiming Brooks can't wrestle is always the fallback for people who are looking to pick a fight with him. I roll my eyes, and when I glance in the opposite corner of the room, Amos stares at the screen in front of him with pursed lips. He's not loving this. They need to do something to get this moving.

"We're the ones who work every damn day to make these shows what they are! And you...you walk in here and expect everything to just be handed to you."

Brooks looks bored, rolling his own eyes.

"I want you to see what it's like when someone takes away your dreams, the same way you've taken away countless dreams from every other wrestler in this company!"

"The dreams I've—" Brooks laughs. *"That's all you've got? Come on, Austin. I know you can do better than this. You're saying the same shit everyone has been saying for the last ten years! Don't you think if I had all this 'power' you guys seem to think I do, I'd have that belt around my waist?"* He points to the belt on the chair *Spencer* occupied not long ago. *"You*

say I manipulate everything that happens here in EWE, and yet I haven't won a title in almost three years! Count 'em." He lifts his fingers to count backwards to 2016. *"I haven't held a title since I lost to Damian Drake at Wreck the Halls in 2016."* He shakes his head. *"You want to come out here and act all holier-than-thou, but the truth is, you're no better than me and every other man in that locker room. If I really am the man behind the curtain, pulling all the strings, especially this close to Wrestlefest, you think I'd be in a match with you?"*

That earns a chuckle from none other than Amos and the crowd.

"No, I'd be face-to-face with Fata, Goodwin, or, hell, maybe even that new kid—Aaron Zimmerman—who's been kicking ass down in NextGen." The crowd roars, and *Brooks* glances at *Viviana*, who stands behind her husband. He points at her with a narrowed gaze. *"And don't even get me started on you. What are you doing here? You make this grand 'comeback,' but you've barely stepped foot in the ring since. Your match with me weeks ago was the third time you've been in a ring since you walked through that door. You didn't even compete in that battle royale earlier for the women's title. Why?"* She looks at *Spencer* for an answer, but he only continues to glare at *Brooks*. *"Oh, don't worry, I know why. I just want to see what you have to say. It's because you're too busy being this guy's lapdog."*

That earns a "lap-dog" chant from the crowd, and everyone backstage starts laughing.

"Why is that?" *Brooks* asks. *"Too scared to get back in the ring unless you're fighting someone with their hand tied behind their back? Afraid to take a bump? Afraid you might get hurt? Newsflash! We get hurt for a living. You picked the wrong career."*

"I wouldn't have gotten hurt if it wasn't for your girlfriend!" *Viviana* hisses.

It would appear he's struck a nerve, but it's her use of the word girlfriend that catches my attention, and that of a few others around gorilla, including Noah. He glances my way with a smirk before turning back to his monitor.

"My girlfriend?"

"If it wasn't for her, I—"

"If it wasn't for her, you wouldn't be standing where you are right now, Viviana," Brooks says, venom dripping from his voice. For a moment, I don't see the character, only the man behind the mask. *"That woman did more for the women's division than anyone else—you included! But I guess you wouldn't know because you were too busy fucking this clown. You're too worried about what other people think of you, but you don't do anything to better yourself. And that's the difference between us and the two of you...When Savvy and I fail, we get back up and try again, but you blame everybody else."*

"That's funny considering she walked out on you two years ago."

My heart stops. I knew this was coming sooner or later; I just hoped it would be much later.

Brooks scrubs a hand over his face before his tongue pokes out to wet his lips. He takes a deep breath and glances around the crowd, which has started to chant, "Holy shit." That's the bombshell they've been waiting for since my return.

"You know something, Spencer? You're right, Savvy did leave me. But you want to know something else? She still answered my call. She still showed up. She's been in this ring every damn day since she walked back through that door, and that's more than I can say for either one of you."

That receives a "Savvy Skye" chant, but I'm too focused on the drama unfolding on-screen to care when every eye in gorilla turns on me. Because for the first time in a long time, I don't know where this will lead.

"*You've created this delusion in your heads where everyone is against you, everyone is out to get you. That's not real, and Spencer, it's time to act like a man, stand up and—*"

"*Do you ever shut up?*" Viviana yells, catching Brooks off guard. Maybe Spencer a little, too. "*I know you like to hear yourself talk, but haven't we heard enough?*"

Brooks chuckles, scratching his chin, and what happens next is *not* part of the script. In fact, most of this wasn't scripted. They were allowed to go out and trash-talk each other freely, because a little improv never hurt anyone, but I know for certain this wasn't planned.

Viviana's palm collides with Brooks's cheek when he starts to speak again, and the world around me comes to a halt.

Did she just...

This isn't a fucking segment anymore. I could see the switch happen, slowly turning from banter back and forth to something more real. Personal. Blurring the lines between the role we're meant to play in the ring and reality. I didn't think it would turn into this; otherwise, I would've insisted on being out there. Viviana can say whatever she wants about me—hell, she can talk trash about him—but she is not going to get away with putting her hands on him.

Before I know it, I'm standing up from my chair and walking out of the curtain that will lead to the ramp. I can vaguely hear one of the producers yelling my name into the headset, trying to get the sound techs to play my music before I make it out there. They want it to seem like this was planned, but they can take their program and shove it up their ass.

When I get back to gorilla, I'm probably going to get my ass chewed because I'm not supposed to be anywhere near this segment. I don't care.

Just before I step out, I hear him chuckle over the speakers—like he *knows* what's coming. Knows I'm about to walk out there.

"*You just made the biggest mistake of your life*," Brooks says, and I'm already on stage before he can finish.

The crowd cheers as I run toward the ring, sliding under the bottom rope. I pop up to my feet in a fluid motion, but Spencer has already pulled Viviana out of the ring. He drags her by the hand toward the ramp.

I snatch the microphone from Brooks's hands and climb the rope, glaring down at them. "You fuck with him? I'm coming after you, bitch," I say, and the crowd explodes. "I'll see you on Sunday!"

I throw the microphone to the ground, and Brooks takes my hand when I jump down from the ropes. He lifts our hands into the air, but my gaze remains locked on Viviana. Her husband continues to pull her up the ramp, and only when they disappear backstage do I turn my attention to the crowd. I finally let myself smile.

Brooks motions to the corners, and we climb up the turnbuckles, soaking in the reaction from the crowd. I can feel his gaze on me, warming my skin, and when I turn to meet his stare, he wears a wide, toothy grin that makes mine grow wider.

When we finally make it backstage, almost five minutes later, all eyes are on us. I freeze, but Brooks places a firm hand on my back, urging me forward.

"*Brooks! Skye!*" Amos's voice rings out before he pops up from his chair. We pause in the middle of the room, meeting the wide grin of the man in charge. "That was good shit."

Brooks nods at him, and his fingers gently tap my lower back. *Keep moving*, they say. I half expect him to pull away when I move forward, but he doesn't. He continues to guide me through the small sea of people who've gathered in gorilla, each one offering us some acknowledgement for the show we just put on.

When we finally make it through the curtain backstage,

Brooks clears his throat, about to say something, but he's interrupted by a loud whistle to our right. Spencer and Viviana are posted along the wall. Were they seriously waiting for us? Don't they have anything better to do?

"Put on quite the show out there, Sav," Spencer says, lips quirked to the side.

"Trust me, Austin, it wasn't a show," I say.

Viviana chuckles, drawing my attention to her as she clings to his arm. Her smug smile only adds fuel to the fire rebuilding inside my chest.

"And you. If you ever put your hands on him again, you'll have more than one knee to rehab."

She gasps, and there's a small chuckle behind me.

Spencer's eyes widen with rage. "Come near my wife—"

"And you'll do what?" My glare turns on him. "If your wife would keep her hands to herself, we wouldn't even be having this discussion."

I feel a tug against my waist, pulling me back a step that I hadn't even realized I'd taken. Somewhere in the exchange of words, Brooks had slipped a finger through my belt loop, making sure I would keep a healthy distance from the two cowards on the other side of the hall.

"You'd better be careful, Sav," Viviana says. Her gaze flickers to Brooks. "Or someone might think you still have feelings for him."

"That's enough!" Noah steps through the curtain. "C'mon, break it up, you guys." He shuffles his way into the middle of our little powwow and glances around at each of us. "I mean it. Now go. All of you. Save it for the ring on Sunday."

34

Savannah

FRIDAY, APRIL 26, 2019

INDIANAPOLIS, IN

"If I didn't know any better," Jo Valence says. My friend glances over her shoulder briefly before she turns back around, looking up at me with big brown eyes and a smile. "I'd think you were falling for him again." Her grip tightens on my arm when I try to pull away from her and stop in my tracks to tell her she's wrong, but she urges me forward down the hallway.

"What are you talking about?" I ask, trying to keep my volume down, because the "he" in question walks only about ten paces behind us.

"Have you *seen* the way you look at him?" Jo laughs, and her short brown hair brushes the tops of her shoulders with each step. "And don't even get me started on that show you put on last night. If that doesn't scream that you still love each other, I don't know what does."

"That was just—"

"Just business, I know." My friend rolls her eyes and unwinds her arm from mine when we reach the end of the hallway. There are two options from here: go through the door that leads back out to the signing hall or take a left and go further into the depths of the convention center. We just finished a joint panel where Jo moderated the conversation between me, Brooks, and the fans. Now it's time to say goodbye to my buffer and hello to two hours of alone time with Brooks for a joint photo session. "Well, this is where we say goodbye." Jo waits for him to arrive at my side before she turns to him to say, "Brooks, take care of my girl."

He salutes her, but doesn't say anything, still maintaining a small distance between us.

"Don't do anything I wouldn't do," Jo whispers, winking at me before she struts down the hallway.

When I glance back over my shoulder, Brooks leans back against the concrete wall with his arms crossed. He doesn't exactly look open to conversation, so I do the same on the opposite side of the hallway, and we wait in silence for the volunteer meant to guide us to the session. Our conversation with Jo was fine—dare I say, fun—but the good time ended as soon as the panel did. He shut down, almost as quickly as he did last night, but today he couldn't turn and run the other way. He couldn't put the distance between us. I think that almost made it harder to deal with because it was like poking the sleeping bear.

The wait time for the volunteer feels like a lifetime in the silence of the hallway, when in reality it's only about five minutes before she appears and asks us to follow her. At first, our walk is shrouded in silence, until I hear the simplest word ever said. "Hi."

I glance up at him, confused. "Hi. Hi, me?"

Brooks laughs. "Who else?"

"Well, you've barely spoken two words to me since you shoved me in a cab after dinner and told me to keep my distance."

"Yeah," he says, scratching at the back of his neck. "Sorry about that."

We walk in silence for another moment before he takes hold of my hand, stopping our stride. The young volunteer we're meant to be following keeps walking, unaware that we've stopped, and when she finally notices, Brooks motions for her to give us a second. She taps the face of her wristwatch, but he doesn't seem to care, turning back to me.

"Sav, I—I'm sorry. I shouldn't have put pressure on you or had any expectations. I know we're both just trying to navigate this new territory, and I'm sorry for not making it any easier. It's not fair to either one of us."

He's dancing around the real issue: his confession. He still loves me, or at least, he did four nights ago.

"Friends?"

Friends? Does he really think it's still as easy as saying the word? Because I'm not sure we even know *how* to be friends. We'll have to learn how to be if I'm going to sign a contract and stick around a little bit longer...and I only have three more days before I have to make that decision.

When I look up from the floor, he wears a hopeful smile, and with a sigh, I nod. Brooks motions for me to lead the way, but this time, his hand rests on my lower back, and it's comforting. His touch grounds me as we walk through the open door, and a wave of noise infiltrates the air. A massive group of people crowds the stage we're meant to stand on, and a long line snakes through the stanchions, out the end, and down the main hall. Seeing things like this always shocks me—humbles me—because who in their right mind would care about meeting me? Who would stand in a line this long just for a few seconds of my attention? It's never made sense to me. It doesn't help that I'm standing next to the man who—I decided on the walk to this exact spot—has just broken my heart all over again.

The word *friends* ricochets around my mind, slowly unraveling all of the work I've done these past two years and ripping it to shreds. I didn't come back to EWE with any intentions of falling for him again. I returned intending to stay as far away from him as possible, but the longer I'm here, the more I'm around him...the more I realize that maybe I've never actually fallen out of love with him in the first place.

The next two hours go by quickly, and it's fun being face-to-face with the fans again. The photographer stands at her post, waiting for the last group to leave before she gives a thumbs-up. "You guys are good to go!"

"Wait, I think we missed someone," Brooks calls out when she starts to walk away. What is he talking about? The last person in line just walked out and—*Holy shit.*

Movement from the corner of the stage catches my attention, and my eyes well with tears: every member of the Williams family lines the side of the stage with a beaming smile. When I look back at Brooks, he lifts his shoulders in a shrug. A small smile sits in the corner of his lips. He did this, I know he did, but I don't have the chance to thank him before I'm swept off my feet by the onslaught of hugs from my brothers.

"What are you guys doing here?" I ask when they set me back on my feet. "I thought you guys couldn't make it."

"We wanted to surprise you," Nash says. "Did you really think we'd miss *this*?"

Papá wraps his arm around my shoulders, pulling me into a tight embrace and kissing the top of my head. "You should be thanking that man over there," he whispers, tilting his head slightly toward Brooks. He stands off to the side, conversing with the photographer, but his eyes turn to meet mine, and he smiles again. "He called a few days ago, wanted to make sure we had what we needed to get here. I was supposed to stay home, but he's very persuasive."

"John, come here!" Mamá pulls him into the tightest hug I've ever seen and kisses his cheek. "It is so good to see you. I've missed our morning chats."

"It's good to see you, Mrs. Williams."

"Ah-ah," she tsks, and a blush immediately flushes his cheeks.

"Laine." Brooks corrects himself, and she nods, patting his arm.

"I don't know about the rest of you, but I'm starving," Blake says, rubbing his stomach for added effect. His twin does the same to get the point across.

"When are you not?" I ask.

"When are you not?" They both mock me, and we go back and forth three more times before Crew smacks our little brothers on the backs of their heads.

"Could you at least try and behave?" Crew asks before he pushes them to the side.

"Well, should we get a picture?" Papá asks, and that's our cue to shuffle into our places.

Brooks stands behind the photographer, and part of me wants to invite him back into the picture, but the better part of me knows I shouldn't. Before I can make the decision, Mamá does it for me. She calls out to him, inviting him to join us. Inviting is a nice way to put it because she leaves no room for rejection.

"Oh no, Laine, it's okay. This is a family photo and—"

"And you're family," Mamá says without hesitation. Her words put a stop to his protests, and my heart. My breath catches in my lungs, and I stare straight at him. Did she really just say that?

Mamá flexes her hand again, motioning for him to join us

before she makes room between the two of us. Slowly, Brooks takes the steps forward and fills in the space left for him. When the gaps begin to fill again, his arm reaches around my waist, tugging me close. It feels right, it feels...normal. And without a second thought, I let my head fall against this shoulder.

From the corner of my eye, I can see a twitch in my second-oldest brother's mouth beside me, an amused breath escaping his lips. I feel the gentle weight of his hand patting Brooks's back. We get a few normal photos in before my twin brothers jump out of position and land on their knees in front of the group to get at least one silly photo.

"I hope you guys have a marvelous weekend," Brooks says when we get back to the safety of backstage a few minutes later. Mamá gives him one final squeeze, thanking him again. He gives me a brief smile, says he'll see me tomorrow for our photo session, and walks toward the labyrinth of passages leading outside.

"Okay, I'm with Blake and Bodhi. Can we get something to eat now?" Nash whines.

And while I agree because I'm starving, my focus never leaves the man walking down the hallway. I can't let him walk away. I shouldn't. He should be with us. I know he's busy, we both are, but he's the one who made sure my family got here and had everything they needed. He should at least get to spend a little bit of time with them, too.

"I'll be right back," I say to my mother just as Brooks disappears around the corner. I run down the hallway, ready to call out his name, but it gets caught in my throat as soon as I make the turn.

"Oh, Savannah!" Chelsea's voice bounces off the walls. "I was just asking about you."

"Chelsea," I say, offering her a tight smile before doing the same to the man by her side. "Xander."

What are they doing here?

"I was just telling Brooks that after that promo you guys gave with Austin and Viviana last night, Amos wants to shake things up a bit. We're going to make the match a title match."

"A title match?" I glance at Brooks, and his reaction tells me he already knows the outcome. I ask anyway. "And who's coming out champion?"

Xander answers, "Austin."

"You mean, we have to lose?" I scoff.

"Sav," Brooks warns, but I ignore him. I don't care. This is bullshit. This is not what I came back for.

"You brought me back to help boost this story, to help *Brooks Taylor* win, and now you want to change your mind and—"

I'm not sure what actually makes my words falter—Brooks's firm squeeze on my shoulder or the height of Chelsea's brow that only seems to get higher as I speak.

"Thank you," Brooks says, looking between them, and maintains his grip on me. "We'll speak with Austin and Vee to coordinate."

"Be sure that you do," Chelsea says. She only offers a tight smile to Brooks before her steely blue eyes glare down at me.

They turn to leave without another word, but Xander pauses mid-step. He looks over his shoulder to say, "Oh, and Savannah, Amos wanted me to remind you that he wants an answer by Monday."

My only response is a glare.

"This is bullshit," I say when they're finally gone.

Brooks shrugs, letting it roll off his back, just like he always does. Just like I always did, too, before I left. "Name of the game, Sav. You know that."

To make it in this business, you have to learn to roll with the punches and take the good with the bad, even when you get the short end of the stick.

"It's still bullshit."

"They want to draw out the feud, most likely. And what better way to do that than—"

"Discredit everything you've said thus far?" I ask.

He knows I'm right, which is why he doesn't fight me. Instead, he breathes out and shakes his head, letting the corners of his lips turn up.

"What was he talking about? What's Monday?" Brooks asks.

"I have to let Amos know if I'm going to sign a full-time contract," I say, rubbing the bridge of my nose.

"And?"

"And," I sigh. "I don't know."

"That's in like…three days, Savannah."

"A lot can happen in three days," I say, and when I open my eyes, I jump, not realizing just how close he had gotten. He looks like he wants to say something, the words sitting on the tip of his tongue, and when I think he's about to say it…

"Savannah!" Crew's voice rings out down the hallway, breaking whatever trance we're under. What is it with him and having the worst timing when it comes to our conversations?

At first, I don't look away from Brooks. It's only when I hear the annoyed huff from my brother that Brooks motions down the hall with his eyes. A smirk tugs on the corner of his lips when I finally turn to answer the call. Crew wears a face of scrutiny as he looks between the two of us, measuring the distance with his eyes before he meets my stare. "Nash and the twins are about to die if we don't get a move on."

I roll my eyes, turning back to Brooks, and say, "I'd better go." He nods. "You want to join us?"

"I can't, Sweetheart. I'm sorry. I have a few things I have to do before Sunday."

"Right. This is one of your busiest weeks," I say, nodding along to the words. "Well, thank you…for making sure they got here."

"They were coming anyway."

"But you made sure they got here, and if this is my last Wrestlefest, I want them to be here."

Brooks smiles. "Well, if you ask me, I don't think EWE has had its last Heartbreak, yet."

"So, tell us. How's it been?" Nash sits across the fire pit outside our hotel. The three of us—Nash, Crew, and I—are the last three standing in the family after Amara decided to go to bed about ten minutes ago. It's been a long day for everyone. I was finally released from rehearsal about two hours ago, and my older brothers, plus Amara, decided to wait until I got back before going to bed. That somehow turned into an almost two-hour yap session, and now that it's just the three of us, it seems they're getting to the hard-hitting questions.

"It's been great," I say, letting my shoulders rise and fall to match my breath.

"Even with Brooks?"

"Yeah, what's going on there?" Crew adds. When I glance at my oldest brother, I anticipate a look of disapproval, but instead, he just looks curious. "You guys looked pretty chummy today."

"Did you see them in that picture?" Nash points toward our brother.

"Oh, I saw." Crew smirks, chuckling. "Hard to believe something isn't going on there. Or what was it, she said? They 'grew apart.'"

"Hello! Sitting right here," I say, looking between them.

"Yeah, we know," Nash says, sipping his beer.

"Are you back together?" Crew asks, and my mouth falls open.

"No! We...We're—"

My brothers share a chuckle before Nash says, "You want to be, though."

"I didn't say that!"

"You didn't have to, SJ."

Brooks and I may not be together, but my brothers are right about one thing...I do want to be. However, I didn't expect this kind of ambush from them—Bodhi and Blake, maybe, but not these two. When I came home brokenhearted, they were the ones most upset, even refusing to watch when he would come across the television for the first few months, unless they knew he was about to get his ass kicked.

I never told my family the truth about our breakup. As far as they knew—as far as anyone knew—we had simply grown apart. "It just isn't going to work out," I said when I called Crew to help me pack up and move back to Celestia. I didn't give him details, no matter how many times he asked. Brooks was supposed to be on a plane to Europe, so the chances of him showing up were slim to none. But on the off chance he did show up, the last thing I wanted was for him to walk in with my oldest, most protective brother, pissed off about the truth.

I don't know why I never told them. Maybe in some convoluted way, I hoped it wasn't really over. But what does that say about me?

"You guys are delusional," I say, rolling my eyes. "You've only seen what's on TV, and that's not real."

"Wasn't on TV today," Nash says, and shares a look with our oldest brother. I turn just in time to see his own smirk before he hides it behind a sip of beer.

"Are you boys still bothering your sister?" Mamá asks, walking out the side door of the hotel to the second-story patio we've been occupying. They both answer with a resounding *No* before she begins to shoo them away. "Okay, *mijos*, c'mon. Your sister has had a long day, *y de nuevo mañana.*" *And again tomorrow*, my mother reminds them, motioning for my brothers to rise. "She doesn't need you poking and prodding her for information."

"You just want to do that yourself, Mamá," Nash says, earning an eye roll from her, but she doesn't deny it.

"She's right, it's been a long day for everyone, I'm beat," Crew says, standing from his chair.

Nash mumbles something under his breath along the lines of *suck up*, before he follows suit, stretching his limbs and following our oldest brother to the door.

"How are you doing, *mija*?" my mother asks, sitting down beside me once she is sure they're gone. She wraps a comforting arm around my shoulders, and I sigh. "That good, huh?"

"It's fine, Mamá," I say, snuggling a little deeper into her embrace.

"*¿Es John?*"

"What makes you say that?"

"Well," she draws out, and begins to play with the ends of my hair. "I think it's pretty obvious from the way you two are with each other. Not to mention, you came here to partner with him when I'm pretty sure you haven't settled whatever it was that happened years ago."

"*Ay, Mamà.*"

"*¿Me equivoco?*" No, she's not wrong. But that doesn't mean I want to hear it. I sigh again, letting my face fall into my hands. "What's going on, Savannah?"

"He told me he loves me."

My mother throws her head back in laughter, like I just told the funniest joke on the planet. "Well, yeah! A blind man could've told you that. You two seem to be the only ones who can't see it, just like before. And what did you say?"

"Nothing."

"Nothing?" She practically jumps from her seat. "*Ay,* Savannah, why did you say nothing?"

"Because..." Do I tell her? Do I finally tell her the truth about things? "Because we agreed to just be friends, Mamá. And saying that I love him isn't exactly staying within the friend zone."

"So, you both spoke and settled things from the past before you agreed to this, or did you just say '*Let's be friends*?'"

I swear this woman has cameras everywhere with the way she knows things. Sure, we talked—kind of—but I wouldn't call that conversation putting things to rest. There are still things that need to be said before Brooks and I can be friends again...if we can even be that.

Mamá sighs, pulling away to look me straight in the eye. "Savannah, I may not know what really happened, but I know that it hurt you. You were talking about marriage, he'd already asked your father's permission—"

"What did you just say?" I interrupt. He had already asked for Papá's permission?

A sad smile crosses my mother's face. "That's why I was so confused when you said you wanted to move back home. I thought things were going well."

John had...

If he'd already asked for my parents' blessing, how close was he to asking me? Yes, we'd talked about it. A lot. But I didn't think...

"You didn't just 'grow apart,' did you?" She asks.

I close my eyes, raking my bottom lip between my teeth as I try to hold back the emotions swirling in my chest. "No," I say, tearfully.

"What really happened, *mija*?" My mother pushes the hair back from my face and wipes away a tear that escapes the corner of my eye.

I sigh and open my eyes to meet her concerned stare. "John...only dated me because of a bet."

"¿*Qué?*" *What?*

"It's a long story, Mamá, but a group of the guys were saying some gross things, and—"

"About you?"

I nod. "He stepped in. And by doing so, they dared him to sleep with me before a certain day."

"And he did this?"

"Not technically. We didn't sleep together until after that. John says the only reason he agreed to it was to protect me."

"Do you believe him?" she asks, calmer than I expected her to be.

"I want to," I say, looking away from her. "But—"

"Savannah, I wish you had come to me about this sooner, so I could have been there for you. So you weren't alone." She pats my hand before giving it a gentle squeeze. "You had every right to be upset, but my love, I think it's time that you let it go. That man loves you. He's always loved you, far longer than you two had ever been together. I knew it from the first time I laid eyes on the two of you."

"The John I know—"

"The John you *know* would have done anything, *anything*, to protect you."

"But agreeing to a bet—"

"Why did he agree to it?" Mamá asks. The tone in her voice tells me that I'm not going to win this. I can't because I know where it's going, and I know she's right. "*Exactamente,*" she says when I don't answer. *Exactly.*

"But his mom hates—"

"Has her own healing to do. Her issue was never with you, Savannah." She cradles my cheek in her hand. "*Mija,* it's okay to want this. It's okay to want him. To admit that you were hurt and upset, and you made a decision based on those feelings. It's okay to admit you made a mistake; you both have made some mistakes. The past two years that you've been home, we could all see you weren't happy. The light inside of you dimmed, and it wasn't until you came back here that I saw it return...When you walked on that stage three weeks ago, it was there, brighter than ever. This is what you love, *corazón*. Not coaching. Not the ranch. This. And him."

The warmth of tears burns my eyes. I look away, trying to regain my composure.

She gently grips my chin and pulls me back, wiping away the moisture collected in the corner of my eyes. "Even if you choose not to pursue a reconnection with John, I think you need to stay here...with EWE. Sign the contract, SJ. Do you what you love. What you're meant to do."

After a moment, my mother sighs before she leans forward to kiss my forehead and whisper that she loves me. Just before she walks through the door, she looks over her shoulder and, with a brow raised, she orders me to get some sleep.

35

Savannah

SATURDAY, APRIL 27, 2019

INDIANAPOLIS, IN

"You look hot," my sister-in-law says when I step out of the bathroom. I roll my eyes but can't fight my own smile. She said the same thing on her wedding day when I walked out in her chosen bridesmaid dress, except I hated that dress. It was a one-shouldered tie-neck in a burnt orange color, and while it made her happy, the rest of the bridal party couldn't stand it. This dress, though, was handpicked by my former stylist specifically for tonight.

The moment he pulled it off the rack, I knew it was the one. It was the only dress hidden within a garment bag, and as he unzipped it, he said, "I was saving the best for last." The vibrant red, floor-length chiffon gown with a sheer overlay was the perfect mixture of classy, romantic, sexy, and red-carpet chic.

"And if Brooks doesn't think so, then he's blind," Amara says with a twinkle in her eye, handing me the earrings my stylist paired with the ensemble.

"Amara!"

"Am I wrong?" Her brows raise in question.

I'm not getting into this discussion when I'm about to spend the better part of my evening with the man in question. It's Legends Night, and while we don't have to spend all night together, Amos expects at least a few photos and a little bit of combined face time. The press and fans have been eating up this story, and the owner of this company has no issue giving them exactly what they want.

"No, I'm not," Amara says over her shoulder, walking down the hallway to answer the unexpected knock at the door.

"Wonder who that could be," Mamá says, coming up behind me in the mirror. She re-fluffs my hair, letting it fall into the perfect curls down my back. I was surprised when I met my parents for breakfast this morning that neither one of them brought up the bombshell I'd dropped on my mother last night. She hasn't said much about Brooks at all today, and I'm not sure how to feel about it, but that's a conversation for tomorrow. I need to get through Wrestlefest before I worry about whether she told my father or not, and how well he's handling it.

"Probably Rae," I say, checking my makeup one last time. I'm supposed to meet her and Brody downstairs in the lobby in five minutes. Normally, I could be ten minutes late and they'd have no idea, but maybe Brody has finally been able to break her of her bad habit.

"You're joking, right?" Mamá laughs. "That girl will be late to her own funeral one day, and you think she's running ahead of schedule to something like this?"

I offer her a grin over my shoulder before applying a final layer of lipstick.

"Oh!" Mamá gasps, her eyes wide as they look past me down the hallway. "Well, don't you look handsome?"

When I turn, I expect to see Brody standing there in his monkey suit, as he called it last night, ready for the night ahead of us, but it's not Brody at all.

Brooks stands in the door, dressed in a full suit and tie, face freshly shaven and hair styled to look like it hasn't been styled at all. There's a red tie that coincidentally matches the color of my dress in the center of his chest beneath the deep navy blue suit jacket. Handsome is one way to put it, but a few other words come to mind. His eyes trail down the length of my dress and back up before he lets out a soft breath, and I don't even realize I've taken the steps to shorten the distance between us until my sister-in-law inches past me.

"Hi," I say, my eyes never leaving his.

Brooks smiles. "Hi."

"What are you doing here?"

"I came to see if you needed a ride. I figured we could go... together."

"Together," I repeat, and he nods. For such a small word, it carries a lot of weight. What does *together* mean? "As friends?"

His throat swells with a hard swallow before he nods again, a tight smile tugging at the corners of his lips. "Friends."

"I'm supposed to meet Rae and Brody in a few minutes, but I don't think they want me going as their third wheel anyway," I say, and he laughs. I've only been a thorn in their side for the last three weeks. I'm sure they've been happy to get some alone time since we've been in Indianapolis, where they've had their own space. "Let me grab my—" My mother stands behind me with my clutch in hand, ready and waiting. "Purse."

"You two just look breathtaking." She swoons. "Don't they, Amara?"

"Best looking couple there," my sister-in-law agrees. I give her a pointed look, and she only giggles behind her hand, turning on her heel to pick up the mess we'd created in my room.

"Go! Before you're late." Mamá pushes us out the door without a chance to say goodbye, and as soon as the door slams behind us, I can imagine the shit-eating grin on both of their faces. I'm sure Amara has already told Crew, and the news is spreading like wildfire amongst the Williams family.

"Shall we?" Brooks asks, offering me his arm. I adjust my purse in my right hand, threading my other arm through his, and he leads me down the hall. The elevator doors open immediately when he presses the button, and we part to stand on either side of the car.

> I found a ride.

> Raelynn Carson
> THANK GOD.
>
> I'm running behind.
>
> I was about to text you.

"Running behind?" Brooks asks from across the elevator, and I give him a knowing look. I'm not shocked my best friend is, in fact, running ten minutes behind. If she weren't, I'd think the world was coming to an end, but tonight, I find myself feeling a little extra grateful for her bad habits.

Brooks leads me out of the elevator and through the side door of the hotel, where a car awaits. Our ride to the stadium is filled with a comfortable silence, one that draws us close as our fingers brush on the seat between us. Slowly, his hand envelops mine, and his fingers thread through my own, thumb tracing a pattern on the inside of my palm. He doesn't let go when we get out of the car, instead using the connection to draw me in close, leaning in to whisper in my ear, "You are the most beautiful woman here." The words are simple, and my insides clench at the familiarity. When I meet his stare, Brooks smiles before bringing the back of my hands to his lips.

All eyes are on us when we walk in. While I can't help but notice, Brooks ignores them. He kisses my temple and pulls me onto the red carpet, where we talk to members of the media. They ask a flurry of questions, and I'm relieved they don't ask the same one we were bombarded with at LNX Upfronts in New York: "Does this mean you guys are back together...like *together* together?" I can see the question on the tips of their tongues, but they never ask. I wonder if that's an Amos thing or a Brooks thing.

Never-ending vibrations come from my phone, which I shoved inside my clutch before we started with the media. I can guess who it is, and when I catch Raelynn's stare across the room, she swims through the crowd until she reaches me. She waits impatiently for us to finish our final interview, and I guarantee her foot is tapping beneath the length of her plum-colored gown.

"I know you said you found a ride, but I wasn't expecting this," she says, looking between us when we're finally released.

Brooks shrugs. "I knew you'd be late, and I knew she wouldn't want to be."

Rae narrows her gaze up at him. "I take offense to that."

"Well, if you guys weren't the talk of the town before, you are now," Brody says, joining us and slapping a hand on his best friend's shoulder.

"Nosy fuckers," is Brooks's only response as he slips his hand back into mine. "They put you by us?"

"I haven't been inside yet." Something catches Brody's attention across the room, and his smile falls. "Don't look now, but your best friend is on his way over."

Before I can ask what that means, none other than Miles Drake steps through the crowd with a dainty blonde on his arm. I wonder where he picked her up. Somehow, I've been fortunate to avoid much interaction with Drake since my return. Now that I think about it, I can't remember seeing him at all. "Well, if it isn't my favorite group of people?"

He sounds overly excited to see a group that can't stand

him.

"Someone call security, they let a stray dog in," Raelynn says.

"Oh, come on, Rae. Don't be like that. I've missed you guys!"

Rae scoffs. "We didn't miss you. It's been nice without you around here."

"Be nice," Brody says, not even trying to hide his laugh.

"Thank you, Brody," Drake says. "I'm glad somebody here is happy to see me."

"Oh no, I'd kick you out myself," Brody says. "But if they want to let you back in for some reason, that's none of my business. I'm not here to get into a tussle with you, Drake. Not tonight. This is supposed to be when we put our differences aside and celebrate the careers of our peers."

"That's all I'm here to do."

"Somehow, I doubt that," Brooks says under his breath, but it's loud enough that it catches all of our attention. The gaze of the man who put a wedge between me and Brooks, not once, but twice, finally turns on us. His eyes trail up my body in a slow, steady pace that makes my skin crawl. When he meets my gaze, his brows raise suggestively, and I can feel the tension building behind Brooks's grasp. I take a steadying breath and plant my other hand on his forearm, giving it a gentle squeeze. This is not the place.

"I was wondering if the rumors were true," Drake says, his gaze flickers to where our hands meet and back. "You know, I guess you didn't need my help all those years ago, after all. You always were good at sweet-talking them into your bed, Brooks." He laughs when Brooks lunges forward, but Brody steps in front of him.

"Get the fuck out of here, Drake," Brody hisses over his shoulder.

"Yeah, you're right. I don't want to be around a bunch of

pompous, washed-up has-beens anyway." Drake turns back to me with a smile. "Oh, and Savannah, if you decide to stick around for a while, come find me when you're ready to be with a real man. I'm sure one night with me will remind you why you left in the first place."

"Fuck you, Drake," I say, knowing full well this is what he wants. He wants to get under my skin, wants to antagonize me, and I know I shouldn't let it show, but I don't care. Glancing around him, I look directly at the blonde and say, "If I were you, I'd run the other way before he places a bet on you, too. This guy doesn't know the first thing about being a man."

Her mouth falls open before she stalks away. That shuts down his laughter, and he glares my way before chasing after her.

"Well, that was fun," Wolf's voice rings out from behind us.

Brooks walks one step ahead of me, putting the same distance between us that wiggled its way in as the night went on. His hands have been shoved deep in his pockets since we got out of the car, eyes trained on the carpet ahead of his feet. Things had been fine until he disappeared backstage to prepare for his speech introducing *"Top Dollar"* Clarence Kennedy.

Clarence Kennedy, who donned the ring name *"Top Dollar" Clarence Kennedy*, was one of the first wrestlers Amos signed and developed in EWE under his leadership and is still a fan favorite. Clarence stands a few inches shorter than Brooks, and since retiring five years ago, doesn't maintain as much muscle mass, but he's "always ready to answer the call and jump back in the ring." Brooks gave a heartfelt speech about the impact "*Top Dollar*" had on his career, starting on his first day in NextGen sixteen years ago. But from my seat, I could see there was something on his mind, and it wasn't just the speech.

When Brooks returned to his seat following Clarence's speech, I placed my hand over his, giving it a gentle squeeze, but got nothing in return. Eyes forward, he didn't even seem to notice when I slipped my hand out of his, but Rae did. So did Brody and Wolf at the after party as the space continued to grow, until he asked if I was ready to head back to the hotel.

"Tonight was fun," I say after a moment of silence outside my room.

Brooks finally looks up, and his blue eyes are as dark as the deepest parts of the oceans.

Clearing his throat, he rocks back on his heels and crosses his arms. "Thanks for coming with me."

"How could I resist a night with *the* Brooks Taylor?" It's meant to be teasing. I hoped it would put a crack in his armor, and it does the trick because I see a twitch lift the corner of his mouth.

Brooks rolls his eyes and takes a step back, ready to turn and leave. "Goodnight, Savannah."

That's it? That's all I get?

He starts to walk down the hallway, and the realization hits me that it's now or never.

"Brooks," I call out, and his feet plant firmly into the carpet, pausing his retreat, but he doesn't turn around. "That's it? After all of this...you're just going to say goodnight and leave. Is this about what Drake said earlier, because if it is—"

"This has nothing to do with *Drake*." He all but spits the name, scrubbing a hand down his face with a heavy sigh. "What do you want me to say, Savannah?"

I don't know, but I know it's not this. I know that I don't

want to walk away from this weekend without having bridged the gap between us a little.

"Look, it was never my intention to cause any confusion. I was—"

"Then what was your intention? Because if I'm being quite honest, it hasn't been very clear the past ten years."

Brooks scoffs. "That's the pot calling the kettle black. You've been hot and cold from the second you stepped out of that curtain three weeks ago. One minute you want me to stay as far away from you as possible, and the next you're begging me to fuck you."

"Begging you to—"

"You want your cake and eat it too, Sav. You want to stay mad at me, but you want me in your back pocket at the same time, and I can't—"

"That's not true."

"Yes, it is!" Brooks takes a centering breath following his outburst. "I can't do this. I'm sorry that I've made things worse because I thought...I thought we could try to be friends, or friendly, but the truth is, I don't want to be your friend. I can't. I can't just be friends with you, Savannah. If there's one thing I've learned these last few weeks, it's that if you're not mine, I can't be in your life."

His confession knocks the breath from my lungs, and without waiting for an answer, he walks away.

I want to call out to him, beg him to come back and talk to me, but I can't get his name past my lips. Tears burn my eyes as I watch him walk away, because this time I know it's for good, and I feel the final piece of my heart crack.

Pushing inside my room, I fall on the edge of my bed. When did my life become such a mess? A mess that I had been trying to avoid, but one that was almost certain to happen if I returned...I'd hoped to have enough willpower to stay away from him. To avoid this exact moment. If I've learned anything the past few weeks, it's that I'm drawn to him like a moth to a flame, ignoring the burn to fly a little closer to the sun. The truth of the matter is, John has been honest with me on more than one occasion. He's told me how he feels—how he's felt—but I haven't done the same. I haven't been honest with him because I haven't been honest with myself. I thought I could fight these feelings that lingered, but…I can't, and I don't want to.

My fingers move on their own volition, dialing the number that I know will give me the one answer I don't have. He answers, but I can barely hear him over the sounds of the party in the background. A minute later, the sounds fade into the background. "Sav, everything okay?"

"Brody, what's his room number?"

There's a soft chuckle from the other end of the line before he answers.

One foot in front of the other leads me down the hallway to the elevator bank and up two floors. I can't think about what I'm doing because if I do, I might turn around. I need to do this. I have to. Counting the numbers on each door, I find the one I'm looking for. It feels like an eternity before the door swings open after I knock.

"Dude, I'm not in the mood—" His words falter when his eyes meet mine. *What is she doing here*? I can practically hear the words just from the look in his eye.

He obviously thought it was Brody, or maybe Wolf. I know they've been texting him since we left the party. I could hear his phone buzz every few seconds on our way back to the hotel, but he ignored it, almost like he didn't notice the messages flooding his screen. Too lost in his thoughts.

He crosses his arms, guarding the doorway. "Savannah, what are you doing here?"

"What if I don't want to be friends?"

His gaze narrows. "What do you want to be?"

"Your last." I step closer. "Your last first kiss, last first date, last time waking up next to someone new, the last hand you reach for in the dark, and the person you tell all of your secrets to and not worry if it's too heavy. I want to be the last woman you come home to and your last I love you...Because I do, John." Tears cloud my vision as I let the words flow freely. I had no idea what I was going to say when he opened the door. I had no plan other than to knock and hope he answered. "I love you, and I'm sorry that I let my fear of the future and the unknown get in the way of this...Us. I'm sorry I didn't give you a chance to explain, not really. I had already made my mind up, and it wasn't fair. I'm sorry I ran, but if there's one thing I've learned the last few weeks, it's that I can't be friends with you, either. Not if it means I can't love you."

John stands there a moment longer than I hoped before he stoops down to claim my mouth in a hard kiss. He kisses me like an answered prayer. An all-consuming, mind-erasing kiss that will be imprinted in the depths of my brain for the rest of my life. Fire spreads throughout my system, overtaking all thoughts I had moments before. The only thing that matters right now is the way his body feels pressed against mine, the way his mouth feels on mine, and the desperate ache growing in my chest to be one with him.

A soft whimper spills from my parted lips when he pulls away, his teeth grazing my bottom lip. His thumb swipes across my cheek, discarding the tear I hadn't even noticed trailing from my eye.

"It's always been you, Sweetheart," he whispers. "It will always be you. And as long as you'll have me, I'll choose you every day for the rest of my life."

With a crooked finger, he tilts my chin up and pulls me forward into a kiss much softer than before. I melt into him as he kisses me again and again, until gentle kisses turn needy and hungry.

John tugs me by the hand over the threshold of his room, letting the door close behind us, not a care in the world that its slam echoes down the hall. My hands grip the front of his shirt, making busy work of the buttons, and I shove it off his shoulders. The fabric catches on his biceps, but he slips his arms free, and it falls to his feet in a white heap. The pad of his thumb skates across my bottom lip, and the corners of his mouth tug upward. "I love you, Savannah Josefine Williams."

I don't answer with words; instead, closing the gap between us again, tasting the hint of red wine on his tongue from the single glass he had at the party. I take my time, letting my fingers slide up his bare chest, re-memorizing every crevice, every ridge, every mark that makes him...him. That's when I notice the new scar on his shoulder. The one from his surgery in March, after I left. My fingers ghost over the discolored line, but he gathers them in his hand, bringing them to his lips.

"I'm okay," he whispers.

"I called," I say. "Ari. I called Ari. When it happened."

"I know." John smiles. "She told me."

"I'm sorry I wasn't there. I should've been there. I should've—"

He cuts me off with a kiss. "I love you."

One of his hands braces the wall. The other tangles in my hair to tilt my head back, angling my neck to give him full access to my throat. His mouth moves from my mouth to my jaw, down the column of my throat, and sucks the skin at my collarbone between his teeth. His tongue laps over the bite before his teeth find the skin again, repeating until I'm sure the skin becomes discolored. I should push him away, tell him to stop, or Anna from the makeup department will have my head tomorrow, but the feeling is too good.

John gently bunches my dress in his hands, lifting it off the ground, and nudges my legs apart. His eyes follow the trail his right hand leaves, disappearing beneath the red fabric. I gasp when his fingers graze the wet fabric of my underwear. "Shit, you're fucking soaked. That's all for me?"

I nod, biting down on my bottom lip, but gasp when one of his fingers slips inside and over my slit.

John leans down to whisper in my ear, "Tell me what you want, Savannah."

He parts me with his fingers, dipping inside me, and my body reacts immediately, clenching around him. It's been far too long since I felt his touch.

"Fuck," I moan, gripping his shoulders. "You, John. I want you."

"That's what I like to hear." His mouth finds my neck again, just below my ear.

With my eyes screwed shut, my head falls back as his thumb circles my clit. He continues to pump his fingers in and out of me, and I grind against him, desperate for release. The burning weight in my stomach grows stronger as his mouth moves down my throat and my shoulders, to the swell of my breasts.

The sweet glint of arousal coats his fingers when he rips them from me without warning. His eyes darken at the sight before sucking them clean. A hum of satisfaction, his eyes roll into the back of his head, before meeting my stare.

"I was so fucking close."

"I know," he says, the hint of a smirk on his lips. "But the first time you come isn't going to be on my fingers or my tongue, Sweetheart. It's going to be wrapped around my cock. I want to watch you as you come undone, feel your pussy milk me for everything I've got, because there hasn't been a day the last two years that I haven't thought about this moment." His eyes soften, a new level of emotion filling them. "You can't imagine how many times I thought about jumping on a plane and flying to Texas to bring you *home*."

Home. The sting of tears coats my vision. Celestia isn't home anymore. Hell, it isn't even at EWE. It's right here... with him.

"I love you, John Brooks," I whisper, tears brimming in my eyes. He wipes away one that falls down my cheek.

"Say it again," he pleads.

I repeat the words, and his eyes flutter closed. "I've always loved you, and I always will."

Warm hands slide down my back, palming my ass, he lifts me off my feet and slings my legs over his hips. My hands lock together at the base of his skull before I lean in close. Breath mingling. Hearts pounding. Our lips brush, but we don't close the gap yet.

John's gaze drops to the space between us, and his fingers dig into the flesh of my thighs, underneath the fabric of my dress. His throat bobs, swallowing hard, before he lifts his gaze back to mine. "You have too many clothes on."

36

Savannah

SUNDAY, APRIL 28, 2019

INDIANAPOLIS, IN

My eyes flutter closed at Anna's direction. She's been working on my makeup for the last thirty minutes while Fallon works on getting the perfect curl in my hair. I won't lie; I've missed days with the glam team. It's nice having someone else to do your hair and makeup two to three times a week.

There's vibration on the underside of my left thigh, and I reach for my phone, cracking open one eye to see if it's *him*, but it's only a message from The Inner Circle—the Williams sibling group chat. My brothers, minus Crew, have been extremely chatty today, and if they don't shut up soon, I'm going to block them until after my match. I've been waiting for any communication from John after he left the hotel this morning, but I haven't seen or heard from him since.

I don't know what roused me from sleep, but the sheets were cool beneath my fingertips as I reached out for him. The room was empty when I opened my eyes, and my first thought was: *This cannot be happening.* Had I made a fool of myself? Was this another fucking bet, and I had fallen for it, again?

The bathroom door cracked open before he walked out, fully dressed, his hair damp from a shower. When he saw me, he smiled and leaned down to kiss the top of my head. "Mornin', Sweetheart. I didn't wake you, did I?"

My heart hammered in my chest, and adrenaline coursed through my veins, my mind trying to catch up to what I was seeing. When I spoke, I tried to steady my voice, not to give away the panic I had felt moments prior. "Going somewhere?"

"I have a meeting this morning." He stepped into a pair of his shoes that lined the hallway mirror.

"A meeting?" I glanced at the clock. "John, it's seven in the morning. Who are you meeting this early? Is everything okay?"

"Everything is perfect," John said, turning back to me. He leaned down and guided my mouth to his. It dispels all worries I had moments before. "Get some sleep. You have a little bit of time before the girls come looking for you to get breakfast."

I groaned, pulling a pillow over my head when I fell back onto the bed. He laughed. "I'll see you at the arena, okay?"

I couldn't go back to sleep after he left, though. I could barely focus on what Raelynn and Jo were talking about over breakfast, too preoccupied trying to figure out what was going on with my...boyfriend? Is that what I'm supposed to call him now? We didn't exactly state that last night. Sure, I think we made it obvious how we felt, but we didn't slap a label on it, or was it supposed to be implied?

What meeting could he possibly have at seven in the morning, the day of Wrestlefest? I know the Raffertys like to make last-minute changes, but if that's the case, shouldn't I have been part of the meeting? Austin and Viv, too. We're all part of this match. Or maybe it wasn't the Raffertys at all. Maybe it was something else entirely. Why not just tell me? The whole thing seems strange.

"Close your eyes," Anna demands. "That boy has waited two years; he can wait a few more minutes." She chuckles when I glare up at her before I let my eyelids close again. She applies the finishing touches before misting my face with the setting spray as Fallon adds a layer of hairspray. "Alright, you're free to go and find him."

"I have no idea what you're talking about," I say, jumping down from the chair, earning an unconvinced chuckle from both women. If there is anyone around here who knows every bit of gossip, it's the hair and makeup team. They hear and see everything.

I smile at my reflection in the mirror, admiring their work. They've outdone themselves, per usual. Everything looks perfect from the curl of my hair to the amount of blush on my cheeks to the carefully selected red hue of the lipstick. Anna found the shade years ago and deemed it "Savvy's Scarlet," because she said it was my perfect shade. What's the real name? I have no idea, but the first time she did my makeup upon my return, she told me she'd been keeping a new tube handy for the day I decided to come home.

It's going to look great with the shirt I'll be wearing tonight. The merchandise team and I had partnered to create a custom *Brooks Taylor* shirt to commemorate tonight. The design matches his current T-shirt with a white *BT* encased in a shield that spans the front. However, instead of black, they'd found a teal blue fabric to match the color of John's ring pants.

With a final thank you, I turn on my heel to search for my tag partner, only to run straight into the broad chest of a different man. The one I've been avoiding. "Oh, shit, Noah! Hi."

"You have a second?" he asks, not looking at me, his eyes scanning the hallway.

"Sure."

447

Noah guides me down a hallway perpendicular to the one we were just in, and the farther we get, the more nervous I become. I know what this is about, and I'm still not ready to make a decision. Amos wants an answer, and apparently, he doesn't want to wait until tomorrow to get it.

We come to another turn, and Noah slows his pace, glancing around the corner before he stares down at me. "Have you given any more thought to what you're going to do?"

I sigh, crossing my arms.

"I'm not trying to pressure you, Savannah. I'm just curious, and Creative wants to know where to go after tonight. There are different directions for what happens, and it all depends on *you*."

"Like?"

"Well." Noah clears his throat, straightening out his tie and rebuttoning his suit jacket. "I want to explore you and Brooks some more."

I scoff. "You mean putting us in an official love storyline again?"

"Savannah, people were eating up that fucking promo the other night. You and Brooks feed off each other better than most—you know it, I know it, and so does everyone on the writing team. The fans live for that shit. They love watching you two together—it's why we wanted you to come back as his partner in the first place."

"Noah—"

"I know that you guys aren't on the best of terms, despite what I saw last night."

"I don't know what you're talking about." I look away from him. Now is not the time to confirm his suspicions, not when I need more answers.

"That's because you didn't see what I saw." The smirk I know he's plastered on his lips makes me roll my eyes without even looking at him. "If I asked you right here, right now, to sign that contract. What would you say?"

My face falls, and when I glance up at him, his raised brow begs me to answer. If I had to decide right now, I would say—

"Noah!" Chelsea's voice bounces off the concrete walls. We both turn to see his wife strutting toward us, and the echo of heels fills the silence that follows. She only addresses me with a quick nod. Chelsea and I have never been close; I don't think she's close with anyone on the roster, maintaining that clear divide between talent and corporate. But she doesn't seem to mind that Noah and I have a mutual respect when it comes to the business. He has been my rock during this entire return, helping me navigate through the waters of my return and keeping Amos off my back when it comes to signing a permanent contract. "I'm sorry to interrupt, but they need you in gorilla. Amos wants to go over a few things for tonight."

Noah straightens, placing a hand on her back to guide her down the hall, but he stops and looks over his shoulder. "Just think about what I said, huh?"

Only after I nod does he lead her back down the hallway.

When they disappear, I fall back against the wall. Was I really about to tell Noah that I would sign the contract?

Yes.

Had Chelsea not interrupted us, I would have. The thought stirs awake the butterflies in my stomach, and their constant motion makes me nauseous. I haven't even talked about this with John. I had planned on bringing it up this morning, but he ran off to whatever meeting he supposedly had. What fucking meeting was it anyway?

My phone vibrates in my hand, and I almost ignore it, because it's probably just my brothers again, but just in case…

John Brooks
You here?

Looking for you.

Hair & makeup

John Brooks
I'll be there in a min

The latest message on The Inner Circle chat catches my eye before I close out my phone. Nash asks if anyone has seen Crew or Papá today.

What the hell? It's four o'clock in the afternoon. They should all be getting ready to come to the arena. I swear, if they are late, I'm never—

"There you are," John calls from the other end of the hall.

"And there you are," I say, stuffing my phone into the pocket of my leggings, ignoring whatever problem my brothers have going on. One problem at a time.

John doesn't hesitate to pull me into a kiss, and it melts some of my resolve to be upset with him. No, not upset. Concerned is a better word. In the past, we did our best to maintain a professional relationship backstage and at most events—we kept our hands to ourselves, never kissed (okay, *almost* never), and checked personal lives at the door (for the most part). We slipped up a few times, but we agreed the respectable thing to do was to keep our relationship at work just that: work. But now, his lack of hesitation to pull me straight into a kiss when anyone could walk around the corner and find us in a secluded part of backstage tells me this time, things aren't going to be the same.

"Where have you been?" I ask when we part. He's still dressed in his street clothes—jeans and a white button-up— which tells me he hasn't been here long. "I haven't seen or heard from you since you left this morning."

"I had a meeting with…Halle." His agent, whom he picked up years ago. She has been trying to convince him to branch out of EWE for as long as I've known her. She has always wanted him to do more than just a television guest spot here and there, but it was hard for John. EWE is home, and he'd always had a hard time considering stepping away to do other things. "Then I met up with Brody before I had to meet with Xander and Brian when I got here."

"Xander and Brian?" Head of Talent Relations and Head of Creative.

"There is a very real possibility that you're looking at the next Cade Jennings," he says. I gasp, and a slow smile spreads across his lips.

Cade Jennings?

Cade Jennings is the beloved character of a cult classic show called *Rock Ridge*, about a small town in the Great Plains run by outlaws that keeps all criminal activities out… minus their own. The show ended over twenty years ago, on a cliffhanger due to the studio being shut down before it could be renewed, and the end of the story is one people have been begging for ever since. In the final moments of the show, Cade Jennings had just become the new leader of the group, one he had secretly devised to dismantle from within, given the chance.

"They're rebooting the show?" I ask.

"A movie." John smiles. "They approached me first, and I'd be lying if I said I didn't want it." His smile is infectious as he tells me how the directors reached out to Halle once the script officially got picked up. They knew they wanted him to come in and read for the role, but there hadn't been much word since he left the office, until now. John used to watch *Rock Ridge* at least once a year, and each time the unexpected finale would come back around, he'd shake his head and murmur that someone should finish it. And now, he has a chance to be part of that...Who am I to stand in the way?

"So, what does this mean?"

"Well, Hal received the official offer last night. That's why she wanted to meet today. To tell me in person. The company is willing to make it work, keep me on televised shows only. I won't be doing any other events until I'm finished shooting." Which means if I sign a contract with EWE, I won't see him much for the next year or longer. "Have you decided what you're going to do about your contract?"

I take a step back and wrap my arms around my torso. "Had you asked me ten minutes ago, I would've told you that I was going to sign it, but now—"

"You still can, Sav."

"And then, I'll never see you."

John sighs, untangling my arms from my midsection and pulling me to him again. He drapes them over his shoulders, and my fingers intertwine at the base of his skull. His hands rest on my hips, thumbs lazily tracing over my skin just above the waistband of my leggings. "I just got you back, Savannah, and the last thing I want to do is push you away, but I know you want this," he says, motioning to the world around us.

Tears prick my eyes, and my shoulders lift in a small shrug. I do want this, and I miss it, but I want him more. I didn't come back looking for anything—not a contract, and certainly not him—but if I had to choose between the two, I'd pick him every time.

"I won't sign the contract," I say like it's the easiest thing in the world. "It's okay. I'll come back next year. I'll—"

"I don't want you to do that," he argues. "We can make this work, and I want to, or..." His smile falters ever so slightly, and he rolls his lips between his teeth.

"Or?"

"Or we wait. We've waited this long. We can go another year, right?"

"You mean take a break from being together. Wow, that comeback didn't even last twenty-four hours. That must be a record of some kind."

John chuckles and kisses my forehead. "I'll do whatever you want, Sweetheart. This isn't...I'm not here to push you one way or another, because I don't want to go another day without you in it, but I don't want to hold you back, either." John pushes a few stray hairs from my eye, letting his fingers trail down the side of my face to lift my chin. He kisses me, but his lips are gone too quickly for my liking, and I stick my bottom lip out in a pout. "Anna will have my head if I mess up your makeup. She told me as much before I found you." The image of the five-foot-two dirty blonde woman staring up at him as she threatens him makes me laugh. "You don't have to give me an answer right now. Let's get through this match and see how you feel then. Deal?"

WRESTLEFEST XXXVII

Live Broadcast

APRIL 28, 2019

INDIANAPOLIS, IN

"Can you believe what we just witnessed? It's going to be hard to follow that match," Scott says. *"Wolf Bennett and Brody Wilder just successfully unseated the Sanchez brothers to become the new tag team champions in a brutal match."*

"Yes, but we're going to try. Up next is our main event here at Wrestlefest XXXVII. Mixed tag team action with the EWE Championship on the line. Brooks Taylor and Savvy Skye will face current EWE Champion Spencer Austin and his wife, Viviana Austin. That's right, Spencer is so confident they'll be able to beat Taylor and Skye that he put his title up for grabs."

"That's a new one, Jude!"

"Indeed. It's not often we see the EWE Championship on the line in a tag-team match, let alone a mixed tag match."

"Kind of a risky move if you ask me, especially considering this is a No Disqualifications match. Anything goes!"

"I agree, especially after that confrontation between the two couples this past Thursday when Viviana slapped Brooks Taylor."

Scott chuckles. *"What were you thinking when that*

happened?"

"I was thinking she's lucky Savvy Skye isn't out here right now."

"That didn't last long!"

"No, Skye was quick to make her presence known, sending Spencer and Viviana running."

The announcers are interrupted by the sounds of Spencer Austin's music ringing through the arena.

"And here comes 'The Showstopper' himself, Spencer Austin, and his wife, Viviana," Jude says as they make their way down the ramp, waving to the crowd, who greet them with a chorus of boos. "You know, Scott, these two have really been a thorn in Brooks Taylor's side for a while now. I'm interested to see how this will go now that the playing field has been evened out with the arrival of Savvy Skye."

"Me too, Jude. I think they're underestimating Skye because she's been gone, but we've seen what she's been doing since her return, and I haven't seen a lick of ring rust on the three-time women's champion."

"Not just a three-time champ, but still the longest-reigning women's champion of all time."

Spencer and Viviana continue to receive a mixed reaction from the crowd as they climb into the ring, only for a louder one to erupt when Brooks Taylor's music hits. He walks through the entrance with a wide grin, pointing down the ramp at Spencer and then motioning toward his waist. He doesn't walk any further, though, glancing back over his shoulder, and his music cuts, replaced instead by Savvy Skye's. The crowd roars with only cheers for the first time when she steps into view. Pausing for a moment, she takes it all in before she looks at him, and they share a smile.

"Ready?" Brooks yells over the crowd. She nods, and they take off down the ramp, sliding into the ring beneath the bottom rope. They pop up to their feet seamlessly, standing face-to-face with their opponents, but the referee steps between them, forcing them apart.

"This is mine, Brooks!" Austin yells over the referee, hoisting the title into the air, and the ring lights glimmer off the belt.

Brooks lets out a breathy chuckle before he ushers Savannah back into their corner. He rips the teal shirt over his head, tossing it into the crowd, and bounces on the balls of his feet.

"Brooks Taylor is entering his twelfth Wrestlefest. Spencer Austin, his eleventh," Jude Paul says as the two couples stand in their separate corners at the direction of the referee.

"You can't forget Savvy Skye, who returned only three weeks ago to even out this match for her seventh Wrestlefest," Scott adds. "She left the company over two years ago after turning on the man she's tagging with tonight. It makes you wonder how that's going to work, and if she has any other tricks up her sleeve."

"That's true, Scott. The last time we saw Skye, she performed her finishing move, the Heartbreaker, on Brooks Taylor, helping Damian Drake win at Wreck the Halls in 2016. However, since her return, she and Brooks seem to be on the same page."

The bell rings, and Brooks winks at his partner before he steps through the ropes to stand on the apron. Spencer kisses his wife and does the same, leaving the women to start the match.

"Typically, in a mixed tag match, men face men and women face women; however, these four have said they'd allow mixed opponents if it comes to that," Jude Paul explains as the two women circle one another.

Savvy takes a step toward her opponent, but Viviana retreats into the corner and slaps Spencer's chest, tagging him in. She throws a smirk over her shoulder before leaning over the top rope to kiss her husband. They switch places, but Skye refuses to do the same.

"The tag was made, but it looks like Savvy Skye still wants to start this match off against Spencer Austin," Jude says.

"You got this, Sav!" Brooks calls from his spot on the apron, watching them circle each other.

"Clothesline!" Scott Harrington calls as Spencer charges, but Savvy ducks and hits the ropes. When her opponent spins back around, she nails him in the chest with a dropkick, sending him stumbling back almost over the ropes.

She jumps up, bouncing on the balls of her feet as they circle each other again. Spencer lunges, but she sidesteps and grabs his wrist. She yanks him forward and shoots him into the ropes.

"Beautiful Irish Whip by Skye," Jude says.

Spencer rebounds, and she leapfrogs into the air, avoiding collision. He rebounds again, off the opposite ropes, but this time she jumps up and wraps her legs around his head. She uses the takedown to launch him into the corner of the ring, where her tag partner awaits.

"What a headscissors by Skye, angled perfectly to land him right in enemy territory," Scott says, his excitement matching that of the crowd.

Savvy walks toward Spencer, fingers trailing along the top rope as she approaches. She glances up at Brooks, who wears a proud smirk, and he slaps her hand when she reaches out to him.

"Tag made, Brooks is now the legal man."

"Did you see that look between them before the tag?" Scott swoons. "That isn't just strategy, that's a kind of chemistry you can't fake, and that's dangerous for the Austins."

The crowd yells as Brooks meets his partner in the ring. Their shoulders graze, eyes locked for one beat too long. The referee gives her the count, but they ignore him, attention focused solely on each other. His brow raises, and her face splits into a grin, nodding. Savvy hauls Spencer to his feet and whips him into the awaiting boot of Brooks Taylor. When he stumbles, Savvy jumps, planting her hands on Spencer's shoulders and her knees on his back, and drags him down to the mat.

"A brutal backbreaker by Skye!"

"Beautiful combo by the team of Skye and Taylor," Jude says.

"This duo doesn't need long conversations. They know what the other is thinking. That's rare."

Savvy rises to her feet, meets her partner's stare, stepping through the ropes out to the apron.

Spencer rolls under the bottom rope, out of the ring, staggering toward the barricade. Brooks rolls his eyes, but does the same, hoping to bring his opponent back into the ring and finish this quickly. Steadier on his feet, Spencer picks up his pace, running around the other side and sliding back into the ring.

"Brooks puts Spencer on the run!" Jude calls as Brooks tries to catch up to his opponent. Spencer is ready and waiting, gripping the top rope as he stomps down on Taylor's head, shoulders, and back. "Oh, the champ suckered him in, attacking Brooks as he tries to get back in the ring."

Satisfied, Spencer climbs up to the top turnbuckle. Brooks rolls into the middle of the ring, attempting to stand, but when he makes it to his feet, Spencer launches off the top turnbuckle with a flying clothesline, leveling him.

Viviana slaps the turnbuckle beside her, rallying her husband and the crowd, shouting words of encouragement. Spencer lands blow after blow before whipping Brooks into the ropes. He leapfrogs and delivers a spinning heel kick to the jaw. Spencer pulls Brooks to his feet for a belly-to-back suplex, driving his opponent headfirst into the mat, rolling through, and doing it again.

"Spencer with the cover!" Scott's excitement is palpable.

"And Brooks kicks out in two. That was a close call, Jude."

"Brooks needs to get back to his corner and make the tag so he can recoup," Jude says.

Spencer pounds the mat in annoyance before he rises to his feet, stalking Brooks. When he finally stands, Viviana lifts her foot to kick Brooks in the head. He staggers into the center of the ring, where Spencer goes for a superkick, but Brooks catches it.

The announcers chuckle. "Spencer's in trouble now!"

The champion shakes his head vigorously, hopping on one foot, trying to regain his balance. Brooks chuckles, shaking his head, and twists the leg hard, sending Spencer belly-first down to the mat.

"Taylor is going for the Legacy Lock," *Jude Paul says as Brooks grasps Spencer's ankle. He wraps his arms firmly around the joint, interweaving his hands to create a headlock that will be almost impossible to get out of. He twists the foot, applying an intense torque on the joint. Spencer cries out in pain, reaching for the ropes, but he's nowhere close.*

"The Legacy Lock is one of those submissions you don't want to be caught in. The pressure on the ankle is intense, and it hurts long after you're out."

"Tap!" *Brooks yells, but Spencer shakes his head, doing his best to inch toward the bottom rope. His fingers almost graze the rope, and Brooks realizes he's too close. He releases the hold, only to pull his opponent back to the center of the ring and reapply the Legacy Lock.*

Viviana vaults over the top rope, stunning Brooks with a dropkick, forcing him to break the hold. Finally free, Spencer limps to the corner, where he makes the official tag with Viviana. Brooks does the same.

"Oh boy," *Scott chuckles.* "Here we go. This is what Savvy Skye has been waiting for."

A grin appears on Savvy's red lips as she slowly steps

through the ropes. She meets her old rival in the middle of the squared circle, and the crowd buzzes with anticipation. They stop mere inches apart, toe-to-toe, neither willing to back down.

"Why don't you just go back to whatever hole you crawled out of, Skye? You're just a washed-up has-been, looking to see her name in lights one more time."

Skye's tongue swipes across her teeth with a chuckle, looking out at the crowd, before she kicks Viviana in the knee.

"Skye attacks Viviana's knee!"

"That's the same knee Viviana injured in their street fight a few years ago," Jude explains as Savvy continues to attack the bad knee.

Viviana cries out in pain, trying to claw her way out of the ring. Skye doesn't let her, dragging her to the adjacent corner and climbing up the turnbuckle. She perches on the top rope with perfect balance, looking out at the crowd as they cheer her on. She winks at Brooks before launching into a moonsault.

"The Last Kiss by Skye! Will it be enough?"

The referee falls to the mat when Savvy hooks the leg to cover her opponent. 1...2...Viviana lurches forward, kicking out.

"No! Kick out at two and a half."

Skye sits up, frustrated, and climbs to her feet to meet her partner for a hushed conversation. He pulls back in shock, but she nods, encouraging him. His shoulders fall with a sigh, dropping from the apron to the ground. Brooks lifts the skirt to dig around under the ring.

"Hey! What are you doing?" Spencer yells, but goes unanswered. The crowd roars when Brooks yanks a ladder out and slides it into the ring. "What in the hell do you think you're doing?"

"This is all legal in a No Disqualifications match," Jude explains as the referee takes a step back from the chaos

happening in the ring.

Savvy forces her opponent up to her feet and stoops down to hoist Viviana onto her shoulders in a Fireman's Carry. With the ladder laid out on the canvas, Skye turns in a circle to look Spencer in the eye as she launches his wife onto the ladder. Viviana's legs take most of the impact, and she screams out, clutching her leg as she rolls away in agony.

"Fireman's Carry onto the ladder, but instead of going for the back, she went for the injured knee," Jude explains. "Skye is showcasing her veteran skills tonight. She didn't come back just to win, but to dismantle her opponents piece by piece. I don't think Viviana will walk out of this match the same, Scott."

"She's reminding everyone why she still holds the record for longest reigning Women's Champ," Scott adds.

"You bitch!" Spencer yells, leaning over the ropes to sneer at Savvy.

"You haven't seen anything yet," Skye retorts, shoving him off the ropes and onto the ground. She grabs the ladder, lifts it upright, and snaps it open in the center of the ring. She doesn't climb it, though. Not yet. Instead, she drags Viviana over and threads her injured leg through one of the bottom rungs, trapping it. Climbing the nearby turnbuckle, it looks like she might be preparing for a dropkick, but Spencer jumps up on the apron and swipes her feet from under her.

"Spencer knew he had to do something," Jude says. "If she landed that blow, this match was over!"

The crowd gasps as Savvy falls to the apron and then to the ground. She clutches her back as Brooks drops from his spot and rushes to her side.

"This is awesome!" The crowd chants as the four wrestlers try to regain their bearings.

"They are right, this is awesome!" Scott exclaims.

"These men need to get the women on their feet so they can tag in and finish the match, though. Neither one is the legal

man right now," Jude says.

Spencer drags Viviana to their corner to do just that. Now the legal man, he dives through the ropes straight into Brooks and Savvy. The impact sends all three of them into the barricade, and the crowd erupts.

"Suicide dive by Austin! There are bodies everywhere, Jude!" Scott yells at the sight of the three wrestlers sprawled on the floor.

"Austin knew he had to do something to change the course of this match," Jude says. "But he took a good hit to the head with that dive, and it looks like Brooks will be the first to his feet. He needs to get Skye back into the ring and make the tag."

Brooks Taylor helps his partner back into the ring before he returns to their corner, where he climbs out of the ropes, planting both feet on the apron. Holding the tag rope attached to the turn buckle, he extends his hand out to Savvy, who quickly slaps it, rolling out of the way.

"Tag!" The referee shouts.

Spencer Austin returns to the ring, locking eyes with Taylor. Each man sprints, meeting in the center and striking one another with hard punches.

Brooks ducks to avoid a final punch, stepping behind his opponent. He wraps his arm around Spencer's waist and lifts him off his feet.

"German suplex!" Jude calls.

Spencer rolls through, but Taylor nails him with a running knee to the jaw. The crowd cheers as Spencer falls to the mat and Brooks goes for the Legacy Lock.

Locking in the submission hold, Spencer cries out in pain, too far from the rope, but not too far from the ladder. He musters up enough resolve to roll forward, twisting free from the hold and sending Taylor into the ropes. Spencer scrambles to his feet and up the ladder, perching himself at the top.

"What's he doing up there?" Scott questions no one in

particular. "Is he gonna do what I think he's gonna do?"

"I sure hope not. There's no way he can do it without injuring himself," Jude says.

Spencer watches Brooks regain his bearings, waiting until the very last moment to jump off the top of the ladder. He somersaults through the air in his signature four-fifty splash. Brooks shifts out of the way, and Spencer's landing misses. He lands awkwardly on his already sore ankle, and a sickening crunch echoes through the ring. Spencer screams out in pain.

"That's the same ankle Brooks Taylor has been targeting all night. This could be a game changer," Jude says. "I think it might be seriously injured."

Brooks takes advantage of his opponent's newest injury, rolling him up for the pin. The referee slams his hand down on the mat.

1...2...3...

37

SUNDAY, APRIL 28, 2019

INDIANAPOLIS, IN

Spencer cries out in pain when I secure the Legacy Lock, struggling against my hold in an attempt to free himself, but the rope is too far. His gaze flounders from the rope to Viviana to the ladder, and it seems he's made a decision when it remains on the weapon in the center of the ring. He bounces on the ball of his free foot a few times before rolling forward, twisting his ankle free from the hold, and the momentum shoots me into the ropes. It gives Spencer the chance to climb the ladder and find his perch on top.

I stumble a little when I stand, and when our eyes lock, I get a bad feeling in the pit of my stomach. There isn't enough room for him to do what I know he's about to do. If he goes for the four-fifty splash from that angle, someone is going to get hurt.

Spencer somersaults through the air in his signature four-fifty splash but misses his mark when I step out of the way. First, I hear the pop, and then the crunch of bone when he lands, followed by a cry of pain.

Holy fuck.

My opponent clutches his left ankle, which is facing the opposite direction it should be. I glance at Mike, the referee, and he's seeing the same thing I am. With a subtle nod, I slide into a quick pin, hooking Spencer's good knee, and force his shoulders down to the mat.

"Stay the fuck down," I say, and I'm shocked when he listens.

1...2...3...

The roar of the crowd mixes with the sound of my theme music, but I can barely hear it over the drumming in my ears. This wasn't supposed to happen. Austin wasn't supposed to get on the ladder. He was supposed to throw me into the ropes and go for the four-fifty off the turnbuckle. There wasn't enough room for him to execute that properly off the ladder, and now...now his ankle is hanging on by a fucking thread.

Despite the reason, I'm sure Amos will have a few choice words for me when we get backstage, but I don't care. I didn't have a choice. I had to end the match. There was no way we could continue. The medics pull Austin under the bottom rope, and he fights them when they try to coax him onto the gurney. *Stubborn ass*, I think, but it does make me feel a little better to see him walk out. A round of applause fills the air as the medics help him limp to the back.

Turning back to the ring, I'm caught off guard when Savannah jumps into my arms, wrapping her legs around my waist and landing against me with a hard kiss. It stuns me at first, but it helps ground me back in the current moment after what just happened. I didn't expect her to do something like this, not in front of...well, everyone. When she doesn't pull away, I let my fingers tangle through her hair and deepen the kiss. The crowd goes nuts, I can tell by the wave of sound that hits me like a wall, and the way the ring vibrates beneath my feet. Her soft moan against my lips drives me wild, combined with the way her body moves against mine. A countdown begins in my head of the minutes until I can carry her over the threshold of my room, lock the door, and have my way with her until morning. "The whole world just saw you do that," I say.

"Good." She breathes the word out. "Then they'll know you're mine." I smile when she pecks my lips, finally letting her legs unwind from my waist and slide down to the canvas. She asks, "How mad do you think they're going to be?"

"It had to be done. Let them strip me of it, I don't care. I have everything I need already."

"If you two are done making out in front of the whole world," Mike says with a smirk. He is one of the two most veteran referees in the company and is almost always the referee I have in a match. He knows my cues, my tells, and tonight I was glad to have him out here because he knew instantly something wasn't right. He didn't hesitate on the three count before turning his attention to grabbing medical staff. "I have something that belongs to you."

Mike holds the title out, and it shines beneath the stadium lights. Taking it from his hands, I take a deep breath and try to hide my smile, but I can't. I know I'm not supposed to be walking out with this, and the only reason I am is because Austin got hurt. We always try to avoid injuries, but there's never a guarantee in this business, especially when someone takes a risk like Austin did tonight. That's why we practice so damn much, trying to prevent the avoidable (and escape the unavoidable as much as possible). But damn, I'd be lying if I said it didn't feel good to have its weight in my hands again.

He steps between me and Savannah, taking one hand each and raising them in the air to a new chorus of cheers.

After a few more minutes of reveling in our victory with the crowd, Savannah steps through the ropes that I step on to hold open. She jumps down from the apron, making a beeline for her family that sits in the corner of the front row.

The Williams family piles into an awkward group hug over the barricade before Laine beckons me forward. She hugs me, despite my warning about the layer of perspiration on my skin, patting my back. Wes offers me a knowing smirk—one that Savannah catches. Her gaze narrows as she glances between us.

"We gotta go," I whisper against her temple.

"I'll see you backstage?" she asks them before I take her hand, tugging her back into my side.

I pause at the top of the ramp and lift the belt into the air, earning another round of cheers from the crowd. The response surprises me. It makes my heart ache. How am I supposed to leave this? How am I supposed to walk away when this means everything to me?

Glancing to my side, I meet the warm brown eyes of the woman who stole my heart years ago. Her beaming smile quells some of the nerves, and I can't help but return the gesture. Wrapping my arm around Savannah's shoulders, I kiss her temple. "Let's go."

She laughs. "Yeah, let's go get our asses chewed."

The applause that follows our emergence through the curtain shocks us both. This is far from the response we expected, and a glance around the room shows everyone on their feet—Chelsea, Theo, Noah, and all the producers. I look down at Savannah, whose facial expression is how I feel on the inside—utter confusion. We just screwed up the end of the main event match of the biggest show of the year, and they're...clapping?

Amos is the last one to stand with a raised brow, crossed arms, and that infamous fucking smirk. He weaves his way out from his corner, through the crowd, and meets us in the center of the room. He extends his hand, and when I take it, he pulls me into an embrace. "Hell of a match," he says, patting me on the back. A gentle squeeze on my shoulder when he pulls back to look me in the eye one last time before he turns his affections on Savannah. "You both looked fantastic. Hell of a job, all of you. Let's chat tomorrow morning around nine o'clock."

"Yes, sir." Savannah nods, and the corners of her lips lift briefly. I can't help but wonder if she's made up her mind, but that's not a conversation to have here. It should be behind closed doors.

Amos knows about the movie. He's known. I told him months ago, well before I was supposed to, and I think that's why he changed his mind on the winner tonight.

The truth is, I've known about the movie for a few days. Halle told me Thursday evening, and the first person I wanted to call was Savannah, but I called Amos instead. And while I did meet Halle this afternoon, it wasn't to hear about the deal; it was to sign it. This morning, I had an entirely different meeting—one that Savannah couldn't know about, not yet. I invited Wes and Crew to join me for breakfast at one of the hole-in-the-wall diners nearby, where we could discuss some of my future plans in private...

As much as I want to beg her to accompany me to New Mexico for filming, I know her heart aches for this place. I saw it the moment she stepped out on that stage three weeks ago, and every moment since. I could be selfish and ask her to come with me anyway, but I won't do that. We can make it work. It'll be challenging, but we can do it. Unless she wants to wait, and as much as it would kill me, I'd do it for her. The idea came to me because I don't want to make things harder on her. If she signs the contract, I know Amos will use her every chance he gets. It will be hard on her, on us, and I don't know if she wants another thing to worry about.

"Brooks, we need to discuss your transition further. I'll see you *both* in the morning then," Amos says, with a brief nod before he steps to the side.

Walking out of gorilla, we're ambushed by an ecstatic scream before Raelynn rips her best friend from my arms. Brody isn't too far behind, with an accompanying eye roll, dressed in gym shorts and a zipped-up black hoodie. His match against Wolf earlier was brutal, both of them walking away with their fair share of spots that are sure to leave them sore in the morning.

"That bag goes great with your eyes," I say, motioning toward the glittering clutch at his side, and he rolls his eyes. "Heard anything about Austin?"

"I saw him being loaded into a car 'bout five minutes ago. I think they're taking him to the hospital to get checked out," Brody says, and I sigh, scrubbing a hand down my face. Naively, I hoped it wouldn't come to this, that Doc would tell him to rest and ice it for a few days. That he'd be fine. "What happened out there? I thought they were supposed to go over."

"They were, but Austin didn't land right off that last four-fifty. I heard it, and when he didn't get back up, I knew something wasn't right. When I went to cover him, I saw his ankle was fucked up."

"I wondered about that when I saw him land."

"Didn't even fight me when I told him to stay down," I say, earning a raised brow from my best friend. Austin and I might have our differences, but I respect his work in the ring (for the most part). He might think he deserves more than his work ethic warrants sometimes, but he knows how to put on a good show when he wants to, even if it means wrestling with an injury. "You know that shit was hurting if he didn't pop back up."

"Well, he couldn't put any weight on it. They had the cart ready to move him into Doc's office once he got back here. I have a feeling it's going to be a while."

"You guys up for some food?" Raelynn asks when she and Savannah join us from their hushed conversation a few feet away. "I could go for some carbs."

"Only if we can join," a voice calls from further down the hallway. Nash leads the rest of the Williams family before Raelynn runs down the corridor, jumping into his arms. I swear, they are the friendliest exes I've seen in my entire life. I'd never tell Brody this, but I quietly rooted for them while they were together, despite my best friend's affections for her. The end of their relationship was something I saw coming a mile away, despite Savannah's optimistic attitude. She had hope for her best friend and her brother, but in the end, the schedule was too much for Nash, and they ended things (almost amicably).

Nash sets Raelynn on her feet and shakes Brody's hand, pulling him into an embrace.

"Where are we going to eat? I'm starved," Bodhi says, and his twin brother echoes the sentiment. That starts the back-and-forth discussion of where to go. Too many restaurants are called out, almost every one of them closed, as Crew's wife tries to keep up with the map search.

I anxiously await some comment on the display Savannah and I put on in the middle of the ring after our win, but no one says anything, not even Laine. I wonder if Wes told her what I asked him and Crew earlier. If so, no one gives any indication. Standing here with them feels like no time has passed at all, like the last two and a half years were nothing but a fever dream. There are no awkward pauses, no sideways glances, no hesitancy about including me in the celebration, and no strange looks when I drape my arm over Savannah's shoulders to pull her against me and kiss her temple. She smiles up at me, but there's a hint of hesitation in her eyes, maybe even sadness, and I think I know why. "I love you," I whisper, and she nods.

"So." The word falls from my lips with a soft sigh, my fingers ghosting over the bare skin of her arm as she lies beside me. It's three o'clock in the morning, and we have to be up in a few hours to go to the gym before we meet Amos at the Fieldhouse. She echoes the word, pushing up from my chest to look me in the eye. "Have you made a decision?"

Savannah sighs and rips her gaze from mine, her tongue poking out to wet her lips. "I-I don't know, John. I don't know what to do. It's like I said, had you asked me before, I would've said that I was going to sign a contract with them, but now—"

"You can't base this decision on me, Savannah. You already did that once, and I'm not going to let you do it again." I pull her to sit up with me and take both of her hands in mine, bringing them to my lips. The thought of letting this beautiful woman go kills me, but I don't want to stand in her way of getting everything she wants, either. She was ready to extend her contract before, but my selfishness got in the way. My fear of what Drake might do or say during the time they spent together clouded my judgment, and I abused her trust. "Sign the contract. It's only a year that I'll be gone, and then I'll be right back here with you every day."

"Until you get another one," she says with a sad smile. "And then it's another year, and another, and the next thing you know, we're living two separate lives again."

"One year, Savannah," I say, and stop her when she tries to interrupt. "Sign a contract for one year. You do that, and I'll do the movie, and after that year, no matter what we decide to do—whether you stay here or I have another movie or I come back—we'll make it work. I'm not saying we can't talk or spend time together, unless that's what you want. I only want what's best for you, and I think that's staying here. The EWE needs their Queen back, and I think she needs them just as much."

She closes her eyes, taking a deep breath, and they're glassy when she reopens them. "So, one year, and then..."

"And then, I'm all yours."

38

Savannah

TUESDAY, JULY 30, 2019

CRIMSON VALLEY, TX

"This is what you were so excited about?" I ask, standing in front of Ash & Thorn—the local dive bar on the outskirts of Crimson Valley. It's been three months since John and I decided to spend the next year navigating the waters of not quite being just friends but not quite being together, either. Three months of only seeing each other once a week, and sometimes not even that much if the company doesn't require him to show up for the weekly Monday taping. Three months of talking on the phone for five minutes here and there before one of us gets interrupted.

We had *Monday Night Rage* in Alexandria last night, and today is the first time in three months John didn't have to jump on a red-eye flight Tuesday morning to get back to New Mexico. He practically got down on his knees last night begging me to let him tag along to visit my family today. He crashed in my room last night and was asleep before his head hit the pillow, but just knowing he was beside me was more than enough. The comforting weight and security of his presence are things I have been missing for years, and I never

473

miss the opportunity to relish in them.

This morning, he woke up bright-eyed and bushy-tailed, bringing me a coffee before I could even get out of bed, asking if we could make a pit stop on the way home. He refused to tell me where we were going, but when I saw the twinkle in his eye, I couldn't say no.

"My old college dive bar?" I ask, looking up at him.

"And the place where we met," John says.

I shake my head with a small smile. "You're a sap."

He shrugs. "I'm sentimental, sue me."

I walk through the door he holds open, and it feels like I'm transported back in time. The inside looks exactly the same. Smells the same, too. Musty and musky with a twinge of cigarette smoke they've never been able to get out of the wood ceiling, even this long after smoking indoors was outlawed. A few patrons belly up to the bar—two enjoy a liquid lunch, watching the sports channel, three others eat burgers—and a group of girls who can't be older than I was when I first walked through the door huddle in the corner with cocktails in hand. One of them catches sight of us, and her eyes widen. She kicks her friend under the table, earning a glare before she points toward us. Soon, five pairs of eyes are on us, and I wiggle my fingers in a small wave before John guides me to the bar, unaware of our admirers across the room.

The bartender approaches, and we order a pair of burgers and two beers before I feel the weight of his hand on my thigh. He jumps under my touch when I place my hand on his wrist, but he doesn't pull away. He's been like this all day. Jumpy. Spacey. I noticed it this morning when I came out of the bathroom. He practically jumped out of his skin when I leaned in for a kiss, too lost in thought to realize I had been calling his name.

I turn his hand over and caress the faded black ink on his wrist—the simple black heart with *SJ* in the center. Leaning in, I ask, "Are you okay?"

John takes a deep breath, closing his eyes, and exhales. Before I can ask him again, he kisses me. It's a soft, gentle kiss, but it melts away the anxiety I've been feeling all morning. "Marry me," he whispers against my lips.

Did he just…Did he ask me to *marry* him? I pull back with wide eyes. What does he mean, *marry him*?

"John…You can't—Are you…You're serious? You can't be serious."

"Wanna bet?" John sets a small blue box on the bar between us, and I must look between it and him five times. Every time I meet his stare, his smile grows wider, until I can't look away from him, even when he pops open the lid.

"Savannah Williams, marry me." The words bring tears to my eyes. "I was drawn to you from the second I saw you in this bar eleven years ago. Call me crazy, but I've known from the moment I met you that you were the one. You weren't going to be like other girls…and you've proven me right. You prove me right every day. I don't want to go a day without you. I love you."

"But…I thought—"

"If these last three months have done anything, it's proved that I don't want to go without you. Even if that means flying you in and out of New Mexico in between shows or flying to you for five hours between shoots before turning back around, I don't care."

I try to find a reason I should say no, like we haven't been back together that long, but that seems silly. We were together for almost five years before and have been friends for twice as long. He knows me better than anyone, better than myself most days, and he makes me want to be a better person—to be a better me. The longer I try to find a reason to say no, I can only find reasons to say…

"Yes."

John smiles, and his mouth covers mine. He slides the ring onto my finger, and I gasp when I finally look at it. A sparkling double halo surrounds at least a five-carat cushion-cut center stone that rests atop a diamond-studded band. This is the exact ring I've always wanted, but...I've never told him about this. We never even looked at rings.

"John, where did you get this?"

"I've had it."

My gaze lifts. "You've *had* it?"

"I had it made before...everything happened. I was going to propose at New Year's. Actually, I was going to propose before that—way before that—but the timing never worked out." My heart clenches at the confession, and it reminds me of what Mamá told me that night on the hotel terrace before Wrestlefest. He'd already asked my parents for their blessing. "I've always known, Sav. It was always you. From the second we walked out of this bar...it was always going to be you."

"You didn't even know me."

"But I wanted to. I would've found you. Actually, I started trying to, but in the end, I didn't have to try very hard because you were stalking me," John says with a toothy grin.

I smack his chest. "I was not!"

John chuckles, reaching down to grip the bottom of my chair and dragging the stool closer to him. "No, you weren't, but that would make a pretty good story."

"Please don't give Amos any ideas."

Pushing my hair behind my ear, his fingers trace the line of my jaw before he lifts my chin. "Happy birthday, Sweetheart."

"That's Mrs. Brooks," I say, lifting my left hand in the air, and the light catches on the stone.

He laughs and leans in to kiss me. "I like the sound of that."

EPILOGUE

Brooks

A mixture of emotions swirls through me as I stare at my reflection. I look exactly the same as I did yesterday, but something feels different, and that feeling is overwhelming. When I first started wrestling twenty-seven years ago, it felt like this day would never come. I felt invincible, like I could do this every day for the rest of my life. Sometimes, I still think I can, but I know better. For the first time, when I wake up tomorrow morning, it will all be over. No more spending over two hundred days a year on the road, no more late-night drives to the next city, no more feeling like I'm stuck in a time loop, living the same day over and over again. No more seeing some of my favorite people every day, no more all-nighters in the ring trying to perfect a new move, no more races down the ramp to the one place that became my home when I was an eighteen-year-old kid trying to survive.

Twenty-one years ago, I signed with Elite Wrestling Entertainment, and I was just happy to wrestle in the biggest company in the world. I never thought I'd be where I am today. Never thought I'd be a sixteen-time world champion, three-time tag champion, named a Sports Illustrated Sportsperson of the year, an Associated Press Male Athlete of the Year, and so much more. This company—the fans—has given me everything…I only wish I had more to give them in return.

The rustle of sheets catches my attention, and when I step out of the bathroom, she greets me with a sleep-drunk smile. We didn't get into San Diego until closer to three in the morning after Wrestlefest, where I lost my title to Wolf in a triple-threat match between me, him, and Knox Sterling. I didn't get much sleep—I couldn't—but Savannah was asleep as soon as her head hit the pillow.

I climb back into bed and pull her into my arms, kissing the top of her head. She buries herself further into my side, and her breathing seems to even out again, signaling she's gone back to sleep.

Despite her reluctance to admit it, I couldn't have done any of this without her. I couldn't have continued going without her support. When she decided to retire three years ago, I considered joining her, starting our next chapter right then and there, but she knew I wasn't ready, not really. I still had a few years left in the tank, and she pushed me to keep going. Since then, she's been holding down things at home while I continued to travel with EWE, even when she was pregnant, despite my protests that I should be there with her. She has been my rock, and when I told her I wanted to do this, her response was: "As long as you're ready."

"When did you get up?" my wife asks, pulling me out of my thoughts. Her fingers trace light, invisible circles on my chest, near the scar on my right shoulder from my deltoid surgery years ago.

"Not long ago."

"You didn't sleep very long." She lets her hand trace a line down my side before gliding back up across the planes of my chest.

"Got some stuff on my mind," I say, enveloping her hand in mine and bringing it to my lips. She plants her hand firmly on my chest and presses a kiss to the column of my throat. A trail of warm, wet kisses up my neck as she slowly lowers her hand. "Sweetheart," I warn, and she hums against my skin. My dick comes to attention when her hand slips beneath the waistband of my sweats and wraps around the base. I hum in approval, not trying to escape her hold, even though I say, "I have to get dressed."

"It's your last day. What are they going to do? Fire you?"

Who am I to argue with that?

I wrap my arm around her waist to roll her beneath me, capturing her mouth. There's nothing urgent in this kiss; it's soft, thoughtful, just enjoying the connection. Her hands smooth up my chest and glide around the back of my neck, coaxing my mouth open, and I sigh. Her tongue sweeps over mine, and my need for her only grows. I let out a satisfied hum when I roll my hips into hers.

I slip my hand beneath the waistband of her shorts, pushing them down her legs and leaving her completely bare to me. I push my fingers inside her, and she moans against my mouth, back arching off the bed. "Fuck, you're so wet already, Sweetheart."

"I missed you," she says.

Savannah didn't join me in Los Angeles for Wrestlefest week until yesterday morning, and I hadn't seen her for two weeks before that due to a spring European tour. Two years ago, the company decided to start adding an overseas trip once a quarter. While it's great to break it up over the year, that kind of travel wears you down faster because there's not a lot of downtime. We move from country to country without a break for one to two weeks straight. Needless to say, I had missed the woman beside me like crazy.

I pump my fingers in and out of her, letting my thumb circle her clit lazily, loving the feel of her slowly coming undone beneath my touch. I take one of her hardened nipples into my mouth through the fabric of her T-shirt—my T-shirt—and she moans in reply. Her hips move against my hand, her body desperate for more friction, for release.

"Patience, Sweetheart," I say, releasing her right nipple, pushing up the fabric of her shirt, and taking the left in my mouth. Savannah squirms beneath me, and a breathy chuckle escapes my lips when I release her with a pop.

Leaving open-mouthed kisses, I move down her body, nipping at the soft skin of her hip. She whines softly but can no longer contain herself when I suckle her clit between my lips. My name escapes rolls of her tongue like a siren song as her back bows off the bed, fingers carding through my hair in a hard tug.

"Please," she begs, and my dick strains in my sweats at the sweet sound.

I pull my fingers from her and shove my sweats down my legs, kicking them off the bed. My cock strains up toward me, and Savannah watches with hungry eyes as I grasp my length, fitting the head to her entrance. As I glide up and down her folds, my mouth waters with anticipation, and I stroke my cock two times before thrusting inside her.

And whatever comes next, I know this is one thing I'll never get tired of.

Savannah

"Is he hurt or just selling?" one of the producers calls out from behind their monitor while the others scramble to get an answer from ringside.

"Stay on *Brooks*," Noah directs into his headset, and the monitor hung in the corner switches to show my husband on the floor, not moving. My breath catches in my lungs, and only when he begins to stir do I breathe out.

"He's just selling!" another production aide answers. "Looks like he's hurt the shoulder, though."

"Tell them to wrap it up before someone gets hurt. That's the last thing we need tonight." Noah glances over his shoulder at me, but I ignore him.

Brody hauls *Brooks* to his feet, and I see him whisper something before John gives him a quick nod that you wouldn't notice unless you knew what to look for. *Brody* shoves him into the ring, but before he can climb in, *Brooks* pops up to his feet and stomps down on his head, hands, and back. Satisfied with his attack, *Brooks* climbs up to the top turnbuckle and launches off the turnbuckle into a frogsplash, sending them both down to the mat. He hooks the leg, but *Brody* kicks out at two.

Brooks takes hold of his opponent's ankle, wrapping his arms firmly around the joint and threading his hands together to create a lock. He turns the ankle, applying an immense amount of pressure for the Legacy Lock, his submission move. There's a flash of pain in his eyes when he lifts *Brody*'s foot further in the air, dragging him away from the bottom rope, and it tells me that the fall out of the ring was more than just selling.

Brody shakes his head, refusing to tap, even when *Brooks* torques the joint further. He attempts to roll forward, but can't.

Brooks plants his feet firmly on the mat, tightens his grip, and lands a blow to his opponent's calf. *Brody* cries out only once before he internalizes the pain, harnessing it, and when his captor loosens his grip to readjust, it gives him the opening he needs. Slingshotting *Brooks* into the ropes, *Brody* hits him on the rebound with a hard clothesline, leveling him. He pulls his opponent up by the wrist, lifts him onto his shoulder, and carries him—slowly, shakily—to the turnbuckle. He pauses momentarily, and to anyone else it would look like he's just trying to catch his breath, but I know better. He's letting it all sink in. The meaning behind this match is finally catching up to him.

"Why is he climbing the turnbuckle?" I whisper. His movements catch me off guard—with John still on his shoulder, Brody climbs the ropes until he's standing on the top one. What in the fuck is he doing? "You cannot be serious."

I rise from my chair, watching the scene unfold. They haven't done this spot in so long, and they're both exhausted after wrestling for almost an hour at this point. Why in the hell would they try this? They know better.

The crowd gasps—hell, even some of the producers gasp. Only two people don't seem surprised: Noah and Callum, the recently discovered long-lost son of the late Amos Rafferty. They both watch intently, waiting for the final spot.

Brody pauses at the top, steadying his feet.

"Noah," I call out, my eyes still glued to the screen, but he doesn't answer. I'm starting to understand why John told me they hadn't decided on a finisher. He didn't want me to know because he knew I would have lost my mind. Death Valley is one of *"The Reaper" Brody Wilder*'s old finishing moves, one that he retired years ago, but apparently, he's bringing it back for this special occasion. A dangerous move if done improperly. One wrong move, and you could paralyze your opponent.

With a final breath, *The Reaper* sails off the top turnbuckle. He drives his knees into the mat, tossing *Brooks* off his shoulders and slamming him sideways into the mat. His upper back and shoulders take the brunt of the fall, digging into the mat in a hard, but proper, fall. It's still too close for comfort. The entire ring shakes from the impact as both men lay arms wide in the center of the ring.

Neither man moves for what feels like hours until, slowly, *Brody* drapes himself across *Brooks* and hooks the leg.

One...

Two...

Three...

The bell rings and the crowd erupts.

Neither man moves at first, catching their breath before *Brody* pushes himself upright. He looks around the arena and then back at his best friend, a genuine smile tugging on his lips. Standing, he reaches his hand down to *Brooks*.

That's when the walls come down, and it's no longer *"The Reaper" Brody Wilder* and EWE golden boy *Brooks Taylor* in the ring. This is Brody Wilder and John Brooks, best friends... brothers. Brody pulls his best friend into a tight embrace, whispering something to him that makes them both chuckle, eyes shining beneath the arena lights. A low rumble forms among the crowd, and I think they're starting to catch on to what's happening.

A warm hand squeezes my shoulder as I stand in the center of gorilla. Tears burn my eyes, and when I glance over my shoulder, Noah stands there. He pulls me into an embrace as we watch John take a microphone from a ring-side aide.

My husband stands in the center of the ring, and Brody finds home in one of the corners. They're both battered and bruised, a layer of perspiration reflecting off their skin, and both men are still visibly emotional. He chuckles, rubbing his chin and running his tongue over his teeth, trying to keep it in check a little longer.

"I don't really know where to begin, but I'll start with thank you. Twenty-one years ago, I stepped foot in the EWE ring for the first time, and it changed my life forever. *You* guys changed my life forever. Without you, none of this would be possible. I wouldn't be able to do what I love, and none of us would. I'm so very grateful that you have allowed me to share this space with you for over two decades."

Visible emotion begins to cross the faces of those in the front rows, hanging on to every word he says, waiting for the inevitable.

John runs a hand over his recently cropped hair, his shoulders rising and falling with a heavy breath. He glances over at his best friend, and Brody gives him a reassuring nod. "Brody, we've been doing this for a long time together…Over two decades. My brother. My road buddy. My ultimate rival and best tag partner. You're the only person who knocked me on my ass, and I thanked him for it. Brody, we started this journey together, and it was only right that it ended that way, too."

"BRO-DY!" the crowd chants, and Brody waves them off with a bashful smile.

"The last twenty-one years with Elite Wrestling have been the journey of a lifetime. You've watched me grow up in this ring. Watched me win titles, lose titles, bleed, overcome injuries that should've taken me out for good, and stand toe-to-toe with the best in the business." His face softens. "But the best thing this ring ever gave me is my wife." A wide grin echoes the sound of the crowd, and I swear I feel the building shake beneath my feet. "How I ever convinced her to marry me, I don't know, but—"

Brody cups his hands around his mouth and yells, "You got lucky!"

"Damn straight," John says, pointing at him. "She came into my life unexpectedly and took my world by storm. She's made me a better person, a better wrestler, and an even better man."

The sound of my name fills the arena, and it's surreal. Since my retirement almost three years ago, I haven't spent much time back at the company. I elected to stay home and take care of things there, to take care of our two-year-old daughter. I recently started working at NextGen, replacing Juliet as one of the trainers—I've found that it helps keep my longing for the ring at bay. I usually join John for big events like Wrestlefest and Beachbash, but in terms of week-to-week shows, I haven't made many appearances. This Monday, however, was a must.

"I've had a lot of matches in between these ropes. Big ones. Brutal ones. Bloody ones. But tonight...tonight is my final one." A collective gasp fills the air, rippling through the crowd, followed by a chorus of "Nos." I watch him fight back the wetness coating his eyes. He rolls his lips between his teeth and nods. With another heavy sigh, he says, "Tonight, I announce my official retirement from EWE."

"You should go out there," Callum says, appearing beside his half-brother.

"This is his moment." I shake my head. "I don't...I don't want to take away from that."

"Trust me, Savannah. Having you out there is going to make it a lot easier to say goodbye."

John sighs on the screen. "I know, I know," he says softly, swallowing back the wetness that makes his eyes shine beneath the stadium lights. "Nobody likes goodbyes, me included, but I've been doing this for a long time—almost twenty-eight years total—and while I love it...I do, I love it. There is nothing in the world like standing here in this ring, nothing like being here with you guys, with the people in the back, but there comes a time in life when you have to say goodbye to the things you love to make room for more."

"Thank you, Brooks!" fills the air, and this time, he can't hold back the tears.

Walking through the curtain, I smile at the two men on the other side before I walk into the arena—no music, no special entrance, nothing to draw the attention away from what's happening in the ring. Brody claps a hand down on John's shoulder and pulls him into an embrace, patting his back. When he pulls back to say something, his words stutter as we make eye contact.

One by one, the members of the crowd start to realize someone else has joined them, until finally my husband looks over his shoulder to see what has caught their attention. A new wave of emotion crosses his face, and his eyes shine beneath the stadium lights. Climbing the stairs, I step through the ropes that Brody holds open. We don't say anything before he pulls me into a soul-crushing embrace. Around us, the audience loses it, chanting a mixture of my name and his. John kisses the top of my head before he pulls away to cradle my face in his hands and kisses me.

"I'm sorry for crashing your party."

"Sweetheart, you can crash my party anytime," he says with a toothy grin. "I couldn't have done it without you."

"Now you're just being corny," I say, rolling my eyes. He could have easily done this without me, and in a way, he has after I retired, but he never wanted to, and that means everything to me. I tighten my grip around his waist as he drapes his arm over my shoulders and turns back to the crowd.

"I wouldn't be here without all of you in the seats, everyone watching at home, and every person in the back. Whether we've been friends for a long time or we just met, this small-town boy from Indiana would've never been able to live his dream if it weren't for all of you. So, from the bottom of my heart, thank you." John crouches down, resting the microphone in the center of the ring. "Let's go home," he whispers in my ear, as the crowd chants "Thank you, Brooks!" louder than ever before.

THANK YOU

Did you enjoy *Heartbreaker*?
Please consider leaving a review on Amazon, Goodreads, etc!

Interested in more from Jensen Parker?
Scan the code below to sign up for the newsletter

Turn the page to read a brand new EWE short story:
Showstopper.

SHOWSTOPPER

AN EWE SHORT STORY

BY JENSEN PARKER

Viviana

FRIDAY, OCTOBER 13, 2017

7:11 A.M.

"*That's my girl,*" are the first words that come to mind before I open my eyes. Cold, heavy limbs weigh me down, disobeying the adrenaline pumping through my veins. A balloon is trapped beneath my skull, and the pressure continues to mount, slowly inflating and begging for release. My mouth tastes like a tangerine peel left in the sun for too long. My tongue is dry and heavy, in desperate need of rehydration. The longer I'm awake, the numbness across my limbs slowly dissipates. I feel the whisper of something against my bare skin. *Why am I naked*? No, not naked, just half-naked. The straps of my bra dig into my shoulders, and I can feel the chord of a waistband on my hips.

Peeling my eyes open, I squint against the morning sunlight slipping through open shades. *What happened last night*? *Where am I*? *Did I—Holy shit.*

The body beside me stirs, exhaling a soft hum as muscles stretch beneath sun-kissed skin beneath white sheets. His left hand reaches out, caressing the soft fabric. He squeezes his shoulder blades together and takes a deep breath before his eyes open to meet my stare.

I bolt up, lifting the sheet to cover myself, and soft, brown eyes stay locked on my every move. "What are *you* doing here?"

"I could ask you the same thing." He pushes himself

upright and leans against the headboard. Large hands run through his short brown hair, massaging his scalp.

I wish he was doing that to me.

No, Vee. You do not wish he was massaging you instead. But damn, I imagine that would feel so good against my skin, relieving some of the pressure settled beneath my cranium.

I squeeze my eyes shut, pinching the bridge of my nose, and try my best to do just that. "This is *my* room, Austin. Get the fuck out."

"Actually, Sweetheart," he says, clearing his throat. "It's my room."

"Shit," I breathe. An image from last night—or maybe from a long time ago, I can't be sure—floods my mind and sends a pulse straight to my core. My legs squeeze together at the mere thought of him being inside me. I push up from the bed, needing to get as far away from him as possible. "This cannot be happening. I thought it was a fucking dream. I didn't—I didn't think we actually—" I can't even complete the thought.

How could I be so stupid?

Austin's eyes trail the length of my body, and I swear they turn from brown to black with each passing inch. I've seen that look too many times to count, and when his gaze finally reaches mine, I know it's taking everything in him not to pull me back into bed. Austin's tongue swipes across his lips, leaving behind a smirk. "Glad to know you still dream about me, Vee."

"This isn't funny, Austin."

"I wasn't being funny." He meets me at the foot of the bed, and his six-foot-one stature towers over my five-foot-three, but I stand my ground. My arms are crossed tightly over my chest, bringing his attention briefly to my breasts, covered in a black lace bra. He plants his hands on his hips, almost like he's trying to restrain them from instinctively reaching out. "Vee, come back to bed."

"Come back to bed?" I shake my head, disbelief laced in every word. "You're unbelievable! Austin, this wasn't supposed to happen. We were supposed to keep our distance. This weekend isn't about—"

"I know what this weekend is about, Viviana."

"Then why are we here?" I ask.

We shouldn't be here...we shouldn't be together. This weekend is supposed to be about Maddie and Drew and their wedding, slated to take place tomorrow afternoon. It wasn't supposed to be about us or how we left things eleven months ago or how we've avoided confronting the situation since. And right now, I can't differentiate between what was a dream and what is reality trapped behind a drunken haze.

I can't remember the last time I got that drunk, but we are in Vegas, and what happens in Vegas stays in Vegas, right? When Maddie handed me the first shot of the night in the hallway outside her room, I had no choice but to snake my arm through hers and down the burning liquid. After that, the drinks never stopped coming...

Without breaking his stare, I ask, "Why am I here? Please tell me we didn't...do anything last night."

"And if we did?" Austin asks, but I ignore his question. If we did...then I'll be back at square one, and I don't want to start all over on the road of trying to forget him. He scoffs, scrubbing a hand down his face to wipe away the remnants of sleep. "You were drunk off your ass and someone had to make sure you didn't choke on your own vomit."

"And that someone had to be you?"

"Well, it sure as hell wasn't going to be Mads." Austin chuckles. "She was in just as bad of shape, if not worse than you."

That means the rest of the girls are feeling about as good as I am right now. *Great, that's going to make today a real joyride.* What were we thinking? The five of us hadn't been together in one place in the last five years, so I shouldn't be surprised we rode a little too close to the sun. Besides, it's technically a bachelorette party...We're supposed to cut loose and have a little fun!

"Please tell me that we didn't sleep together," I beg, pushing the heels of my palms into my eyes. I hope to God that drunk-me was smart enough not to let something happen, or that the man standing before me was gentleman enough not to take advantage of the situation.

"What kind of man do you take me for?" Austin scoffs. "You know I'd never do that, Vee."

"Then where are my clothes?" I motion down my body. I'd love to know why I'm dressed in only my bra and his sweatpants.

"Mads spilled her whole drink down your front." He motions to a heap in the corner, where my hot-pink sequined shorts sparkle in the sunlight underneath the matching pink blazer and white tank top that's not so white anymore.

A wave of nausea rolls through me, the acid clawing its way up my throat, but I force it back down. I have to get out of here. I need to get back to my room so I can get my shit together before brunch.

"C'mon, Vee," Austin pleads, reaching out to me. "Come back to bed. I'll get you some Tylenol and order room service. It'll help you soak up what's left in your system."

"No." The small word has a big bite. "Get out of my way, Austin," I say, attempting to move past him, but he doesn't budge.

"I'm serious, Vee," he says. "Please, let me help."

"I don't want your help!" I grab the black T-shirt he'd been wearing last night and pull it over my head. When I gather up the pile in the corner, I get a strong whiff of tequila and fruit, making it hard to fight back the nausea. *Thanks a lot, Mads.*

Austin stands at the end of the hallway, blocking my only

way out, unless...I glance over my shoulder at the sliding door. I could scale down the balcony. It's only one story, I could make the jump...No, Vee. We left those kinds of shenanigans back in college. But it could be fun in a "what happens in Vegas stays in Vegas" way.

Yeah, kind of like that dream.

Fuck, I almost forgot about that.

I glance back at him, and he stands with his hands on his hips, feet planted on the carpet I'm sure has seen more action than me in the last eleven months. A small bout of disappointment forms in my stomach—a heavy weight that ripples through my entire system.

Waking up next to Austin Murray after having a dream about him professing his love and making love to me is what I imagine waking up from a head trip must be like. The dream was obviously just a result of his actions the night before, dredging up feelings from the past. Feelings I shouldn't be having. Dream Viviana jumped at his confession, hearing the words I'd always wanted him to say. The problem is that those five words will never come out of Austin Murray's mouth, because Austin Murray doesn't do *feelings*, and he certainly doesn't do relationships.

"Would you please get out of my way?"

"Vee—"

"Look, I appreciate you looking out for me, but you should've just taken me back to my room. We haven't spoken in months and—"

"Whose fault is that?"

I scoff. "I'm not having this fight, Austin."

"You mean you don't want to have this fight." He crosses his arms over his broad chest, and I have to fight to keep my stare from moving to his bare skin. "You're the one who ended things with me, Viviana, not the other way around."

"Because you refuse to grow up. Now, get out of my way. I

need to get ready. We can't be late for brunch."

Finally, he lets me shove past him, and only when I make it back to my room on the other side of the building do I allow myself to take a deep breath. It's unstable, the exhale even worse, before a quiet sob falls past my lips.

Austin

FRIDAY, OCTOBER 13, 2017

7:32 P.M.

This weekend is the first time I've been around Viv in almost eleven months, and it's gone about as well as you'd expect. We have successfully avoided each other at work since she ended our...arrangement. The separation has been easier than I anticipated because she's been off the road recovering from an injury. At least, that's what I tell myself. But we knew running into each other this weekend was unavoidable. Two of our closest friends are getting married, and there was no way we'd miss Maddie and Drew's big day. Maddie was Viviana's roommate from freshman year of college, and Drew and I have been friends since high school. He was my biggest supporter when I decided not to go to college and pursue a life in wrestling.

The duo met three years ago at a pay-per-view show where Viv began her first major championship title run, and I lost mine. Viv and I had always been friendly, but never anything more than a casual nod in the hallway or a quick hello at an event until two years ago. I caught her eye across the pool table at the bar a few of us hit up after the show. Her narrowed gaze watched my every move, only half listening to the conversation at her table, and when she realized she'd been caught, the right corner of her lips lifted slightly, followed by her brow, urging me to finish the game. The look in those brown eyes stirred something in me—a hunger, you could say—awakening something I couldn't properly name at the time. Sinking the last striped ball into the left corner pocket, I looked up, but she was gone. I watched her backside as she casually swam through the crowd toward the back hallway, and before I knew it, I sank the eight ball in the side pocket and dropped the pool stick, following her. That was the start of our arrangement...Neither of us wanted anything serious, just a way to let off a little steam, no strings attached.

When I got a call from Drew last July asking me to help him ring shop because he wanted to propose to Maddie on their Labor Day trip to the mountains, I never thought Vee and I would be in this place. I thought we'd be living the high life, celebrating the union of two of our closest friends. Instead, she can't stand being in the same room as me. As soon as I received the invitation in the mail six months ago, I knew this weekend was going to be tense and awkward as we navigated this new territory as exes—if you can even call us that, ex-flings (permanent booty calls?) might be more appropriate.

The moment I saw her walk into the rooftop bar last night, I knew I was in trouble...A tight pair of shorts that showed off the delectable curve of her ass. A white tank top kept riding up, revealing the tanned skin of her stomach beneath a hot-pink blazer that signified her as part of Team Bride, as if the white across her body wasn't enough. Keeping my hands to myself while undressing her when we got back to my room was the hardest fucking thing I've ever done in my life. But I'm nothing if not a gentleman, and I wouldn't take advantage of her in that state. She was drunk off her ass. None of the girls were in any shape to watch out for her or themselves, and I refused to let any other groomsmen near her. I'd already decided to bring her back to my room before Drew suggested it as we watched her and Maddie stumble with laughter at something one of them said.

However, this morning was a different story. My dick strained at the sight of her before me, watching her pace the end of the bed. Her milky skin was barely covered in her black lace bra and my sweatpants, and she raked a hand through her hair as she paced. Her brown hair was shorter than I ever remembered, the ends just long enough to kiss the tops of her shoulders. And the image of her riding me—tits bouncing with each movement of her hips, her fingers delicately playing with the sensitive bundle of nerves—infiltrated my mind before her words of panic cut through the mental image. It had been a struggle to regain control over the blood rushing to my lower brain, but I'd done it...because the last thing I needed was her knowing I had a hard-on thinking about screwing her senseless right then and there. She would've killed me.

Viviana ended things between us on a Saturday night, simply citing the reason as being done with the arrangement. She ended things over a text message from the other side of the country and didn't give me a chance to ask questions. She avoided me backstage on Monday night and every night after that. Anytime I tried to get a second alone with her, someone would swoop in and save her.

Later that month at Clash of the Titans, the November pay-per-view, Viv was injured in a street fight match with Savvy Skye for the women's title. The two women were exhausted; they'd beaten each other to hell, and it was coming down to the wire. Savvy landed three chops on Viv's chest, sending her into the barricade, before taking hold of Viv's hair and tossing her into the steel steps of the ring. Viv should've loosened up to prepare for impact. Instead, I watched from the monitor backstage as she planted her left foot and her leg twisted in the opposite direction. That was only the initial blow, and I could tell that something was wrong from the way her face twisted in agony, but she didn't stop. Viv finished the match, which included taking a few chair shots to her injured knee, before Savannah finished it off with a chain rope. Needless to say, Viv didn't walk out of there on her own and refused to let me help when I tried, accepting help from Miles Drake instead (that fucker). At the time, it seemed odd. Miles was known for being the backstage asshole. He always inserted his two cents where it didn't belong, and Viv detested him. When we were putting on a show, Mile was known as Damian "The Anarchist" Drake, and sometimes it felt like he blurred the line between reality and fiction.

"She doesn't want to talk to you, Austin," Wolf Bennett, whose real name is Bennett James, said as I watched Miles lift her onto the backseat of the golf cart. "Harp says they've been talking, whatever that means."

My head whipped to the side. What did he mean they were *talking*? Harper Valentine was Wolf's fiancée and the biggest gossip backstage. If you wanted to know something, you went to Harper, but there had been plenty of times she was wrong...I could only hope this was one of those times.

"Don't shoot the messenger." Wolf chuckled, lifting his hands in surrender. "You had your chance, and you blew it."

"Shut up, Bennett." I rolled my eyes and walked away. What did he know? What did any of them know?

Viv had surgery two days after that, and there hasn't been so much as a whisper about her return to the company. But at least I know she and Miles aren't together because he's been back to normal for a while now, sleeping with the ring rats—groupies for wrestlers—in almost every city.

"Why won't you just talk to her?" Drew asks, bringing me back to my current position. The server sets the bill presenter between us, and we both reach for it, but I win the fight. "Oh, give that here!"

"No," I say, and stuff my credit card into the presenter. I slam it shut with extra oomph just for good measure.

"No, to which?"

"To both, I suppose," I say with a tight smile and hand over the check to the waiter.

I know I shouldn't have let Viv leave without talking this morning. It was probably my one opportunity to get an explanation about what happened...and I let it slip right through my fingers. The thought has plagued me all day, knowing the truth was right within reach and I didn't take hold of it when I had the chance. After the rehearsal brunch, the wedding party was released from our duties, free to do whatever we wanted. The bride and groom's only request was not to have too much fun since we had an early morning of preparation ahead of us. I walked down the Strip, hoping to clear my mind of the woman at the far end of S. Las Vegas Boulevard.

It didn't work. Everywhere I looked, there was a happy couple. It was inescapable, and each one begged me to turn around and finally tell Vee everything I've wanted to say the past few months.

When Drew called and asked if I wanted to grab dinner at Hell's Kitchen, I thought that might do the trick...

It didn't.

"Austin," Drew says, catching my attention again. "It's been what...a year? Isn't that enough time for the dust to settle and talk about things? Seems like fate is giving you the chance to fix things this weekend."

Guess I'm not the only one who thinks so. Or at least to talk about what happened.

"Dude, what happened? I thought you were trying to lock it down."

"I was...She wasn't interested."

"Did you tell her, or did you just say okay when she ended things?" Drew sits back in his chair, hands laced together over his stomach.

"She didn't *say* anything, she texted me."

"I know, you've said, but you never get past that part. What happened?"

Our arrangement became complicated when our lives began to intersect more and more. Our best friends were dating and getting married. I'd taken her home for my brother's birthday. She'd taken me home for Thanksgiving. "We're just friends," we'd say when someone asked, but I think everyone saw right through the lie. There was something there, something more than just friends, but I was too scared to admit it...and when I was ready, she'd already moved on.

"I'm going to take that as a no," Drew says, shaking his head. "Look, Ace, it's time to pull your head out of your ass and do something. Either move on or tell her how you feel."

I smile at the old nickname and sign off on the bill when the waiter returns, throwing a one-hundred-dollar bill in the presenter. Sitting back in my chair, I swirl the remainder of my whiskey in the glass and sigh. "I have moved—"

"*Don't* finish that sentence." Drew tosses another twenty-dollar bill on the table and points his finger at me. "Don't you dare, because we both know you're lying."

Viviana

FRIDAY, OCTOBER 13, 2017

7:50 P.M.

I offer a silent prayer up to God, the angels, and whoever else is looking out for me today. I managed to get through the bus ride to Red Rock Canyon, the rehearsal, the ride back to the Strip, and all of the rehearsal brunch without running into Austin. There were more than enough people to keep us both occupied and maintain a healthy distance, which is exactly how I envisioned this weekend going.

But just because I managed to stay away from him didn't mean I was in the clear. Before the end of brunch, the bride-to-be joined me on the restaurant terrace for a final look at the Bellagio Fountain show, but that wasn't all she wanted...

"Want one?" Maddie asked, standing beside me with an iced coffee. I noticed earlier that she and I were the only ones avoiding alcoholic beverages today. I found it strange. How were the others dealing with such a nasty hangover and still going? Bouncing back is not as easy as it once was, now that I'm not in my early twenties. When Maddie's sister Emmy shoved a cocktail in my face on the bus earlier, I was sure I was going to vomit.

"What's going on with you and Austin?" she asked, leaning back against the banister. She placed her straw delicately on her tongue, taking a sip as she stared up at me with big blue eyes.

"What are you talking about?"

"Oh, come on, Viv! Don't play coy." Maddie laughed. "I've seen you making googly eyes at each other. And before you deny it, you were doing the same thing last night."

I rolled my eyes. "We were not."

"Yes, you were! Not to mention that..." She looked around to make sure none of the lingering guests were listening. "He took you home last night."

I scoffed. "And nothing happened."

"You sound a little disappointed, Vee." A smirk spread across her bright red lips, taking another sip of her coffee. "Did you *want* something to happen?"

Did I want something to happen?

That was a great question. One that I didn't have an answer to. No, I didn't want something to happen because that would only reopen the wounds I had been fighting to heal. Being away from the company for the last nine months while recovering from surgery has been good and gave me a chance to work through my feelings without having to see him. But I won't lie that part of me wished something had happened...Or maybe it was just my delusion talking. I knew better than to believe the delusion. This was Austin Murray. Better known to the world as Spencer Austin, the Showstopper. One of Elite Wrestling Entertainment's top entertainers. If he were tied down—as he so eloquently put it in years past—he wouldn't have the freedom he desired. That's why he loved our arrangement. No feelings. No strings attached. Just sex.

"You guys were cute together—"

"We weren't together, Maddie."

Maddie snorted. "Yeah, okay. Spew that bullshit to someone else, because I don't believe it for one second. Drew and I were convinced you guys would get married before we did. I was shocked when he told me Austin wasn't with you during your surgery. You didn't even tell me you guys broke up; I found out from Drew, who found out from Ace! You've still never told me what happened."

"There's nothing to tell. Austin didn't want anything serious. He made that very clear from the beginning. You know that. We were just friends, and he wanted someone consistent to get his dick wet when he felt the urge." The words rolled off my tongue with ease because that's what I'd been telling myself for months. We were just friends (if that), and that's all we'd been because Austin Murray didn't do feelings. "So, I ended things before I got hurt."

"And how did that go?"

"Not well," I whispered.

"Vee, I love you, but you brought this on yourself. You broke up with him over a text instead of—"

"It wasn't a breakup!"

"You should've talked to him and told him how you felt. How you feel." Maddie offered me a sad smile. "Vee, maybe this is a sign. You guys can hash things out before you go back to work. And if nothing else, you can at least be friendly. It'll make your return a little less awkward."

Maybe it was, but it wasn't a sign I would explore this weekend. Besides, I didn't know if I was going back to EWE... Maddie didn't need to know that, not right now.

"Promise me something, Viviana. Before you leave this weekend, you *will* talk to Austin. And you'll be honest with him about everything."

"That's not—"

"Promise me," Maddie interrupted me. "I think if you give him the chance, you'll see that you were more than just a...What did you call it? 'Someone consistent to get his dick wet'?" She gave me a look that shut down my protest almost immediately. I rolled my eyes and walked away from her, but I knew the next time she had the chance, she'd bring the conversation back around.

After brunch, Maddie and Drew released the wedding party from their duties until tomorrow morning. I took the opportunity to spend my day relaxing by the pool with a book and an Aperol Spritz. It only took an hour after brunch to not get queasy at the thought of consuming alcohol again.

Am I trying to avoid a repeat of last night? Maybe…but I'm telling myself I'm just being a good bridesmaid and avoiding any issues that a long night could cause tomorrow morning.

Issues like a certain brown-eyed man who's been a lingering thought since I left his room this morning (let's be honest, it's been a lot longer than that). Have there been a few times the image of being in bed with him for other reasons than just a good night's rest slipped through the cracks of the wall I've been trying to keep up? I'd be lying if I said no.

Different scenarios have entered my mind, each one better than the last, and as I step off the elevator, another one enters my mind…I glance down the hallway that will take me to his room on the other side of the floor, but I remind myself I'm not supposed to be looking for trouble.

"Just go to your room, Vee," I whisper. *Go to your room and don't look back.*

That's exactly what I'm going to do. Go straight to my room, take a hot shower (maybe a nice long bath), and order some room service while I scroll through the endless movie titles before finally settling on one I've seen a million times.

Walking into my room, I toss my pool bag on the chair across from the bed and strip out of my swimsuit. Room service says it'll be an hour before they deliver, giving me enough time to shower, run through my skincare, and get dressed without rushing.

I let my fingers dance through the warming water until it reaches maximum temperature, and I stay in the shower until the water runs cold. Slipping the plush white robe over my shoulders and twisting my hair into a towel, I swear I hear a knock on the door. As I step out of the bathroom, the world seems to stand still, and every sound of the world around me is sucked into a vacuum of silence. Only to be broken when another knock sounds. This time, with more weight to it.

The first thought I have is: *What the hell? They shouldn't be here for another thirty minutes.* And the second is: *What if it's not room service?*

Austin

I was not expecting *this* when I knocked on the door. The only thing between me and the woman before me is a plush, white robe. She pulls her hair out of the twisted towel and lets it fall to her shoulders. Raking a hand through it, she tries to comb it out as best she can. The front of the robe loosens with the movement, drawing my attention to where the opening exposes the swell of her breasts.

"What are you doing here, Austin?"

I clear my throat, forcing my eyes back to her face. "You've been avoiding me."

Viv scoffs. "And what have you been doing all day?"

"What you wanted. Keeping my distance. But I thought we'd at least pretend to get along for Maddie and Drew's sake."

"I refuse to let this ruin their weekend, Austin." Her lips pull into a firm line, and she plants her hand securely on the door. "Just stick to your side of the aisle, and when this is all over, we never have to speak again."

Gripping the door's edge, I stop her from closing it. She takes two steps back when I push inside, closing the door behind me. "Would you just listen to me for a second?"

I pace across the short hallway, wringing my hands together, trying to think of the best way to say this. When I look at her, I expect to see impatience written across her features, but it's not there. She's moved to the edge of the bed, her legs crossed, and she watches me try and find the courage to do what I came here to do. To be honest with her and tell her how I feel. How I've felt. I should just say it, right?

Just put it all out there...Lay it all out on the table and whatever happens, happens.

"I know...I know what I said two years ago. I know I told you I couldn't give you more, that we couldn't be more, but Vee...that's not true. It's not...That's not what I want. I don't want some casual fling. I want you. I've wanted you, all of you, and I wanted to tell you that last year, but I never got the chance."

It's quiet for a few heartbeats, and with each passing breath, her eyes narrow until she's glaring through me. "Are you fucking kidding?"

Not exactly what I wanted to hear, but I'm not surprised, either.

"Fuck you, Austin Murray." Viviana steps off the bed, walking toward me like a lion stalking its wounded prey. "Fuck you and your bullshit excuses. Did you really think you could—"

Without thinking, I kiss her, halting whatever insult she's about to hurl at me. An insult that I probably (definitely) deserve, but all I could think about was feeling her lips against mine. So, I kiss her. Her hands land on my chest, a feeble attempt to push me away, before her fingers twist the fabric of my button-down. I sweep my tongue along her bottom lip and kiss her deeply, my tongue searching her mouth when she opens to me. Viv moans softly when I suck her lower lip between my teeth, parting from the kiss.

Her eyes have grown dark, and her breaths come out in soft pants. Part of me expects her to slap me for that, but I'm pleasantly surprised when she doesn't.

"No," I breathe. "No, it wasn't my plan to come here and try to make you feel bad or guilty or to act like the victim...

because I'm not, Vee. I know I'm not. Neither are you. We're both at fault and we've hurt each other, but fuck, I love you, Viviana Grace Ridley." I take her face in my hands and kiss her again. "I love you so much and it scares the shit out of me—"

"Austin, I—I've waited for this. To hear you say those words, but how do I know when the next ring rat or the next new girl tries to—"

"I haven't touched anyone since you," I say, tucking a strand of hair behind her ear. "Sure, we said that it was okay, but it felt wrong, Vee. Like I was betraying your trust."

"Why didn't you just tell me you felt this way?"

"Why didn't you?" My question takes her aback, and she swallows back whatever quip she is about to unload. "Neither one of us is blameless here, Vee. Not to mention, you moved on pretty quickly to Drake."

"Drake?"

"Armageddon. Harper told Wolf you were seeing each other."

Viviana laughs. "I was not dating Drake. We were supposed to begin a storyline together the next week. His only interest in me that night was to see if I could still walk well enough to wrestle."

"Asshole," I say under my breath.

"I wish it had been you...helping me, standing by my side before they rolled me into surgery...But I was trying to move on, trying to forget you. I-I couldn't do it anymore, Austin. You said we couldn't have more, that we couldn't be more. I didn't want to be the girl you called just because you felt lonely. I wanted you. All of you."

"I wanted that, too."

Viviana scoffs, biting down on her lip. "Why didn't you just say that?"

"I tried to! You wouldn't listen, and you kept interrupting me...and I-I snapped. Then you sent me that text and...I-I should've just said what I had to say, but I was hurt. I thought I didn't mean as much to you as you meant to me...Who breaks up with someone over a text?"

Viv sighs, poking her tongue out to wet her lips and lowering her gaze. "Can I ask you something?" she asks, and I nod. "What if I never come back...to EWE?"

"Come back, don't come back...I don't care. Whatever makes you happy makes me happy. I love you, Viviana." Finally saying those words lifts a weight off my chest. I step forward, closing the space between us and taking her hands in mine. "Fuck the agreement we made. I want more with you. I want the ups and downs, the wins and losses, I want it all because I love you."

A warm glaze covers her eyes, staring at the carpet beneath our feet as she mulls over my words. My heart races, both from my confession and her lack of a response. What if I just fucked this up even more? But this is what she wanted... Isn't it?

Pulling my bottom lip between my teeth, I drop her hands and step back, stuffing my hands in my pockets. "Now would be a really good time to say it back."

Viviana laughs softly, finally looking up, her doe-eyed gaze full of tears. She steps forward, cupping my face, swipes her thumb over the stubble on my cheeks, and whispers, "This is all I wanted, Austin...I love you, too."

I don't waste another moment, stooping down to capture her lips in a hard kiss. Her body fits against mine like we were made for each other, two missing puzzle pieces finally put together. She drapes her arms over my shoulders, and a soft hum rumbles deep in my throat when her hands glide up my shoulders and around my neck. Her nails coast through the hairs at my nape, sending a shiver down my spine and reaching out to every one of my nerve endings. The kiss turns soft and leisurely, exploring and getting reacquainted with each other.

I play with the tie of her bathrobe, undoing the knot, and a soft gasp falls from her lips when cool air rushes across her burning skin as the front of the robe falls open. The sound mixed with the sight before me sends all the blood rushing to my dick. *Holy fuck.* My tongue sweeps across my top lip.

"You gonna do something or just stand there and stare?" Vee challenges, and it's enough to lift my gaze from her body to her eyes.

I take her face in my hands, infiltrating her space a little more, and the pads of my fingers skim across her bottom lip. "This isn't a dream, right?"

"If it is, you'd better make it a damn good one." There's a twinkle in those brown eyes that plunges a syringe of pure adrenaline straight into my heart.

I slide my hands down her sides, grazing the sides of her breasts and trailing down her curves before I squeeze her hips affectionately, tugging her forward into a tight embrace. We remain in the stillness for about ten heartbeats, and her fingers draw invisible circles on my back through my starched white dress shirt. I lace one of my hands through hers, bringing her fingers to my lips to kiss each one before holding our embraced hands against my chest. With my other hand, I push a strand of chestnut brown hair behind her ear and kiss her. "Let's get married," I whisper against her lips.

"What?" Vee stares at me like I suddenly grew four heads. After a moment, she laughs, but stops when I don't join her. "Austin, you can't be serious."

"Why not? We're in Vegas! They do weddings until midnight or one around here…Let's do it."

She shoves a hand through her damp hair. "This is Maddie and Drew's wedding! We can't—"

I grab her hand, pulling her back into my embrace. "So, we don't tell them. We wait until after their wedding—hell, after the honeymoon, and then tell them."

"You're serious about this?"

"Serious as sin."

Vee laughs, and it's the most beautiful sound I've ever heard. She shakes her head in disbelief. "I can't believe I'm gonna say this, but okay."

Viviana

MONDAY, APRIL 8, 2019

8:35 P.M.

"Noah," Austin says, shaking hands with Noah Callahan, Chief Content Officer and husband of Chelsea Rafferty—daughter of Amos Rafferty, the man who started the EWE empire.

"Austin," Noah says with a smirk that makes my stomach queasy before he turns to me. His hand engulfs mine with a tight squeeze that does nothing to help the nerves firing off in my stomach. "Mrs. Murray. How was the honeymoon?"

Austin and I finally had a proper wedding in Scotland before enjoying a week in the Maldives. Now, after two weeks off, we're back to find out who will be joining our current storyline feud with *Brooks Taylor*, whose real name is John Brooks, as his tag team partner. Brooks is *the* guy in EWE. When you think of EWE, you think of *Brooks Taylor*. Austin and Brooks have a complicated relationship. They're not exactly friends, but they're friendly, and for the most part respect each other...

I think my husband holds a grudge against Brooks because the Raffertys chose Brooks over him when the time came to push someone, but (and I'd never tell Austin this) I think it was the right choice. Austin is the guy people love to hate, while Brooks is the guy people either desperately love or absolutely hate—either way, he elicits an enormous response from every crowd.

"You guys ready for tonight?" Noah asks.

He's been leading the charge on our feud, which has consisted mainly of losses for Brooks. It started two months ago when Austin's character *Spencer Austin* confronted *Brooks* because he was getting a title shot...again. My husband aired his frustration with the company on national television, telling Brooks he needed to hand over the opportunity to someone who had earned it. Someone like him. The fourteen-time champion laughed in my husband's face and said, "*If you want it, come and get it.*"

After weeks of back and forth between the two, it all came to a head six weeks ago when *Austin* won the title in a triple-threat match between *Brooks*, *Austin*, and the former champ, *Brody Wilder*.

Brooks Taylor has been itching for revenge ever since.

"Only if you're ready to tell us who's coming out tonight," I say when Noah extends his hand to me. Making my official return to the ring last year, I entered the Women's Battle Royale at number twenty-five, earning one of the biggest pops from the crowd that night. After our weekend in Vegas almost two years ago, I started traveling with Austin, and the itch to get back out there was instantaneous. It didn't take long for my husband to notice the twinkle in my eye every time I set foot in the arena, and he encouraged me to start training again. That first day back in the ring was brutal, but the best I'd felt in years.

"No can do, Viviana," Noah says with a shrug. "You'll have to wait like everyone else."

We've been waiting since they proposed the idea. The feud with *Brooks* took a turn when he and I went head-to-head in a handicap match—*Brooks* would have one hand tied behind his back—before the wedding. The idea had come from none other than founder Amos Rafferty himself. He thought it would be great television to include me further in their story, and tonight everyone finds out who will join us in the storm. It's been very hush-hush since Noah and Brian, head of Creative, sat the three of us down about the idea. We'd thrown out names of who we'd like to work with, but they disregarded each one, saying they already had someone in mind.

Noah adjusts the button of his sports coat and rolls his shoulders. "Well, if you'll excuse me, I have to meet with Amos and Brian before showtime to go over a few things for tonight."

"I have a bad feeling about this," I say when he's gone, looking up at Austin.

When he meets my gaze, he offers me a soft smile and kisses my temple. "Whoever it is, we'll face 'em together."

"Who do you think it is?"

"Honestly, it has to be someone from developmental. Why else would they be so secretive?" Austin shrugs, wrapping his arm around my shoulders. "Let's get something to eat. I'm starving."

Austin

"*You think you can beat me?*" I scoff, glancing at Viviana, who laughs behind her hand. The crowd begins an *Austin* chant, which makes me smile. "*Hear that, Brooks? They don't want you. They're tired of you.*"

Brooks stands at the top of the ramp with an unamused look. The character of *Brooks Taylor* doesn't find any of this comical—he hates every bit of what he's been put through—but the person behind the mask has been eating this shit up.

I adjust the oversized championship belt on my shoulder, the same belt I won in the triple-threat match against *Brooks* and *Brody* at Capitol Punishment six weeks ago.

"*And you know, I think it's comical you think you can beat me when you couldn't even beat Vee with a hand tied behind your back.*" They'd gone head-to-head in a handicap match the Monday before we took a small hiatus to get married properly. "*Should we see a clip? I think we should. Roll the clip!*" My demand is met with an instant replay of a highlight reel from the match.

The ref tied Brooks's hand behind his back, and he tested the give of the rope before he rolled his neck and shoulders, loosening up. I whispered to Vee outside the ropes from the apron, and she cracked her knuckles, bouncing on the balls of her feet. This was going to be a piece of cake. It was something Brooks wasn't happy about when Amos suggested it, but when he saw how excited Vee was at the opportunity, it quelled his refusal. The ref motioned for the timekeeper to ring the bell, and I jumped down from the apron to the floor just as Vee moved toward her opponent. She chopped Brooks in the chest three times, backing him into the corner of the ring before she jumped up on the ropes on either side of him and began to punch his head. Vee looked out at the crowd before landing a final blow and jumping down from the rope as Brooks slumped farther into the corner.

She moved to the opposite corner, watching for a moment, and when he began to stir, she pushed out of the corner to perform a somersault and landed a hard kick on his chest. The impact sent him back into the ropes, but the force springboarded him back into the ring, straight into her foot.

When he fell to the mat, she took a moment to celebrate, a little too long in my opinion, giving him the chance to recoup. Vee attempted to kick him on his way back up, but he took hold of her foot and twisted instinctively. She yelped in pain, and Brooks dropped her foot.

"Enough, Vee!" Brooks yelled. "Enough, I'm not going to fight you."

"Finish him," I said from under the bottom rope, and the crowd began to chant the same thing. As Brooks tried to talk sense into her, Vee climbed the top rope and landed another dropkick, this time onto his head. Brooks fell to the mat, in a quick 1...2...3, Vee was declared the winner.

The camera pans to Vee, and I watch her smirk grow on the jumbo screen hanging above *Brooks*. A loud chorus of "boo" fills the arena. Their response surprises me. This is the first crowd that has mostly been behind him since the start of our feud.

There's been a strange energy in the air tonight. I think everyone feels it. I tried to pry the name out of him before the segment earlier, but he swore he didn't know. The Raffertys have kept the name of his tag-team partner under lock and key. No one is supposed to know who will walk through that curtain until they are on the other side.

"*You didn't even try, Brooks,*" I say. "*You could've at least tried to put up a fight, given her something to work with.*"

Brooks stands tall and confident at the top of the ramp, maintaining the stereotypical *Brooks Taylor* façade. The same one that used to bug me every time we were forced to work together. The best part of this feud has been knocking *Brooks* down a few pegs over the last few months, even if it was only in story form. Everyone knows there isn't anyone who can oust *Brooks Taylor* from his place on the throne of EWE... There isn't anyone prepared to take his place because no one is willing to do what he does. Not even me.

"*Are you serious?*" He scoffs.

Intergender matches aren't a normal thing at EWE, and if they did happen, there was always some handicap to protect the women. I think the concern is a safety precaution. We work in a business where you can do everything right, and there will always be a risk that something could go wrong. But if there is any man I'd let Vee get involved in an intergender match with...it's Brooks.

"*I wasn't going to fight your wife, Austin. Are you insane? Vee is good, but...I refuse to do that.*"

There's a spark in the air following his words. A hum in the crowd as I watch a smirk lift the corners of his mouth.

Brooks wets his lips and chuckles. "*But I know someone who will.*"

Showtime.

The arena goes dark, and for exactly ten seconds it's so quiet you can hear a pin drop until the opening riffs to a familiar song fill the air, followed by "*Get on your knees and bow down...*" But I can barely hear the words, drowned out by the crowd.

"There's no fucking way," I say, but my words are lost in the madness, and I swear the building quakes on its foundation.

The chorus hits, and *she* steps out. Savannah Williams, better known to the world as *Savvy Skye*. The woman who disappeared from the company two years ago after turning on the man next to her. She stood by his side, cheered him on from the sidelines, and then cost him the championship before she disappeared.

Savvy's eyes scan the crowd, soaking in every ounce of energy thrown her way, and I can't deny I'm a little envious. I can't remember the last time they were this loud for one of us.

"I see why they didn't tell us," Vee says, glancing up at the ramp. Her tongue swipes across her lips, never taking her eyes off the other woman. She'd never admit it, or maybe she would behind closed doors, but seeing Sav up there makes her nervous. Don't get me wrong, Savannah was one of the best women wrestlers in EWE and one of the safest people to work with, but the last time she and Viv worked together, my wife got injured. "Wonder what Brooks thinks about this."

The crowd begins to simmer, and I take the opportunity to keep the show moving—that's what Noah and the head of Creative told us to do once her identity was revealed. "You can't do this!"

"*It's already done*," *Savvy* says, wearing a proud smirk, and the crowd cheers. "*You already signed the contract.*"

"*I didn't sign—*"

"*Did you even read that contract before you signed it*?"

I scoff. "*Did I read the contract? Of course, I read the—*"

"*She's right*," Vee says, holding up the contract I signed less than ten minutes ago. I snatch the folder from her hands and scan the words.

Holy shit. I should've looked at that damn contract.

Right there—in bold printed letters—is the name of *Brooks Taylor*'s tag-team partner, and I didn't even see it.

***Spencer Austin** and **Viviana Austin** will compete in a _____ match between **Brooks Taylor** and **Savvy Skye** on April 28, 2019, in Indianapolis, Indiana, at "Wrestlefest" as the Main Event of the show. Match stipulations can be set by Taylor and Skye at any point leading up to the event.*

"You've got to be fucking kidding me." I scrub a hand down my face, scratching through the scruff on my chin.

"*Signed, sealed, and delivered,*" Savvy says. "*We'll see you in three weeks. Oh, and I hope you're ready because the match…it's going to be No Disqualifications.*"

No Disqualifications? Is she fucking serious?

No Disqualifications means it's basically a free-for-all… There are no rules, except one: pinfall or submission must be in the ring to win. Why wouldn't Noah warn us about this?

"*You don't even work here, Skye! Not to mention, the last time you were in the ring with my wife—*"

"*Scared your wife can't hold her own?*" Brooks asks.

Normally, I'd expect the two of them to share a smirk or a look or something, but they haven't made eye contact *once* since Savannah came out. Barely even acknowledged each other…Oh no, are Viv and I going to have to play referee between these two?

I did not sign up for this.

"T*his is between you and me, Taylor! Leave the women out of this.*" I can feel the heat radiating from my face, and the crowd boos in response. "I'm not putting my wife in the ring with her."

"*Your wife would be lucky to step foot in the same ring as her.*" Brooks practically sneers. It would seem I've hit a nerve. "*Maybe she could learn a thing or two about wrestling.*"

Viviana gasps and looks at me with fake tears in her eyes before she buries herself into my chest. Her reaction is over the top, even for her character, but the crowd eats it up.

Wrapping my arm around her waist, I comfort my wife and glare at my opponent. *"This isn't over, Taylor!"*

"You're right." Brooks chuckles. *"It's not over until I bring the title back where it belongs."* He drops the mic and motions toward his midsection with his thumb and index finger on each hand to represent where the belt should hang on his hips. *"We'll see you in three weeks!"*

WHAT'S NEXT?

More books in the Elite Wrestling Entertainment series. Stay tuned for more to come.

You can check out my other books on jensenparker.com!

Strangers Series
Until Now
Strictly Business
Terms & Conditions
Begin Again

Elite Wrestling Entertainment
Showstopper (short story)
Heartbreaker

Acknowledgments

Heartbreaker is the longest book I've ever written, and this universe is large and exhausting, but I loved every second of it. This book wasn't even supposed to be a thing, at least not right now. I had plans to work on a completely different book, but sometimes you have to pivot to the thing that's right in front of you. Wrestling has always been a major part of my life. As a lifelong fan of WWE, writing this book has been so much fun because I get to combine two of my favorite things: writing passionate, angsty romance with wrestling, and all of its glitz, glamor, body slams, and drama. My goal with this series is to capture the in-ring performances mixed with the real lives of those bigger-than-life personas, and put it on paper without losing the magic of professional wrestling.

The idea for this book came while I was in bed, almost asleep, and I immediately had to get up and write it down. A few nights later, I ran the idea by my longtime friend, Stephanie, who said, "Sign me up for this now because I NEEED it." We've been friends for almost twenty years (that is actually crazy to say), and over that time, we've shared many stories. She is someone I can bounce ideas off, and she isn't afraid to tell me if something doesn't work, and vice versa. But that night, she helped me decide that transitioning from the Strangers series to this was the right move...

This book is not just a love story between two people. It's a reminder, for those of us who need it, that it's okay to start over. You're not going to get everything right the first time, or second, or even the fifth. That's okay. Give yourself some grace, and start over.

First, I need to thank the Lord. I couldn't do what I do without the gift of words that He's given me. I mean, how else could I string together 26 letters to create 139,000+ words?

Second, my husband. I couldn't do this without you. You believe in me even when I don't believe in myself. I love you to the moon and back.

Third, B. I truly couldn't have done this without your help. With your insight, my own experiences, our "gossip" sessions (as my husband has called them lol), and the many texts about this crazy world we both love, I've been able to create a universe and a story that I'm extremely proud of.

To my editor, Sophie B. Murphy. This is a shameless plug. If you need an editor, go to: https://www.eloquentinkblot.com/. Okay, now that I'm done, let me start by saying thank you for sticking with me on this one. Wrestling isn't your thing, but you didn't back down from the challenge when I first told you about this new universe. I know I said this in Begin Again, but can you believe we just finished out (now) three books and two short stories in less than a year? We need a vacation—a real vacation. Not the vacations we've been taking this year.

A few other people I want to name who supported me in making this book: my mom, my incredible alpha readers, Ashley, Samantha, Miriam, and Alexandra, My SPN Loving Sam to My Dean Chick, Claire Isenthal, Holly Whitworth, Kristin Mulligan, and Taylor J. Bridgeforth. There are so many other people to name here, but it would be nearly impossible to do so. I appreciate and love you all.

I told myself I was going to take a break after this, but my brain had other plans and I've already started working on a little surprise for you...

—Jensen ♡

GLOSSARY

Alliance A cooperative relationship between two or more wrestlers. (see tag team)

Angle A storyline.

Apron A platform area of the ring extends beyond the ropes, covered by a skirt to hide the ring's framework.

Audible A message delivered from backstage (to the refs or commentary team).

Audible Finish A match finish that occurs sooner (and differently) than planned. Often used when a wrestler is legitimately injured and cannot continue, when the match is approaching the time limit, or after a botch that significantly changes the plot.

Babyface See face.

Backbreaker Wrestler drops their opponent so the opponent's back receives the impact, or is bent backward against a part of their body.

Belly-to-Back Suplex See German suplex.

Body Slam Wrestler lifts opponent and slams them into the mat.

Book To determine and schedule events of a wrestling card.

Botch Something doesn't go as planned. Also, a move that is messed up.

Bump To fall to the mat or the ground.

Bury The worked/staged lowering of a wrestler's status in the eyes of fans. The act of causing a wrestler to lose popularity, momentum, and/or credibility.

Call To instruct the other wrestler on what is going to happen in the match. This also refers to the commentators detailing what is happening during a match.

Call it in the Ring When wrestlers make up moves and storytelling on the fly, rather than rehearsing them in advance.

Card	The show lineup.
Carry	When a more experienced wrestler is guiding a less experienced performer through the match.
Character	See gimmick.
Cheap Heat	When a wrestler incites a negative crowd reaction by insulting the crowd, usually bringing up something non-wrestling related, and puts it in a negative light.
Cheap Pop	When a wrestler incites a positive crowd reaction by "kissing up" to them.
Clean Finish	A match ending without cheating or interference.
Clinic	A match where one wrestler or faction completely dominates their opponent through superior technique, skill, and strategy. Nothing over the top, but demonstrating their mastery of the sport.
Clothesline	A maneuver where a wrestler runs toward their opponent, extending their arm out to the side of their body (parallel to the ground), and striking the opponent in the chest or neck.
Collar-and-Elbow Lock Up	A stand-up grappling position where wrestlers grip their opponent's neck area with one hand and elbow with the other. Creates a neutral position where one wrestler can attempt to gain an advantage, typically with a takedown.
Cross Armbreaker	Submission hold, where a wrestler uses their legs to trap one of their opponent's arms, pulling upwards, causing hyperextension of the elbow and shoulder.
Crossbody	A maneuver where a wrestler jumps onto their opponent, landing horizontally across their chest or torso, and forcing them down to the mat.
DDT	Wrestler places their opponent into a front facelock (aka inverted headlock), and they fall backwards to drive the opponent's head into the mat. This can be done with the opponent's legs hanging from the middle rope.
Dirt Sheet	An insider newsletter/website that tries to "get dirt" on what is happening behind the scenes of the

professional wrestling business.

Double-leg Takedown Wrestler attacks both legs of their opponent simultaneously, forcing them down to the mat.

Dragon Sleeper Submission hold targeting the neck and upper spine. A wrestler starts behind their opponent, wrapping their legs around them to create a body scissors, then hooks their arm under the opponent's chin and neck. The opponent's face should be looking up and back.

Drop-kick An offensive maneuver where the wrestler jumps, either off the mat or from an elevated position, and kicks an opponent with both feet.

European Uppercut Strike technique where a wrestler throws a forearm in an uppercut motion, making contact with their opponent's chin or chest.

Face The good guy. (see babyface)

Facebuster Wrestler forces their opponent down into the mat face-first without a headlock or facelock.

Faction Similar to a stable, but without the "leader" or spokesperson.

Feud Staged rivalry between two wrestlers or a group of wrestlers. Feuds may last months or years or be resolved quickly, within the course of a single match, depending on the story.

Figure-Four Lock Wrestler performs a single leg takedown, landing their opponent flat on their back. Twist the opponent's ankle, and the wrestler swings their leg over the opponent's while keeping the leg trapped. Bringing the opponent's leg around the wrestler's leg, hook it against their knee. Wrestler places the Achilles on top of their quad and sits back to be in line with the opponent, then places their left leg over their opponent's foot to secure the hold.

Finisher A wrestler's signature move usually leads to pinfall or submission. Sometimes called a "gimmick."

Fireman's Carry Wrestler lifts their opponent onto their shoulders and throws them over to the other side.

Flying Clothesline A maneuver where a wrestler runs toward their opponent, leaps into the air, extends their arm out to the side of their body (parallel to the ground), and strikes their opponent in the chest or neck. (see clothesline)

Four-Fifty Splash
High-flying move where the wrestler is in an elevated position (typically the tope turn buckle), and spins 450 degrees mid-air before landing in a splash position on their opponent. While impressive, this is a risky maneuver, requiring precise timing and execution.

Frogsplah
High-flying move where the wrestler is in an elevated position (typically the tope turn buckle), and leaps forward and outward, stretching their body horizontally in the air. Mid-air, the wrestler typically pulls their arms and legs inward, resembling a jack-knife position or frog. They extend their body again upon impact, landing on their opponent, usually lying on the mat below.

Front Facelock
Often used to set up for bigger moves, it's similar to a headlock. The wrestler wraps their arm around their opponent's neck from the front, pulling them into a bent-over position.

German suplex
Wrestler crouches and wraps arms around their opponent's lower waist (not the chest), then lifts them off the ground until they are overhead. The opponent should continue to fall, landing on the lower part of their neck.

Gimmick
The character portrayed by a wrestler. This involves their in-ring persona, behavior, attire, and distinguishing traits while performing, created to draw fan interest.

Go over
To win a wrestling match.

Gorilla
Headquarters of backstage. The staging area behind the entrance where wrestlers come out to the arena. This is where producers, writers, and other members of the creative process sit during the show.

Grappling
Close-quarters combat, where wrestlers use grips, holds, and throws to control their opponent and gain dominance.

Handicap Match
A match where one wrestler (or team) faces their opponent with some type of disadvantage,

creating an unfair advantage for the heels (i.e., larger group of opponents, hand tied behind their back, etc.)

Headlock   Often used to set up for bigger moves, the wrestler traps their opponent's head under their arm, squeezing the skull and neck area to control and immobilize the opponent.

Headscissors   Wrestler positions their legs on either side of their downed opponent's head, crossing over to encircle the opponent's chin, creating a "scissor" grip. They tighten their leg grip, compressing the opponent's throat, which could be used for a chokehold or submission maneuver.

Headscissors Takedown   Wrestler uses momentum from ropes or running forward to leap and wrap their legs around their opponent's neck, then use their legs and body weight to force their opponent down to the mat. (see headscissors).

Heat   Negative reaction from the fans. Also, real-life tension or ill will between two wrestlers.

Heel   The bad guy.

High Flyer   A wrestler who specializes in the execution of gravity-defying moves, including launching themselves off the ropes, turnbuckles, or other elevated platforms. They use aerial moves to target opponents.

Highspot   A high-stakes move that is perceived to be risky and dangerous.

Independent Circuit   A collection of smaller, independently owned wrestling promotions that are not part of major or international organizations.

Independent Promotion   A smaller wrestling company that operates at a local level and usually employs freelance wrestlers. (aka Indie Promotion)

Independent Wrestler   Freelance wrestler, usually not signed to exclusive contracts. (aka Indie Wrestler) Indies

Indies   See Independent Circuit.

Irish Whip   Not a damaging move, but used to set up for bigger sequences or moves. Wrestler grabs their opponent by the wrist, then pushes them into the ropes or another obstacle. Upon release, the opponent bounces off the ropes or hits the obstacle. Followed up by an attack or counterattack.

Jawbreaker
Wrestler grips their opponent's head and uses momentum to drive their opponent's jaw into their knee, head, or shoulder.

Job
To lose a wrestling match, typically the goal is for the losing wrestler (see jobber) to make their opponent look strong and advance a storyline.

Jobber
A wrestler who routinely loses to build the credibility of other wrestlers.

Jumping Facebuster
Wrestler grabs their opponent's head/hair and jumps or drops to their knees, forcing their opponent's face into the mat.

Kayfabe
The presentation that professional wrestling is entirely legitimate or unscripted. This is not as well-maintained now.

Kendo Stick
A prop weapon made from hollow bamboo sticks taped together at the ends. It creates a loud cracking sound when struck.

Kick-out
To kick or power out of a pin and lift shoulders off the mat.

Leapfrog
A maneuver where the wrestler jumps over their opponent with their legs spread wide to avoid an incoming charge.

Legacy
Frequently used to describe wrestlers who come from families with deep roots in pro-wrestling.

Mark
A wrestling fan who enthusiastically believes professional wrestling is not staged, or loses sight of the staged nature of the business while supporting their favorite wrestler. Often used to refer to people who have little or no knowledge about the business.

Mid-Carder
A wrestler who is seen as higher than a low-card wrestler, but below a main eventer. They will often wrestle for the secondary title of the company.

Missed Spot
A move or series of moves that are mistimed.

Missle Dropkick   A diving version of the dropkick, usually from the top turnbuckle. (see *dropkick*)

Moonsault   A wrestler will face away from their opponent and backflip, landing onto their opponent, forcing them down to the mat. (generally attempted from the top rope)

Near-Fall   When a wrestler's shoulders are pinned to the mat for a two-count, but the wrestler manages to escape before the count of three.

No Contest   A match that ends in a draw without any clear resolution.

No Disqualifications (No DQ)   A type of match where wrestlers are allowed to use weapons and outside interference without the risk of being disqualified. The match must still end in a pinfall or submission.

Over   When a wrestler achieves the desired crowd reaction, the audience buys into the performer or gimmick.

Over-Sell   When a wrestler shows too much of a reaction to their opponent's offense. This could be done accidentally (i.e., during a missed spot or botch).

Phantom Bump   A wrestler or referee takes a bump without a plausible reason.

Pin   See pinfall.

Pinfall   A wrestler's shoulders are pinned to the mat for a three-count, resulting in a win.

Pop   A cheer or positive reaction from the crowd.

Powerbomb   A wrestler places their opponent in a standing headscissors position, then takes hold of their opponent's hips and flips them up so their opponent's legs rest on their shoulders. Once up, the wrestler slams their opponent back-first onto the mat.

Premiere Live Event   High-profile wrestling events outside of the normal, weekly programming. These events are often the culmination of long-running storylines and feature highly anticipated matches.

Promo

An in-character interview or monologue. Typically includes an in-ring or backstage interview or some type of skit by wrestlers to advance a storyline or feud. The act is referred to as "cutting a promo."

Put Over

A wrestler helps boost the status of another, often by losing a match or selling their opponent.

Receipt

A term for returning a particularly stiff move in return to a wrestler. This is usually when a wrestler is legitimately hit by their opponent, and they will send a legitimate move/hit back as a wordless reminder not to hit so hard.

Rematch Clause

When a champion loses their title, this clause may be invoked as a storyline plot device to procure a title rematch in the future (usually at the next premiere event) to continue to feud.

Reverse Irish Whip

Not a damaging move, but used to set up for bigger sequences or moves. The wrestler grabs their opponent by the wrist, then attempts to push them into the ropes or another obstacle, but the opponent counters and sends the wrestler into the ropes instead.

Ring Rat

Similar to a groupie, one who frequents wrestling events to pursue sex with wrestlers.

Ring Rust

A detriment to wrestling ability resulting from a lack of practice during a hiatus.

Roll-Up

Pinfall maneuver. The wrestler moves behind their opponent, rolling them backwards onto their shoulders for the pin, often grabbing one or both of their opponent's legs.

Rope Break

Breaking the pin count or submission hold when a wrestler places his hand or foot on the rope or under the rope.

Roundhouse Kick

Striking technique where a wrestler pivots on one foot, rotating their hips, and extends the kicking leg in a semicircular motion to deliver a powerful kick to their opponent, typically aiming for the head, body, or legs.

Running Forearm

A strike where the wrestler runs toward their opponent, leaps into the air, and hits them with their forearm, typically in the upper body.

Running Knee	A strike where the wrestler runs toward their opponent and launches their knee, striking with their knee or shin. Typically targeting their opponent's head, neck, or back.
Running Lariat	A strike where the wrestler charges their opponent and delivers a forceful blow with their arm, aimed at the chest or neck area, often sending their opponent to the ground (or over the ropes).
Running the Ropes	A maneuver where a wrestler rapidly moves across the ring, grabbing the top rope with their hand and leaning into it to gain momentum and spring back into the ring. Often used to set up for a powerful offensive move.
Seated Dragon Sleeper	Submission hold targeting the neck and upper spine. The wrestler wraps an arm around their opponent's neck and sits (either on heels or on the mat) before pulling their opponent's upper body backward into a bow. (see Dragon Sleeper)
Sell	To react to something in a way that makes it appear believable and legitimate to the audience. Typically refers to the physical action by a wrestler to make their opponent's move look impactful.
Shoot	Going off-script deliberately, either by making candid comments during an interview, breaking kayfabe, or legitimately attacking an opponent.
Shoulder Tackle	A strike where the wrestler runs at their opponent, their shoulder makes contact with the opponent's chest, sending them to the mat.
Side Headlock	Headlock position where the two wrestlers are positioned side-by-side, with an arm wrapped around their opponent's head from the side. (See headlock).
Sleeper Hold	A classic submission move, designed to cut off blood flow to the brain. A rear chokehold, where the wrestler wraps their arm around their opponent's neck from behind, applying pressure to the sides of the neck, often securing the hold to provide additional pressure. When applied correctly, it could cause the opponent to lose consciousness.
Spear	A powerful offensive move where the wrestler charges at their opponent from a distance, then drives their shoulder into the midsection and takes

them down to the mat.

Spinebuster
Wrestler grabs their opponent around the waist, typically after the opponent has charged them. They use the momentum to hoist them up (often overhead) and slam them back-first onto the mat.

Spinning Heel Kick
Wrestler spins in a 360-degree rotation, often including a jump, and strike their opponent with the back of their leg or heel. Typically, striking the opponent in the face, neck, or chest.

Spot
Any planned action or series of actions in a match.

Springboard
A wrestler using any of the ring ropes to bounce upwards. Most high-flying techniques can be performed after this.

Squared Circle
The wrestling ring.

Standing Dropkick
Wrestler jumps from a standing position and kicks their opponent with both feet.

Stiff
Using excessive force when executing a move, deliberately or accidentally.

Strike
Any contact made with an opponent.

Suicide Dive
A high-risk aerial maneuver where the wrestler creates momentum from ropes to dive through the ropes with their arms extended, typically targeting an opponent who is outside the ring on the floor.

Superkick
Wrestler delivers a side kick to their opponent's face or chin, typically with the sole of their foot.

Suplex
Wrestler places their opponent in a front face lock. Wrestler place their opponent's opposite arm over their neck before lifting them off their feet and throwing them backwards, causing them to land on their back.

Takedown
The wrestler brings their opponent from a standing position to the mat.

Technical Wrestling
A style of wrestling focused more on holds, takedowns, submissions, and grappling.

Texas Cloverleaf
Wrestler performs a single leg takedown, before placing their opponent into a Figure-Four. The opponent's extended leg goes underneath the

wrestler's armpit, and they thread their arm through the opponent's legs. The opposite arm comes underneath the same heel, locking hands together (s-grip). Wrestler lifts the opponent to their shoulders, then turns onto their stomach, maintaining an upright posture. Wrestler squats down over the top of their opponent.

Timekeeper

A supporting role responsible for ringing the bell to signal the official start and end of each match, keeping track of the duration of each match, and often involved in other production duties.

Triple-Threat Match

Three wrestlers compete against each other until one achieves pinfall or submission to win the match.

Turn

A switch in alignment of a wrestler's character. Usually, when a wrestler turns from Face to Heel, or vice versa.

Turnbuckle

A rigging device used to adjust the tension of the ring ropes. There are typically three in each corner, covered in soft pads for the safety of the wrestlers.

Up and Overs

Maneuver where the wrestler is sent towards the ropes by their opponent (typically in an Irish Whip). The wrestler avoids hitting the turnbuckle by gripping the ropes on either side, jumping up, tucking their legs into their chest, and then kicking out. The aim is to clear their opponent who runs toward them, allowing them to run into the turnbuckle instead.

Valet

A person (usually female) who accompanies a performer to the ring.

Visual Fall

A pinfall the referee does not see, but the crowd does. Usually followed by a late kick-out when the referee does see the pinfall and starts the count.

Work

(n) Anything planned to happen in a match.

(v) To methodically attack a single body part throughout the match. Also, to deceive or manipulate an audience to elicit a desired reaction.

Worked Shoot

A wrestler seemingly going "off script," often revealing elements they shouldn't of the production, but it's actually a fully planned part of the show.

Jensen Parker

Jensen Parker is a wife, mother, and contemporary romance author. She studied English at Loyola University in Chicago and Harvard University in Boston. Coffee, wine, and travel are her love languages (especially when they all coincide!). When she's not working on her next project, she likes spending time with her family, cooking, or planning her next vacation. She currently lives in Indiana.

For sneak peeks, giveaways, and more...Sign up for Jensen's newsletter! https://www.jensenparker.com/subscribe

Follow her on social media!

Instagram : instagram.com/jensenparkerauthor

Facebook : facebook.com/jparkerauthor

Threads : threads.net/@jensenparkerauthor

Twitter : twitter.com/jensenpauthor

Goodreads : goodreads.com/jensenparkerauthor

Amazon : amazon.com/author/jensenparkerauthor

TikTok : tiktok.com/@jensenparkerauthor

"I urge you to live a life worthy of the calling you have received. Be completely humble and gentle; be patient, bearing with one another in love."

- Ephesians 4:1-2

#MadeforMore